Praise for Jeffe Kennedy's Twelve Kingdoms

The Mark of the Tala

"The fairy-tale setup only hints at the depth of world-building at work in this debut series. What could be clichéd is instead moving as Andi is torn between duty to her father and the pull of Rayfe and his kingdom . . . This well-written and swooningly romantic fantasy will appeal to fans of Juliet Marillier's Sevenwaters series or Robin McKinley's *The Hero and the Crown*."
—*Library Journal*, starred

"A tale that is both satisfying and tantalizing. This promises to be a trilogy th

"I thoroug   y created here. It was the   to get lost in, thanks to the interesting characters, the bit of mystery surrounding Andi's mother, Salena, and their otherworldly heritage."
—*Harlequin Junkie*

"This magnificent fairy tale will captivate you from beginning to end with a richly detailed fantasy world full of shapeshifters, magic, and an exciting romance!"
—*RT Book Reviews*, 4½ stars, Top Pick

"I loved every page and the conclusion simply left me stunned."
—*Tynga's Reviews*

The Tears of the Rose

"Kennedy creates a well-constructed world, and Amelia has a solid character arc, moving from unlikable to heroic in her own way."
—*Library Journal*

"New readers will have no trouble following along. . . . Amelia's journey from pampered princess to empowered woman begins with sorrow and pain, until she begins to see her purpose and embraces her newfound strength and power. She is a surprising female character, as is the scarred and mysterious Ash. One of the highlights of the Twelve Kingdoms series so far is that the women are charged with saving themselves and creating their own happily-ever-after, with the men surrounding them just one part of the process."

—*RT Book Reviews*, 4½ stars, Top Pick Gold

"*The Tears of the Rose* strikes gold . . ."

—*Fresh Fiction*

"Certainly, Jeffe Kennedy's characters are not perfect. No, they are flawed, even Andi in the first book, but their flaws are believable and make them relatable. So, even if you don't like them (like I didn't like Amelia at first), you can definitely understand where they're coming from."

—*The Romance Reviews*

The Talon of the Hawk

"The saga of The Twelve Kingdoms returns in grand style! This is a complex world full of danger, subterfuge, and secrets with empowering female characters who are not afraid to fight for their future."

—*RT Book Reviews*, 4½ Stars, Top Pick

"Excellent character development and strong action continue to characterize the Twelve Kingdoms, and I'm thrilled beyond belief to know that we will see more of this world in future Kennedy books."

—*Fresh Fiction*

"Riveting."
—*The Romance Reviews*

"This series has left me with a serious book hangover. Do not read this as a standalone novel—buy all three and enjoy the marvelous world that Jeffe Kennedy has created for us all. . . ."
—*Urban Girl Reader*

"This is powerful stuff. Epic fantasy!!! I absolutely adored this book!"
—*Tea and Book*

"*The Talon of the Hawk* is everything a lover of high fantasy and romance can expect: action, adventure, closure, and sweet romance."
—*Romance Junkies*

"The third installment of Jeffe Kennedy's Twelve Kingdoms fantasy series tears sharply and deeply into the books' mythology as well as into the heart of its core family. *The Talon of the Hawk*, Ursula's story, doesn't hesitate to draw blood and, in the process, proves also to be incredibly healing."
—*Heroes and Heartbreakers*

"Ursula is such a great character. She doesn't take people's crap and she tells it like it is. No matter if anyone likes it or not."
—*Night Owl Reviews*

Books by Jeffe Kennedy

The Master of the Opera

The Twelve Kingdoms:

The Mark of the Tala

The Tears of the Rose

The Talon of the Hawk

The Uncharted Realms:

The Pages of the Mind

The Edge of the Blade

Published by Kensington Publishing Corp.

THE
EDGE
OF THE
BLADE

JEFFE KENNEDY

KENSINGTON BOOKS
www.kensingtonbooks.com

KENSINGTON BOOKS are published by

Kensington Publishing Corp.
119 West 40th Street
New York, NY 10018

All Kensington titles, imprints, and distributed lines are available at special quantity discounts for bulk purchases for sales promotion, premiums, fund-raising, and educational or institutional use.

Special book excerpts or customized printings can also be created to fit specific needs. For details, write or phone the office of the Kensington Sales Manager: Kensington Publishing Corp., 119 West 40th Street, New York, NY 10018. Attn. Sales Department. Phone: 1-800-221-2647.

Kensington and the K logo Reg. U.S. Pat. & TM Off.

ISBN-13: 978-1-4967-0426-9
ISBN-10: 1-4967-0426-6
First Kensington Trade Paperback Printing: January 2017

eISBN-13: 978-1-4967-0427-6
eISBN-10: 1-4967-0427-4
First Kensington Electronic Edition: January 2017

10 9 8 7 6 5 4 3 2 1

Printed in the United States of America

To Jillianne Wilkinson
You were on my mind as I wrote this book—maybe you'll
understand why, if you ever see this. I think of you often,
with hope and love.

Acknowledgments

Many thanks to Carien and Sullivan McPig, for many services rendered, including beta reading, assisting on All the Things, and in particular for photos of Fraeylemaborg, the inspiration for the Imperial Palace in Dasnaria.

Thanks to Marcella Burnard, for notes on all things nautical. As always, any errors are due to my obtuseness or willfulness, possibly both at once. She tried to teach me about sailing, folks— she really did. Also thanks to Anna Philpot, for close reading on a short timeline. And for bubbly in the grape arbor.

Hat tip to Jeremy Brazille, Karen Hardie, and Worldbuilders. You all know why.

Thanks to Peter Senftleben, editor extraordinaire, for loving Jepp best of all. (And not letting me kill her off in a previous book.) Attendant thanks to everyone at Kensington, all of *whom* work so hard to make these books wonderful and get them into readers' hands, especially Rebecca Cremonese, Jane Nutter, Vida Engstrand, Lauren Jernigan, and Kristine Mills.

As always the terrific team at Fuse Literary gets my gratitude, particularly fabulous agent Connor Goldsmith and savvy agency partner Laurie McLean.

Many thanks to all the reviewers, readers, and book bloggers who've supported these books—I would be lost without you.

Love to bestie Megan Hart, forever and always an LH. And to Margaret, who remains my source of light.

Hugs to Veronica Scott, steadfast supporter and loyal friend. Same to Katie Lane, who always makes me smile.

Huge thanks, love, early morning coffee IMs, and cupcakes to Grace (Darling) Draven, for help with a difficult scene. No raw chicken parts hitting the floor—I just couldn't go there—but I used most everything else, you gory wench.

I'd be a sad and lonely writer without my professional organizations. Here's a shout out to the Science Fiction and Fantasy Writers of America (SFWA)—especially the Keepers of the Flame in the chatroom—and the Romance Writers of America (RWA), with special hugs to the wonderful folks in my local chapter, the Land of Enchantment Romance Authors (LERA).

Finally, much love to my family. I was writing this book over Thanksgiving and Christmas—and no one blinked that I spent hours at Starbucks. My stepsister Hope even met me there a couple of times for a quick latte and left quickly. There is no greater love.

Always, to David, who's with me every day. No cottages and picket fences for us either—and we've made it work brilliantly. I love you, my dear.

1

The dragons loomed in silent menace against the rosy dawn. They'd given me a serious chill the first time the *Hákyrling* sailed between their fearsome snarling mouths. This time their daunting size and gleaming black coils seemed to mock me.

Running away, little warrior?

No—just abandoning the field of battle, deserting the woman entrusted to my protection by the High Queen, and flinging myself headfirst into a mission completely beyond my skills. Nothing to write home about. If anyone at home had cared. Ha!—and if I could write very well. Stupid saying, anyway.

As Glorianna's sun tipped over the ocean's horizon, the rays caught the sharp edges of the dragons' scales, glinting as on the finest blade's edge. Carved from the island rock and built up from there so they reared ten times the height of the *Hákyrling*'s mast, they looked about to spring to annihilating life. Great bat wings lay folded against the back of one, half-mantled on the other, massive snakelike tails winding down the rockfall to dangle in the seawater. Impossible creatures, I'd thought—until I'd seen one flying through the air.

The guardians delivered an obvious warning that I'd nevertheless neglected to heed. Now Dafne, my friend and the person I had been supposed to protect, lay prisoner in the clutches of the dragon king. I gripped the polished rail of the ship, keeping myself from looking back. *Bryn never look back.* More than a superstition, less than a magic spell, I'd heard that caution all my young life, told me first by my mother, and echoed by my grandmother, aunts, great-aunts, sisters, cousins, friends, and teachers.

Bryn never look back.

I wouldn't shame their legacy by doing so now. Much as it pained me. Had I been gifted with Zynda's shape-shifting magic, I might not have been able to hold out. How she kept from leaping into the water and swimming back to Dafne's side, I didn't know. Maybe that was why she'd gone below, an unusual move for her, as much as she thrived on being outdoors. Likely the worry wormed in her gut also, wondering what Dafne might suffer even at that very moment. Alone among a foreign people, likely married to a tyrant—a mark of the muddle we'd made of it that we weren't entirely sure of even that much—and barely able to speak the language. Walking away in the dark before dawn had been one of the hardest things I'd ever done.

And I'd done plenty of hard things.

Where I came from, you did hard or you gave up and died. Easy decision. Usually.

We passed beneath the silently roaring dragon guardians, and my gut lurched. No, the ship did, leaping to the wind outside the protected harbor, wine-dark sails billowing with a series of booms as the Dasnarian sailors scrambled to adjust them. Within moments, the island, and any hope of reneging on my decision to shirk one duty in favor of another, fell behind me.

"She'll be all right—don't fret yourself so much."

Oh joy. Kral. Just the megalomaniac to make my morning perfect. "Is that an order, General Kral of Dasnaria and Imperial Prince of the Royal House of Konyngrr? Ooh—or perhaps you're relating a vision from Danu herself!"

He growled in his throat and leaned his forearms on the rail next to me, bracing against the pitch of his ship as we crossed into the choppier open sea, away from the lee of the island. "In Dasnaria we do not heed your three goddesses. Perhaps the women do, to succor hearth and home, but such weakness would not be fitting for a warrior of our people, much less one of the royal line."

I rolled my eyes, ostentatiously so he wouldn't miss it, turning so I stood hipshot, daring him to take a good long look at what he'd never again lay a finger on. "Danu is the goddess of clear-eyed wisdom, the bright blade, unflinching justice, and self-discipline. I can see your point—not manly virtues at all."

He turned his head, blue eyes glittering. Not like the sea, but like the deep ice of Branli near the Northern Wastes, where cliffs of it rose so thick, the white darkened to blue. Chill and ruthless as any of my blades. "If you were a man, I'd challenge you for such words."

"Challenge me anyway. I could use a minute or so of exercise. Though I might not need even that long to take you down."

"My honor does not permit me to challenge a woman. Now, if you care to attack first . . ." he trailed off invitingly, jaw hard behind the short golden beard he'd grown on the journey.

I ground my teeth. "You know full well my pledge to the High Queen prevents me from doing so."

"A woman making a vow to another woman." He shook his head, assuming an expression of innocent wonder. "You're all so adorable."

My grasp of Dasnarian still lagged miserably behind fluent, but I thought I had the meaning there. Even if not, his condescending tone expressed plenty. My fingers itched to pull the twin daggers from the sheaths at my hips. How fine it would be, to see the bright blood springing red against his tanned skin, shocked surprise burbling into that cold gaze as he clutched his throat, collapsing at my feet. Unable to even beg for the mercy I'd never offer.

"What?" Kral's brows drew together in suspicion.

I raked his long body with a deliberately salacious stare and grinned. "Just enjoying a little fantasy."

That got him. Petty revenge, perhaps, and a smidge compared to how I'd love to make him suffer for his many sins. Lust flared in his hard-lined face and he clamped his lips down on it. A pity, as that mouth had provided me with considerable pleasure that one ill-advised night we'd spent together. As had those big hands with their fierce strength. Hung like a stallion, with the stamina of a man half his age and oh, Danu, the devastating and meticulous patience to use it all to drive a woman crazy.

Goddesses take me, I was getting all hot and bothered thinking about it. Thanks to Lunkhead and his tyrannical edict that none of his men touch me, I already suffered from longer privation than I had since I figured out someone else's hand felt even better than my own.

He iced it over fast, covering it with neutral arrogance. "Learn to squelch your fantasies. I will not have you again, *rekjabrel*."

"I didn't offer. You will never be so lucky. Oh, and it wasn't *that* kind of fantasy."

"Wasn't it?"

"No." I yawned deliberately, which turned into a real jaw cracker. Nothing like missing two nights of sleep. Zynda and I had taken turns guarding Dafne while she slept, but I'd never quite managed more than a light snooze. Odd, as I'd long ago mastered the soldier's art of taking restorative sleep instantly at the opportunities afforded by circumstance. It might have been because I'd never before had sole responsibility for another's life—and at the charge of my captain, now High Queen. Who I'd already failed by fucking up with this very man. *You pissed off a prince of the Dasnarian throne, general of their armies, with whom we just created a very new and even more tenuous peace?* Dafne's incredulous voice still echoed in my head. How was I supposed to know Kral expected some kind of fidelity? After one encounter. Well, six or seven—I'd lost count somewhere in the early dawn hours—but only one night. One of the best I'd ever had. Unfortunate, given his obstinate irascibility.

"No," I repeated. "I don't want to hurt your fragile manly feelings, but really the fucking was quite forgettable. I thought maybe you'd improve with practice, but alas." I shrugged for the inevitability of it all. My Dasnarian might be far from fluent, but I knew most of the sex words, and it had proved to be a language excellent for delivering insults.

Kral straightened, folding his arms as he faced me, muscled legs impressively absorbing the ship's movement. I'd like to be able to do the same and not hang on to the rail, but pitching overboard would be an even bigger blow to my pride.

"I seem to recall otherwise." His turn to look me over with hot eyes, taunting me. "Once I had you on your back, you squirmed like a *kottyr*, purring and helplessly happy to have her belly rubbed just so."

The image shouldn't have made me as hot as it did. My susceptibility was no doubt due to his thrice-damned enforced celibacy. Well, and my unreasonable attraction to him. Gathering up all that too easily aroused lust, I funneled it into a prayer. *Danu, accept my sacrifice for you.* If the goddess talked to me— which, ha! Goddesses didn't really do that kind of thing—she would be snorting in disgust. Her priestesses offered Her their celibacy as a sign of devotion, dedicating their bodies to being instruments of war and justice, channeling sexual energy into devotion to a cause, not to the softer, hedonistic delights. I was pretty sure being hard up didn't exactly count as a sacrifice.

Thing was, Kral *had* rubbed me exactly the right way, and I'd done more than purr. I was never helpless, though—an important lesson the Dasnarian had yet to learn. "I seem to recall," I echoed him, pursing my lips as if in thought, "that you had me on more than my back. You had me any number of ways—on my stomach, on all fours, on *your* back . . . Tell me, lover, which was your favorite?"

We hadn't closed any distance, but it felt like we had, the heat thickening the cool morning air. Oh, yeah, that got to him. He didn't shift to adjust his arousal, but he wanted to. I let my eyes linger there and smirked. Then blew him a little kiss.

"Witch," he said, with narrowed, hard eyes. The same word his brother Harlan had used to name the late unlamented Illyria, priestess of a foul Dasnarian religion, Deyrr. An evil worker of magic indeed. Low blow comparing me to the resurrector of corpses.

"Resorting to that?" I snickered. "Though, from what I've heard of your Dasnarian women, what I did to you must have felt magical all right."

"You know nothing of our women and yet you defame them with your sly insults. You will make an ill ambassador indeed. I will be hard-pressed to keep you from getting yourself killed."

"Aw, so sweet. I didn't know you cared. Oh, wait! You don't. You made a promise to your brother. Tell me—does Harlan know you manipulated events to draw Dafne out of Ordnung in order to deliver her to King Nakoa KauPo?"

The accusation caught him unawares, guilt mixing with surprise before he covered it. My keen-edged question had flashed through his guard before he saw it coming, and I had my answer, thrice-curse it.

I shook my head, tsking sadly. "You pretend to make amends with a brother you wronged and lie through your teeth. Does your Dasnarian honor come with laundry service? I'm afraid yours is a bit soiled."

Kral's jaw bulged, and the fingers holding one forearm dug in, clearly longing to draw on me. Oh, I wished he would. Danu take him for what he'd done to Dafne. This wasn't at all how an ambassador should think—or behave—but I'd been field promoted and likely wouldn't survive to face Her Majesty's censure regardless. Or, if I did manage to get through this and she cut me loose, I'd just go elsewhere. I'd re-created myself before and could do it again. Everyone needed good scouts.

The Tala shape-shifters might lump me in with the unchanging mossbacks, but I'd never stayed anywhere long. Not since I'd left home.

"I did not forswear myself to my brother," Kral replied, his voice measured against the rage boiling behind the icy blue. "I promised to watch over the scribe in the Dasnarian court. If she is not at court, there is nothing I can do."

My own anger burned at his perfidy. "You promised that, knowing all along that you would deliver her into a forced marriage with Nakoa. You have a large mouth that you can lie out of both sides at the same time. And to a brother you already wronged at least once. You shave the boundaries of your honor pretty thin."

"What do you know of what passed between Harlan and me?" Kral flung out the question as a challenge, but he wanted to know the answer. Too bad. I wouldn't give up my advantage by owning up that I had no idea. Dafne hadn't known either. If Harlan had confessed the truth to High Queen Ursula, she'd kept his secrets well.

"Enough to know you've betrayed him yet again by failing to protect Dafne as you swore to do."

"I neither betrayed him nor failed to protect your queen's ambassador." He held out a hand, ticking off the points. "I did not know King Nakoa KauPo's intentions, only that he handed me a drawing of a woman and asked to meet her. I do not believe her to be in danger, as he clearly regards her as a much-treasured wife. Any woman should be grateful for such fortune. Harlan's judgment may be questionable, anchoring himself in servitude to a foreign queen as he has, but any true son of Dasnaria would recognize the truth of this. Finally, the *expressed* goal of his mistress and your queen was to send an ambassador to the Dasnarian court. You might be a pitifully inadequate substitute who will no doubt immediately shame your Twelve Kingdoms, but the mission arguably continues intact as described in the treaty."

I fumed, wanting to argue seven different points at once. Failing that, I curled my lip in my best sneer. "You are an ass."

He nearly lost it, fingers twisting and body quaking as he almost lunged for my throat. I had my blades out and ready to strike before he viciously yanked himself back. "Because you are no proper female, I could justify taking you down for that, but I won't."

"Afraid if you bend that honor any further, it will break? Understandable, as you've stretched your vows thin enough to be flimsy threads in the wind."

"What is it you want with these taunts, Jepp? I could break you in half without trying."

"You'd have to get past my blades first."

He unfolded his arms, fisting hands on his hips instead. Once under sail, he'd shed the black armor that made him and his men look half again as big, but still he towered over me by a head. "I already did," he said softly.

"You won't ever again."

"I wouldn't lower myself. As you pointed out, the rewards were hardly worth the sweat. I'll now point out that you didn't answer my question."

"I want two things," I spat at him, sheathing my knives. Might as well lay it out now. "I agreed to leave Dafne behind because me taking her place as ambassador is more important in the grand scheme than her personal happiness. She made the sacrifice and I won't diminish it by gainsaying her."

"And because you had no choice in the matter."

That rankled. I still thought we could have broken her out somehow. Nakoa's open-air palace had no physical security. Even with her unable to walk, we could have maybe . . . Eh, no help for it now. Dafne had made the decision—including handing me responsibility for the secret part of her mission—and she outranked me. "Therefore," I continued as if Kral hadn't made his petty point of clarification, "I'm calling on you to uphold your promise to your brother and aid me in navigating the Dasnarian court."

He set his mouth mulishly. "That regarded the scribe, not you."

"Oh, I think you bent that vow plenty already to accommodate covering me also. Don't forget—we're not in Dasnaria yet.

You've yet to be allowed to cross out of Her Majesty's realm. Queen Andromeda will meet us at the barrier wall, and if I tell her what's transpired, she may not choose to let you pass. You need me if you want to get home. Also, if I send a message back to Harlan, detailing what you've done—how do you suppose *he* will interpret your rearrangement of the rules?"

"My little brother has long been estranged from me. What would it matter to me if he renewed his snit?"

Logical, and yet . . . I thought it did matter to him. Just as it mattered greatly to him to get his ship and men back to Dasnaria. Nothing like spending a skin-slicked night learning a man intimately to give a woman insight into his psyche. One reason sex made an excellent venue for spying and extracting all sorts of information. Kral was an indisputable, unmitigated ass, but family mattered to him. Whatever had happened, it had affected them both profoundly. He and Harlan had mended fences over a bottle of *mjed*, a Dasnarian liquor Harlan had saved during his travels for just such a special occasion—once the treaty had been signed. Several of the other Hawks and I had matched them shot for shot, the *mjed* deliciously light, belying the sucker punch that rivaled that of Branlian whiskey. Which may have led to the aforementioned ill-advised sexual encounter.

The scent and flavor of it certainly twined in my memory with the taste of Kral's skin and the heated thrust of his body. *No thinking about that.* I needed to focus on carrying forward with Dafne's quest. Like it or not, I'd need Kral's help.

"I think it would matter to you. More, I think it would matter to him. Shall we find out?" My dare whipped out like the whisk of a blade against his resolve. Oh, yeah, he flinched ever so slightly.

"I will help you act as ambassador," he conceded. "As I had already planned to do. Not because of your weak threats, but because it would shame me to have you blundering about offending one and all. Thus my first piece of advice—learn to dress and move as befits a lady. Your mannish ways will only offend."

"You didn't find me so mannish at Ordnung."

He ground his teeth, the click of his jaw audible. Not healthy at all. "Sampling the exotic fare travel brings is not the same as stomaching unpleasant foreign tastes in one's own home. You asked for my assistance; that's where we begin. No one at the Dasnarian court will speak to you garbed as you are and behaving as you do."

"Do you think putting me in a gown will make me less dangerous? I could gut you before you knew I'd drawn a blade."

Kral narrowed his eyes. "I am not young Blagor. You would not take first blood so easily."

"Heard about that, huh?" Ursula, back then not the High Queen, but heir and captain of the Hawks, had chosen me to demonstrate to Harlan and his Dasnarian mercenaries, the Vervaldr, just what a well-trained woman with a pair of delicate blades could do. Surprising them had been most satisfying.

"An exaggerated tale, I'm certain," he said.

"I'm happy to demonstrate anytime, General Killjoy, no matter what I'm wearing."

"Ah. I'm glad you agree, then, that wearing a proper garment will not be a problem for you."

Danu save me, I couldn't back down from that. Besides, I would need every advantage I could muster. "Fine. Once we arrive in Dasnaria, I will obtain some of the local clothing."

"Best to practice before then."

"I didn't exactly pack a lot of ball gowns." My job had been bodyguard, not prancer-about-in-pretty-outfits woman.

"There are some traditional Dasnarian costumes appropriate for females aboard. I will arrange for them to be sent to your cabin."

On a shipful of men? I probably didn't want to know. Kral read it on my face, however, enjoying my discomfort. "Occasionally our *rekjabrel* accompany their men on shorter journeys. And we bring gifts back to them and our wives. The wise man keeps his woman in pretty things, as her happiness may not guarantee his, but her unhappiness will surely create his misery."

"You're just chock-full of advice today, aren't you?" I almost preferred his studied refusal to acknowledge my existence.

A strange expression crossed his face, as if he'd also only just realized he'd reversed his recent behavior. "As you will be ambassador whether either of us enjoys the prospect, then yes—it occurred to me that I'd best take you in hand to ensure I am not censured for bringing a disgrace into His Imperial Majesty's court."

Sweet talker. I sent a prayer to Danu for patience. And wisdom. Maybe a double helping of both. This prayer felt far more sincere. *Look at all this celibacy I've offered, Danu—my idea or not, I'm doing it. A little assistance in return wouldn't go amiss.*

I managed to swallow my pride at the "take you in hand" remark. What would Dafne say? "I am . . . grateful for your advice and assistance, General Kral."

He grinned, not at all nicely. Couldn't even be gracious in victory.

"What was the other favor you craved of me?"

Excuse me? I bit back the seventeen different retorts that sprang to tongue at *that* one. I almost regretted that I'd announced I wanted two things, but oh, well. Hurt nothing but my pride to ask. "Lift your edict on no one having sex with me."

Ridiculous that I had to ask, but I was getting thriced-desperate. Neither Dafne nor Zynda had been persuadable on the topic; the couple of days on Nahanau had been entirely in crisis mode with no time for dallying. Now I'd be trapped with Kral and his men for Danu knew how long, and not a one would go against his order that I was hands-off. Goddesses knew I'd tried.

Kral smiled with only half his mouth, a definite smirk. "Feeling the burn, *kottyr*?"

My turn to clench my teeth together. "As I'm sure you must be also."

Instead of delivering a scathing remark, he inclined his head in acknowledgment. "Though it seems to me you scratched your itch more recently than I have mine."

No dallying with the pretty island girls, then? Interesting. "By hardly a day," I pointed out. Which was the wrong thing to say. Kral had taken it quite badly that I'd fucked Brandur hours after leaving the general's well-used bed. I wasn't even sure why I had. Kral had left me thoroughly sated. Brandur and I had never been exclusive, but Brandur had invited me in a persuasive way and . . . Okay, maybe I'd felt the need to scrub the lingering and overpowering feel of Kral from my body. No lover, man or woman, had ever stayed on my mind like that, for most of the next cursed day. Danu's tits—who knew the man would be possessive of a woman he'd just met?

"Are you asking for an apology?" I asked, sounding reasonably neutral.

His gaze sharpened. "Are you offering?"

"No, I'm determining the terms of this particular treaty."

"An apology for offending my honor and betraying my trust would go a long way, yes. Along with the acknowledgment that you agreed to be mine and will not stray again. At that point, I might be able to be persuaded to assist with that itch of yours. If you ask nicely." He grinned, a definite challenge.

"Not going to happen. I never agreed to be yours, you misogynistic tool." I added that last insult in Common Tongue, as—no big shocker there—Dasnarian didn't seem to have a word for the concept, though they might as well have invented the practice.

His smile vanished, face going as icy as those Branlian glaciers. "You did agree, when you accepted the invitation to my bed."

I threw up my hands in exasperation. "Sex! I accepted the offer of sex, not lifetime servitude."

"I offered you the protection of my body, a guarantee of food and shelter. Those are the terms."

"Dasnarian terms."

"Of course," he replied, frowning a bit. At least he might be processing some of his mistake there.

"Look, Kral." I made an effort to sound reasonable. "I realize you think the Dasnarian Empire is the center of the universe, but there are other cultures, other ways of doing things. I protect my own body, work for my own food and shelter. In my world, an offer of sex is just that. We had a good night. We parted ways after. Now we have to work together. Can we call a truce already?"

"Certainly." He smiled again. The smile failed to reassure me. "But my orders stand."

I cursed him, a vicious one from old Bryn, which only made him look more pleased.

"I'm responsible for my men and for your welfare as ambassador. The Tala sorceress, too. I would be remiss if I allowed any trouble to ensue." He looked me up and down. "But if you wish to renegotiate the terms of our truce, you know what to do."

He sauntered off, whistling, much too pleased with himself.

2

Full of restless energy, I couldn't bear to go below. I should likely check on Zynda, but she knew how to find me. It wasn't that big a ship. Instead I headed for the wide area near the stern, where I could train without being in the way of any of the sailors. My body felt creaky with inaction and sleep deprivation.

Not to mention being nearly gutted alive.

Don't think about it. Still, that moment when High King Uorsin burst out of his barricaded rooms, insanity and bloodlust in his eyes, seized my brain in the occasional surprise choke hold. Like his namesake, he'd charged like a bear startled out of hibernation, crazed, starving for the first flesh he came across. I'd seen that once, when I was a kid and accidentally awakened a brown bear. It had been a warm winter, with the scant snowfall already receding well before actual spring. A fringe effect of the drought in Aerron, though my little clan hadn't known much about that—or anything in the larger world. Bored with the tree stand my aunts had staked out on the deer trail, my cousin and I had wandered off. Found the cave and foolishly explored. Awakened the bear. Then ran screaming right back for safety.

Our shaman later said the bear was too skinny, that the lean summer and fall before had sent her to sleep with too little fat and she likely would have emerged anyway. Just bad luck we happened on her cave when we did. Worse luck for my cousin and two of my aunts, who were disemboweled by those heinous claws before enough spears and arrows stuck to bleed out the bear. I'd had nightmares for months after. Occasionally still did after a bad fight.

Or after Uorsin, mad bear in his own right, did the same to me.

In my head, I knew that was why I'd frozen. The sight of him, sword drawn and spittle flying, had rocketed me straight back to being nine years old and terrified. Marskal, Lieutenant of the Hawks, had berated me even as he'd packed my guts back in and staunched the bleeding with his shirt. *Why in Danu didn't you dodge?* If Queen Amelia's consort, Ash, hadn't been there, I would have died.

I should have died, both times, way back when, with my cousin, and again barely a month ago.

Perhaps the third time would be the charm. Did they have bears in Dasnaria? Perhaps whatever they did have would be the third and final iteration of the monster that sought my death.

Dark thoughts needed to be dispelled, so I elected to go for Danu's Dance, instead of one of the more demanding, strength-building series of forms. A bit easier on the body, promoting flexibility, with the added benefit of allowing me to draw my twin blades and let them fly flashing through the morning light. A sight that always made me happy.

Ash didn't get why I hadn't healed completely. With the barrier between Ordnung and Annfwn down, magic flowed more freely, so he should have had plenty. Though, by the stories my scouts brought back, the magic acted more like spring squalls, hitting hard, then vanishing—leaving monsters and altered landscapes behind. Ash had brought Harlan back from the brink of death, and Queen Amelia, too, if the rumors were true. Which they had to be, because my people didn't bring me false rumors. He should have been able to get me back to full health, but I felt more like that monster we'd encountered on the River Danu—out of place and twisted up.

Working out helped, though. Good, honest sweat always did. Let Kral get a good gander. Dafne had said he watched me when I wasn't looking. Hopefully he'd get an eyeful of what I could do. I'd take first blood, all right, and the killing stroke, too. The fantasy energized me, and I imagined taking him apart, sliver by sliver, while *he* begged for mercy.

An apology . . . offending my honor . . . betraying my trust . . . acknowledgment that you agreed to be mine . . . will not stray again . . . persuaded to assist that itch of yours . . . if you ask nicely. Ha! I punctuated each odious phrase with a swipe of my blade. There his icy eyes slashed. Gone his smug smile. So much for those muscles, those abs, that damned cock he was so proud of.

Danu's Dance allowed for plenty of creative embellishment, but I finished it with her salute, right hand holding one dagger pointed up over my heart, the other above my head pointed to the sky. Her noonday sun blazed nearly overhead, so I counted my timing perfect. Even if it did mean I'd been at it for hours. Now that I'd stopped, my muscles trembled with exhaustion. Probably I needed to eat.

A great seabird swooped over the deck, dropping beside me and shimmering into Zynda, who gave me an assessing look. "You look like you were the one to take a dip in the ocean."

I sheathed the blades and wiped my face, then tunneled my fingers through my hair. Completely drenched, short as it was. "I had a workout, yeah."

"And a loud argument with General Kral."

"You heard that? I thought you went below."

"Neither of you is exactly a soft speaker. Something you might keep in mind in taking on Dafne's mission as ambassador." As spy, she really meant. Her Majesty had tasked Dafne to penetrate

The Edge of the Blade • 17

the Dasnarian court under the guise of ambassador and determine if rumors that a deposed high priest of Glorianna, Kir, had
thrown in with Illyria's Temple of Deyrr. Personally, I didn't care
why the sanctimonious creep had vanished. And Illyria had been
nicely burnt to ash. Still there was more afoot than curiosity. Ursula wasn't one to squander people and resources on a whim. Me,
she might send on a fool's errand as punishment, but not Dafne,
her most trusted adviser. All that added up to Dafne's fact-finding
errand being of critical strategic importance. A responsibility now
firmly squirming in my lap. And where Dafne had been able to
read and write in Dasnarian and possessed a diplomatic tempera-
ment—yours truly *so* did not. I was doomed to fail. Zynda was absolutely right, but that didn't make me any less cranky about it.

"Because you know so much about diplomacy?" I grumbled.

The Tala woman raised her brows. "As a member of Salena's
powerful clan? Actually, yes. The Tala may not have as complicated a government as the Twelve or the Dasnarian Empire, but
we have intrigue aplenty. Especially when you factor in all the animal natures, which add multiple levels of antagonism and alliance—sometimes all within the same person."

"How many animal forms can you take, anyway?" I asked.

Predictably, she ducked answering, with her slow, easy smile.
"Several."

I'd seen her change into at least five—a tiger, the seabird, a
dolphin, a hummingbird, and a horse—and I had reports of a seal
and probably a snake. Apparently those who claimed relationship
to Salena, former Queen of the Tala, later Uorsin's wife, then
mother of Ursula, Andromeda, and Amelia, could shape-shift into
many forms. As opposed to other Tala, who could take on only
one or two, sometimes none at all. The fact that Zynda boasted so
many meant that she possessed an extraordinarily strong ability,
something she tended to be cagey about. She could also work
magic, though she wouldn't come completely clean about that either.

Too bad I couldn't seduce more out of her. Long limbed and languid, with the characteristic streaming black hair and intense blue eyes of the Tala, she was lovely indeed. The simple, filmy dresses she favored hinted at a nicely curved figure, and that sheen of magic . . . could very well make things interesting. Add that to the fact that she was the only person in leagues not forbidden to hook up with me . . .

"Sure you're not interested in a little sex play?" I invited, only half teasing.

She shook her hair back, winding it into a rope that she coiled on the back of her head and fixed in place with a jeweled pin. "Knowing you'd be thinking of Kral all the while? No, thank you."

"I wouldn't," I insisted. "I'd totally focus on you. You said you've never lain with another woman; why not give it a try? I promise to make it worth your while."

"Jepp," she said gently, laying a long-fingered hand on my arm. "I know you're worried about Dafne. I am, too."

I blew out a frustrated breath and let myself look at the receding horizon. Nahanau had long since faded from sight. "We shouldn't have left her."

"We had no choice." Zynda followed the direction of my gaze. "She's a smart woman. She'll make it through."

"Did you go check on her?"

Zynda shook her head absently. "Tempting, but I thought I'd better not. When we reach the barrier, I want to get back to Annfwn as fast as possible, to get word to the High Queen about Dafne's predicament. I figure I'd better save my strength—just enough moving around to keep limber."

I sighed for that. Smart thinking. And once she left, I'd be on my own. Not that I hadn't been before in my life, but surrounded by the Dasnarians . . . Even the Vervaldr on the ship I'd thought I'd known well had reverted to their native language and customs. I was not looking forward to this.

A strange sound cut across the ubiquitous creaking and snapping of a ship in full sail running before the wind. Something . . . animal? Zynda heard it, too, lifting her head in a way that reminded me of a predator pricking its ears into a downward wind. Or prey.

I drew my blades, muscles singing from exhausted to hyper-alert. "What is it?"

"I don't know. It sounded like a hunting cry. It registered like a wolf calling to the pack that prey had been sighted, but . . . avian?" Her eyes went deeper blue. "So much for conserving energy."

Scanning the skies, I spotted nothing. Kral came skidding up, broadsword in one hand, a huge knife in the other that, on a smaller man or woman, would suffice as a sword in its own right. "Lookout spotted something strange ahead. Advice?"

We'd come a long way, at least, since the battle with the river monster, when I'd had to browbeat Kral into listening to us. He gave Zynda an expectant stare, pressing his lips over the evident desire to ask her to use magic—she hadn't responded well to the last request. Tala were funny about doing things only on their own agenda, according to their own moral code. Their values were nearly as far from those of the other twelve kingdoms as the Dasnarians' were, only in another direction.

"Strange how?" she asked crisply, all languid ease gone. The tiger looking out of her eyes.

"Climb to the crow's nest with me and see. We can haul in sail to slow momentum, but we'd lose maneuverability. If we're going to turn her, I'd rather know sooner than later." Kral was already striding to the rigging, taking time to sheath the broadsword on his back, but keeping the knife out. He climbed rapidly, even one-handed, and Zynda and I exchanged a glance before she followed, climbing with agility.

With no intention of being left behind, I followed them on the rigging—after sheathing my blades. I'd rather climb two-handed and have to draw than risk missing a handhold. I hadn't scaled anything this high since the forest pines when I was a kid.

At the very top of the mast, the swaying motion of the ship became more pronounced. Charming. I'd thought Kral's name for the thing a Dasnarian euphemism, but a couple of hobbled crows cawed a greeting, and I stepped up at Kral's impatient gesture.

"Ma'am." The lookout, a Dasnarian I didn't know, handed me a scoping device, using an honorific Dafne had said applied only to women of high status. At least somebody had manners. He held it for me, showing me how to adjust the focus. What had looked like a black cloud on the horizon resolved into whirling pieces.

"Avian. I think you called it, Zynda. Hard to get perspective, but I'd guess smaller birds, no more than hand's length, flock structure like swallows, moving in waves. Could be feeding on something? Definite sheen of magic. Colors are all wrong—unnatural greens. Brighter even than the Nahanaun birds. Can't get much more detail from this distance. I don't like this, though."

Zynda snatched the glass from my hand, muttering something in Tala.

"Never seen anything like them, but you're right, Jepp," she said. "Definite feeding pattern. Looks like they're taking something apart—I can make out blood and, oh, yes, bones. Stripping flesh at an amazing rate. Whatever it was, we can't help it."

"Curse helping it," Kral growled. "We want to avoid the things."

Zynda handed the long-distance glass back to the lookout with a smile that had him nearly choking, though she seemed not to notice, turning it on Kral. "Good luck with that—we're headed straight for them."

"No, we're already taking evasive action."

I squinted at the glinting cloud. Excellent long-sight had been one of the reasons I first became a scout. "They're shifting to intercept. Looks like a couple of them are tracking us for the flock." I pointed out the circling specks of green above, the source of that shrill cry I'd heard. Now that I had a fix on the creatures, I could pick them out against the searing blue more easily.

"That means intelligence," Kral declared.

"Not the sentient kind, necessarily." Zynda watched them, too, thoughtful. "Lots of pack animals display that behavior. Hmm. A hawk or eagle could take out the scouts."

I put a hand on her arm. "No. Don't engage them in bird form."

"A bigger, more vicious bird form," she argued, with raised brows.

"Don't do it. What if they swarmed you? I've seen smaller birds in groups harass bigger ones. Corvids like these take on eagles." The crows cawed and preened, as if pleased with my observation. "Why are these crows even here?"

Kral gave me an impatient look, then transferred his gaze to the shifting, glinting cloud, now decidedly less black and more green as we closed. "If we get fogged in, we release them and they fly to the nearest land. We follow. Good safety tactic."

"Better get them under cover," I advised, "if you want them to live. That goes for every living thing on this ship."

He glared at me, disbelieving. "Hide?"

"Danu, Kral." I rolled my eyes at him. "How do you propose to fight the thrice-damned things? They'll swarm us like they did whatever that goddess-forsaken thing is out there. Surely there's some Dasnarian saying on the wisdom of retreating to fight when the odds are better."

His chin firmed and ice blue glinted coldly. "The odds are always in a Dasnarian's favor."

Danu save me. "You asked for advice; that's mine. Zynda?"

She studied the birds overhead with pursed lips. "There's more of them every passing moment. I suspect Jepp has the right of it. Perhaps if we hide and seal all openings, we might be able to wait them out."

Kral blew out an explosive breath. "With no one manning the sails? A recipe for disaster."

"Drop the sails," I suggested.

"Oh, wonderful idea—we'll be dead in the water while they

pick us apart." After snarling at me, he rounded on Zynda. "Can't you do some kind of magic thing to wipe them out of the sky?"

Zynda went still. "This is their place and they have a right to live. I will not simply extinguish them on the chance they might harm me."

He thrust an open hand at the flock. "They're stripping flesh from bone. I'd say the threat is clear."

"What if whatever it was attacked *them*? What if it's their natural prey?" She lifted her chin. "I will not use magic in such a way."

Kral ground his teeth. Happy to see him frustrated with someone besides me, I stayed out of the line of fire and kept an eye on the scout birds. There were indeed more all the time. It would be good to get somewhere less exposed, but I didn't want to leave with the risk of Zynda taking it into her head to shift and go after them.

"You just offered to turn into an eagle and kill those," he ground out. "What in *hel* is the difference?"

"That's animal to animal. Using magic is . . . cheating."

Kral turned his glare on me. "Can't you reason with her?"

I gave him my sunniest smile. "With the Tala? We of the Twelve have been trying for generations. I've got nothing." A bright green flash zoomed between us. Kral flinched and a line of blood appeared high on his cheekbone. Good reflexes, or he could have lost an eye. "Except for my previous advice that we get under cover. Let's move!"

Zynda thankfully obeyed, clambering down the ropes again, much slower than going up. I kept close, ready to defend her. The lookout followed us, holding the jesses of the crows in one hand as he came down. If we survived this, I'd have to practice climbing one-handed. As it was, I had to pause to hold on, drawing a blade to slice at another bird that came too close. Way too close. "Faster!" I shouted to Zynda.

Kral remained above a moment longer, relaying orders in Dasnarian too fast for me to follow, and sails began flapping around us as the sailors hauled them in. The deck swarmed with activity, not unlike the shifting flock of carnivorous birds, Shipmaster Jens and Kral tag-teaming on coordinating the frenzy as the sails were roped into place. Shouts of command gave way to cries of pained insult as more of the green birds zoomed in.

"Get below," I ordered Zynda. With a blade in each hand and my feet on a reasonably stable surface, I felt better. The Whirling Wind pattern might work nicely against the creatures.

"Not until you do," she replied grimly. "I'll shift and—"

"Conserving energy, recall?" I sang out, moving into the Whirling Wind pattern, creating a field of slicing steel between Zynda and the birds. "Guide me and I'll cover us."

Her fingers slipped into the back of my sword belt, pulling with firm insistence. She had a good feel for it, not interrupting my rhythm, but keeping up a consistent direction to lead me. The position also allowed her to more effectively crouch behind my shield of blades. Kral ran up, knocking one of the birds from the sky with his broadsword, much like the kids' game of hitting balls with big sticks. Impressive speed on that man, despite his bulk. So sexy.

"What are you girls doing up here?" he shouted. "Get below, you idiots, before I chop you into pieces and throw you into the hold."

There he had to go and ruin it every time. So not sexy.

"We're there," Zynda yelled. "On three, turn and dive. One, two"—solid thunk of her heel on the door—"three!"

Blindly trusting, I turned and dove, sliding through the just-opened door and skidding on the polished floor of the hall beyond. Zynda had a bleeding scratch on her forehead and her hair was wildly tousled but otherwise looked fine. Another thunk on the door and the Dasnarian manning it opened it fast, yanked his brother sailor through, and slammed it again. Two birds followed. I caught one with a midair swipe with my left blade and threw my right knife, pinning the other to the wooden wall.

Both Dasnarians gaped at me.

"Nice move," one of them noted, with a salute that smacked ever so slightly of irony.

I pulled another blade, to be ready. Normally I wouldn't throw away a knife, but I had plenty on me and in these close quarters I could be reasonably certain of getting them back. Zynda edged over, pried the dagger from the wall, and the limp body with it, studying it curiously.

"Dead?" I asked.

"Thoroughly. I'd like to study it."

"Fine. Take it to our cabin. I'll help here."

"I can help here by—"

Thunk on the door. Open, grab, two more men in. More man flesh than air in the hall all of a sudden. You'd think the Dasnarians would build ships to match their bulk.

"Too crowded!" I called to Zynda. "Go!"

After that the men arrived thick and fast, some covered in the birds. I was hard-pressed to keep up with the scurvy green bastards. Most of the men had switched to shorter swords and big-bladed knives, but the small space hampered their powerful swings, and the nimble birds ducked them easily. Between razor-sharp beaks and freakishly strong talons, the birds were thrice-damned hard to kill once they dug into a man. If we encountered the vile beasts again, I'd don my leather gloves first. As it was, I could hardly skewer the birds in place without further injuring the man they clung to, which meant pulling the creatures from their gnawing frenzy to get enough room to cut their gluttonous throats. My hands were sliced to a bleeding mess.

Kral, of course, was the last man through the door. Him and his damn honor. He'd probably be one of those to go down with the ship if it came to that. Good to remember as a potential method of assassination if he pissed me off once too often.

He came through so covered in the birds and bleeding wounds that it seemed murder might not be necessary. Methodically, I wrested the birds from his flesh, pinning them with a boot when I could and cutting off their heads. Several of the men had observed my technique and emulated it. These Dasnarians—always with the big, bold moves first, instead of finesse. Finally we got the last bird dead and rolled Kral onto his back. His icy blue eyes glared at me from a mask of bright blood. "I'm going to kill your Tala friend," he snarled. "As soon as I can stand."

And promptly passed out.

3

Kral's men carried him off to his cabin, presumably to be healed, though no one bothered to inform me.

"You're welcome," I said in Common Tongue to their retreating backs. Not that they cared, but it made me feel better. Especially with the stings of a thousand cuts making themselves known, along with the crashing exhaustion that comes after any fight, win or lose. Nevertheless, I paused a moment longer, listening. With the sails furled, the ship creaked only with the movement of the waves, water slapping against the hull.

The Dasnarian who remained on the door raised one shoulder and let it fall, a classic Harlan gesture of resignation in the face of what fate would bring. *Hlyti*, he called it. "Quiet now," the man commented.

Yeah, right. Maybe the birdies would get bored and fly away. Ha! Nevertheless, since I seemed to be in the habit of praying to Danu lately, I sent her a fervent wish to make that happen. Me and Danu, best of friends, chatting all the time.

I made my way to the cabin Zynda and I—and previously Dafne—shared, the door left invitingly open for me. I'd grown used to seeing Dafne at the lone desk with her stacks of books, an absorbed frown on her face as she studied some scroll or another, and now it irritated me to miss her. Instead Zynda sat there, the iridescent bird spread out, wings extended. If all went well, soon I'd have the room to myself except for both their ghosts. A screwed-up definition of things going well.

"Did everyone make it in?" Zynda asked, a concerned line between her brows.

"So far as I know." I went to the washbasin, resisting the urge to sit. Once I did, I wouldn't want to get up, and then I'd be stiffer than Danu's tits in an ice storm. "Kral came in last, bitten nearly to death, and I don't think he would have, even then, had any of his men been left standing. He said he wants to kill you, however, so you might watch your back."

She grimaced at that but didn't apologize. "I've never seen an animal like this."

"How so?" I peered at the cursed thing, my first opportunity to study one at leisure. Wickedly curved beak, long, fiery-orange talons I'd come to know well. Shiny, bright green . . . feathers? But with sharp edges. No wonder my hands were a mess.

"It's like part fish, part bird," Zynda explained. "The motion of the flock, that's the same that some schools of fish do. And there are warmwater fish that behave this way, converging on prey and consuming all flesh in a short time. It's almost as if . . ."

She trailed off with a deeper frown.

"Might as well say it," I prompted. "Won't make it any more or less real."

"Well." She sighed, then eyed me. "If you made me guess, I'd say these were that kind of fish that changed and gained the ability to fly."

"Because of the barrier shift?" Now that she said it, the gleaming green did look more like scales than feathers.

Zynda shrugged, a liquid roll totally unlike the fatalistic Dasnarian gesture. "Maybe? Probably. If the barrier extending and bringing magic to the world outside Annfwn could awaken the river monster and the dragon in the volcano at Nahanau, why not these fish-birds?"

"Not to mention the other stories we've been hearing." Stories my scouts used to bring me, before I got exiled due to stupid sex decisions. Another thing I missed, hearing from my network of people. They'd made me feel connected to the world. In control, in that I could at least see and hear beyond my small circle of physical ability. "I don't like this. Animals shouldn't be able to change from one thing to another—it goes against all rational sense." I winced, throwing Zynda an apologetic smile. "Not you. That is . . ." Me and my big mouth.

She laughed. "Well, a piece of good news is that these fish-birds don't seem to be anything more sinister than magically affected animals following their natural instincts."

"I'm sure that will mollify Kral," I replied drily.

She remained serene. Could be a trait they'd all inherited from Salena—none of her get seemed easily shaken. I could pretty much count on one hand the occasions I'd seen Ursula rattled, and I'd served with her for more than five years.

"It's possible that once they can no longer see or hear us, they'll move on."

"They can probably smell us."

She shook her head slightly. "Bird forms are usually heavily visual, with auditory second, depending on the species, and fish forms need the water for olfaction. I think we should give it a little time and then check. I could shift into—"

"No." I paused in cleaning a dagger and pointed it at her for emphasis. "No more shifting. You have to conserve energy, you said."

"That was before—"

"Zynda," I interrupted her again. "You're the one who said you're not sure how far it is to Annfwn from here, as it's never been mapped, or that it's anything but open water in between. If you exhaust yourself—or if you get attacked by something like these creatures—you could die on the journey."

"An unlikely scenario."

"But possible. We've already made sacrifices to ensure the success of this mission. Getting to the barrier safely and making sure you have the best chance of taking information back to Queen Andromeda and Her Majesty trump the rest. If we can't get through the barrier, there won't be any of me going to Dasnaria and sussing out what Kir and the Temple of Deyrr are up to."

"Unless *you* get eaten alive by fish-birds and never make it to Dasnaria," she pointed out.

"I have no doubt Emperor Hestar would send another ship after his beloved brother, difficult as it may be to believe anyone would miss the cantankerous bastard. There would be other opportunities to send an ambassador from Her Majesty. Besides, the fish-birds have to go find other food sometime, right?"

"I could take a quick look—it would tell us much."

"You don't know these creatures—you said as much. What if they're like the mountain cats of the Noredna forests, who'll lie in wait for days for prey they've run to ground, ready to pounce the moment the hapless thing pokes its head out?"

She gave me a surprised look. "Speaking from experience?"

"Bitter ones, yes. I grew up in that region. Hunters had to be very careful not to become the hunted. I'll go report your findings to Kral and see if they've managed to sew him together."

"Speaking of which, want me to bandage your hands?"

I'd gotten most of the blood off—the washing a torture on those myriad bites—and changed into clean leathers as we talked. They were a well-worn, comfortable set, which only reminded me of the pending trial of wearing traditional Dasnarian female garb, whatever it turned out to be.

Being devoured by fish-birds might be the better prospect.

"Thanks, but I'll let the cuts bleed a bit, in case there's any nasties." I took a scrap of cloth with me, to blot with, however. Probably not polite or womanly to drip blood on Kral's floor.

"Jepp?" Zynda said, just before I walked out the door. She looked unhappy but resigned. "If it comes to that, I can kill the

fish-birds with magic. It might mean killing everything outside
the ship for a certain distance in every direction, but I can."

I nodded at her. "I'll tell Kral."

They had Kral propped up on a bed ridiculously large for the
smallish cabin—especially as that appeared to be the only furni-
ture in it—tucked up under a ring of thick glass panes that looked
up at the sky, taking advantage of sloping space there. A row of
fish-birds perched along the edge of them, staring in and occasionally stabbing at the glass with their sharp beaks. So much for hoping they'd gone away already. Kral returned their baleful looks in
kind. Wasn't there a joke about birds of the same feather? Same
scales? Sharks and fish-birds, kissing cousins.

Kral transferred his scowl from them to me, taking in my smirk
with a decided lack of change in expression. Me and the carnivorous fish-birds, both banes of Kral's existence. The thought
perked me up considerably. And helped distract me from his
blazing nudity.

The man who worked on him glanced up at Kral's turn of attention, then stood to block me. "The general is indisposed; you
should not—"

"Stand down, Trond," Kral stopped him, sounding weary.
"She is my *rekjabrel*, so it will not matter."

Trond regarded me with such intense curiosity that I wondered if he'd never met any other of Kral's lovers.

I kept my eyes studiously on Kral's face. Even beat up, he
looked good enough to eat in great, big, greedy bites. My great
weakness, this passion for him.

We seldom marry our great passions. My mother had said that.
More than once. Enough times, in fact, that I'd always suspected
my father had been one of those great passions—and a man not
suitable to be any kind of a life partner for her. Apparently the

fawn didn't stray far from the doe on that one, an irony that might amuse me under other circumstances. Ah, well, so it went.

"Going to survive to fight another day?" I asked.

"So I'm reliably informed," he replied in the same dour tone. "How is it you barely have a scratch on you?"

I gave him my sauciest grin. "I'm really good."

He opened his mouth to fling back a reply, slid a glance to Trond, and shut it again. Discretion from General Killjoy—who knew it was possible?

"I also got under shelter a lot earlier than you did," I conceded. "You were out there much too long." Hmm. I sounded like I cared.

Kral caught it, too, eyes glinting. "And yet you didn't come save me."

"I'm only a weak female," I countered. "I cowered indoors, as is appropriate. If it makes you feel better, my hands are rawer than a skinned deer." I held them up in demonstration.

He made a snorting sound that might have been a smothered laugh. "I had to make sure all my men made it in once the sails were properly furled. A matter of the honor you so deride."

I let that one go, uncomfortably aware that I respected the hell out of him for doing that. "Why did you take in the sails? I thought you were more worried about us sitting here stuck while they swarmed us." I gestured needlessly at the avidly watching fish-birds.

Kral flashed me a disgusted look. No, it might have been a frown for the needle going into his forearm, the sinew pulling together a particularly deep slice.

"Bit some flesh away," Trond grunted. "Gonna scar."

"Ah, well. Women like scars." Kral grinned at me, a challenge in it. "Recall, Ambassador, that there lurks a barrier wall out there. That easterly wind had us nicely on course to reach it within half a day. If we'd hit it at full sail . . ." He lifted one shoulder, let it fall.

Ah. Good point.

"So, Zynda thinks the birds are actually fish-birds, magically mutated with the barrier shift, and that they'll go away if they can't see prey anymore." A few more of them arrived on the glass above Kral's head. "She's betting they're visually oriented, with hearing probably second. She thinks they can't smell us all that well."

"And is she some sort of fish-bird expert?" Kral asked, decidedly mocking.

"She's a person who has been both a fish and a bird," I pointed out in my sweetest, most reasonable tone. "Seems like that kind of experience wins over any other expertise. Oh, wait, unless you have fish-bird scholars among your men?"

Kral glowered and Trond cast me a sideways glance of either warning or astonishment. Not like I could get in worse with the man, but . . . yeah, maybe a little less mouth. I made the worst ambassador in the history of the world.

"Anyway, if she's right, it could be a good idea to cover your windows, tell everyone to be quiet. Then wait it out." There, that sounded reasonably diplomatic. To be honest, Dasnarian tended to be pretty didactic, with words suited more to giving orders than to making suggestions. At least the ones I knew.

Kral heaved out a long breath, then told one of the men on the door to bring the storm shutters and pass the word to cover all portholes similarly. Should have known they'd have some system for that. The men retrieved the things in short order, sturdy wooden pieces that fit into grooves and locked into place with ingenious fittings. Dasnarians could be counted on for clever solutions, if nothing else. Once they finished, Kral bade them all to leave him and spread the word to keep quiet, which all but Trond hastened to do. Given their general's tone, I didn't blame them a bit. In fact, I made to do likewise, but Kral stopped me.

"Stay. Trond is nearly done with me; then he can see to your hands." Now he sounded like *he* cared, Danu take him.

"They're not that bad. Most of the slices are shallow and already closing up."

Trond snorted. "I can see from here at least three need stitches. Stay as you were ordered."

Stitches. Ugh. The needle piercing Kral's flesh made me vaguely ill to watch. "Um, well . . . I should, ah . . ."

"Afraid?" Kral taunted. "And here I thought nothing scared my little *hystrix.*"

"Those fucking fish-birds scared me, and look—here I am considerably less injured than General I'm Afraid of Nothing. Fear can be healthy."

Predictably, he scowled at that but had no immediate retort. I awarded myself the win for that skirmish.

"Done," Trond pronounced, then—Danu bless him—covered Kral with a blanket. An opulent one, embroidered in metallic threads with intricate designs on the burgundy silk that matched pillows mounded behind him, all similar shades to the *Hákyrling*'s sails. Kral's signature color. "Being quiet until those creatures disperse will do you good, General. If you don't reopen the wounds, they ought to heal clean quite quickly. All right, Ambassador Rekjabrel, let's see those hands."

"Don't you have an office or somewhere we can go?"

"I am a moving medic. Dasnarians have no leisure to sit in offices and be tended to."

Thickheaded, the entire race. Trond examined my extended hands, glanced at my face, and nodded at the bed. "Sit. You're already green and I don't need a woman fainting on me."

How about projectile vomiting? No, I'd keep it down. I'd already choked on my own pride enough for one day. No need to add actual bile to the mix. I plopped my butt on the end of Kral's bed and glared at his amused expression. Mainly because it saved me having to see that cursed needle. "Would it kill you to have a couple chairs in here?"

He lifted his shoulder, let it fall, and winced. I was petty enough to take bit of gleeful pleasure in that. "I'm not in my cabin except to sleep." He added a leer. "Or for sex. Why would I need chairs?"

"Clearly your sexual experience is sadly limited if you don't know what can be done with a chair or two," I retorted. "Ouch! Danu's tits—that hurts worse than the original bite did."

"Because you're flirting, not fighting," Trond returned mildly. "You'd do better to argue with your *cvan*—it would distract you better."

Kral's amused leer broadened, so much so that I bit down on the retort that leapt to tongue that flirting with Lunkhead was the *last* thing on my mind. Any protest would only intensify their teasing.

"Nothing to say?" Kral asked softly, an edge of danger in it.

"I'm concentrating on not hurling on your nice, clean bed." I expected him to taunt me for it, but no.

Instead he grimaced in what appeared to be sympathy. "Why is it that I can carve up a man in battle, take a thousand hits, but the medic's needle makes me want to crawl under the bed?" he asked the ceiling, then gestured at the closed shutters. "And this. I hate being closed in. I'd rather face those razor-beaked bird-fish and get sliced up to bleeding to death again than lie still behind closed walls and wonder."

"Keep your voice down," I advised, "and they might be more likely to leave."

Kral fixed me with his intense gaze, more heat in it than should have been possible. It hadn't been only the *mjed* talking. I'd flirted, sure—I always did. Flirting was to sex what training was to martial expertise, a woman had to keep limber, make sure her head and body stayed in shape for the game. Didn't pay to get rusty or flabby in either arena. But something about the way the man looked at me, then and now, like he'd never seen a woman before . . . Yeah, he really got to me.

"Do you have suggestions for muzzling me?" His voice went rough on the words, reminding me of the way it had sounded that night, all the things he'd said, most of which I hadn't understood and had written off as unnecessary to parse when his body told me everything I needed to know. Part of me wanted to hear them again, now that I had a stronger grasp on the language. Fortunately, a bigger part of me knew better this time. Could I be growing wiser? That would be helpful.

"Not if it involves being invited to share your bed again. I've been enlightened on what *that* means."

Trond was holding his breath, doing his best imitation of a fly on the wall. A fly with a big painful needle poking in and out of my palm, one I'd love to swat, particularly if he took any of this gossip back to his fellows. Who was I kidding? Of course he would. I'd never met a warrior who didn't love to speculate about his or her fellows and their liaisons. Fighting and fucking—pretty much all some of them knew, or cared about. When Harlan courted Ursula, every one of the Hawks knew it before she did. Though none of us would have been disloyal—or foolhardy— enough to do more than hint about it to her. It had taken her long enough to indulge in what he offered her. But then, she was royalty and had more considerations than a night's pleasure. Arguably, I should have considered more before accepting Kral's offer. Dafne sure thought so. This being-wiser thing came with an awful lot of second-guessing and dithering.

"And what"—Kral breathed it like a dare—"do you believe an invitation like that entails?"

"Okay, done!" Trond declared, tying the last bandaging cloth into place, obviously relieved to escape. "Unless there's any other wounds on you, Ambassador?"

"Perhaps you should undress," Kral offered blandly, "so I may check you for additional injuries."

"Thank you, Trond," I said to him, deliberately ignoring Kral and rising to go. "My hands were the worst of it."

"Stay, Ambassador." Kral's tone enforced that this was an official order. "Leave us, Trond."

With a salute for his general, Trond beat a retreat hastier than farmers fleeing before shape-shifted Tala. I faced Kral, using the movement to take me a safer half step away from the bed. Not that I feared he'd grab me—though the thought gave me mixed feelings—but to ensure a more formal perimeter. If I'd guessed back at Ordnung that I'd be faced with a solo diplomatic mission reliant on this man, I wouldn't have fucked him.

Okay, maybe I would have, knowing me, but I would have been smarter about it.

Or maybe not, knowing me.

Danu, give me strength. "Look, Your Highness." I jammed my fists on my hips, then suppressed a wince as the stitches pulled. "I may be new to the ambassador game, but I'm not a toddler in the hunting party. You don't get to give me orders, and I don't have to obey them."

"And yet you did obey," he pointed out with a hint of a smile. "Toddler in the hunting party?"

Dafne had taught me Harlan's trick of translating words directly if I didn't know the other language's version of the expression. *Better to get the sense across than say nothing for fear of saying something wrong,* she'd advised. In the face of Kral's bemusement, I reconsidered the wisdom of the advice. Of course, the man seized any opportunity to amuse himself at my expense.

"It sounds better in my dialect. When an inexperienced youngster goes along hunting and causes problems through ignorance." I sounded remarkably patient.

"Oh, I understood the metaphor." He levered himself up on the pillows, pain crossing his face at the awkwardness. "Help me here."

"I'm not your nursemaid."

"I'm wounded battling magical creatures unleashed on the world by *your* queen, while protecting you and your companion, and you refuse me the minor assistance of helping me take pressure off a painful injury—because of, what, your damnable pride?" His voice rose until he finished on an incredulous near shout.

"Hush," I hissed at him, jabbing a finger at the boards over his head, a gesture made considerably less dramatic by the white bandage. When he opened his mouth, a hard look in his eye, I moved in to help, more as a way of shutting the man up already. This was all I needed—to be becalmed, trapped and surrounded by lethal fish-birds, while Kral and I took bites out of each other. And not of the enjoyable variety.

"More on the other side," he directed, indicating the side away from him, where the bed abutted the curving wooden wall, requiring me to lean over him.

"I can get it from this angle." I shoved an arm behind the pile of pillows, adjusting them that way. No compunction to be overly gentle, lest he think me softening toward him. "There."

"Better," he grunted.

"May I be excused, then?"

"Now, explain," he said, as if I hadn't spoken. "Who takes young children hunting?"

"Look, Kral. I'd love to hang out and chat, but I have things to—"

"To what?" He interrupted. "To go sit in your cabin and be quiet?"

He had a point. I'd already driven Dafne and Zynda crazy on the journey thus far with my pacing. Being cooped up didn't suit me any more than it did Kral.

"Stay," he coaxed, in a much more enticing tone. "Talk to me. Don't make me lie here alone to listen to the fish-bird scratches. I hate having to lie abed with injuries."

I could sympathize with that, especially having spent my own time recovering recently. "Conversation isn't exactly our strong suit."

"There." He jutted his chin at the far wall. "In that cabinet you'll find some *mjed*. We can share some to mute the pain."

"Yes, but what will mute the misery of your company?" I replied, mostly out of habit, because I was already halfway to the cabinet. An afternoon bout of drinking with my friendly enemy to kill the boredom. What in Danu could go wrong?

Danu didn't reply. The bitch goddess never did when I needed it.

4

Another ingenious mechanism, the cabinet door appeared to be part of the cabin wall until I pressed where Kral told me to, allowing it to spring open, revealing a fairly deep cavity with several shelves. "Clever," I remarked.

"Thank you."

"The craftsman who built the cabinets, not you." I pulled out the familiar ceramic keg, stoppered with a wax-sealed cork, and two sturdy mugs made of a metal I didn't recognize, etched with the same design as on Kral's blanket. An intricate pattern of something reminiscent of a spider's web, but with a hand in the center. "So, is this a family crest, or what?" Making conversation, cordial chatting, look at me go.

Kral took the mugs I handed him, holding them while I poured. "You've not seen this design before?"

"Other than on every surface in this room? Nope. To Danu of the clear eyes and bright blade." I clunked my mug against his, then tipped it up to the sky I couldn't see.

Kral didn't drink. "To the Emperor, and the Konyngrr dynasty. May both continue until the end of time."

"A little much, don't you think, to celebrate a mortal man instead of a deity? Smacks of distressing arrogance." Dafne had complained of that arrogance, how Kral and the other Dasnarians hadn't bothered to learn enough Nahanaun to really communicate with King Nakoa KauPo. Entirely possible that Kral truly hadn't understood Nakoa's plan to imprison Dafne—which would be all his own lunkheaded fault.

"His Imperial Majesty is more than a man. Arising to the throne via the blessing of the gods makes him semi-divine in his own right," Kral returned, sounding very much as if he were quoting something.

I took a healthy drink of the *mjed* to keep from laughing in his face and to bolster the epic levels of tact this conversation would surely require. "I might not be terribly fluent in Dasnarian, but even I understand that 'semi' means 'not so much.'" I let my gaze fall to the juncture of his thighs and raised my brows. "As in semi-erect isn't going to do much to make me happy."

"You enjoy provoking me, but if you know something of hunting, then you know better than to waken a sleeping bear." He frowned at me. "Don't go all faint on me. If you're going to pass out, do it on the bed. All you need is an injury to that already thick skull."

"I'm not *faint*." Credit to me that I managed to sneer the word, which had the suffix that applied only to females. Dafne hadn't managed to beat much through the aforementioned thick skull of mine, but she had made me aware of those nuances. In general, female forms of address in Dasnarian meant they were thinking of me as lesser, which meant I should pay attention in those circumstances, particularly if I wanted them to take me seriously as an ambassador. Curse Kral for managing to hit on exactly the metaphor that got under my skin. I'd never been missish in my entire life, but I no doubt looked it at that moment. He *had* to pick bears. What were the odds?

"So, your brother is *semi*-divine. What does that make you—quasi-divine?" I toasted my own wit, though my mug had little in it to drink. Shrugging, I poured more, since I held the *mjed* keg still, then looked for a place to set it down. Who had no tables? The floor it was.

Kral was regarding me. "Is there anything at all you hold respect for?"

Restless—and it had nothing to do with those poking-the-sleeping-bear memories, as that was ancient history—I prowled the cabin, testing various panels to discover which held hidden cabinets. "Sure. I respect Her Majesty Ursula, High Queen, and my captain, and also Marskal, my lieutenant, along with all my fellow Hawks, who never fail to have my back. I respect Zynda and her magic, Dafne with her ridiculous bravery, enviable knowledge, and even more enviable ability to learn. I respect the edge of the blade, the sing of the bowstring, the pitiless thrust of the spear, the fang of the mountain cat, the claw of the brown bear, the cornered fighter, and Danu's merciless justice."

"A long speech for you."

"Think so? We haven't spent much time *talking*, I might point out. Still not a long list, all in all."

"I notice I'm not on it."

I turned from a cabinet full of clothing, all in burgundy. "Difficult to dredge up respect for a man who holds me in contempt."

"Is that what you think?"

"Am I wrong?"

Instead of another scathing attack on my moral depravity, he hesitated. "I do not hold you in contempt. Far from it. In fact, I . . . I've been thinking on our conversation of this morning, and it occurs to me that perhaps our problem lies in not understanding each other."

A miracle. Praise Danu for opening the eyes of the blind. "On that we can agree."

He shifted, as if uncomfortable. "Tell me about taking children hunting. Is this the way of your people?"

"I don't get this, Kral. Why do you care?"

"We won't understand each other without knowing more about

each other, and it seems we're stuck in close quarters for some time. We have nothing better to do, so let's tell each other stories. I'll trade one of mine for one of yours. More *mjed*, if you please."

My turn to be bemused, I poured him more. And myself, too. Why not? Again, no Danu popping in to guide me otherwise.

"I'll start by answering one of your questions. No, I am not divine at all. By Dasnarian law, only he who is anointed Emperor ascends to the level of semi-divine. I will only attain that state should I succeed my brother on the throne, which is unlikely unless things change drastically, as he has now sired two fine sons who stand in line before me."

"I doubt a government can legislate a mortal man into godhood."

"True. Only the gods can do so. The law simply recognizes the fact."

"Do you believe it—that your own brother is a god? That you would become one?"

He gave me a long look, as if debating how much to say. "You know, no Dasnarian would ask me that question. It doesn't matter what I believe. It is the way of things in Dasnaria, and no man profits by going against that. Your turn." He tipped the cup in my direction.

"Fine. I will follow no one into godhood. I come from a nomadic group of . . . hill people. Simple folk called the Bryn." I substituted words freely there, but Kral seemed to get the general meaning. "We moved around a lot. No permanent structures. So it's not like we always had safe places to stow the kids while hunting, especially during lean seasons. You leave little ones behind without enough protection, and they end up being the ones eaten. Which runs counter to the whole point of acquiring food, if you're running at a loss. Those are the kinds of people who take little kids hunting."

"Where was this?"

"In the Thirteen, kind of in the middle. Low mountains in the western part of Noredna, northern part of Duranor, depending on who was drawing the lines at the time and which kingdom had a more aggressive tyrant on the throne. Doesn't tell *you* much, but there you go. Isolated enough that I grew up speaking a little-known dialect and had to learn Common Tongue later." Something I hadn't given much thought to, but perhaps that had made acquiring Dasnarian easier. Dafne said that the more languages she learned, the easier it became to pick up new ones.

"I thought you'd grown up at Castle Ordnung, a royal by-blow, perhaps."

"Me? Ha! Perish the thought. My people skirted the line of criminality, mainly because they danced along the edge of starvation, too. If they needed something and the opportunity presented itself, they took it. Disappointed?" Maybe he'd been angling for an in with the royal family when he hit on me. Funny that it hadn't occurred to me before. Though I wouldn't kick myself for missing that possibility. People in general were bad about seeing motivations in others that they didn't themselves possess, and I was no different. I indulged in sex because I liked it and it was a convenient method for extracting information. Using it to climb socially or politically? No. No gray areas there. I didn't have many moral qualms, but that was one.

Kral watched me but didn't dignify my jibe with an answer, instead asking, "How did you end up serving the High Queen, then?"

"That's several questions in a row. My turn."

"You asked me several."

I shrugged, as if I didn't care. As if the memories crowding my head of those days didn't hurt still. The hunger and the struggle. The loneliness of being clanless. "I struck out on my own. Left my home, traveled around a while. Discovered that the skills that had kept me alive in the hills"—I pulled a dagger with my free hand, spun it, and resheathed it in a blur—"made me useful to various militias, royal guards, standing armies."

"You were a hired sword?"

"Yes and no." I found a new cabinet, with books in it. Dafne would have liked to see those. "The Twelve didn't really have mercenaries as such, or didn't until Harlan and his Vervaldr arrived. But each individual kingdom maintains various fighting forces, some for the protection of their own royal families, others to mobilize at the request of the high throne for the common good. I found jobs here and there. Stayed awhile, usually got bored—or kicked out, as I'm not always the best with authority, and don't smirk like that—then I heard that Princess Ursula needed a good scout for her elite guard, the Hawks. So I lit out for Ordnung, trounced the competition in the trials, and got the job."

"Naturally."

I liked when he smiled more easily like that. "Some things you can count on. Eventually I became head of her scouts, too. Served her ever since."

"Despite not being the best with authority."

"Ursula—I mean, Her Majesty—is different."

"I doubt that. She struck me as an exceedingly authoritative person."

She'd created that impression quite deliberately. Not that Ursula didn't give orders when she needed to, but she'd grown up with a tyrant of a father, and that changes how a person views the wielding of power. I'd been in on some of the strategy sessions where they discussed exactly how to play it when Kral arrived at the gates of Ordnung with his battalion of crack warriors. Kral kept his expression bland, but he watched me carefully. I, however, was no stranger to interrogation techniques. He could dig all he wanted and I'd never betray anything vital about Her Majesty. Let him wonder. On the other hand, I was learning useful things about him and Dasnarian culture. Good information to be able to report back. A decent spy learned everything she could, I figured, just as the best scouts did. Might as well spend the shipboard time usefully. "She and I get along just fine."

"What made you leave your people?" A change of tacks from my inquisitor. Recognizing he'd hit a wall. Interesting. A practiced interrogator, then. No surprise, really.

"Why does any teenager leave home? Even wolf puppies leave the pack and go wandering. I wouldn't know about sharks."

"You were a teenage girl on your own in the world?" He sounded indignant on my behalf. Kind of sweet on one level. Insulting on another.

"I was fifteen—an adult in my tribe—and could take care of myself."

"You could have been raped, enslaved."

"That's why a girl's best friends are a pair of sharp daggers."

"I don't understand your people at all. A young, fertile woman should never be treated so casually, as if she has no worth."

"Isn't that why I'm subjecting myself to this interrogation, so you'll understand? And I'll point out that my people—who are many and varied, so it's really not useful to lump them into one way of thinking—place more value on a woman than as a walking womb."

"This isn't an interrogation." Kral frowned still, notably not addressing my last remark.

"No? An exchange of stories, you called it, but it's become solidly me answering your questions and you judging my answers."

He made a reflective sound, relaxed more into the pillows, and waved that away. "Force of habit. Ask me something, then."

"Tell me about this design." I held up a seal with it, probably for stamping scrolls and so forth. I'd carried plenty of sealed messages in my time. "Family crest or what?"

Kral held up his empty mug, so I crossed the room, scooped up the *mjed* keg, and refilled for us both. If he meant to get me drunk, he'd discover that took quite a bit of doing. And even a nice buzz couldn't make me reveal anything I didn't wish to.

"Do you always poke around in other people's things without permission?"

"Ooh, yet another question. First of all, you showed me how to open the cabinets, so I figured that for permission, since we're being all chummy and so forth. Second, you didn't tell me to stop, which you've had multiple opportunities to do. And third, yes, I'm a scout by profession because curiosity is in my nature. I enjoy exploring and digging up clues." Also, I wouldn't pass up an opportunity to gather what information I could. You never knew what might prove useful later. "If you'd rather I sat on my hands, I should warn you that's not my forte. I can just go."

He smiled then, more of that real one, like he'd smiled at me that night, his eyes not at all icy then, but full of warm admiration that I'd drunk up along with his excellent liquor. "I'd rather you stay and continue to entertain me."

Unable to resist, I sketched a quick jig for him, an intricate quick step and hop, followed by an elaborate bow. "Anything to please the customer," I said in my home dialect. "Throw a coin, kind sir?"

He laughed. "Do I even want to know what you said to me?"

I couldn't help grinning back. The *mjed* did make for a happy drunk. "Tell me about the crest. Why so surprised I didn't recognize it? You haven't worn it on your daily stuff or your armor."

"It's a sort of a family crest, though most of the meaning it holds is intimate—for the Konyngrr dynasty, not necessarily as the ruling party."

"Splitting a fine difference there."

"Yes and no. To a member of the royal family, using this symbol is a demonstration of our faith in the Emperor and belief in his divine status, and in the Konyngrr right to rule. We keep it private outside our home territories, but prominently used within them. Not to do so would be a sign of . . . dangerous disloyalty."

"Ah. You think I should have seen Harlan use it."

"That he doesn't use it means he's entirely turned his back on his family."

I shrugged. "Could be he has something of it in private, as you say. I'm not privy to his intimate life. But he also traveled for years with the Vervaldr, as I understand, without handy hidden cabinets to store knickknacks in. Extraneous stuff like that gets heavy pretty quickly when you don't have a permanent place to keep it."

"*This* should be important to him." Kral scowled into his mug, swirling the contents as if it might give him an answer.

"What does it mean?"

He held up the mug, pointing to the hand. "This is the Konyngrr fist, the might that rules all. From there spin out the threads of our family influence. All are connected to the central hand, which in turn holds all strings. We are tied together by blood, loyalty, and obedience. It's who we are. You see? Not simply extra weight."

"Harlan left Dasnaria a long time ago as I understand it, and more than once I've heard him say he never intended to return. People change. What might have been important in our youth can become deadweight over time." And probably he didn't care to be obedient to the Konyngrr fist, but I didn't bait Kral that far.

"My brother's allegiance to family should be at the core of his being, not something to be cast away alongside the road."

"I feel compelled to point out that all evidence indicates that Harlan's allegiance to Ursula is the core of his being these days. Isn't that how it should be? Danu teaches that children grow up, leave their parents and siblings, then put their partners above all else. It's not natural for a person to put the family they grew up with before the person they choose as a life's companion."

"It's natural for a Dasnarian man. No woman could ever mean more than a man's family."

"By which you mean his father and brothers."

A frown creased his brow. "Usually, yes."

"What about sisters—aren't they family? Assuming you don't strangle them at birth."

He nearly choked on that. "Our sisters and daughters are precious to us. We provide for and protect them. It's our sacred responsibility. Harlan, more than anyone, knows *that*."

Something there, for sure. My scout's senses tingled, telling me something unseen lurked, just beyond the perimeter. "Do you and Harlan have sisters? He's only mentioned brothers."

"Two sisters. And you—what of your brothers and sisters?"

"No, no, no. It's still my turn. Your mother had nine children?" The poor thing must've spent half her life pregnant.

"Our father had three wives who bore my brothers and sisters between them. Naturally this does not include children via his concubines."

"Naturally." Kind of mind-boggling to contemplate. Not a family situation I'd love to be part of, but hey—the world took all types. "So the concubines' kids don't get to be princes and princesses? Kind of sucks for them."

"Not at all. Those cousins are valued members of the royal household, holding places as our closest servers and retainers."

A royal family that breeds its own servants. That explained why he'd assumed I was a by-blow of Uorsin's. Thank Danu I had nothing of that man in me. "Oh, joyful life for them."

Kral frowned but didn't correct me immediately. "Perhaps it isn't for some. Those men who are unhappy go to seek their own fortunes."

"But not the women."

"Where would they go?"

"This is exactly what I'm wondering."

"My people would never allow a woman of station to wander the world, bereft of family and support, as yours did. It's unconscionable. I'd sooner put a blade to my sisters' throats than allow them to be so abused and unprotected." Kral's face flushed as he spoke, voice rising until I stabbed a finger at the unseen fish-birds.

"You are so wrongheaded about this." I shook my head as I paced. "I can't decide where to begin on all the stupid in what you just said."

"Insulting my intelligence will not bring us closer to seeing eye to eye."

"Okay, let's pretend you're not a lunkheaded idiot and can take a step back and view this objectively." I set my empty mug on the floor next to the keg and held out my bandaged hands, ticking off the points on the protruding fingertips. "You specified women of station, which means there are women with no station—like yours truly, here—who don't count. You assume a woman wandering the world without family—again with yours truly—has no means of support or protection and will be simply tossed about like a leaf on the autumn winds until she's shredded beyond repair. Finally—and I seriously hope that's some Dasnarian euphemism that's milder than it sounds—you would rather see your sister, or any woman at all, dead, her life forever taken away by your righteous beliefs, than for her to be on her own. Stupid."

Kral glowered. Swigged from his mug and found it empty. I didn't much feel like catering to him, so I didn't make a move. I'd had enough anyway.

"And you hold yourself up as an example of a woman with a good life?" He swept his hand at me. "Where is your husband, your children, your family? A woman without these things is nothing."

"Where is your wife, your children, *your* family, Kral? Not in this room, either."

"None of your damn business!"

Ooh, sensitive there, were we? A vulnerability in his emotional armor just begged to be exploited, and I possessed exactly enough ruthlessness to do it. "No? But my life is your business apparently. I have no secrets. My mother is dead. I never knew my father and never felt a lack there. I never wanted a husband or children, as both tie you down."

"And of course you couldn't commit to being with one man only."

"Back to that? And this coming from the guy whose daddy had three wives and umpteen baby-popping concubines." I licked my fingertip and held it up to the air, pretending to check the direction of the wind. "That stink of hypocrisy coming downwind must be you."

"The Emperor has a responsibility to provide children for the empire. Only the finest women of the highest station become his wives and concubines, producing the best and brightest children to govern the empire. That system works far better than the random selection of mates based on sexual whims. Should your queen produce children with my brother, they won't be heirs to your High Throne, will they? He's her concubine, with another title."

"It's different for them."

"How? Now you're the one splitting hairs, because you don't like my truth."

"Because Harlan entered into that relationship of his own free will. In fact, he settled on her and courted her with great patience and fortitude, and—"

Kral barked out a laugh, interrupting me. "This sounds exactly like my baby brother."

"*And*," I continued, "he wasn't chosen and bound to her by someone else. He's free to go at any time, to wander the world."

"No, he's not." Kral stabbed a long finger at me, face alight with triumph at drawing blood, all shark. "He pledged the *Elskastholrr* to her, which means he's bound to her for the rest of his life, possibly beyond, depending on whose teachings you believe. Thus he is arguably less free than even any of Hestar's wives and concubines."

Caught by a tricky maneuver without the proper weapon to counter. Curse it. But, pretending you knew the answers never got you the real ones. "I don't know what that is."

"Don't you?" Kral nearly preened at that, stretching and tucking his hands behind his neck, showing off his muscled chest nicely. "Pour me some more *mjed* and perhaps I'll explain."

"No." I'd had enough of his games. And him, for that matter.

"No?" He sat up a little, winced, and settled back. "We already went through this."

"What we went through was a subterfuge on your part to get me talking, a poorly disguised attempt at interrogation. You agreed to exchange stories for mine and yet you continue to avoid telling me anything real. I'm not catering to your little tournament of wits any longer. I'm bored with this." I yawned. That's right—I'd been tired before all this. Sleeping off the restless nights, the battle of the fish-birds, and the *mjed* buzz might just serve to kill the rest of the day and night.

"Fine," Kral finally said, in a grudging tone. "What do you want to know? Ask me straight, I'll answer, and you'll give me the *mjed*."

"Pretty cheap you're selling yourself there, Prince—don't you have servants to cater to you?"

"They won't let me have the *mjed*. Trond thinks it's bad for healing. He doesn't know I have that keg hidden away." His mouth quirked in a half smile at the admission, blue eyes lighter with mischief, like an ornery young boy's. Where was *that* man most of the time?

"Here's what I want to know. Explain this *Elskastholrr* to me, tell me why you don't have a wife and children, what went wrong between you and Harlan, and exactly what the whole inviting-me-into-your-bed thing means."

He winced, and not for his wounds that time. "All that for a flask of *mjed*? I'm not that desperate."

"And for my stories, which you promised you'd pay back in kind."

He studied me. "You're more intelligent than I took you for."

"Gee, thanks. You're a lot stupider than I first imagined."

To my surprise, he grinned at that. "I suppose there's something to be said for letting a woman wander the world on her own, if they turn out as entertaining as you are. Come." He patted the bed beside him. "Stop pacing around like a cat in a house with no doors, bring the keg of *mjed*, and sit with me."

"What are you up to, Kral?"

"Maybe I simply want to keep you out of my cabinets."

"Does this count as inviting me into your bed?"

"Why—afraid you won't be able to control yourself with me?"

Danu take him, he knew I couldn't resist that challenge. Also, if he did have seduction on his mind, then praise all the goddesses. I'd even light a rose candle to Glorianna if she'd lead Kral to end this sexual drought.

"Oh, honey." I grabbed the keg and my mug and sauntered over, letting my hips sway. "You offered tuna to the right kitty cat."

5

I climbed onto the high bed after kicking off my boots, and settled back against the mounds of burgundy silk pillows. Luxurious,
bedding a prince, it turned out. My blood sang with anticipation.
Call me impulsive and shortsighted—wouldn't be the first time—but
the prospect of getting laid made it easy to cast aside other concerns.
Besides, if Dafne had it right, I'd incurred the damage by accepting the first invitation. I could hardly compound it further. With a
lovely *mjed* and thank-Danu-I-finally-get-to-have-sex buzz going,
this all made perfectly rational sense.

Kral took a long drink, smacking his lips in satisfaction. "Nothing to ease the burn of fish-bird bites like a decent drunk. The
Elskastholrr is a vow a particular brand of Dasnarian idiot makes,
and I'm fascinated Harlan and your Ursula keep it secret."

Hey, I was a scout, not the High Queen's adviser like Dafne. I
would not have been on any need-to-know list concerning Ursula's sex life. Not that I'd admit as much to Kral. I kept quiet, the
best way to keep a man talking.

"It's full of religious and philosophical nonsense." Kral waved
that away with a contemptuous sweep. "Subsuming the self to

someone else, unconditional love and loyalty, taking the lower path, and so forth. Comes down to that my baby brother pledged himself to this foreign queen and gave up everything for her, for the rest of his life, or else he's forsworn."

All very interesting. I bet Dafne knew about this vow. "Some men would take being forsworn over more dire consequences, should it come to that."

"Not Harlan." Kral shook his head in disgust, sounding a little bitter. "He has an overdeveloped sense of selflessness. Always had to be the hero, saving everybody."

"Perhaps the Konyngrr hand is better off without him." And my High Queen clearly benefited with him, which meant we all did. I had no problem shoring up Kral's disappointment in his brother.

"No hand is better for losing one of its fingers. As for a wife." Kral sobered considerably, staring into his cup. "I do have one, thank you very much. Marrying as the family wishes is another responsibility I shouldered that Harlan evaded."

Very interesting. "And does Mrs. Kral know you sample the exotic fare travel brings?"

"It's the way of things. We have a marriage in name only."

"Really?" And he gave me grief for not wanting a husband. "Why?"

"It's complicated." He turned a little on the pillows and I decided to be helpful and plump a few behind him. He smiled slightly, more an ironic twist of the lips, and stroked my bare arm, as if testing the texture. Mmm. Nice. "She's nothing like you. Blond hair like sunshine and fresh snow, very tall, pretty blue eyes. Very accomplished, as appropriate for an Imperial Princess of the Royal House of Konyngrr."

Was that self-aware irony? More and more interesting all the time. "Accomplished how?"

"The womanly arts, of course—singing, painting, sewing. She embroidered all of this."

Yes, but could she pin a fly to a tree at twenty paces with a thrown blade? "So why haven't you bedded this paragon of womanhood?"

He tapped his mug against mine. "I am a second son, which means my lovely wife shall remain forever virgin, unless I'm needed to fill the Emperor's jeweled shoes."

I choked on a mistimed swallow of *mjed*. "You can't be serious!"

"Oh, yes. No legitimate children for Hestar's lateral heir, lest they get ideas about giving his grandsons competition. It's the way of things."

That particular Dasnarian phrase was going to drive me crazy eventually. "What about your other brothers?"

"They do not matter, unless I should meet a dire fate; then my third brother's son would be put to the sword as a precaution, and any more sons he should have." Kral shook his head, gazing into his cup. "That is the chance he took by having children, but it does serve to keep him invested in my continued well-being."

I could see that. "I hate to point this out to you, but just because *you* aren't fucking your wife doesn't mean she's still a virgin."

His face went deadly cold. "Her father sees to it or our contract is void."

"Though it doesn't apply to you." I sent an apology to Danu for entertaining any uncharitable thoughts about this woman. What a miserable life.

"Of course not. *I* am in no danger of conceiving a child."

"You could spawn one."

"Not a legitimate one, and—as you may recall—I'm exceedingly careful of such things."

Ah, yes, the *lind* he insisted on using. His deal if he wanted to dull sensation. He'd never asked, so I never mentioned my own methods for preventing unwanted babes. Easy enough for a child of the hill people.

"You're telling me that Mrs. Kral—"

"Karyn."

"That Karyn married the guy she was told to, never had sex

before that, will never get to have sex, and she has to live with her parents for the rest of her life?"

"I asked her and she accepted. She's well provided for. She lacks nothing. She's the fourth-highest-ranked woman in the Dasnarian Empire. It's a good life."

"Would *you* like a life like that? I notice you haven't given up sex."

He stirred, brows drawing together. "It's not the same for women. They don't have the same urges."

"Oh, honey. You're saying that to *me*?"

He transferred the frown to me. "I've told you—you are like no other woman I've ever known."

"Okay." I tossed back the last of the *mjed* in my cup. Even getting laid wasn't worth this. Not that I owed this distant Karyn anything. At least, her existence shouldn't bother me. Not doing Kral would hardly change her life at this point. Still. "I've had enough."

He put a hand on my hip. "Don't go. You asked for honesty and I have two more questions to answer. Will you run because I honored your wishes?"

He had a point. "Fine. Tell me the rest. Might as well eat the rest of the rotten meat and extract what nutrition I can."

"More of your people's hunting wisdom?" He stroked my hip, as if fascinated by the curve, making me want to purr again, despite everything.

"We're full of such things."

"So I perceive. As for your third question, the answer is fairly short, as the tale of Harlan and his departure is not all mine to tell, nor is it all his. I'll tell you what I can. Let's just say he and I disagreed on a family matter. He acted on his beliefs, which went against both the law and our father's direct command—and put another member of our family in grave peril. I attempted to intervene and set matters to rights. He caused me to lose the only thing that's ever mattered to me. He won out by default, succeeding in his misguided notions and ruining more than his own future."

"Then why try to bring him back with you if you're so angry with him?"

Kral made an impatient sound, working his fingers under my shirt to find the skin at my waist. "Harlan could come back and apologize at any time. Our father has passed into the *mjed* hall of the gods and His Imperial Majesty would welcome his brother back and forgive his transgressions. I gave that rabbit the perfect opening to be able to return—despite what he did—and yet he continues to refuse it."

"There is the *Elskastholrr*," I pointed out. "That compels him to stay with Ursula, even if nothing else does."

"The fool," Kral muttered, sliding his hand up my ribs. "He could keep his ill-advised vow to her and still return to civilization."

"Hey," I objected.

He smiled, all shark. "Don't fret, tidbit. I like your barbarian ways just fine." His hand closed over my breast and, ooh, yeah. I didn't care about the civilization remark any more. "And you like mine, it's clear to me."

His thumb rubbed over my nipple, tracing the sensitive circle of my areola, and I let it melt through me. The man had good hands and knew how to use them. I arched my neck in invitation and he took it, kissing me there.

"Being invited to my bed is not an insult. Far from it—it's a great honor," he murmured against my skin. "I have only ever offered the privilege to three women. It means I give you the protection of my body, my name, and my treasury. You would want for nothing and have no responsibilities, except for this one, which you so greatly enjoy, as you've pointed out."

Rolling my nipple between fingers and thumb, he raked my neck with his teeth. Nice and sharp, those sensations. I fumbled at the blanket covering him, ready to have at him already, the bandages making me a bit clumsy, but the *mjed* had done its work and my hands didn't hurt overmuch. "Enough conversation; let's get this cock inside me, doing what it does best."

"There are rules, though." He let me grasp his cock in my hand, eyes glittering in pleasure. He possessed plenty of control to enjoy himself without coming for some time, as I recalled. "No more fucking other men."

"Do you see other men in this bed?" I tightened my grip, finding the rhythm that got to him most, using the texture of the bandages to good effect, judging by the rocking of his hips.

"At all," he growled. "You belong to me and only me."

"Patently not true, because—"

"Shut up, Jepp." He effected the order by kissing me thoroughly. I considered it, as I savored the kiss, pinching his tender glans, for a little extra torment. Temporary exclusivity. I'd done it once or twice. Kral would be lover enough to keep me satisfied so that I wouldn't need to look elsewhere. And he'd proved I wouldn't have luck looking elsewhere if I didn't take his deal. I tore my mouth away. "Until we're done with each other."

His eyes narrowed, hand dipping into my trousers to—thank Danu!—part my folds. "What does 'done' mean?"

"Done," I gasped. "I get tired of you. You get tired of me. Or I have to sail home. We say good-bye and part ways full of delicious memories."

"What if you decide you're done and I decide I'm not?" He pushed a finger inside me, stroking me just the way I liked it.

"Either one of us gets veto power."

"What is that word?"

Forgetting myself with Common Tongue. "Either of us can end it at any time."

"We can try that. No weeping from you, however, when I am the one to be done first." He pushed his cock through the ring of my fingers. "I've missed those callused hands, little warrior."

"I missed having them on you. Inside me. Now."

"I'm happy to oblige. All that remains is your apology. Along with you asking me very nicely to fuck you the way you need it."

An apology for offending my honor and betraying my trust would go a long way.

I did need it in a bad way. Enough that I could see my way to asking nicely. A bit of dirty talk never hurt, and I'd be sure to "ask" in such a way that he'd be in no doubt as to his marching orders. But an apology? Spare me the male ego. Still, I'd never been one to let the little deer go just to maybe bag a bigger one. "I apologize, Kral, for bruising your feelings."

He thrust his cock harder in my hands. "For offending my honor and betraying my trust."

"We had no agreement; therefore, I betrayed no trust, offended no honor," I gritted through my teeth, his hand working wonders. Nearly there.

"I am master of my own honor," he growled back. "I say you offended me and I'll have an apology for that."

"Then you'll be waiting for the Northern Wastes to grow pink roses."

"You will apologize to me," he demanded, pumping harder, face going rigid with desire and determination.

"Fuck if I will," I hissed, vising both hands on his thick length.

He convulsed, remembering to swallow back the shout by sinking his teeth into the juncture of my neck and shoulder, spilling his seed over my hands as I milked him through it.

Then he withdrew his hands and rolled onto his back on the mounded pillows, all sated male, and rolled his head to look at me. He smiled, his smug, thin-lipped one. "No fucking until you do."

"You bastard!" I hissed.

He laughed, grabbing my wrists to hold me off him. If I'd thought to draw a blade, I'd have carved new holes in him that even Trond couldn't sew up.

"You satisfied me very nicely today, little *rekjabrel.* Enjoy the pleasure of having pleased me and earned your keep."

I managed to keep from trying to take a bite out of him. "Let me go, you ass."

"So you can draw one of your gnat killers on me? I don't think so."

He wasn't holding me tightly enough. And he called Harlan a

fool. I sagged a little, giving in, adding a whimper for effect, and he chuckled.

I exploded out, breaking his grip easily with the surprise, whipping out my twin daggers—which I hardly needed, as I'd made sure to catch him with both knee and elbow on recently stitched wounds, along with the heel of my foot to those balls he thought so big and manly—all as I flipped off his cursed bed and landed on my feet.

Like a cat, indeed. Never offer one tuna, then snatch it away. You'll get the claws every time.

Kral wheezed, grasping his groin, his face a fascinating shade of pale green. "I should kill you for that," he managed.

"Ambassador, remember? I may be new to politics, but even I know it's not worth starting a war over a bit of pussy." I chuckled at my own joke. Made me feel a bit better for getting suckered into his bed again. Earned my keep, indeed.

"Dasnaria would crush your Twelve Kingdoms."

I bared my teeth at him, filing away that bit of information. Was that plan in the works? "If we were wholly human, maybe. You've barely tasted what magic battles are like. It's a game changer, and you might find your armored boys cracked like eggs. And it's thirteen kingdoms, at least. Plus Nahanau, right, as they're inside our barrier? Guess that means we get whatever treasure it was you kept hinting about to King Nakoa. Must be pretty good stuff for you to want it so badly!"

Kral had a bit of breath back and produced a reasonable glare. "You were eavesdropping."

"Scout, remember? One of my favorite tools of the trade, eavesdropping." Though I also knew he'd given that search as his ostensible reason for being in the islands in the first place when he spoke with Ursula. "Hope you did enjoy that little hand job, as it's the last time I'm laying my hands on you in pleasure. Next time, I'll cut it off." I gave him a slicing smile, pouring all of my anticipation into it. "Don't think I won't, General."

"Oh, don't go spiky on me, *hystrix*. Come back and play with me. We can debate the terms of your apology."

Clamping down on my self-control, I left without another word.

The next morning, Kral sent out a man in full armor to test for the presence of the fish-birds. As Zynda had been arguing again that she could go look, I was just as happy for him to risk one of his men. She'd been asleep when I returned to our cabin—probably as exhausted as I was from watching over Dafne—so she'd been spared my rant about stubborn, pigheaded Dasnarians. In the bright light of morning, and, okay, maybe a teensy bit of a hangover, I didn't feel like reviewing my poor choices of the evening before.

It had been a long time since a guy had gotten me drunk in order to seduce me. Oldest trick in the book, and I fell for it like I was fifteen again. So, though Zynda gave me a number of inquiring sidelong glances, I kept my own counsel. At least practicing discretion made me feel more ambassadorial.

The man reported the area within sight range free of fish-birds, thank all the goddesses, and Jens sent sailors flying up the masts, unfurling the sails to catch the wind with great snaps and billowing that sounded quite optimistic. All that wine red reminded me a bit too much of Kral's bed, so I set to working out. Clear the mind and constitution. A bit brutal with the hangover, but a good penance for all that.

By midafternoon, though Jens had reported we'd drifted off course by quite a bit during our downtime, the lookout's shout announced that we approached the barrier. Zynda stood with me at the prow. I couldn't see a damn thing but ocean, sky, and more ocean and sky, but she squinted, then nodded.

"What do you see?" I asked her.

"A kind of shimmer; see there?"

I followed the line of her finger. No shimmer. And I had the best long-sight of most anyone I'd met. "No. What color?"

She slid me a smile. "Magic colored."

Oh, great. "Don't play enigmatic, Tala sorceress—just describe it." I hadn't seen the barrier before, that I knew of, as I hadn't gone to Annfwn with Ursula. All those times in Branli, though, when she led the Hawks on Uorsin's errand to find another crossing into Tala territory, I'd think I must be coming closer to the barrier, only to find myself going the opposite direction of where I'd planned to . . . Surely I'd seen it then and not known it for what it was. Galling.

"I understand it looks different to Tala eyes than to a moss-back's," Zynda explained, not at all daunted. "To me it looks like a great curtain of magic, stretching from the depths as high as I can see."

"It looks like a mirror, Ambassador," Kral inserted, stepping up beside us, making the honorific sound as sensual as when he called me *hystrix*, whatever that meant.

"Should you be on your feet?" I asked, with plenty of sweet mocking in return. "Wouldn't want you passing out and falling overboard."

"Push me and you'll go, too."

"I've heard non-Tala say it's like a mirror," Zynda inserted.

"The first time we hit it," Kral replied pointedly only to her, "we did so at full sail, damaging the prow enough that it took us days to repair."

"You'd think a big mirror would have shown you your own ship racing headfirst at your idiot self," I commented drily.

Kral set his jaw. Ha! Point to me. "It reflects the landscape only. To us it looked like more sea and sky."

"How is your lookout spotting it, then?" I searched the horizon, irritated with myself for not seeing a great curtain of magic. Something like that should be visible. It violated the laws of nature for it to hide from some people and not others. And there I went, thinking about it like a sentient being. Kral had me all kinds of inside out.

Kral pointed at the crows circling the lookout high above. "They see it."

Great. Even a crow could spot what I couldn't.

"Animals should be able to pass freely through the barrier, though." Zynda gave Kral a puzzled frown. "How did you discover this trick?"

"Our crowmaster is quite accomplished. At my direction, he trained them to fly alongside the barrier, to guide us. Easy enough to teach them, he says, as that's not much different than their usual duties. We Dasnarians are most inventive and clever." He added that last with a snide smile for me.

"Or your crows are," I retorted. "I imagine repeatedly bashing your ship into an invisible mirror wall gave you considerable incentive to figure something out."

Zynda managed to keep a straight face long enough to turn it away from Kral, but I knew I'd amused her. Just as I knew I'd struck a nerve with Kral. I could just picture the scenario, him commanding his men to try again and again. Like me, he wouldn't believe something existed that he couldn't see until he'd nearly brained himself trying to bull his way through it. Or shark his way through. I didn't know much about the toothy fish. Chomp his way through?

Kral managed to swallow the tart response his sour expression transmitted anyway. "Incentive to keep us all from drowning, indeed. Now, tell your Tala friend to hold up your end of the bargain. We've shown you where the barrier is. Call in this enchantress queen to bring us through."

"I'm standing right here," Zynda said in a mild tone that nevertheless raised the hairs on the back of my neck. King Rayfe had a knack for that, too. Like the soft growl of a predator in the shadows. Never paid to forget the power the Tala carried inside their mutable skins, no matter how genial or languid they appeared. Mountain cats looked like that, too.

Kral wasn't a total idiot, because he noted the implicit danger and—no doubt recalling the demonstration in the court at Ordnung when Zynda became a lethal tiger—gathered himself enough to bow slightly. "My apologies, sorceress. I am . . . out of sorts this morning. We await your next move."

"Accepted, General." Zynda still sounded cool. "If you'll give me room to consult with the Ambassador, we'll determine our final strategy."

He didn't like it, his bow stiff and more perfunctory, but Kral strode off.

"What strategy?" I asked her. We already had a plan, the one Her Majesty gave us. Zynda might be worse with authority than I was, but we couldn't not follow those orders.

"Mostly I wanted to talk to you before I go. Do you think it's wise to dally with him?"

"I'm taunting, not dallying."

Her gaze went to my neck. "Did someone else leave that bite mark?"

I clapped a hand over it. Danu! I'd forgotten. A definite weakness that I liked his mouth so well. When words weren't coming out of it. "I blame Danu," I snarled.

Zynda tilted her head, a long, slow blink of her deep blue eyes. "Isn't love Glorianna's realm?"

"Yes, though there's no love lost between me and Kral."

"Just a burning passion you seem to be unable to resist."

"I could resist if I wanted to, which I have enough *incentive* to do now, as the man makes every cursed thing so difficult. Sex is a simple thing. Why can't he see that?"

"And you blame Danu because . . . ?" she prodded.

"She's supposed to guide me. Clear-eyed wisdom and all that. Clearly she's not transmitting any of it to me, because I keep stumbling back into the same thrice-damned mistakes."

Zynda flattened her quick smile into a somber line. "I suspect the point is not for the goddesses to rescue us from our own mistakes, but for us to follow the example of the virtues they embody and learn to do better."

"Had to figure there would be a catch," I muttered, mostly to myself. "Don't worry about me. I'll be fine. Have you settled on a shape?"

"I'm going with a porpoise—good for long distances, less risk of fish-birds, as I can outswim them more easily than outfly. And a porpoise is smart enough for me to keep most of my sentience. Just in case I need to reassess along the way."

"And you're sure you can find this spot again?"

"Another good reason for that form; they have excellent homing instincts. I'll go and be back with Andi as soon as I can."

"Getting word to Her Majesty about Dafne's abduction takes precedence."

"If only I could be in two places at once."

"Use some of that Tala magic. What about shifting into two versions of yourself? That's what I'd want to be able to do. You should practice that."

She laughed, which was much better than the worried frown. "Be careful, Jepp. Maybe try to antagonize Kral a little less. I have a bad feeling."

"Is prognostication among your gifts?"

Shifting uneasily, she looked away. "They were among Salena's, though personally I never get more than vague concerns."

"Even *I* get those. Whiskey helps."

She didn't laugh again, but she smiled. "Don't make me worry about you."

"I could say the same to you."

"I'll deliver the messages. I won't fail you."

"Never crossed my mind that you could."

She hugged me and I held on to her fiercely. Ridiculous to feel abandoned. I'd been far more on my own before in my life. Funny, though, how taking this journey with her and Dafne had forged a friendship among us unlike any I'd had before. We had little in common, the three of us. Neither of them shared my profession, as all of my sisters and brothers in arms had. Who'd have predicted that a librarian and a shape-shifting sorceress would become so much a part of my heart?

The one Kral would say I didn't possess.

Perhaps it would be best for Zynda to go and take that softness with her. I needed to be my cagiest, hardest-shelled self to defend against Kral's determined attacks.

"Good-bye," I told her. "May Danu guide you wisely, may Glorianna keep watch over you, and may your goddess Moranu protect you as the best and brightest of her children."

Zynda smiled through unshed tears. "I'll appeal to Moranu to protect you also."

"I'm no shape-shifter."

"No, but scouts and spies keep to the shadows, which are Her domain. And you may be wearing more skins in the future than you realize. Good fortune to you."

With that, she released me and climbed up on the rail. To my surprise, she gave me the Hawks' salute, fist over heart, then leapt, transforming midair to neatly cleave the waves and disappear.

"I don't like this," I said to the unblemished waves. They had no reply to that. No one ever did.

6

The fish-bird swarm found us again by sunset.

I'd been standing at the rail, watching Glorianna's vivid aged face, fraternal twin to rosy dawn, sink into the ocean beyond the barrier I still couldn't see. If it acted like a mirror, how could I see the sun set beyond it? Magic made no sense at all.

Shipmaster Jens had set us on a gently curving course that followed the barrier for a while in one direction before he brought the *Hákyrling* about to retrace in the opposite direction. The redundant pattern kept us more or less in the same place as best as could be managed without dropping anchor—something I'd been informed we couldn't do at that depth.

Kral had taken his injured and cantankerous self back to bed—at Trond's orders—and to the relief of more people than just me. Once he wasn't around, his men stopped pretending I didn't exist, and some even sang as they worked. It had never occurred to me that fighters could double as sailors, though to be fair, I'd never set foot on a sailing ship before this journey. Efficient of the Dasnarians, though I'd never say so to Kral. His ego needed no help.

Either the fish-birds had grown wilier or Kral's lookouts more complacent, but we had little warning before the creatures fell on us. It meant the lookout had his sword out and carving through the fish-birds, bright green pieces falling to the deck and grabbing my attention at the same time as his shouts. They hit us hard, in great numbers from the outset, several of the men falling under the hordes almost immediately. Seeing Jens swarmed at his critical post, I leapt to his defense, as he could hardly hold to our careful course and fight off the fish-birds also.

"You can't stay out here," I yelled at him.

"Have to keep the wheel," he gritted out, ducking a razor swipe at his cheek.

I went into the Whirling Wind pattern, somewhat hampered by my still-injured hands. Might have been smarter not to worry the wounds by working Kral over, especially as he hadn't been worth the effort. Water under the bow, as it were. Speak of the demon, himself appeared on deck, wearing his gleaming black armor, complete with helm and gauntlets, and bellowing orders. I knew that bellow, and also Kral's lean height and effortless command. He sent men below as he reached them and made his way to us.

"We're helpless pinned against your barrier." He flung up his face plate and shouted the accusation at me, as if it were all my fault.

"Busy here," I informed him, not pausing the spin.

At least he provided some assistance, taking my back and weaving his own pattern with the broadsword to keep the things off Jens. Slower than would be perfectly effective, but fast for the considerable weight of the weapon—and taking into account the previous day's injuries. Another man would not have recovered as well so quickly. I had to admit, donning the armor had been a smart move. The first time I'd seen it, when I escorted Kral and his bodyguards through Ordnung's gates to approach the High Throne, the exotic armor struck me as ridiculously rigid. Daunting, yes, as it made the wearer look much larger, and creepily fierce, like a hard-shelled insect that promised a painful sting. But not at all practical to my mind.

Now I rather envied him the protection.

"Take us away from the barrier," Kral ordered Jens.

"Not so easy with the men on the sails under attack."

As if to answer that, a man up on one of the crosspieces gave a wailing cry as he fell, plummeting from above and hitting the deck with a sickening thud. A flurry of bright green bodies descended on him like flies feeding on fresh droppings, more heading that way with hungry cries that sawed on my nerves.

No, that was the screech of the edge of the ship against the barrier. I still couldn't see the thriced thing, but the sight of wooden splinters flying as the *Hákyrling* ground against nothing would be difficult to miss under any circumstances.

Kral shouted a curse. Then flung a fierce look at me. "Keep him alive and on the wheel or we're all dead and I'll send your corpse personally to your Tala friend so she'll see what her tender heart cost."

I focused on keeping my speed and momentum, admirably refraining from spending any energy on pointing out that Kral wouldn't be sending anything anywhere if all of us were dead. Keeping maybe some of us from being all dead took serious precedence. From the edges of my vision, I spotted Kral climbing the rigging, surprisingly agile in that armor, which had to weigh as much as a small child, shouting in Dasnarian so rapid and thick I couldn't make it out, even if I'd been able to spare the attention.

Sails flapped as the *Hákyrling* wheeled about, moving away from the barrier and going more north and east, away from where Zynda would bring Andi to meet us. Not that I was inclined to argue. But the Three had better have a plan to keep this from being a complete and utter disaster. More bodies accumulated on the deck, at least occupying substantial numbers of the feasting fish-birds and making them less inclined to go after those of us who still fought back.

Still, I was hard-pressed to keep them off of Jens, who gallantly held the wheel as he took us at what felt like a strong diagonal, at a steadily increasing speed as the sails angled to catch the wind. My muscles wept with exhaustion, still not recovered from the previous day's fight. Internally I kept up a singsong prayer that alternated between beseeching Danu's assistance and lamenting my loss of stamina from days gone by. It would have been handy to be in top form.

Kral appeared again, black armor smeared with blood and bits of glistening green scales, accompanied by several of his smaller, faster men, all similarly armored and now using a double-bladed attack as I did. They set up a perimeter while Kral neatly ducked through the opening I made for him in the whirling defense around Jens. "Follow us," he shouted in my ear from behind.

In a wearied fog, I did, grateful that the other fighters helped thin the fish-birds who made it through to my blades. I'd slowed, and slow meant death. *Run as fast as you can or the bear will catch and gut you.* Kral carried Jens over a shoulder, head hunched against the flying razored beaks, as he bolted at top speed for the cabin door to safety.

I should have savored going in and out of that doorway at a leisurely pace earlier, while I still could.

Kral made it through the door, which shut behind him and Jens. Two men ahead of me, one behind. I put on a burst of speed, which curiously upended itself. I'd fallen through that hole before, through the long, slow, dizzying drop of a mortal wound. As I crashed to the planks, I expected the warm rush of my guts spilling out with nauseating pain. No one should feel that and live.

Maybe I hadn't and all this had been a dream as I lay dying at Uorsin's feet. Trading one bear for another. I should have heeded that omen. Apparently I learned nothing from my mistakes.

As my vision went bloodred, then black, I sent a prayer to Danu to find a better warrior to complete my unfinished business. Like mother, like daughter. Failed in the end.

Lost.

I blinked at the wooden shutters above. Not Ordnung. Had I been captured? The Tala, Duranor . . . Oh, right. The sway of the *Hákyrling* brought it all back, along with an excruciating headache. With a groan of self-pity, I lifted a hand to press whatever spike drove itself into my temple to help it finish the job and let me die already.

A man said something and I managed to focus on him. Twisted, hard-edged words. My sluggish brain churned to make sense of them.

"Your head hurts due to blood loss," he said more slowly, and wrapped my hand around a flask. I really didn't want *mjed*—just the thought made my stomach heave. "Water," Trond insisted. "Drink, Ambassador. If you die on us, it will look very bad for Kral."

There was an upside to everything. Except if I died, I wouldn't get to watch Kral squirm as Ursula skewered him.

"It could mean war between our realms," Trond reminded me with a reproving frown.

There was also that. I gulped the water, slowing when he reminded me to sip. Not easy, as my drained body seized on the desperately needed moisture, every tissue screaming for more. I'd been in this place before. Only that time I'd awaked to Ash's scarred face and gentle green gaze studying me with concern, instead of this big Dasnarian medic. And Ash had healed me, mostly. Turned out even only partial magical healing had it all over being bandaged. As my head descended from the numbing cloud of unconsciousness—which had frankly been quite preferable to reality—more and more of my body awakened and began clamoring for attention. That's how pain worked, an alarm call that something bad was happening to the body. Really not all that useful in the aftermath, however. In pitched battle, I never felt the wound, and afterward there wasn't a thrice-cursed thing I could do to change it.

I hated pain. I really did.

Some of the meditation Danu taught worked to mitigate wound pain, but first you had to be able to banish enough of the distraction to concentrate on it. Vicious circle. Also, something nagged at me. Something I'd forgotten.

"Where are my knives?"

Trond gave me a wry smile. "Both of you alike—the general put them under your pillow."

I slid a hand under, immeasurably reassured by the familiar sense of edged metal within easy reach.

"How do you feel?"

I really hated that question, too. What did they think anyone would say? "Like a skinned and bled-out deer must feel when slow smoked over a campfire to be made into jerky, only the deer gets to be dead."

A grin cracked his face. "Excellent."

"Seriously?"

"Yes. Always a good sign when my patients show spirit. The general ordered me to make sure you lived."

"Such a reasonable guy." I scowled at the wooden ceiling, seeing for the first time that even it had the Konyngrr crest inlaid with silver metalworked into the wood. Great for the psyche, to see that fist tugging the spiderweb of control and intrigue on waking and sleeping. No wonder Kral was sideways in the head. "Do I want to know why I'm in his bed?"

"No significance." Trond tucked another full flask next to my hip. "The general's room was closest and gives me more room to work than your smaller cabin. We had you on the floor for a while."

I followed the tip of his head to see the wide stain of drying blood on the wood. "Ouch."

"Considerable blood loss." Trond reiterated, lifting a shoulder and letting it fall. "Surprising that such a small body can contain so much, eh? I thought you were dead more than once."

"Wouldn't be the first time," I commented. How many lives had I used up? At least three now. Kral likened me to a cat, and they supposedly had nine. Could be I had . . . five or six more. That sounded downright optimistic, looking at it that way.

"It amuses you that you nearly died?"

"It amuses me that I seem to be hard to kill. Maybe Danu *is* looking out for me. How long was I out, anyway?"

"All night and the following day. It's coming on sunset again."

Whoa. I tried to sit up, and my head spun so that I couldn't muster any resistance when Trond pressed me back again. "No sitting up yet, until you make more blood."

"What about the fish-birds? Where are we? Where's Kral?"

"Still following, somewhere in the Nahanaun archipelago, and up on deck. The general has everyone going above in full armor."

"Smart of him."

"Kicking himself for not thinking of it before," Trond noted with a wry smile. Heavy bootsteps approached and the door opened. "Speaking of whom," he said, giving me a cautionary look I couldn't quite interpret. Another thing I hated—the significant warning glance that gave no information. All the scouts I trained knew to give detail before vague alarms.

Maybe making mental lists of things I disliked would distract me from the grinding pain.

"Does she live?" Kral asked, striding over to the bed and peering at me before Trond could answer. "You're awake," Kral informed me.

"And you're a stunning master of observation." I didn't like how it unsettled me to see the man in that striking black armor; even with the faceplate up and his broadsword safely sheathed on his back, he looked menacing. The sharp edges of the narrow opening only made his icy-blue eyes more intense and penetrating. Didn't help that I was naked, but for the copious bandages, and too weak to even sit up. I sucked furiously on the water. *Come on, body, make that blood.*

"I'll see about getting you some meat broth, now that you're ready for that step," Trond said, fleeing the battlefield.

"How do you feel?" Kral demanded.

This again. "Like killing about a thousand of those fish-birds and stomping their shiny green bodies into dust," I snapped.

Kral reached a hand to the back of his helm and yanked it off, tunneling through short hair made a darker gold than usual with sweat, and grinned at me. "That's my girl. I figured a leathery piece of meat like you would be tougher to kill than that."

However oddly phrased, the remark warmed me. Probably counted as an actual compliment in the Dasnarian book of male communication. Fascinated, I watched him remove the armor, plate by plate, stowing it in a cabinet I'd not yet found. The armor sections seemed to connect with each other much the way the cabinets fit flush into the wooden walls. He wore padded cotton beneath, also soaked through with sweat, and began stripping that off also.

"You will not go above," he ordered over his shoulder, "until we have seen the last of the fish-birds."

Oh, joy. "That's hardly a workable solution."

"Unless you have armor I don't know about?" He pointed at the bloodstained floorboards. "That's going to have to be sanded out as it is. Nobody is going above without armor, no matter how miserably hot it is. Stupid that I didn't think of it before. I wouldn't have lost five men if we'd taken that simple precaution." Naked, he kicked at the pile of sodden cotton in furious disgust. Then he triggered a panel that folded out into a table, pulled out a basin and pitcher, and began washing himself. The water and the glow of lantern light did fine things for the golden lines of his body. I sipped at the water, appreciating both the sight of his muscular back and ass flexing as he moved, and the entertainment. I could kind of see his point from the day before. Lying abed feeling like a critter caught in a snare too long, starved and gnawing off its own paw became marginally less torturous with interesting company.

I wasn't thrilled at the prospect of being trapped inside for the foreseeable future, but neither was I eager to feed either the fish-birds or the wooden planks more of my blood. "So, what *is* your plan? When Zynda returns with Queen Andromeda, they won't know where we've gone."

"Now who's the master of observation?" He grumbled, though not in a particularly mean way. Almost philosophical. He turned, treating me to a full frontal of his excellent chest, abs, and thighs. Not to mention that generously endowed cock, impressive even flaccid. Too bad it was attached to an obstinate idiot. "We're sailing through shallower waters, so we can anchor if need be, though being in motion seems marginally more effective for keeping the fish-birds from swarming. Fortunately, their numbers don't seem to be growing and we're continuing to pick them off, so they might even be decreasing. Plus, we tipped the corpses overboard, and many of the scavengers followed that food source—and with nothing to eat aboard ship, they seem to be losing interest in us."

He and I shared a grimace for that reality.

"Jens predicts that your people shouldn't arrive back at the magic barrier before another day and a half or two days. We'll head back that direction in the morning by indirect route and hope to have lost enough of the flock that the fish-birds won't attack your people when they meet us."

"Probably Zynda would be persuaded to clear the air and water of them with her magic, should it come to that."

"What makes you think her bleeding heart will be moved to self-preservation this time?" Kral said sourly.

"She said as much before she left."

Kral's hands stilled in midwash long enough for me to drag my gaze up to his face. Not nearly so pleasant, set with that black expression. "And you only see fit to mention that now?"

"We had no reason to think the fish-birds would be back. I

can see her point on that. You don't go around wiping out species that aren't directly threatening you. Kill all the mountain cats and you'll be ears-deep in deer."

"I'd think that would be a good thing for simple hill folk following their food source around."

"Clearly you've never survived off the land. Too many deer means they eat down all the vegetation, which means none left for people and then blood and bone disease follows. There's a reason Danu requires balance in all things."

"I'm rather tired of hearing about Danu, balance, and sympathy for predatory fish-birds. In Dasnaria we either possess or kill. No in-between for women's tears."

"Control or destroy? Fits with what I know of your empire. Can't say I find it admirable. Or all that effective." That last wasn't quite the word I wanted, but my head seemed to be going muzzy again.

Kral shrugged into loose pants and a light shirt, both in a dusky blue that did a great deal to soften the ice of his eyes. He left the ties undone on the shirt so it lay open to his navel. Made up for losing the entire view to some extent. Not entirely, since my new rule—a line never to be crossed again—was looking only. No touching.

"The Dasnarian Empire is nothing if not effective, nor does it require your admiration."

"I'm sure there's something cutting I could say about that, but it's not coming to me."

Kral came over to take the water from my hand. Could be the dizziness, but he looked concerned. Gentle, even. "Sleep, then. Let your body recover and you can fight with me tomorrow."

"Are you being nice to me?"

"No." But he smoothed my hair back from my brow. "It's no fun to spar with you with your weapons so dulled."

"I'm in your bed," I muttered sleepily.

"Where you belong, *rekjabrel*, as you agreed from the beginning."

"Where will you sleep, though? I should move." Though I couldn't. Weariness dragged at me, and his bed *was* hugely softer and more comforting than my hammock.

"I'll think of something."

I fell asleep to his hand stroking my brow, mulling hazily how long it had been since someone touched me that way, outside of sex.

I awoke to the sound of thunder. No, to Kral's deafening snores. Incredible I'd slept at all with that racket. He lay on his side between me and the door, massive back to me, shoulder blocking all but the glow of the lantern he'd left burning on low. Another dragging snore. Danu save me. I thumped Kral hard on that shoulder, and the noise cut off instantly as he erupted up, a knife in his hand. Half a moment later, he relaxed and fixed on me. Impressive reflexes.

"Here." He reached to the floor and handed me a flask. "I'm to make you drink this when you awake."

I took it, bemused by him. From dead asleep to the order of business within three heartbeats. I scooted up a bit—cautiously, though the severe head swimming from before didn't arise nearly so viciously—and took a swallow. Still warm, the meaty broth flowed into my stomach, as comforting as Kral's hand on my brow had been. If I hadn't dreamed that.

The man himself, discharged of duty, lay back again and yawned mightily. "It's a few hours until dawn still, so once you finish we'll sleep again. You're to drink it all, then another flask of water I have here—if your stomach is up to it."

"And if it isn't?" Said stomach had gone from vaguely queasy to voraciously hungry, but I knew well how easily it could go back in the other direction. I'd hate to foul Kral's bed as well as his floor, if only because I didn't want to have to lose its delicious soft comfort.

Kral turned his head on the pillow and grinned at me. "I have a basin for that. I'd offer to hold your hair while you puke, but you don't have any."

"I have hair."

"Short as a servant's."

"Any longer and it becomes a fuzzy cloud. I look like an angry porcupine, only less tasty."

"What is that?"

I'd used my home dialect for the animal and shrugged, finishing the broth and giving it a few moments to decide if it wanted to stay there. "Who knows if you have them? A smallish insect-and-berry eater." I demonstrated with my hands. "With stiff fur that's sharp, like thorns, and stands up when it's threatened."

"Aha! The *hystrix*." He sounded enormously pleased, and I recalled he'd called me that before, just my luck. "The trick with those, as with all prickly creatures, is to flip it onto its back and address the soft underbelly." He put a hand on my abdomen beneath my bare breasts where the blanket had fallen away, caressing what little skin I still possessed that wasn't wounded.

"Address my soft belly all you like, Kral. You're not getting anywhere with me again. My people have a saying: Fool me once, shame on you. Fool me—"

"—twice, shame on me. Yes, yes. This is a Dasnarian wisdom. I have never tricked you."

"I'm ready for the water." I pointedly ignored his still-caressing hand and the arousing shivers it produced.

He rolled over, grabbed the flask off the floor, and handed it to me. "You needn't fret. I would not take advantage of you in your wounded condition. You like a little pain with your sex, but that would be much even for you."

"Such consideration."

"I could say that Trond would have my balls if I jeopardized your recovery by using them on you, but this is for me. I want you hale and hearty before we go at it again."

"No fun to spar with a pathetic wreck, huh? I heard you say so."

"That." He sighed and tucked his hands behind his head. "Also,

I deeply regret that you were so gravely injured in my service. I—all my men—owe you a debt. Jens says he could never have stayed at the wheel without your protection."

I finished the flask of water and handed it back, trying to find a non-sore spot to lie on. Given how much fluid I'd consumed, I'd have a severe need to piss eventually, but so far it seemed to be holding off. Becoming blood, probably. Also, I didn't quite know what to make of Kral being nice to me. And grateful. "You don't owe me a debt—it was in the interests of saving my own skin that I did it. Couldn't stand by while the *Hákyrling* ground herself into sawdust against the barrier." I'd gone for acerbic and uncaring, but it came out sleepy, and Kral chuckled.

"Ironically, it's your skin that you forfeited. Such pretty skin, too, like *svasshnut*."

"What's that?" My turn to ask. Ouch, not that spot.

"Here." Kral stretched out an arm, threaded it under me, and tucked me against his side, my head pillowed in the hollow of his shoulder. "Better?"

Surprisingly so. Skin to skin always soothed me, as did his male scent, faintly spiced with some foreign soap of his.

"*Svasshnut* is a dessert. Very creamy and sweet."

"I'm not food, Kral."

"Creamy and sweet," he repeated, and kissed my brow. "Sleep, my *hystrix*, so your bristles may be sharp enough tomorrow to guard that soft underbelly."

7

Trond was there when I woke late into the next morning, and I told myself I wasn't the least disappointed that Kral had absented himself. The desperate need to pee had arrived as predicted. It took only the threat of letting loose in Kral's bed to convince Trond to let me get up instead of using the basin he thought he'd foist on me.

Because I'd insisted so forcibly, I had to put on a considerable tough act to cover the dizziness and nausea that swamped me as I staggered to the chamber pot. I'd never hurt so much. Not that I could recall. Kral's quip about me not having skin left wasn't far off the mark.

"The stitches hurt the most," I complained to Trond once I made it back into bed. "They pull. I think I'd be fine without them."

"Oh sure, sure," he said affably enough. "Just let me get a tarp so when all those wounds open up again and you bleed out, at least we can feed it to the fish-birds instead of staining the floor."

I scowled at the shutters overhead, pretending it didn't feel infinitely better to be lying down again. Trond handed me another flask of warm broth. "Ugh. Can't I have real food?"

"If you keep this down, yes. If you rush yourself, it will only keep you abed longer."

"We have magical healing in the Thirteen Kingdoms, you know. Goes much faster."

"I envy those healers, then," Trond replied, checking my bandages. "Lucky them to be rid of difficult patients so quickly. You're worse than the general."

Perversely, that pleased me. *Top that, Kral.* Though I felt a tinge of guilt. "I apologize, Trond. I know I'm a terrible patient. Never did master the knack of that particular skill."

He patted my arm on a hand's breadth of unscathed skin. "Bold spirits never do. It's what keeps you fighting when a saner personality would retreat for cover. You were something to see, warrior, your blades moving so fast they seemed to be a lethal fog. I never saw your blades, only the green rain you made of the fish-birds."

"You were on deck?"

"Briefly. Dragging men inside, those still living."

"Kral said he lost five."

"Seven. Two more died of their wounds."

He did look weary. No surprise with tending all of us. "Go rest. I'll be still and behave. No need to watch me."

Trond nodded and rubbed palms briskly on his thighs. "I won't refuse that offer. Can I have anything sent to you, or will you sleep?"

No way would I sleep—I hurt too much, though I wouldn't say so to Trond. He'd heard enough of my complaints. At least Dafne had had her books, journals, and such to keep her occupied when she skinned her feet. I probably looked all over like her poor soles had. She always nagged that I wouldn't sit still long enough to learn written Dasnarian. That was true, though I'd also figured I wouldn't need it. *Hlyti* spitting in my face there. I supposed I could put my inactivity to good use.

"There's a few scrolls, some ink, in my cabin. If you could have those sent?"

"Done. And solid food soon, if you swear you won't touch it if you feel any stomach cramping or other illness."

"Agreed." I doubted I'd feel anything as prosaic as a bellyache through the increasing shouting of my nerves at the painful pulling of the stitches. Some lethal cloud I'd produced, that allowed those beaks to get me everywhere, despite my fighting leathers. Thinking of which . . . "Trond—where are my leathers?"

He paused at the door and shook his head in regret. "Unsalvageable. Cut to ribbons, just as you were."

Great. Just wonderful.

I must have been learning more about being aboard the *Hákyrling* than I realized, because I felt the shift in our direction toward evening. Maybe in the sound of the waves rocking the ship, the angle she leaned in. Headed back to the meeting place, no doubt. I tossed down the scroll I'd been painstakingly copying Dasnarian characters onto. Dafne said the best way to learn to read was to make myself write them. I'd hate to know what the worst way was.

Bootsteps in the hall caught my ear. Kral's tread, if I didn't miss my mark. I'd been playing that game all the long, dull afternoon, listening to the passing of Dasnarian feet, knowing none of them for his, occupying myself with cataloging activity and making mental notes of their routines. The door opened to admit Kral, and I pumped my fist in victory. Amazing what can be entertaining when you're out of your mind with boredom.

"Happy to see me?" He pulled off his helm, ran his fingers through sweaty hair. A man of certain rituals, my Kral.

"Congratulating myself for correctly pinning the sound of your footsteps. Though you have a certain unmistakable aggressive cadence, so it wasn't much of a challenge."

To my surprise, he smiled easily at that, stripping off the armor with quick efficiency. "Tired of recuperation?"

"About ready to gnaw my way through the hull," I admitted.

He picked up the scroll I'd been laboriously copying. "Your handwriting is atrocious. My five-year-old nephew can do better."

"Oh, yeah? Let's see how your Common Tongue looks. Or, hey, how about your written Nahanaun!"

"Bah." He tossed the scroll back onto the bed, much as I had. "That language makes no sense. It gives me a headache to even think about it. How can going '*OO-ay*' mean something totally different than '*oo-AY*'? A madman constructed that language."

I laughed, a welcome feeling after bored misery. It pulled my stitches, however, so ended on a kind of embarrassing wheeze of pain.

"It's the serration of the beaks." Kral showed me one of his own healing wounds in sympathy. "Trond had to pull the stitches tighter than usual, because the edges of the wounds weren't even. Want some *mjed*?"

"Drinking with you did not turn out so well last time," I made myself say, though the prospect of lightening some of the pain made my mouth water.

He gave me a long look, contemplating. "I know you value your independence, and I'm trying to understand that about you, but everyone needs help sometimes. Let me take care of you that much."

"You won't try to use it against me?"

Suppressing a smile, he held up a hand. "I promise not to re-engage our game until you feel better."

Always games with him. Easy to be fooled by those layers of bluster. "Unfortunately, I think we polished off your stash of *mjed*."

That mischievous little-boy grin lit Kral's face. "I have several stashes. An effective warrior maintains his own supply chain."

"More Dasnarian wisdom?"

"Always." He crossed to the far wall, crouched, and opened yet another hidden cabinet, with a number of the *mjed* kegs in it. A man after my own heart.

"In one of the northern kingdoms, Branli, they brew a whiskey twice as strong as your *mjed*," I told him, "though not nearly as smooth on the tongue. I bartered for a case of that stuff and packed it around for the better part of a year."

"And you haven't shared it with me? Cruel woman."

"Finished the last bottle with Dafne and Zynda on the way here," I told him with quite a bit of rue. No more replenishing my supply anytime in the near future, either. I accepted the full mug from him as he sat on the edge of the bed and tapped it to his. "To carrying around the weight of the good stuff."

He raised a brow at me. "Is that an oblique reference to my grievance with my brother not carrying what I call important?"

"Make of it what you will." The *mjed* burned delightfully into my blood, taking the worst edge off my jangling nerves.

"I hadn't credited you with subtlety," Kral noted with a thoughtful frown.

"To be perfectly clear, you haven't credited me with much."

"That's not true." He surveyed me, though I had the blanket modestly tucked over my breasts. Not that I'd be all that tempting—or tempted—in my current condition. I likely looked like one of Illyria's reanimated dead. A more gruesome sight I'd never before encountered and never hoped to again. "You're the best lover I've had the pleasure to bed. You're smart, beautiful, beyond skilled with a blade, with a body equally adept at fighting and fucking."

"Why, Kral. You charmer. And here I thought you didn't care."

"Too bad that smart mouth of yours ruins all the rest," he commented, in that fake philosophical tone he liked to pull out.

"Ha-ha." We sat quietly for a bit, both savoring the *mjed*, me trying to pace myself, lest my churning stomach hurl it back up and blow our little secret. The solid food Trond had promised had been a child's portion of bread and dried meat. Not much joy there. "Feels like we're headed back toward the meeting spot?"

"Yes. With a storm twixt that and us."

"Why do you sound so happy about that?"

"I like a good storm at sea almost as much as I like a trouble-some vixen in my bed." He slanted me a wickedly sexy smile, some rare, real joy in his eyes. Goddesses save us all, he meant it. I squelched the impulse to ask what made him so unhappy most of the time. We weren't friends like that. "And," he continued, "we are hopeful it will drive the fish-birds underwater long enough to lose our trail."

"A storm. Have I ever mentioned I can't swim?"

"Then I advise you to stay aboard."

The storm did indeed hit during the night, waking me from a dead—okay, drunken—slumber into full alertness, my knives in my hands.

"Will you slay the sea herself?" Kral muttered sleepily.

"Excellent idea. I'll get right on that. And least then she'd lie still." The *Hákyrling* pitched up, then down, as if she'd slid down one side of a gulch on fresh snow and rocketed up the other again.

Kral snaked an arm around me and nestled me against his side. "Don't worry, *hystrix*, I'll protect you against the big, bad rain. Put your gnat stickers away."

"It's not the rain, you lunkhead." But I slipped the knives back under the pillow. Even I had to admit they'd do me no good against the angry goddess of the ocean. Probably fell to Moranu, with all her mysterious, dark depths and trickster nature. One moment all aqua serenity and the next a raging sorceress. The ship pitched again, even more steeply, and I would have rolled into the curving wall if Kral hadn't held me in place. "Shouldn't you be up there, making sure the ship isn't . . ." *going to break into pieces and drown us all.* "Is okay?"

"They'll alert me if I'm needed. This is but a minor squall.

Only a landlubber would be awakened by such a small bit of bumping."

"So mean."

"I know. So are you. This is why we suit so well. Go back to sleep." He put his other arm over me, holding me in the circle of them. "I won't let you wash overboard."

Normally I liked to sleep clear of other bodies, as I'm told I kick around in my dreaming, but for once—probably due to the unfamiliar instability of my new world—I liked being held inside those strong arms. Didn't mean anything. Any wounded animal would do the same. My version of denning up and letting the healthier herd members drive off the wolves.

Everyone needs help sometimes. Let me take care of you that much.

Trond let me out of bed the next day, even removing some of the bandages, bringing me a fresh basin of water to sponge bathe with and a fresh change of clothes. Not my favored, now forever lost, best fighting leathers, but at least they were mine. Trond mentioned that Kral had left female garb for me, but I elected not to heap misery upon agony just yet.

"The general says you may come up on deck, if I judge you steady enough," Trond said. "No sight of the fish-birds since the storm cleared. Though I'm to tell you that if they reappear and you don't immediately take cover, the general will toss you overboard."

This would be his new favorite threat. Should never have told him I couldn't swim. "That would hardly save me, as the fish-birds also swim," I commented, hoping a bit of misdirection might keep my weakness from being obvious.

Trond smiled knowingly anyway. "True. He said something about keeping his cabin floor clean."

Sweet talker. However, it felt incredibly good to walk through that doorway onto the deck of the ship again. As I'd promised myself, I savored going through it at a leisurely pace instead of diving through headlong, vicious fish-birds slicing me to bloody bits. The storm had washed the air clean of the thick humidity that tended to lay over the calmer seas around the Nahanaun archipelago, and I took a deep lungful of its freshness, giving Danu thanks for all sorts of things. Kral spotted me and strode over.

"I'd hoped you'd have something more attractive to wear," he said, raking me with a doubtful eye, "having forfeited your usual garb."

"Nope." I cocked a hip jauntily, though it pained me. Totally worth it to present the right attitude. "I make a point of only wearing horribly ugly things, if only to enjoy that lemon-eating look on your face."

"Aha. Verification that you have been waiting for me all your life, if you put such planning into it." He flashed a grin at scoring the point and turned to face the prow of the ship.

"Any sighting of the barrier?"

"Not yet. Two of Ove's crows were lost to the fish-birds." Kral scowled for that. He took every loss of life so personally. But then, all the best leaders did. "So we have only one left for looking. Jens estimates we're close to the same waters, but no sign of another ship."

"They might not arrive by ship," I pointed out, searching the horizon for the shimmer Zynda had spoken of. I more than half suspected she was having a joke on me with that one. Tala enjoyed their tricks, even with friends.

"What do you mean?" Kral gripped the rail in a gesture I recognized. He didn't need the balance, not with his sea legs, but the mysterious ways of Tala magic unsettled him, too.

I shrugged, enjoying being the one on firmer footing for once. "Depends on who Zynda brings with her. Queen Andromeda is a shape-shifter also, as is King Rayfe. Unless they bring others, they can simply swim here."

"You think both this king and queen will come on this errand?"

"Well, Queen Andromeda certainly will, as the barrier answers to her. And King Rayfe is quite protective—he's unlikely to see her go off without him."

"See? This is not always a bad thing, for a man to be protective of his woman."

"I'm not your woman," I retorted.

"So only this Queen Andromeda controls the magic barrier?" Kral looked thoughtful. "Interesting."

If only the Dasnarian alphabet was as easy to read as his face. "Not only her," I lied, because from what I understood, she *was* the only one. "This is an unusual circumstance, where Queen Ursula asked it of her. Besides, I wouldn't get ideas. She wouldn't be able to work the magic from Dasnaria, and the king and queen won't journey without considerable Tala reinforcements. Even if you don't see them, they're deadly. Especially if you don't see them," I amended. "That's when they're at their worst."

"You've battled these Tala?" Kral looked even more interested. And was that a hint of respect? Be still my heart.

"A number of times. They stormed Ordnung when King Rayfe first set to extract the then Princess Andromeda to be his bride. Many engagements after that, large and small, as we chased them before and after the wedding." And the various escaped Tala prisoners and pockets of unrest, which continued to the present, but it would be impolitic to inform the Dasnarians about that. "They have a kind of domesticated animal, staymachs, that shape-shift at a trainer's direction, which they employ in battle also."

"Not unlike having trained warhorses," Kral mused.

"Right. And sometimes their actual warhorses are these shape-shifted staymachs and sometimes they're people in horse form. Keeps things interesting."

"Is a person in horse form as intelligent as in human form?"

Had to credit Kral. He might be a lunkhead as far as human values and social skills, but he thought through the ramifications of an enemy's abilities quickly. I was not, however, going to reveal any of the secrets Zynda had confided. That story she'd told, of how Tala trapped in animal form could lose their human selves entirely, bothered me greatly. For all that I appreciated the convenience shape-shifting would bring—though it would be even better if she could manifest extra weapons at will when converting back to human form—I liked my skin the way it was. Or rather, as it had been before the fish-birds ate most of it. I was still myself, no matter how scarred, but only if I stayed in control of my own life and destiny. Nothing would make me give that up.

I'd die first.

I pushed the dark thoughts aside and focused on prevaricating. "Hard to say. The Tala are cagey with information about their abilities. And it hasn't been long that we've been allies instead of enemies."

"Since your queen conquered their territory."

"Since she arrived at a treaty with the Tala via marriage alliance."

"Though their king abducted the woman in question and forced her into the marriage. Something you seem to object to strenuously with the scribe."

"Totally different. Princess Andromeda made a considered political decision in wedding King Rayfe." Probably an emotional one, too, given the gossip I'd heard. No one blamed her there. Rayfe was as hot as they came. I would have wanted to wrap myself in that long, black hair and let him have his tricksy way with me, too. With a mental sigh, I let that image go. "Dafne had no idea what Nakoa intended. Really still doesn't." Tired of looking for the shimmer, I turned my back to the rail and took in the view in the other direction.

"She'll be well provided for, will lack for nothing."

"Exactly what you said about Karyn."

"Your point, *hystrix*?"

"Just that you have certain mental ruts."

"Ruts?"

I'd used the Common Tongue word. "You know, like a muddy road where the wagon wheels dig in, creating deep ruts. Even if you try to drive on a different part of the road, those ruts drag your wheels in, and boom!" I clapped my hands in emphasis. "You're back in that rut."

"Thinking that there's nothing wrong with a person being provided for so they can have a peaceful, fruitful life is hardly a 'rut.'" Kral sounded all calm and logical, using the Common Tongue word that I had.

"No Dasnarian word for that?"

"All roads in the empire are paved with stone," he said proudly. "No 'ruts.'"

"The roads weren't paved with stone in Nahanau."

"Nahanau is—was, before this barrier took the islands—a protectorate, not part of the empire."

"Apt analogy right there," I commented, squinting. Something in the water? No hail from the lookouts, though. Maybe the Dasnarians wouldn't be watching for people emerging from the waves. Good test of arrogance.

"How so?" An edge in his voice. Danu, I loved needling this man as much as fucking him. Okay, not *quite* as much—but in lieu of the one, the other would do.

"See, as a man, you are part of the empire, enjoying all those pretty paved roads. As a woman, Karyn is like your protectorates, supposedly taken care of, but without the benefits. All of that simply dresses up what is truly occurring."

"And that is?"

His carefully neutral words didn't sucker me in for the width of a blade's sharp edge. I gave him my sunniest smile. "Exploitation."

"How am I exploiting Karyn, when I don't get to enjoy her as my wife? I am childless, alone, without the succor marriage brings." He locked his jaw down on saying more. It surprised me he'd said that much. "If anything, she's exploiting me by having the use of my good name and my fortune, with no obligations in return. Same for Nahanau. The islanders have enjoyed the protection of the empire, having to yield up nothing."

"Only because you haven't been able to get your greedy paws on their treasure."

"I saw no evidence of treasure. On top of everything, I have to face the Emperor with that news, as well."

I wondered. The Tala weren't the only ones cagey about hiding their riches, material and otherwise. "And I'll make you a bet right now that your Karyn would give up the amazing honor of your name and fortune in a heartbeat in exchange for her freedom."

Kral's face cleared into complete bafflement. "You know less than nothing about Dasnaria—yes, less than nothing because your wrongheaded ideas take you in the other direction—and you dispute with me over my own wife's preferences, to the point of challenging me with a bet of honor?"

Hmm. The way he phrased that made it sound a bit more . . . high stakes than I'd intended. Not the dicing-and-drinking version of the word. "I didn't mean a literal bet."

"Oh, no, you don't. You don't get to backpedal on a challenge like that. You made a bet with me and I'm accepting."

Fine, then. I shrugged, making it as insouciant as possible. "Sure."

"I choose the terms."

"No, we agree on them together."

Finally, the lookout's warning rang out. Sloppy. I'd been watching signs of the Tala approach for a good five minutes. My scouts would never have been so slow.

Two porpoises leapt from the water, transformed into birds that were joined by a large black raptor that stooped from above, then pulled up abruptly. All three circled, then landed before us, shifting again into Zynda, Queen Andromeda, and King Rayfe.

I bowed deeply to them, maybe a bit more than I would have normally, to both give Kral the cue and poke at him a bit more. A couple more people I respected to add to the list. "King Rayfe,

Queen Andromeda, may I present General Kral of Dasnaria and Imperial Prince of the Royal House of Konyngrr."

"King Rayfe, Queen Andromeda."

They returned Kral's dip of the chin. Fair enough between rulers of equal rank, I supposed. Dafne would know for sure, but I was all the ambassador they got. The King and Queen of the Tala had manifested in, what was for them, formal court gear, as had Zynda, who raked me with wide and horrified eyes. Compared to Kral's rigid armor, however, their brilliantly colored, flowing silk garb was as far as sunny Elcinea was from the frozen Northern Wastes.

"Ambassador Jepp." Queen Andromeda raised dark eyebrows over storm-gray eyes. I might not be able to see a giant magic curtain, but the magic that shimmered around her had always felt like itchy wool on my skin. Even back when she'd been only invisible Andi, I'd given the awkward teenager a wide berth, as most in Ordnung had. "What under Moranu's gaze happened to you?" Her gaze went silvery as it flicked to Kral. "I demand an explanation. Translate that for me, please."

I grimaced. "It wasn't—"

"I'll hear it from General Kral of Dasnaria and Imperial Prince of the Royal House of Konyngrr," the queen interrupted, using a tone as cutting as Her Majesty ever employed. They might none of them be the tyrants their father had been, but they'd all learned a thing or two about power at Uorsin's knee. "Since Jepp won't do it, Zynda, you speak their tongue. Translate exactly what he says."

Zynda stepped up and asked Kral the question. Her Dasnarian wasn't quite as fluent as mine, but neither was it as lowbrow.

"King Rayfe," Kral said, addressing him while Zynda translated, "perhaps you and your wife would care to join me for refreshments after your journey, and I can explain our adventures at length." I winced at his stupidity, and Zynda shared my chagrin with a bare shake of her head.

Rayfe regarded him with wolfish amusement, the ocean breezes whipping his hair around his lean body like a cloak made of night, deep-blue eyes nearly as dark. "Condescending to my queen, who has journeyed to assist you in crossing back into your own realm, seems hardly wise, General Kral of Dasnaria and Imperial Prince of the Royal House of Konyngrr. We're pressed for time. If you still wish our assistance, I suggest you answer Queen Andromeda's question."

Kral actually faltered at Zynda's translation. Not so as anyone who didn't know him well would notice, and not that I blamed him. He'd thought Zynda representative of the Tala. She possessed powerful magic, certainly, and more shape-shifting ability than her king, but Rayfe had the ruthless air of a man who would do—and had done—anything in pursuit of his goals, much like a sword forged in the hottest fires. Keeping a considering eye on Rayfe, Kral composed himself and nodded more respectfully to them both.

"Forgive me, Queen Andromeda. I meant no offense," he said. Using male language, too.

"Didn't you? My sister the High Queen told me something about you, General Kral of Dasnaria and Imperial Prince of the Royal House of Konyngrr, as did her consort, my heart-brother Harlan. I believe I have an idea of what offense you do and don't mean to give."

Kral set his teeth. "Please, Your Highness, call me Kral."

She only waited, expectant, as if they had all the time in the world. Why had they said they were pressed for it? Kral glanced at me, put a mailed hand on my shoulder in a protective gesture. I managed to tamp down the snicker, though it took yanking my gaze from Zynda's expression of wicked amusement to get there.

"Ambassador Jepp incurred her wounds nobly defending the ship and my men from a second attack of the fish-birds your cousin Zynda saw. We feared Jepp dead more than once and only great effort by my medic saved her life. We are all greatly in her debt, for surely without her actions, we all would have died."

Color me shocked that he pulled off that speech, with all apparent sincerity. And that he managed to refrain from snarling at Zynda about it or pointedly referring to the danger of the invisible magic barrier.

The queen tilted her head, examining me, not so much the teenage Andi I recalled ducking arms practice. "Exactly the valor I'd expect from one of Ursula's Hawks," she murmured in Common Tongue to me, "but it looks like it hurts."

A mere scratch was always the joke among the Hawks and other fighters, though I thought the queen wouldn't appreciate that brand of humor. "I'm healing, Your Highness. Thank you for your concern."

"You might have my concern, but my sister would have my head if I left you to continue on your journey in this condition, no matter how important this mission to her."

She glanced at Rayfe, and he acknowledged. I didn't catch the signal, but a seal leapt from the water, flipped through a bird form, and landed on the deck as a green-eyed woman with long, silver hair.

"We do have rope ladders they could use," Kral muttered at me, which nearly made me laugh.

"Our healer can tend to you, Jepp," Queen Andromeda told me, then lifted an inquiring brow to the woman, saying something to her in the liquid Tala tongue.

She nodded and, moving with that uncanny Tala quickness, took my head in her hands, eyes taking on a glow. Nearly as fast, Kral knocked her aside, a knife in his hand. The queen and king exchanged interested looks at that, while I barely stayed Kral's strike.

"A healer, Kral." I caught and held his eyes, which had gone cold as frozen steel. "She can help me."

As fast as he'd gone on the defensive, he relaxed again. A practiced and deliberate effort. "Good. You looking like carrion was putting me off my feed."

"Ha-ha."

Andi gave me a slight smile, assessing gaze flicking back to

Kral. "Meanwhile Zynda can translate while I prepare to move the ship through the barrier."

"Your Highness, I made it this long. I can wait to be healed."

She shook her head. "Not on the other side of the magic barrier you can't be."

"Would it be better for you to rest than work immediately?" Rayfe murmured, in Common Tongue, apparently for my benefit. "Let Jepp get thoroughly healed."

"I'd like to, but . . ." She looked away from me and into his eyes. "The longer I'm far away, the less power I have. I can feel it draining by the moment. I need to do this now."

He looked grim. "If you're determined, then do it."

"I promised Ursula—she seems to think it's important." She turned back to me. "Just tell me this, does the ship have a name?"

"The *Hákyrling*," I told her, Kral going alert at the sound of the word.

"Not the Dasnarian word, a meaning I can latch on to."

"*Lady Shark*, as Kral's name means 'shark' in their language. Why does it matter?"

She smiled, the sense of magic gathering about her like an impending storm. "Names matter, Jesperanda. Sit where you can see. We're making history today."

8

Queen Andromeda decided on a position near Shipmaster Jens, by the wheel, so I propped myself in a sitting position nearby, the Tala healer working on me in silence, since neither of us shared a language and Zynda was busy translating for the Dasnarians.

It took all the patience I possessed, a virtue that admittedly did not run deep in me, to both sit still and refrain from jumping up whenever there was a pause in the arranging, in order to ask Zynda what she'd found out about Dafne. There would be time for that later. I really hoped.

The healer worked rapidly, to finish the job before we crossed, which made all those already uncomfortably pulling stitches itch like I'd fallen into a stinging-ant nest. Trond made his way over to observe, thankfully cutting the stitches as she healed each major laceration, which helped immensely. It could have been the relief from the grinding pain, but as I healed, restless sexual desire began to boil through my veins. Not an unusual state for me, especially given the recent extraordinary privation, which would strain any woman's resources, but brighter and bolder than I'd ever felt.

So not what I needed. *Head in the fight.*

I wasn't close enough to hear, but I read Kral's expressions well enough—the incredulity followed by resignation before he passed the order that everyone aboard the ship come on deck. It made for a tight squeeze, though many took to the rigging, which helped. King Rayfe stood at his queen's back, an arm around her waist, not tight enough for stability, so for some other reason.

She closed her eyes, one hand on Jens's shoulder—who looked fascinated; the other on Kral's arm—who managed to look dubious, annoyed, and excited all at once. Gradually, that sense of static, of a storm looming, grew denser and tighter, making me sweat. The ship turned, the sails caught, and she glided forward.

A murmur of discomfort began at the prow, growing in volume until Kral's cracking command cut it off. The *Hákyrling*, however, continued to creak louder than ever, shuddering and shaking. Queen Andromeda's voice rose above it, speaking in Tala, singsong, but as if she spoke to the ship herself.

The Tala healer put her hand on the top of my head and sent a final burst through me, something that felt much like I'd jumped into a cold mountain spring, both shocking and refreshing.

I knew the moment we passed through the barrier, though I never did *see* anything.

It raked through me, though, like Uorsin's sword had, only on an insubstantial level, and I clamped my lips down on the desire to growl as the Dasnarians did. The world dimmed, or my eyes lost keenness, and pain from my wounds, so briefly relieved, rose again—though nothing like before. The Tala healer gave me a sympathetic look that said she'd done her best in the time she had. Considering she'd filled in any number of bits of missing flesh, I counted myself far better off than before.

Then, with a sudden lurch, as if the *Hákyrling* were a cork popped from a keg long sealed, we emerged on the other side. I knew it as surely as I knew my own name—though how Queen Andromeda had known *that* was an entirely other question. The sea remained as lovely, as serene and sparkling, but somehow . . . less. Not quite as deeply colored or vibrant. Hard to describe exactly, and I'd made a career of observing and reporting salient details.

A massive change nonetheless.

Queen Andromeda sagged abruptly, Rayfe catching her and sweeping her up in his arms. That explained his previous caution. And the presence of the Tala healer, because she abandoned me to tend to the queen. She and the king exchanged concerned expressions. Zynda caught my eye. My cue there. I got to my feet. Not perfect, but exceedingly better than I'd been.

Kral had a speculative look in his eye I mistrusted. "If the enchantress is exhausted by her effort," he said, "we can provide them with accommodations."

"I'll mention that," I lied, and turned to Rayfe, asking in Common Tongue, "Does Queen Andromeda need anything, Your Highness?"

King Rayfe flicked me a wry glance over her limp body. "Soon you'll be more a diplomat than even Lady Mailloux. She needs to get back across the barrier and into Annfwn. She predicted this might occur. Unfortunately, I don't have a form that can carry her, which means we need Zynda."

Oh. Zynda gave me a rueful shake of her head, making me realize how stricken I must look. "I'm sorry," she said. "I hoped that I'd be able to stay, or that we'd at least have more time after to talk."

"Kral, please ask Jens to stay close to the barrier," I asked, very politely, I thought, though he predictably scowled at me.

"It's not wise."

"No fish-birds here," I retorted. "Call it a favor I'll owe you."

That speculative gleam deepened. Great. "Done," he replied, and folded his arms, armor clinking. Clearly going nowhere.

"Quick," I said to Zynda in Common Tongue, "what of Dafne?"

"No news, but the High Queen herself is on a ship to Nahanau even as we speak. She gave me this letter for you." She pressed a scroll into my hands and I clung to it without looking. I'd choose hearing the words over reading them every time.

"She's going in person? What ship? Did she commandeer one? It will take weeks to get around the Crane Isthmus and the weather will be terrible. They could wreck. What in Danu—"

"Jepp!" Zynda took my shoulders, Rayfe impatiently glaring behind her. "Listen. She got a ship from—" Rayfe cleared his throat, eyeing her. "A friend," Zynda amended, flicking her eyes in Rayfe's direction from an angle he wouldn't be able to see. Interesting. Very interesting. "I went ahead of her over the pass, so she's taking a *shortcut*. Got it?"

The pass could only be Odfell's, between Ordnung and Annfwn, which fit with the ship in question belonging to the Tala. If she sailed from there, she could possibly be at Nahanau already. Zynda nodded, seeing my relief. Though I hoped Ursula had taken plenty of reinforcements.

"Did Harlan go with her?"

"Yes."

"Good. If anyone can handle Nakoa, she and Harlan can."

"Them and Dafne."

"Cousin," Rayfe said, steel in his tone.

Zynda kissed my cheek. "I'll come back and find you. I'm not leaving you out there alone."

"No, you don't know the way and—"

"I'll find you if I have to swim all the way to Dasnaria!" she repeated, then scooped the unconscious Andi into her arms, ran for the rail, and jumped, Rayfe pacing her, then snapping into the raptor at the last moment.

I ran to the rail also, wondering how in Danu—no, in Moranu's name—she planned to hold on to the queen, when I saw her shift midfall into the impossible. She remained recognizably herself from the waist up, though bare breasted and with her fair skin scintillating in a way that reminded me of the fish-birds' scaly gleam, and with a powerful silver fish tail below. No sooner did she cleave the water than it churned with other aquatic creatures, including the healer in seal form again, and they all swam out of sight, vanishing behind the barrier.

As if they'd never been.

"Was that . . ." Kral beside me, helm tucked under his arm, now that we were safe from the fish-bird scourge.

"The tales in my part of the world call them mermaids," I replied, still feeling stunned at that, the gamut of emotions, physical sensations, and the speed with which my friends had come and gone. "I never thought to see one in the flesh. Of course, I never thought to see a dragon either, so there's that."

"It's a strange world we're living in," Kral agreed. "I must say I'm thankful to be back in the nonmagical part of it."

I wondered at his confidence in that, given what I'd been sent to discover in Dasnaria. Their Temple of Deyrr had worked magics that made Zynda becoming half fish—or maybe more than half, given the appearance of her scaly skin—look pretty mild by comparison. I didn't mention that, however, as keeping up the appearance that all I cared about was making connections in the Dasnarian court would be key. Couldn't have Kral watching over my shoulder as I infiltrated one of their most powerful, quasi-illegal temples.

However I planned to do that. I'd skin that deer once I brought it down.

Kral was still eyeing where the Tala had vanished. "Mirrorlike on this side, too. Will it have the same properties, keeping us out?"

"So past experience informs me," I said, remembering the frustrations of Branli.

"Yet they passed through as if it weren't there."

"That's Tala magic for you."

"Magic that spans much more than Tala territory."

He had a point, but I shrugged. Not my expertise, and I sure wasn't going to give him more detail on that aspect of the Thirteen. Especially with Ursula away from Ordnung. I wondered at the wisdom of her leaving the High Throne so early in her reign, but what did I know? I was a simple Bryn woman of the hills, a decent hunter and an excellent scout. The running of kingdoms belonged to others.

"So." Kral's tone had gone quieter, more intimate, and he leaned over me. "About that favor you owe me."

I turned in the circle of his arm and indulged myself by running my fingers through his sweat-damp hair. A sweaty man always worked for me. Made the muscles glisten and him ever so much more masculine. Both men and women worked for me, for different reasons. But with my libido up and Kral right there, filling my head with his scent, well . . .

"What have you got in mind?" Maybe it was an aftereffect of the magical healing, but I wanted him like never before. Enough to feel all hopeful about it.

"Looks like you're feeling better," he noted. "And I've heroically restrained myself, having you in my bed these last days."

"Me looking like carrion shouldn't have tested your restraint much."

"Nevertheless." He pressed lips to my temple. I nearly climbed him like a tree right there. "Come to bed with me, *hystrix*. Let me rub that soft underbelly."

I put a hand on his chest to stop him, and his lips tilted in question. "How about *you* come to *my* bed—no nasty bloodstains on the floor."

"You have a hammock," he pointed out. "Not nearly so comfortable. Or expansive enough for what I have in mind."

He did have a way of whetting a girl's interest. "No strings or expectations?"

"Not beyond what you already agreed to."

"My memory isn't that short, General Killjoy. Do you plan to attempt to extract promises, or that stupid apology from me, and leave me hanging if I won't go along? Because I can tell you right now that, tempted as I may be, I'd much rather take to my uncomfortable hammock and my own hand than go through that again."

His sultry smile dimmed ever so slightly, and he ran fingers through my hair, much as I'd done to his. He'd shucked the gauntlets, too. "That had not been my intention. I miscalculated, not realizing how seriously you took the game—or the depth of your obstinacy."

"Oh, honey, I have depths you haven't even guessed at."

"I hope you'll show me." His gaze went to my mouth, the shark in his eyes. "We still have that bet to discuss, as well."

"I have some ideas there."

"No doubt you do. I must consult with Jens; then I'll meet you in *my* cabin."

"Fine, fine." He did have a point about the room. "Any special requests for this favor?"

His face lit with surprise and desire. Hey, I can play nice, especially if he'd give me what I wanted. No, what I needed with burning intensity.

"In the cabinet with my clothes, at the back, there are several outfits you can investigate. Any will please me, though it's difficult to say if any will fit."

Not intended for me, then, but for those mysterious Dasnarian females who must be as tall as their men. "If I know you, these outfits weren't intended to cover much anyway."

"True." His smile went wolfish.

I stood on tiptoe and bit his earlobe. "Don't take long. I might get bored and turn to practicing my handwriting." Putting on my best sashay, I headed for Kral's cabin with his eyes on my back. Not how Dafne would have done the ambassadoring, but the key to learning martial arts of all kinds was making them your own. It would never be enough to imitate the moves of others, no matter how clever or skilled. Taking those techniques, internalizing them, and bringing them out again with your own personal polish—that was the way of Danu. I'd see how much of Her Majesty's letter I could puzzle through later.

Hlyti had conspired to send me into the Dasnarian Empire with only one ally, and I intended to keep him close. Being Kral's lover would make spying that much easier. The rest was completely a side benefit.

Danu, I loved my job.

The dark recesses of Kral's clothing cabinet held more than a couple of outfits. I put back the stacks of what looked like lengths of folded silk and examined several of the toys, some I knew the purpose of and others that sparked my imagination in delicious ways. Clearly a man of interesting appetites. I considered using one of the toys on myself, just to take the edge off, but I'd waited this long; I might as well hold out for the grand prize.

Had I been another sort of woman, I'd have wondered who else had worn and employed these things. But that train of thought led to the pitiable Karyn, who Kral had never offered or delivered any kind of exclusivity, nor did she get to indulge in variety herself. She might as well be one of the White Sisters, forever locked in their cloister, doing whatever in Glorianna they did all day. It wouldn't alter Karyn's life a whit if I fucked Kral or not, but I still didn't like thinking about her.

If it wasn't me, it would be another woman. Or many women, the way Kral talked about it. I didn't have any particular moral problem with Kral catting around on his virginal wife. Followers of Danu tended to be either celibate or promiscuous. Most fighters weren't terribly monogamous either way, mainly because the life rarely allowed for the kind of roots spouses and children required. I found it ironic, in truth, that Kral insisted on exclusivity from me, whereas I didn't much care who he diddled.

Easy for the only woman on the boat to decide, perhaps—and I was pretty sure Kral wouldn't give any of his men a try, if only to preserve the chain of command. Mmm. Nice image, though, to picture him with another man. Like Harlan and Blagor staging that wrestling match, all oiled skin and bulging muscles. Then whoever won could peg the other.

What a sight that would be to see.

Embroidering on that in my mind, I picked out a flimsy little chain-mail number. Amusing, given that none of the Dasnarian women were fighters, from what I understood. Still, it suited my style and my mood. When I took the scroll from the High Queen to my cabin, I also grabbed a pair of high leather boots for riding that might suit the outfit, along with a dressier knife belt than I normally used. Too bad I'd given my mother's jeweled one to Dafne, as it would have matched perfectly.

But then, some things were sacred even to me. I'd never have worn it for dirty sex. Giving it to Dafne had been an impulse, but the right one. Perhaps my mother's spirit, wherever it might be, would watch over the librarian and guide her.

I set that thought aside as no more productive than contemplating poor Karyn.

The cabin had a disused feel from being empty the last few days, just a place to keep my things, along with all of Zynda's. Though neither Kral, nor anyone else on the ship, could read Common Tongue, I felt better hiding the scroll in there. No one seemed to go in and mess with our things, but I felt discreet and spy-like tucking the scroll away in some of Zynda's clothes.

At the last moment, I unfastened one of the chairs from the floor and took that with me, too. Back in Kral's cabin, I put down the cabinet door that served as a dresser, found fresh water inside, and used that for an additional sponge bath.

I finished in time to strike a pose at the sound of Kral's distinctive tread, one boot on the seat of the chair, hand on cocked hip, tits out, and head high. Judging by the way he halted midstride, expression going avid, I'd succeeded in my mission to begin driving him out of *his* mind. I had all kinds of revenge planned for him.

He closed and bolted the door, tossed aside the helm and gauntlets, then advanced on me with a slight smile quirking his clever mouth. "Trust you to find the hardest-looking outfit in there."

"If you don't like it, why do you have it?"

"Oh, I like it all right." He settled big hands on the inward curve of my waist. "Though another woman would have left off the blades."

"You should know by now that I'm not much like your Dasnarian women."

"Or any other woman I've met, for that matter." He ran his hands up my rib cage and down again, one stroking over my upraised thigh. Oh, yes. "I see you found a chair."

"Thought maybe I'd teach you a thing or two."

"You think you can?"

"I look forward to the attempt, anyway."

"It's good to see your lovely skin in one piece again," He dropped a kiss on my bare shoulder. "And to know you won't scar."

"There's days ahead to acquire more of those. Plus I have others, old ones."

"I know, but I prefer you don't gain more serving me."

"I'm not serving you." I nipped his neck in reproof. "I'm serving my captain and High Queen."

"Still," he growled, part arousal, part annoyance. "I find them—and you—as fascinating as your callused hands. Put them on me, *hystrix*."

"You're wearing rather a lot of armor for that."

He grinned, all shark. "Yes, you'll have to take it off for me. Bathing me afterward wouldn't go amiss either."

I gave him a considering look. Not that it wouldn't be a joy to make free with his truly excellent body and relearn every bit of it, but . . . "Is this the favor?"

"Yes."

"You have kind of a fetish for me being your handmaiden, don't you?"

He stroked my thigh thoughtfully, not going close enough to where I really needed those diligent fingers. "I do," he said slowly. "Does it help if I confide that it's all the sweeter for knowing you're the farthest thing from a handmaiden? Knowing you could take me apart with those delicate blades makes seeing your tender underbelly that much more delicious."

He made me all kinds of warm and mushy with those words, and not in my belly, but somewhere in the vicinity of that heart I'd lost somewhere along a well-worn campaign trail.

"Makes you feel more manly, huh?"

"Yes, you do. Both more and less manly. I don't quite understand it."

I licked my lower lip, then pursed them, drawing his eye. "But you like it."

"Gods help me, I do." He growled the words.

"You make a persuasive case, so I'll agree to that, but I need something from you first. Call it proof of goodwill. I promise it won't take long. And you'll enjoy it."

His eyes darkened, further intrigued and aroused. "Will you ask nicely?" Teasing me this time, mouth quirked in a half smile.

Taking my foot off the chair, I leaned into him and rose on tiptoes, wrapping my hands behind his thick neck. "Please, General Kral, prince among men. I need you in a bad way. Will you indulge me and give me a good fucking? Hard. Fast. Ruthless." I punctuated each word with a kiss, writhing against him, giving vent to genuine need, not needing to playact at all.

"I'm still in my armor," he breathed, wrapping a viselike arm around my waist and crushing me to him anyway, returning my kisses in greedy bites. "I'll bruise you."

"Oh, Danu, I hope so. Do it, Kral, and I'll play handmaiden like you've never seen."

That did it. With a snarl, he spun me around and bent me over the high back of the wooden chair, pushing me down with a firm hand on my neck and kicking my feet apart. If I hadn't already been slicker than a spring mudslide, I'd have gone there immediately. Kral yanked on the skimpy chain-mail bottom, snapping the threads and sending metal pieces flying. Next I knew, he thrust into me to the hilt, cold metal armor hitting my ass. Stretching me to oblivion and back.

I came instantly, with a grateful scream.

Danu bless him, he didn't even pause, just kept fucking me with all the relentlessness I craved. Hand vised on my neck, the other holding me by the hip, he pumped in and out of me while my breath sobbed. I climaxed again, digging my short nails into the wooden chair for whatever purchase I could manage while the rest of me spun off into a haze.

Yes. This was all I wanted. Him, his magnificent cock filling me, the man grunting Dasnarian sex words at me, taking me up higher, so I climaxed yet again before he slammed against me one last time on a shout, grinding into my ass.

Danu! The man sure could fuck.

We held for a few endless moments, ragged breath synching, diverging again. Sweat dripped into my eyes and I blinked it back.

"I know how to use a chair for sex," Kral said, slapping my hip with affection and withdrawing to wash his *lind*. Amazing he'd had time to put it on. Must have had it handy.

Levering myself up slowly, I took a moment to let my spinning head settle. Then solved the problem by plopping my butt in the chair. "Danu, I needed that."

Kral flicked me a glance. "Thank me, not your goddess." He had a hinged plate open in his armor, his generous cock hanging out.

"Handy, that," I commented gesturing to the opening.

He slanted me a wicked smile. "Useful for pissing in enemy territory and satisfying impatient females." He washed the *lind*, laid it to dry, and took out several more.

"I'd take exception to that if I weren't so exceptionally satisfied." I stretched. *So* much better. "You don't need that, you know." Might as well cut the guy a break.

"They prevent babies," he replied, not looking at me.

"I know, I know. I'm saying you won't get me pregnant."

Now he did look at me, with suspicion. "Are you calling my manhood into question?"

Oh, Danu. Not with this. I rolled my eyes at him and turned on the chair. Considered taking off the boots, but I liked how they looked still. Let him take them off, if he even wanted to. "No, General, I'm telling you that I won't conceive."

"Why not? Are you infertile?"

"Temporarily. Unless and until I decide to have a child. My people have ways."

"Forgive me if I don't trust those 'ways.' "

Really? Trusting souls, neither of us, and for good reason, but still. "What do you care, anyway? If I did get with a babe it wouldn't be legitimate; therefore, no complicating the Konyngrr lineage, according to you."

"And have my child grow up without a mother? Never."

I waved at him. "Hi. Mother here."

He rounded on me with a hard expression that hid much. "Would you stay in Dasnaria, then?"

"What? No. Doing my job, then going home."

"Which would leave my child motherless."

"I'd take *our* child with me."

"No," he replied evenly. "If you tried that, I'd have to kill you and then my child would still be motherless."

I regarded him for a long moment. The son of a bitch meant it. "You're a ruthless ass, aren't you?"

"You liked it well enough when I ruthlessly fucked you over the chair."

Much as I wanted to argue that point, I couldn't muster the words. I'd more than liked it; I'd loved it. With anyone else the conflict wouldn't be a problem. I could enjoy the sexual side of that personality without subjecting myself to it in the rest of my life. Not so much on this venture.

I stood, stretched again, my body humming. Arrogant and impossible though he may be, Kral was a great passion, indeed, satisfying me like no other. "Suit yourself, then," I told him. "Where do I start on this armor? I might need clues."

He stayed my hands, holding my wrists, searching my face. Both angry still and bemused. "Just like that?"

I shrugged as best I could with my wrists anchored. "You and

I were never planning on settling down and playing mommy and daddy. I offered you an out on using the *lind*, but if you prefer to use it, it makes no nevermind to me. I knew you for arrogant and ruthless the moment I laid eyes on you, so that hasn't changed either. But you're right—I do like the way you fuck me, enough to let you be the only one to do it while this lasts, so . . . let's not waste more time. Where do I start?"

He let go my wrists, something dark crossing behind his eyes and disappearing again. "Since you're half-naked, might as well finish the job."

I glanced down at the chain mail top still clinging to my tits. "Guess this wasn't made to stand up to any kind of actual fight."

"Not the point, no." His lips twitched, a bit of levity returning to his expression.

Putting my hands behind my neck, I attempted to look like a meek handmaiden. "Care to do the honors?"

With a hard look, he put his hands on me, ripping the threads as easily as brushing aside a spiderweb, making me gasp and my blood surge in answer, even though I'd expected something of the sort.

Danu love the man.

9

Islipped out of bed the next morning, leaving Kral to sleep, and stretched, assessing my body. Bruised in places, yes, but deliciously so instead of the sick ache of wounds. I felt sated for the first time in weeks. How Danu's priestesses managed total celibacy, I'd never fathom. I absolutely grasped the sacrifice aspect, however, in a way I never quite had before. Maybe Danu would be content to leave me be for a while and throw a bit less trouble my way.

Until we reached Dasnaria, where I assumed there would be plenty.

Now that I'd satisfied the other need, my body cried out for exercise. Magical healing did great things to sew up and even rebuild flesh, but it didn't make up for days of stagnant lying about. Tanking on my endurance during that fish-bird attack had been a warning slap upside the head. I'd take advantage of the boon of the healing—hey, maybe Danu arranged it through Moranu, to help me out, cheerful thought!—and get myself in the best condition possible to face the Deyrr witches.

First, however, I'd be a diligent spy and read Her Majesty's letter. Our cabin was as private as it got for me on the *Hákyrling*, so

I locked the door, withdrew the undisturbed scroll, and—feeling all scholarly—sat at Dafne's desk to read.

Once I unrolled the scroll, I heaved a sigh of relief. *Thank you, Ursula!* For this was indeed my captain and sister-in-Danu writing to me, not the High Queen. She'd remembered my marginal reading skills and used the shorthand we'd employed for missives within the Hawks—in her own hand, too, and hastily written. It made for a sort of encryption, I supposed. No doubt with Dafne gone she hadn't wanted to dictate the message, either. To my surprise, it made me feel . . . I didn't know. A little misty-eyed, maybe, at the sight of her writing. It brought back those early days with the Hawks, when—though she'd been a princess and heir to the High Throne—it had been easy to forget that half the time. We'd had some good conversations over a bottle a time or two. I'd even once told her my mother's story, the only person I'd told it to. So far as I knew, she'd never told another soul, either.

This was why I'd taken on this mission instead of simply walking when she dressed me down for the screw-up with Kral. I'd follow her to Glorianna's arms, if it came to that.

> Got word from our shifty friend. None of it your fault. You did good. Don't beat yourself up for the dragon king's actions. That's an order. Things will work out. I'm handling it. Maybe even better this way. Know our librarian relayed some of what she and I spoke of, but she may have been uncertain what to keep secret.
>
> In case there's doubt:
>
> Determine if Ami's annoying friend who visited her before we did can be found. Do not engage. Recon only.
>
> Questions to answer regarding mak-

ers of our troubles, IF you can without ANY danger:

What do they know of a special jewel, how badly they want it, plans to acquire, plans to use. The why is critical.

Keep it simple. Do the job. Come home. Don't be a hero.

You are, and always have been, my best scout. I picked you for a reason five years ago. I picked you for good reasons this time, too. Not the ones you think. When boulders speak, they give good advice. I listened and acted accordingly.

If this finds its way into a fire, all the better.

I read it over several times, an unaccountable knot working its way into my throat. I'd assumed from the beginning that Ursula's anger over the Kral Incident had spurred her to send me along as Dafne's bodyguard, but clearly not. She could be tailoring the history to make me feel good, but I doubted it. Our captain had always been fine with letting one of her Hawks believe she might be angrier than she was, in order to motivate them. I'd witnessed her employ that technique several times with new recruits.

It had never occurred to me that she might pull the same trick on me.

Taking the scroll up to the deck, I mulled over her message while I set the scroll aflame from a watch lantern, holding the parchment over the rail at the back of the *Hákyrling*, so the ashes scattered themselves in our wake. Fitting somehow, especially as Glorianna's sun was just tipping over the flat ocean almost directly behind us. I felt frisky and cheerful enough, from the reassurance of the missive and from a night well spent, that, after I dropped the last flaming fragment, I drew a circle in the air toward the fickle goddess of dawn and sex, humming her morning song. I'd never observed Glorianna's rituals beyond what was politic, though that had been substantial, as hers was the official worship under High King Uorsin. Because of that exalted status, Her temple sat on Ordnung's grounds. The ringing calls to worship, along with the sunrise and sunset hymns, permeated life there, and evading them simply hadn't been possible.

Even rushed, the Tala healer had packed quite the whammy, and I felt better than I had since before the unfortunate gutting episode. Either that or I could credit Kral's truly talented and vigorous fucking. Could be a brilliant combo of both. We'd gone at each other hard pretty much all night, in between catnaps and pauses to feed each other food and *mjed*. As long as we didn't talk, things went great.

And fortunately, I possessed a lively inventiveness for keeping his mouth otherwise occupied.

Because I felt so hale and hearty, I started into Midnight Form, the first of a set of twelve forms technically intended for longer blades. Ursula, like many others, preferred to run them with her sword, but she had the lankiness to make that work. Though I could pull it off without bringing shame on my tribe—or lopping off my own ear—I preferred a shorter blade. Not the twin knives I favored for Danu's Dance and close infighting like the Whirling Wind pattern, but a bigger knife that I also used for hunting. That blade allowed me to accelerate the speed, while the heft made me work for it, which always gave me the best conditioning.

Nice to have the morning quiet to myself, the early watch crew far less boisterous than in the full day. Done correctly, the set of twelve forms brought on a centering, meditative state. I wasn't much of a contemplative person, but given enough peace and quiet, I came as close as I ever did while running those forms. The physical work let my mind drift over the contents of the scroll. I might not read and write well, but my memory worked like a charm.

Ami's annoying friend had to be Kir, former High Priest of the Church of Glorianna, who visited Queen Amelia at Windroven just before Ursula diverted us from Branli so she could be with her sister for her lying-in. And the makers of our troubles were undoubtedly the Temple of Deyrr, origin of the unsavory Illyria. I'd heard various whispers of what she'd been at Ordnung to obtain, as she'd asked around about it, and even demanded it outright the night Uorsin announced their engagement. The Star of Annfwn, which no one in my network had any knowledge of. However, Illyria had asked for Salena's jewels, then demanded this Star when she didn't find it. Ursula's reference to a jewel in her note couldn't be a coincidence. If Illyria had expected to find this Star in Salena's jewels, it made sense that Ursula had inherited same from her mother. No one had told me as much, but I'd have to have been a blind fool not to notice that the cabochon topaz had gone missing from the hilt of Ursula's sword, sometime after—or while—she killed Uorsin. It had been a talisman to her. Every fighter has them, and I'd noticed many times how she touched it while contemplating a problem. Or heading into a fight.

So, if the topaz was the Star of Annfwn, where had it gone? Deyrr wouldn't have it, because I was to find out how badly they wanted it and their plans to get it since Illyria had failed to do so. The fact that Ursula wondered what they wanted it for spoke volumes. Apparently Salena hadn't told *her*. Magic users keep their secrets and so do mothers. Double nasty when the two converge in your life.

If Kir had thrown in his lot with Deyrr, that added a whole extra layer to it all. I had avoided him along with most of the priests of Glorianna. Not my goddess.

Running the full set of twelve forms to completion, even at a brisk pace, takes more than an hour, so by the time I hit Noon pose—an excruciating position to hold, up on one toe, other leg poised for a snap kick, knife stretched over my head, coiled to lash into Snake Strike, my other hand palm out, steady in Danu's salute—the sun had risen quite high. The *Hákyrling* sailed through a grouping of rounded islands, enough like Nahanau that it seemed they must be part of the same archipelago. I half expected to see Dafne in her nook of the prow, busily sketching her maps. I did spot Kral, talking to Jens, but observing me with burning intensity.

I sauntered over to him, treating him to my best smile. After his efforts of the night before, he deserved that and more. "Good morning, General, Shipmaster Jens."

"You're unusually gracious today," Kral noted.

"I slept really well."

Jens made a snorting sound and Kral took me by the arm, guiding me off to the side. "I was surprised to find you gone when I awoke."

"Did you have some handmaidenly duties in mind for me?" I let my gaze travel over the golden skin exposed by his open shirt collar. Much better than the armor, though that turned me on well enough, too.

Kral trailed a rough fingertip down my arm. "You make an exceptional handmaiden, it's true."

"You were sleeping so hard I didn't want to wake you. And I was restless."

"I thought I'd worked that out of you. I'll have to try harder tonight."

"I'm up for that challenge."

He ran his hand down the rest of my forearm, lifting my wrist to examine the blade I still held. "An impressive-looking knife. Larger than your gnat stickers. I don't recall seeing it before. May I?"

I reversed it, handing it to him by the hilt. "It's a bit large for me to comfortably wear, so I usually keep it in my packs unless I know I'm going to be fighting. Or training."

He hefted it, holding it up to the sun to examine the double edges—one serrated, the other razor smooth—and the grooves etched down the middle of each flat side. "Functional for many activities. Where did you get it?"

"My mother gave it to me. She never said, but I believe it belonged to my father. Or another man who happened to be her lover around the same era."

Giving me an opaque look, he handed the knife back to me. "Why do you think that?"

"She never said directly, but no one else among our people had one like it. I know she picked it up sometime during the Great War, but I've never seen another with the same design, so I'm not sure where it came from. Also, it held sentimental value for her. One of her shieldmates made the long journey to bring it back to me after she died, saying it was my mother's last request." Along with the knife belt I'd given Dafne. The knife and the belt didn't match each other, anyway, even if that blade had been a comfortable carry for me. No sense keeping both.

"My sympathies." Kral studied me, still a strange look on his face.

I shrugged that off. "It was long ago. She died an honorable death, on her feet, as would have been important to her."

"How did she die?"

"Blade in hand. I'm surprised we're going through islands again. Is this the Nahanaun archipelago still?"

Kral turned, surveying the islands with me. "Yes, we're taking an indirect route through them, which is still the faster route. We dipped to the south by some distance to cross the barrier in open water, as that seemed the wisest approach, since we couldn't be sure what would meet us on the other side and that at least upped our chances of making it through without trouble. By evening we'll be out of the islands, and then tomorrow afternoon, landfall in Dasnaria proper, at Jofarrstyr."

"Port city or capital city?" Dafne probably knew that. Another thing I should have asked. Maybe Ursula would extract her from Nakoa's bed and send her along to Dasnaria. But no, that would require a barrier crossing, and judging by what it had taken out of Queen Andromeda, she wouldn't be doing that again anytime soon, even if King Rayfe would allow. For the first time it occurred to me that I had no guarantee I wouldn't be spending the rest of my life in Dasnaria, after all. Or at least outside the barrier surrounding the Thirteen. Had Her Majesty thought of that? She always thought to the long game, so surely she had a plan. I might have lit myself on her expendable list, but she considered Dafne practically a sister. There would have been some plan to get her home. It was all the conversation about my mother and what happened to her that had me paranoid.

"Both," Kral replied, giving me a puzzled look when I blinked at him. "The port city is also where the palace is located, though some distance from the harbor. Isn't that what you asked?"

Head in the fight. Bryn never look back. "I was contemplating the wisdom of having the capital city of an empire perched on the vulnerable coast."

"As opposed to the center of the subject kingdoms, where it could be surrounded on all sides?"

Including its greatest enemy at its back, I mentally added. But Kral wouldn't know about that, how Uorsin built Ordnung where he did to guard the pass to Annfwn, object of his undying obsession, due to its material wealth of all kinds. Waving any kind of wealth under Dasnarian noses was like showing meat to hungry dogs.

So, I cheerfully shrugged at that and let Kral believe he'd won the point. Then narrowed my eyes at a movement around one of the islands. "Friendly natives?"

Kral tensed. "Where?"

"There. Lee side of the third island to the right." I pointed.

"I don't see—" And the lookout's warning call went out, interrupting Kral and making him scowl at me like I'd been at fault somehow.

"Best long-sight in the Hawks," I informed him with a sunny smile. When something wasn't stupidly magically invisible, that was. Kral strode away, snapping out orders that sent men drawing weapons and setting up defensive stations. Others climbed the rigging, adjusting the sails for maximum maneuverability. Not so friendly, those natives, it seemed. No surprise, as I made out at least a dozen longboats, with more appearing all the time. Good thing I'd kept the big knife out. Good homage to having stirred awake those memories of my mother, to whet the blade with some blood.

Thinking of you, Mom, wherever you may be.

"Get below," Kral snapped at me as he passed in the other direction. I pictured his brain matter splashing into a mental rut and jolting along.

Oh, I don't think so. But, to forestall the inevitable argument, I headed in the direction that would take me below—the picture of obedience—then slipped out of sight while Kral had his attention elsewhere. My muscles loose and limber, my blood high, I was spoiling for a fight and had no intention of hiding out.

Particularly as I counted at least two dozen boats, all bristling with at least ten Nahanauns carrying various weapons that glinted in the light, with more boats rounding the lee every moment.

Wishing I could look through the long-distance glass, I edged around to a different vantage point, keeping a low profile from both the Dasnarians and the Nahanauns. Stealth works in a number of ways, all requiring escaping notice from both the stalked and the ones who stalk. Fortunately, among the *Hákyrling's* many clever features—though I really doubted Kral's boast that he influenced the design—were some view holes tucked under the curve of the rail near the prow, and well out of sight of most ship activity.

That overhang, and my caution, proved quite useful when several arrows whistled overhead and thunked into the wooden deck behind me. In no danger of being pinned, I scanned the boats for the archers, spotting them in the semi-stable center sections of several boats, with impressively sized longbows, which explained the range. Kral's battalion of soldier/sailors tended to be more hand-to-hand focused, so they likely couldn't match that . . . and ha! Yes, there went easily a dozen Dasnarian arrows splashing harmlessly in the water, far short of the shallow boats.

If I had even two or three of the Hawks' archers with me, they would not have missed. I could see Her Majesty's point in denying me that request, however, as I supposed it wasn't politic to take a crew of warriors on an ambassadorial mission. Thinking more like a diplomat all the time.

The arrow volley was enough to make the Nahanauns slow their approach, though. Odds were that Kral planned to let them attempt to board the *Hákyrling* and pick them off in small groups. From Harlan's accounts, Kral's men could each take on ten trained warriors. Even with their number reduced by a quarter over these adventures, they should be able to handle a force of around seven hundred, possibly more, possibly less, depending on strategic positioning. By my count, the Nahanauns had fielded nearly a thousand, with more coming. Therefore, Kral's best bet would be to keep the invaders from swarming the rails, to keep that ratio below ten to one.

I didn't have much—okay, any—experience repelling boarders from a sailing ship. I had no idea what my fighting ratio might be, though I supposed it depended a great deal on my own strategic positioning. I held my own one-on-one, but my strengths lay in speed, stealth, endurance, and surprise. No captain ever placed me in the center of the front line, if they knew their stuff. Send me to the trees and I'll nibble away the edges.

Good plan of my own, then.

The lead boat grew closer. Covered by a steady barrage of arrows, several of their warriors leapt from the boats, diving into the water like blades themselves, swimming rapidly for the *Hákyrling*. My fault that the maneuver surprised me. You see in others what you see in yourself. I couldn't swim, but these island people moved through water as easily as through air, sleek brown bodies like the seal forms the Tala favored.

Kral's archers took out a few of the swimmers, but not all by any stretch. A number popped up from the water directly against the hull. I hadn't seen them swimming, so they must have been deep under. Kral had muttered about rope ladders before, but presumably those would be deployed only for friendly boarding and strategically withdrawn under these circumstances. The Nahanauns didn't seem to need ladders any more than the Tala had. They climbed the wooden sides of the *Hákyrling* with remarkable agility, blades in their teeth, spears and quivers riding their backs, finding finger- and toeholds that shouldn't support a man or woman's weight. But clearly did.

Farther down the deck, shouts went up as a group mounted the rail, battered back by two of Kral's men, who indeed seemed to dispatch the invaders with reasonable ease. I kept an eye on a woman bristling with weapons who climbed near my position, and on two more men who leapt from the sea and began their ascent a bit farther down. Two more of Kral's men could be in position for them quite readily, and my gal climbed faster, anyway.

I lost sight of her as she ascended the curve under my position, as the viewhole didn't allow me to see that much of the periphery, but I had her speed figured, so coiled myself into a crouch. She made the rail exactly as I anticipated—not quietly at all—and one of Kral's men spun with a shout of warning. I already had her, up and in, big-bladed knife to the gut, and back over the rail she went.

After that, the battle blur took over. Another sort of meditative state, but the opposite of peaceful and contemplative. I kept to my self-assigned quadrant of the deck, dispatching the men and women who stormed the rail only to find the surprise of my blade. Kral's men left me to it—particularly after one rushed to rescue me from a big Nahanaun levering himself up with impressive muscles, and who fell again with one of my throwing knives in his eye.

Regrettable, the loss of that knife. With luck, though, the handsome fellow would survive. Pity for the world to lose that physique.

There's a tenor to a pitched fight, even when one's in the middle of it. A good warrior knows when the advantage shifts, like recognizing the shifting of a wooden deck beneath her feet, hearing the crack of wind in the sails that signals a change in direction. This is why Danu is also the goddess of clear-eyed wisdom. The frenzy of the fight is one aspect, the knowing when to pull back another.

That's as close to philosophy as I get. Still, I knew it the moment we'd successfully repelled the attack.

A few stragglers still tried, here and there. I took a moment to survey the waters, gratified to see the fleet of longboats paddling away, occupants crouched under shields to ward off the following rain of Dasnarian arrows. Looping around to walk the long way back, I satisfied myself that no more boarders attempted that end of the *Hákyrling*'s steep sides. She was a good ship, and well constructed in a way I hadn't previously appreciated. Kral's battalion, too, had lived up to their fighting reputation. I'd wondered a bit, after that river monster managed to gobble so many, and with the fish-bird attack incurring such damage.

Keeping in mind my maturing, diplomatic self, I mentally excused them, taking back any uncharitable thoughts I'd harbored. When faced with human fighters, a known quantity, they'd done brilliantly. I would stop judging them for falling to the unknown. Magic skewed everything, after all.

The Dasnarians rounded up the bodies that remained on board, those still breathing and those not. Aha! That man had one of my knives in him. I crouched to retrieve it, cleaning the blade on my own shirt, as the Nahanaun wore nothing more than a loincloth. Another beautiful man. Such a waste.

"Idiot," I said to him. "Why would you attack a ship this size—what could you have hoped to gain?"

"What does anyone want?" Kral spoke behind me, and I twisted to squint up at him. None of the blood looked like his. "They probably thought we carried treasure and sought to steal it."

"Did you interrogate any of the wounded to find out for sure?"

"I'm about to, if you'd like to listen in, Ambassador. Since you're on deck, instead of where you're supposed to be."

"Ah-ah, General. I decide where I'm supposed to be."

"My ship."

"Anywhere I am counts as neutral territory."

He actually sputtered over his reply. Point for me. "That is not how diplomatic immunity works."

"And you know this how? From all the other ambassadors the Thirteen Kingdoms has sent to the Dasnarian Empire?" I was beginning to get the diplomacy game. Not unlike sparring. Inventiveness counted here, too. As with a fight, the only rule that counted was winning and protecting what mattered. I smiled as Kral stewed, but resisted patting his cheek. "Let's go ask some questions."

With a gallant bow that oozed irony, he gestured for me to precede him. "Is any of that blood yours?" He muttered the question as I passed.

"I don't think so. Didn't feel anything hit. You?"

"A few scratches, nothing more."

He led me to a man, bound with rope, too young to have much bulk yet. Probably his first battle, certainly his first against the Dasnarians, as he took in the armored warriors around him with eyes wide and black with shock. He spoke quickly, babbling some explanation in the islander language. Dafne had complained quite bitterly about what a challenge that language presented. It sounded almost like singing to me, which I now knew indicated that pitch influenced meaning. A woman of the world, the new Jepp.

"Why did your people attack us?" Kral demanded.

The boy shook his head, speaking more of his tongue.

"I don't think he speaks Dasnarian," I pointed out, most helpfully, I thought.

"Brilliant observation, Ambassador." He heaved out an impatient breath. "You . . . spear . . . me . . ."

I could just picture Dafne's expression as Kral butchered the islander language. We really needed her. No wonder she'd been

so annoyed with the Dasnarians calling the Nahanaun archipelago a protectorate while not being able to talk to the people.

To keep from kicking Kral, I surveyed the other prisoners.
One woman, hair matted with blood on one side, watched us with
alert interest. More than the expected interest in keeping her skin
intact, and quite a bit more alert than the head wound would suggest. I didn't much care for the way several of Kral's men discussed her while ogling her scantily clad, quite lovely body. Not
that I didn't do my share of ogling. I didn't like their intent behind it. She didn't either.

I ambled over to her, hunkered down. "Do you speak Dasnarian?"

Her liquid dark eyes sharpened, calculating her reply, though I
already had my answer. "Here's the deal," I said. "Answer my
questions and I'll see you get off this ship without difficulty."

She considered a moment longer, her gaze flicking over the
men, then spoke very softly, in Dasnarian. "No rape?"

"Not while I'm alive. Though if you'd like to try one or two, I
can vouch they give a good time."

She shuddered lightly. "I don't care to. I have a husband, children."

So much monogamy going around. It was like an epidemic.

"I have heard tales," she continued, so quietly I had to lean in
to hear, "that the Dasnarians abduct females and keep them sequestered. Not exactly slaves, but close enough. I'd rather you
killed me, so my family can grieve and my husband move on."

I sat beside her. "How about you talk, and I'll handle the rest.
My vow to you that you'll go home to your family. Why attack us?"

10

Her name was Nani, and after she started talking, I asked her to wait a moment while I brought Kral over. It got him off browbeating that kid, too. He hadn't started any actual beating, maybe also realizing that the Nahanaun boy had gone past terrified. Sometimes interrogations required force—I'd witnessed my share, though I never much liked it—but they also took a certain level of skill. Terrified prisoners tended to babble anything they thought would save them.

Nani had enough experience and maturity to stick to the important information and keep her cool. "This one speaks Dasnarian, if you'd like to listen in," I told Kral.

"Absurd." He locked his jaw. "None of the Nahanauns speak Dasnarian. Where would they learn it?"

"More of us understand it than you know," Nani said. "It's only wise to know the tongue of the oppressor."

While he was still backpedaling, I went for the killing strike. "I promised Nani she can go free, without being harmed in any way, if she answers our questions."

"You have no authority to make those promises," Kral ground out. Really, the man needed to relax more.

I drew an invisible line around Nani and me with my hands. "My island of neutrality, where Jepp's word is law. She goes free in exchange for information."

"One of these days, I'm going to kill you." Kral sighed, sounding weary and not much like he meant it.

"You can try." I shrugged it off. "Keep in mind which of us took a few 'scratches' from that battle versus who's unscathed before you issue ultimatums you lack the skill to uphold."

Nani's keen gaze flicked back and forth between us. "Do you agree or not, General?" I didn't want to say it where Nani could hear, but I'd make sure she went free regardless.

Of course he didn't like it, but Kral grudgingly agreed. He even managed to back off and let me ask the questions once it became apparent that Nani spoke much more freely to me. She kept a wary eye on Kral and his men but showed me a level of trust I probably didn't deserve. After all, had I met her in battle, I'd have likely stabbed her in the heart rather than clunking her on the head. Her good luck in a way, that the Dasnarians hesitated to kill women. Though I agreed with Nani that I'd rather have my throat cut than be locked up as some Dasnarian's concubine for life.

Her people had been cut off from the rest ever since the barrier shifted—to right down the middle of their island. Nani normally lived on the main island near King Nakoa KauPo's palace but had been home visiting family when the shift occurred. An enormous mudslide wiped out several villages, and a magical storm had caused all sorts of monsters to appear. Once the fury died down, the most magical beings disappeared as if they never were. The barrier, however, remained, which none could cross. Unfortunately, Nani's husband and children were on the other side.

What a headache.

When the *Hákyrling* appeared, popping through the impenetrable and clearly hostile barrier, the island chief mustered all able-bodied warriors to attack. "We reasoned that the magical assault was sent to first wound and frighten us, for the Dasnarians to then follow to enslave us and take our treasure."

Kral bristled at this. "Have we enslaved any of your people? Stolen any treasure? You impugn the honor of the Dasnarian Empire."

"You leapt to the same assumption, as I recall," I reminded him. "Isn't that one of the charges you leveled at Her Majesty? In open court at Ordnung," I added, "which I happened to hear."

He threw me a look full of daggers, and I smiled sweetly in return. "I suggest we explain to Nani what occurred, so she can take the information back to her people."

"You know more about it than I do," Kral pointed out. "I know full well your High Queen did not reveal everything."

Nor had she wanted Dafne to explain too much to King Nakoa KauPo, though I wasn't certain exactly where those lines were drawn. Theoretically none of them would have told me, simple scout and bodyguard, anything too politically sensitive. I knew more than the average citizen, largely due to my network of scouts and—hey, call a pig a pig—gossipers.

"This is what happened," I told Nani, keenly aware that Kral also listened intently. "I am from the Thirteen Kingdoms, many days' sail from here. Once upon a time, we were Twelve Kingdoms, with the thirteenth behind a magical barrier that none could cross. It sealed them away from the world, with magic inside, and none outside. A great calamity occurred and the magic barrier moved."

I congratulated myself on that wording, making it sound like we were taken by surprise, too—which was true—and that the barrier had moved as an act of nature—which was false, as the three sisters had somehow caused it to happen when Ursula essentially assassinated the High King. She hadn't moved the barrier consciously, so the scuttlebutt speculated, but it had happened as a result of her actions and some great magic the three wove together. I didn't pretend to understand it and didn't want to. Leave me to the practical realm.

"Once the barrier stabilized," I told Nani, "all the magic on the outside died away again. Only people from certain . . . families can cross on their own. Others need help from friendly sorceresses."

Hope, bright and daunting to me, lit up Nani's face. "Then I can get back to my husband and children."

Ugh. I hated to dash her hopes, but who knew if or when that would ever happen? Still, Her Majesty would feel compelled to deal with this. High Queen Ursula took responsibility for her people very seriously, whether her small troop of Hawks, the denizens of the Thirteen, or now all these islanders, so impacted and divided through her actions, however inadvertent. Once she met with King Nakoa KauPo and extracted Dafne, Her Majesty would be taking steps to right these wrongs.

Of course, I had no idea what she'd do. Being an ambassador required even more autonomy than even long-distance scouting, spying, and guerrilla fighting. Fortunately, I counted lying convincingly among my many skills.

"Yes, you will get back to them," I told Nani, feeling like I might be making a promise I'd have to find a way to keep. "It's all being sorted out. Have patience. Go back to your people and pass the word. Her Majesty High Queen Ursula will treat with King Nakoa KauPo and find a solution to serve everyone." That sounded really good. At least if word came that Her Majesty had slaughtered Nakoa and his entire household to free Dafne, I wouldn't be here to look into Nani's desperately hopeful gaze.

"I will tell them," she promised, then cast a cagey glance at Kral. "I may go now? What of the others?"

"They need a boat, General Kral. Nani shouldn't swim with that head wound."

"They?"

"You're letting all the prisoners go, aren't you? There's no reason to keep them, and much goodwill to be gained by letting them go. You won't ever get their treasure by being an ass to them."

Kral narrowed his eyes. "Your mouth is far too big, Ambassador."

I shrugged, pretending he didn't intimidate me a bit. My mother had once said my mouth would be my undoing someday. Looked like that day was bearing down on me like . . . well, like a crazed and starving brown bear.

"Fine. Arrange for them to go," Kral ordered one of his lieutenants, then took my arm. "You and I will discuss more in private."

I slipped his grip, diplomatically not pulling a dagger on him. "I'll just see Nani safely off, as I promised her. Shall I meet you in a bit?"

He growled an inarticulate threat and stalked off. Nani watched him go with wide eyes that went thoughtful as she turned them on me. "You're either very brave or incredibly foolish, to taunt a man like that."

"Definitely the second," I informed her cheerfully. "However, if you do get the opportunity to deliver a message to either a woman named Dafne or Her Majesty High Queen Ursula, would you please tell them that you met Ambassador Jepp and relate what I told you today and all that occurred. Maybe, ah, leave out the bit about me arguing with General Kral. In fact, if you wanted to dress that up a bit and make me sound wise and diplomatic, that would be ideal."

Nani snorted out an actual laugh. "I've only just met you and I suspect that anyone who knows you well would know that story for a lie."

Probably true. It was worth a try, at least. "Any way you can make me sound good at my job, then?"

She put a palm over her heart, as the Nahanauns in Nakoa's household had done. "I owe you a debt today, Ambassador Jepp. I promise to deliver your message and to tell of your bravery and fairness to my people."

Ha! I'd go down in history as a totally different person after all.

After seeing Nani and the other erstwhile prisoners away in one of the *Hákyrling*'s rowboats, along with the bodies of their dead brethren, I went to find Kral. He and Shipmaster Jens had their heads together over a series of charts in the room that served as both a sort of officers' dining hall and study.

Kral barely glanced up at my entry. "Done losing me a boat along with my prisoners?"

"I'm sure you can acquire another boat with the vast wealth of the Dasnarian Empire, and the prisoners would simply have been more mouths to feed."

"I should make your High Queen reimburse the empire for the *gyll* those prisoners would have fetched on sale. The woman alone would be worth a fortune."

"She's a free human being, Kral. She wasn't yours to sell."

"She gave up that right when she attacked my ship and my men—and you, I might point out," Kral snapped. Jens, apparently oblivious, made a note on the chart.

"So if I defeated you in battle, you would lose your freedom and be mine to keep or sell?" I flung at him.

"Of course." Kral held up his hands as if that were obvious. "*If* you could defeat me. That is the way of things."

"Not everywhere. *Nor* is it remotely honorable."

"Honor has nothing to do with it. Being the strongest, having the most power, does. Either you win or you lose. You rule or you serve. There's no in-between." That bitter sound in his voice again. "Perhaps you of the Thirteen Kingdoms don't understand that, but you are in the Dasnarian Empire now, Ambassador. I suggest you keep that in mind."

I shut my mouth. Heroism comes in all forms.

"Change of course?" I asked, all cheery politeness.

Jens glanced up with a nod—and a sparkle of something in his eyes. "Yes. The general has deemed it wisest to stay away from the islands. It means a longer journey to Jofarrstyr but will prevent further difficulties."

"Excellent strategy, General." I spoke with sincerity, but Kral took it for sarcasm.

"So kind of you to say so, Ambassador. Jens, proceed with the course we outlined."

Taking the dismissal for what it was, Jens hastened out. Kral leaned against the table, legs crossed at the ankle and arms folded. The silence thickened, making me itch to draw my daggers. *Not that kind of battle. More diplomacy.* I only wished my wits could be sharpened as easily as my blades could. Holding on to stubborn resistance, I refused to break the détente. He had things to say; he could say them.

"I realize I do not make your list of people you respect," he finally said, in a forbidding tone. "And it amuses you to call me by my titles. The fact remains, however, that I *am* general of the Dasnarian military, Imperial Prince of the Royal House of Konyngrr, and captain of the *Hákyrling*. You may have a certain amount of diplomatic immunity and you may be my *rekjabrel*, but you will not undermine my authority. I will consider that an act of war on behalf of the queen you claim to represent."

"Claim?" I fastened on that, to help dispense the chill of failure. Kral had a point. Me, my mouth, and my difficulty with authority. "I *am* the ambassador."

"I know as well as you do that no one intended you to be the ambassador to the court of the Dasnarian Empire. The scribe, Lady Mailloux, made for a logical choice. I even understand your High Queen's rationale in sending you to be her bodyguard. However, you stepping into her place was an accident—and we both know it."

"Well, gee, Kral, if only we'd known you planned to surrender Dafne to Nakoa, then Her Majesty the High Queen would have sent a better backup. I might not be the top choice and, okay, you're right. You and I both know it. But I'm the High Queen's avatar in this venture, like it or not, as well as Danu's, the goddess we both serve. I'm going to do my best to be wise, clear-eyed, and just. I may be a green recruit as ambassador, but that doesn't mean I'll retire from the fight."

He assessed me. Was that a glimmer of respect behind his anger? "We need to establish some rules, you and I."

"As well as the terms of the bet."

"That, too, since you had the balls to make that challenge. First rule: You will show me respect and obey my orders."

"Agreed, as long as those orders are the same as you'd give any of your men. No sending me out of a fight."

"It's my responsibility to see you safely to Dasnaria."

"Yes—as it was to see Lady Mailloux there, and look what happened."

He set his teeth. I was beginning to suspect he did that instead of ripping my throat out with them. "Fine. But if you get your fool self killed, it's not on me."

"Fair enough. If I disagree with you, I'll do so in private and you will promise to hear me out."

"I need agree to no such foolishness."

"You do if you don't want me mouthing off in public."

"I could kill you now. Cut your throat, heave you overboard, and tell your people that you died in the Nahanaun attack. No man on this boat would say otherwise."

Nani would say otherwise, but I wasn't going to direct his attention there. Instead, I let myself coil into battle readiness. "I'd like to see you try." I laid out the challenge in my softest, deadliest tone.

"Tempting." He said it reflectively, as if weighing the possible outcome. "And yet, I enjoy stopping that mouth of yours in other ways."

Funny how I'd thought the very same thing. "Perhaps we should agree not to try to kill each other," I suggested, half in jest, but he frowned seriously.

"A large concession, but perhaps necessary." He spit in his palm and held it out. "Let us make a pact of it, then."

"Seriously? You want me to touch your spit?"

He grinned, abruptly and with wicked mischief. "Seeing as how you've had my mouth, tongue, and spit lavishly applied to every part of you, it seems late to be claiming missishness over that."

Did other ambassadors have to deal with this? Surely not. I spit in my palm and clasped his. "A pact, then. I promise not to kill you if you promise not to try to kill me."

"So promised." He held on to my hand, tugging me closer. Ah, romance. "How can I want you so much when you drive me out of my mind?"

"Because I'm a fantastic lover?" I suggested, going for flip be-cause his words and expression sent me straight to full-on arousal. He posed a fine question. Why Kral did it for me so thoroughly when I disliked so much about him had become one of the great mysteries of my life.

"We're well matched that way, it's true," he murmured, spread-ing his legs and pulling me between them. Still holding my hand, he bent his head to kiss me, thoroughly, deeply, and filled with passionate anger and desire. I returned in kind. Maybe this was how we had to play it; having agreed not to kill each other, all that remained was to devour the other sexually.

A challenge that bothered me not in the least.

"Lock the door and let me have you," he growled against my mouth, his free hand snagging my ass and pulling me hard against him.

"Don't we have more rules to establish?" I managed to get out between drugging kisses. That's me—a thinking woman.

"I'll negotiate more rationally with this edge off."

So would I, in truth. No better way to work off the aftereffects of a battle than a good round of healthy sex. "Okay. Stay right like that." I untangled myself from him, locked the door, and shimmied out of my boots and pants. Kral watched with glittering interest, letting me apply myself to freeing his erect cock. Glad he wasn't wearing his armor, I pulled the cloth aside and—for my own pleasure—opened his shirt as well. "Hold this for me."

With some bemusement, Kral took himself in hand, holding his cock at the angle I requested. "What are you—"

He broke off when I put a foot on the table beside him, then, using that leverage along with my hands on his shoulders, climbed up and lowered myself onto him. We both let out long, gratified breaths at the connection, which pulled us together into a tangling kiss. That position is a miracle worker, and I took full advantage, going for the depth I loved, flexing my thighs to pump up and down on him.

"Wait." He broke the kiss, but not the rhythm or our embrace. "No *lind*."

"Feels good," I agreed, nibbling on his neck.

"I don't—augh!" His hands vised on me when I turned the nips into a bite.

I lifted my head and looked him in his hot blue eyes. "Trust me or don't, Kral. You can't have it both ways."

He wavered, deep suspicion in his face with something raw beneath. How long had it taken to make him into this hard man, this scarred and wary warrior? Probably all his life, and a difficult one at that. I'm not a woman much given to sensitivity, but my heart wrung with compassion. That or the depth of his penetration. "Just fuck me, honey. You know you like it." Using my internal muscles, I squeezed.

Which put him over the edge.

Holding me by the hips, he pumped in earnest, eyes searing me hotter than the noonday sun on the Onyx Ocean. The deep pleasure bordering on delicious pain, I let him control it, clinging to him until we both dissolved in mutually devastated bliss.

I finally gathered enough wherewithal to climb off him again, grateful he'd had the presence of mind to keep me from falling to the floor. Figuring I'd have to bathe soon regardless, to get the blood off, I pulled on my already soiled trousers without bothering to clean up. Kral did likewise, watching me with an odd look on his face.

"What?" I finally put my fists on my hips. "Don't yell at me for distracting you from our argument—that one was your idea. A fine idea, but still yours."

He huffed out a dry laugh, shaking his head, then standing to pace the small room. "What is it about you that turns everything upside down?"

"My natural charisma?"

"You are unlike any woman I've ever met."

"We've pretty much established that."

"Jepp." He stopped in front of me, then cupped my cheek with surprising gentleness, his face grave, eyes dark. Not in anger, but . . . worry? Surely the great and terrible Kral didn't fret things. "I don't know how I'm going to keep you alive in the Dasnarian court. Lady Mailloux would have listened to my advice. You . . ." He shook his head again. "You're going to say the wrong thing to the wrong man and he won't hesitate to strike you down for it."

"I'm not so easy to strike down."

"Which would result in you being given to the Emperor for judgment, which would mean execution for the crime. Even as an ambassador from a foreign realm, a woman simply does not have the right to strike a man, even in self-defense. The law is very clear. I wouldn't be able to stop it and I don't know how to get that through your thick head."

"Would you care?" I had started the question as sarcastic, partly to break the tension. Tender, concerned Kral gave me the nerves. Instead, though, my voice came out throaty, and my heart perched like a bird on an unsteady limb, ready to flap away at the least jolt.

"It defies rational explanation," he said slowly, "but yes. I can't bear the thought of it. Don't make me watch you die." His mouth brushed mine, lips soft, searching.

My jittering heart folded its wings, happy to be held, warm and secure, if only for the breath of a kiss. Kral pulled back and searched my face, awaiting an answer.

"I'll listen to your advice," I said. "I'll learn to wear the girl clothes and speak softly. I can swallow insult and stay my blade, but I have to do my job, too. Even if it means getting myself killed. If that's what it takes to do what Her Majesty requires of me, that's what I'll do."

"Your recklessness terrifies me."

"Says the man who marched a hundred men across the breadth of a foreign kingdom he knew nothing about to confront the fortress at its heart."

He laughed softly and combed fingers through my hair, cupping my skull. "It's easier to do it than watch someone you care about face that kind of danger. The Emperor's court is fraught with peril, and not the kind you understand. It . . . worries me, to think of you there." He took a long breath, as if suddenly aware of the strange intimacy of our exchange, and stepped back, releasing me. "What are the terms of the bet, *hystrix*?"

I'd forgotten about Karyn, all while I was cozied up here with her husband, even if in name only, exchanging sweet nothings and discussing executions. I put more distance between us with the excuse of putting on my boots again. Not that it changed anything, but I felt less hypocritical. "You ask Karyn if she would give up marriage to you in exchange for her freedom."

"You have no idea the enormity of what you're proposing."

"It's a question. How hard can it be?"

"What if she says yes?"

"Then let her go."

"It's not that easy to dissolve a marriage. Certainly never at a woman's behest. Usually it's only in cases of adultery, and then usually she's executed."

"Let me guess, having witnessed where you've been dipping your wick lately—no such penalty for men."

"That's the way of things. A man cannot carry a babe, so there's no need for fidelity from him."

"And yet you and I are fucking with no intention of making babies."

His brow lowered as he frowned at me. I let it go. "So, if she says yes, you divorce her."

"Why would I do that?"

"Because you don't want her."

"Whether I want her or not is immaterial; the Emperor's decree says I cannot have her except in name."

"What is the point of being married to her, then?"

"It was His Imperial Majesty's desire, and I had no choice but to do what I was told." There ran some of his bitterness.

"Why her?"

"Her family, the Hardies, hold an important region with fertile orchards in one of the rare parts of Dasnaria proper that does not suffer harsh winters. Our marriage cements the family alliance to the Konyngrr regime."

"How does her family feel about the alliance?" A stretch for me to contemplate the politics, but I could think this way. Just a different kind of strategizing between foes and allies. Kind of an interesting give-and-take, another good sparring match. "I'd think being aligned with the semi-divine Emperor would be useful."

"Yes, it's good for them, too."

"Then if Karyn says she wants out, have her sign something that keeps the alliance in place."

He frowned. "Sign what?"

I threw up my hands, having reached the end of my cleverness on this topic. "I don't know! You're the prince—you figure it out. That's the bet I propose, that if you offer her freedom, she'll take it."

"Where would she go?"

"That's the beauty of freedom, Kral—only she will get to decide that."

"If she's not married to me, I won't be able to protect her. She won't be an Imperial Princess anymore."

"That's her call, then. The price she'll pay. I'm betting she'll be willing to pay it."

"I'd have to send for her," he said thoughtfully, clearly turning over the logistics in his mind. "Have her brought to the Imperial Palace to have this conversation."

I shrugged. "This is a problem for an Imperial Prince of the Royal House of Konyngrr?"

"No, she would have to obey, whether she wanted to make the journey or not. It would require a considerable entourage with chaperones, but I can afford it."

Hopefully this Karyn wouldn't hate me for putting her through that. "It would probably be worth it to her. She's a young woman, right? Visiting the palace would be exciting for someone like that, in my realm. Has she ever gotten to enjoy the shiny part of being an Imperial Princess of the Royal House of Konyngrr?"

He laughed, blue eyes sparkling like the calm seas. "The shiny part?"

"You know." I waved my hands, picturing Queen Amelia when she'd been a young princess still, with her ladies, decked out like flowers whirling through the halls of Ordnung. "The gowns, jewels, and fancy hair. Girl things."

"What do you know of shiny girl things?"

"I may not be a royal by-blow, but I did live at the seat of the High Throne of the Twelve Kingdoms for years. I have eyes in my head."

He made a noncommittal sound, contemplating me. "What do you win, then, if you're proved correct?"

That took me aback. I didn't have anything I wanted to win—except for this woman I'd never met to have something of the chance I'd had, to make her own way in the world. Whatever that would take. If necessary, I'd find a way to help her do it. That fell within my skill set, most likely. But I found it difficult to believe that she would have zero options—that had to be more of Kral's rut-brained thinking. "What do you want if I lose?" I countered.

We eyed each other, Kral similarly unwilling to put claim to anything. Too much lay between us, our time together too short to predict what we'd want from the other, should the bet ever be resolved.

I spoke into the uneasy silence. "How about we each agree to a favor, to be claimed at any point in the future?"

He raised his brows at me, his face free of surliness for once. "A great leap of faith, for both of us."

"That's what makes it special. We commit equally . . . and trust that the other won't ask something we can't give. Or won't want to."

"It seems to me that we're both people who tend to be ruthless in going after what we want. Why wouldn't we exploit this kind of advantage over the other?"

"I don't know." I felt a little wild, contemplating it. A great advantage, indeed. A little thrilling, too. "But I'm game if you are. It *is* a challenge, after all."

"Done," he replied. And spit in his hand.

Danu save me from Dasnarians.

11

In a gesture of magnanimity, Kral arranged for me to have a proper bath, albeit in a fairly small tub that two of his men hauled in and filled with hot water from the galley. Still, it was Dasnarian sized and so big enough for me to soak in it—utter bliss.

I'd grown up bathing in snowmelt mountain streams and progressed to snatching dips in whatever body of water lay convenient to the campaign trail. Taking a real bath in hot water always implied the safety of home to me. A dangerous thought, as I couldn't fall into being comfortable around the Dasnarians, particularly Kral.

But it was nice while it lasted.

I was toweling myself dry when Kral joined me. "Good," he grunted, stripping off his bloodstained clothes. "I'll use your water."

"You sure you don't want fresher and hotter?"

"No. A Dasnarian warrior doesn't need such things. We're made of sterner stuff than that."

I rolled my eyes at his back and refrained from commenting. Witness the dramatic growth of my diplomatic skills.

"There's some perfumed lotion at the back of the clothing cabinet," Kral suggested, squinting at me as he stood—he was much too big to be able to sit in the tub—and soaped his hair.

"Are you saying I stink?" I wandered over to rummage through the cabinet anyway. Perfumed lotion, huh? Speaking of girl things.

"No." Kral had that tone, the one that emphasized how patient and even tempered he could be. Ha! "But I do like the scent."

I found the squat glass jar, uncorked it, and sniffed. Kind of like an evergreen forest, but with sweeter elements, too. Something like the cinnamon pastries they made in Elcinea, something else I didn't know. At least it didn't have the cloying density of the pink rose unguents the followers of Glorianna used far too liberally. Still. "Anyone would be able to smell me from a distance, maybe even leagues, if I'm upwind."

Kral stepped out of the tub, sheeting water on the floor, crouched and dunked his hair to rinse it. A fine sight, with his thighs and buttocks flexing, a glimpse of his man jewels between. I'd never shared quarters with a man this way, but I began to perceive the many advantages. Kral grabbed a drying cloth and rubbed it over his face, then gave me a look. "Are you planning any stealth missions in the near future?"

"You never know," I retorted. But I dropped the towel and took my time smoothing on the lotion, enjoying his attention. I liked my body just fine, scars and all, and it served me well as long as I took care of it. Kral, though . . . somehow his regard made me relish my curves, the softness of my skin. Danu help me, I wanted to smell pretty for him.

"I have dinner this evening with my officers." Kral, with one last hot survey of my nakedness, moved to the cabinet and pulled out one of the folded cloths. "I'd like you to join us."

Ugh. I must have made a face to match, because he laughed, running a big hand over my skull, smoothing my short hair, then handed me the cloth. "Call it practice."

I had a bad feeling about this, unfolding the length of crimson silk. Not Kral's deeper red signature color, but close. That's all there was to it—a long length of nearly sheer silk. "This counts as clothes?"

"Yes. Female clothes." Kral had gotten out the washbasin, dipped it in the bathwater, and set it next to a razor.

"I have zero idea how to wear this. I'm thinking like a big bandage or a funeral shroud. I'll just wrap it around myself until it's all used up and tie a knot, yes?"

He came over and took the silk out of my hands. "I can help. Pay attention."

"It's clothes, not like learning to read and write Dasnarian." I paid attention anyway, watching as he expertly wound the cloth snugly around my torso, letting it drape more loosely on the outer layers, finishing with a long piece that swept over my bosom and trailed dramatically over my shoulder and down my back. "Dressed many women, have you?"

He grinned, full of sexy, wicked mischief. "I've undressed plenty. A man learns."

I could just imagine. The outfit definitely felt . . . weird. Not bad, necessarily. Almost like wearing nothing at all. Aside from being unusually snug around my midbody, the silk provided a fair amount of range of motion. I tried a few of my favorite sword-form movements, satisfied with the freedom the silk afforded. "You realize, however," I told a rapt Kral, "that an attacker's weapon would go through this like I'm wearing nothing at all."

"This is not normally a problem for women," he admitted. Ironic, that. The men armored themselves like tortoises set to bury themselves in the mud to last out the dry season and the women went virtually naked—but it was the *men* who thought they had all the thick skin and bravery. Kral trailed a hand over my one bare shoulder, down my arm, then to my waist and over the slight curve of my hip. "You look ravishing," he murmured. "You could be a Dasnarian lady. If you had different coloring and longer hair, of course."

"I'll have long hair at the same time it turns blond and my skin goes peaches and cream." I moved away, gathering my knives from the bed where I'd left them while I bathed—and the two from the floor by the tub. Finding places to secret them in that outfit posed a challenge, but not an insurmountable one. The drape of the lower part allowed for thigh and ankle straps. The bare shoulder meant my arm sheath showed, but the delicately tooled leather made it decorative enough.

When I finished, Kral shook his head from his observation point on the lone chair. "Rather less like a Dasnarian lady now."

I cocked a hip and grinned. "Better, then. What do I do for shoes with this getup?"

"Dasnarian ladies go barefoot. Many of them wear lovely ankle and toe jewelry. I'm sorry I don't have any for you."

Barefoot, huh? Well, I'd spent the lion's share of my early life running barefoot in all weather; I supposed I could relearn. Time to toughen them up again, apparently. "I think I can live without foot jewelry."

"Good. Will you shave me?" Kral cocked his head at the bowl and razor.

"Is this a handmaiden thing?"

"Less sexual than practical. I never seem to get the shave as close as another can."

I stood in front of him, between his long, splayed legs, and dug my fingers through the silky hair. "I like the beard."

"It itches. And it's not appropriate for—"

"Let me guess. For the general of the Dasnarian military and an Imperial Prince of the Royal House of Konyngrr."

His lips that I loved so well twisted in a rueful, wry smile. "Exactly. Though our sail will take an extra day or so, we'll be in more trafficked waters soon. I need to be presentable."

"I've never shaved a man before."

"You've a deft hand with a blade; I'm sure you'll do fine."

I shrugged for that, checking out the razor, and followed his instructions for soaking a cloth in the warm, sudsy water. Kral tipped his head back, gaze on me as I brought the finely honed edge to his throat. I caught his eye. "So much trust."

"You made a vow."

Interesting. Working carefully, I found the ideal angle, bringing the gleaming razor just so along his golden throat. Indulgent, even, to follow the ridges of his corded neck, the hard bulge of his larynx, the etched line of jaw, for once relaxed and not set in aggravation with me. As the light hair fell away from his fine cheekbones, the tanned, smooth skin of his face showed a darker shade. I followed the sharp edge with my fingertips, checking the closeness of the shave, the softness of the newly hairless skin. Another way of enjoying a man's body, this. With his eyes closed and face relaxed, Kral seemed almost a different person. Whatever demons drove him lay still in the moment. Perhaps part of why he liked to be tended to this way.

Of course, being me, I couldn't help needling him a little. "Vows can be broken."

He opened one eye, the pale blue diamond bright in the light of the lantern I'd set on the ledge. "Can they?"

I shrugged, then set the blade against his other cheek. "Depends, I suppose. But I've yet to see one of the Three descend from wherever They lurk to chastise someone who broke a vow made in Their name."

"What of living with yourself?"

"You tell me."

His jaw flexed. "At some point you're going to have to let go of what happened to Lady Mailloux."

"I'm not much for letting things go."

"Why does this not surprise me?"

"Don't taunt the woman with a sharp razor at your throat."

He closed his eyes again, mouth curving in a pleased smile, and tipped his head back even more. "You won't hurt me."

His smug confidence tempted me to slice him, just a little, if only to see his surprise. I resisted, however, and quite easily—because I didn't want to hurt him, a realization that took me aback.

"I've never fucked a woman without a *lind* before," he remarked.

Aha. I turned that bit of information over in my head. "What of all those concubines?"

"Even with them. A concubine with an Imperial Prince's child holds power. I couldn't afford for anyone to have that kind of control over me."

Weren't we in a confessional mood? It seemed a good opportunity to worm information out of him, and yet . . . I didn't like this. It felt wrong. And I'd been down this path before and met with trouble. . . . *the point is not for the goddesses to rescue us from our own mistakes, but for us to follow the example of the virtues they embody and learn to do better.* "Kral," I said, and waited for him to open his eyes. "That might have been significant for you, but it's business as usual for me."

"So?" His voice carried a faint edge. This is what came of being honest, apparently. Still I plunged on.

"I just don't want you getting ideas, like you did before. I'm being clear on things."

He wrapped his fingers around my wrist, holding me there. "Are you reneging on your promise of exclusivity?"

"No." The thought hadn't occurred to me, which was unusual. If nothing else, however, Kral had a knack for keeping me sated. Now that he was on board. "But when my job is done, I'll have to leave. I don't want you getting . . ." *attached.* I didn't speak it aloud, faintly horrified at the thought. Is that what I meant?

Satisfied, he let me go, running his hands over his face, then snagged me onto his lap. "Well done. I'll miss this quiet time with you, once we reach Jofarrstyr." He kissed me, and I leaned into it, enjoying the newly soft skin around his clever mouth. Though I missed the contrasting texture of his beard. Ah, well, something of pleasure to be found in both, I supposed.

"We can make time, can't we?" I murmured against his lips.

He kissed me a bit longer, then set me on my feet. Stood himself and went to get fresh clothes. "You should be aware that . . ." He trailed off, searching for words, his back to me.

Uh-oh. "Just give it to me straight, General."

"Fine." He yanked on trousers in his signature color.

I almost asked why the ever-faithful Karyn hadn't embroidered the Konyngrr fist on his ass. At least he hadn't dressed me in something with it. I would have to take exception to that. Too bad I didn't have any reproductions of the new flag for Her Majesty's reign. *That* I would wear, and proudly. Following Uorsin's death, the Hawks had gathered and made a ritual of removing his bear from our uniforms. It wouldn't have been politic for us to wear our own symbol, not with the former High King's level of paranoia. When I got back, if Her Majesty would let me remain in the Hawks, I'd have to ask about us wearing something of our own. Or at least her symbol, as her elite guard.

"The Emperor's court is a dangerous, delicately balanced community," Kral was saying. I nearly yawned in his face. That described any king or queen's court, ever. Power—and the lure of it—did that to people. "Very few ladies attend court or other official business. The ones who do are noble wives, or my sisters, the Imperial Princesses." He cleared his throat, casting me a cautious sidelong glance.

"Kral, I'm not going to knife you for giving me good advice. Let me guess—all of these fine ladies are wives. No *rekjabrel* among them."

Surprise ghosted over his face. "You know what that means?"

"Essentially 'bed slave,' right? Dafne translated it for me."

"I thought you might be offended by that, should you discover it."

"And yet you call me that anyway."

"It is an accurate representation of our relationship. My men needed to know. It's not an insult."

Restless, I drew my favorite throwing knife and twirled it, prowling the room. "Seriously, Kral, it takes far more than that to bother me."

"Good. I've been thinking about how to put this to you. When your High Queen said she intended to send three women to Dasnaria as her emissaries, I thought that would be all the better for our advantage. I could have told her that, for any emissary of hers to be taken seriously, she should send a man, but . . ." He lifted a shoulder, let it fall, and pulled a shirt over his head. "I had no intention of helping her cause. In all honesty, I'm surprised Harlan did not warn her of this."

Because Harlan knew exactly why Ursula picked Dafne for the job. No one had her same skill set to be the spy the throne needed in Dasnaria. Unfortunate how things had worked out.

"Okay, so you're saying I'm not anyone's wife, virginal or otherwise, nor am I a concubine."

"Correct. Even concubines are formally contracted, a kind of lesser marriage. But no concubine would show her face in court."

Perish the thought. "I can only guess where a *rekjabrel* falls in this hierarchy."

"At the bottom," Kral admitted. "You should know that this does not reflect my regard for you. I would offer to marry you or make you officially a concubine, but—"

"Absolutely not."

"As I assumed you'd answer. Besides, you have no one to sign the papers for you, so it would be impossible to set up the contracts."

I went to Kral's secret cabinet, pulled out a fresh flask of *mjed*, uncorked it, and took a long pull. Kral's hands settled on my shoulders, his mouth brushing my cheek from behind.

"I'm sorry for this," he said quietly. "I would give you status if I could. As it is, I've determined your best chances for acceptance lie in not being any of the usual things, which includes *rekjabrel*. No one can know of our liaison. No one there will know what to make of you any more than I did."

I managed to stifle several sarcastic replies and didn't even shrug off his hands. The man meant well. Not his fault he was an idiot. Not entirely.

"That's very sweet of you. Thoughtful. I think I can endeavor to keep our forbidden love a secret." Okay, I didn't quite squelch *all* sarcasm. "But what of the seventy-odd men on this ship who do know?"

"Loyal to me. They won't betray our secret . . . relationship. Nor will any but a few officers be at the Imperial Palace." Kral had an odd sound to his voice, so—figuring I had schooled my expression sufficiently—I turned in his arms. Sure enough, he seemed bothered by something, though I couldn't discern what.

"It's a plan, then." I took another drink of *mjed* and offered him the flask. "To secrets kept."

He took it and drank, watching me as he did.

By the time Jens informed me we'd reached within half a day's sail of the harbor at Jofarrstyr, I'd grown quite proficient at donning the *klút*, as the Dasnarians called the female garb. In many ways I liked the ease of it—no buttons, laces, or stifling undergarments needed—but the weather chilled as we approached the coast, and I was thrice-damned cold.

Keeping my promise to Kral, and in a greater sense to Her Majesty, I'd turned my entire attention to learning to dress, speak, and behave as a proper Dasnarian lady. I feigned the meek subservience well. Not looking directly into men's eyes went against every instinct I'd honed as both a fighter and a scout, but Danu taught to turn disadvantages to advantages. While obeying that particularly stupid social rule, I practiced attention to peripheral vision. As with my long-sight, it was excellent. Even better, it seemed I could observe more peripherally, all because people thought I wasn't watching.

The interminable dinners with Kral's officers proved useful for practicing that and the others in my new quiverful of spy skills. The men tended to fall into boasting, telling stories of various battles and hunts, particularly when Kral broke out his stash of *mjed*.

Once I would have been the first to join in, matching them shot for shot and tale for tale. With the prohibitions against proper Dasnarian females drinking—kill me now—and speaking up unless directly questioned, I found myself distressingly sober, and able to observe a great deal. The men, including Kral, frankly seemed to forget my very presence, revealing themselves in ways I might not otherwise have noticed.

Much like stalking deer from a blind, I remained in plain sight, yet camouflaged, able to witness how they behaved. Lurking in prime position to take them down, should I wish to.

Of course, I had no problem with Kral's men in general. The officers shared the usual annoying thickheaded ways of most Dasnarian men, with the salient exception of the Vervaldr, but they possessed intelligence and—if their stories were to be believed—excellent strategic and fighting skills. They made perfect sparring partners for me to learn upon, though ignorant of their role as I honed my skills for the true enemy.

The biggest surprise came from how all the Dasnarians reacted differently to me in the traditional female garb. In a seeming contradiction, I became both the subject of intense male attention, to a level I'd never before experienced—and someone easily dismissed. When it didn't stick in my craw, I considered their behavior in terms of Kral's remark, that he'd considered Her Majesty's decision to send three females a sign of her ignorance and stupidity.

Some of that came from his own foolishness. Even with his many changes in attitude toward me, he still couldn't wrap his mind around a woman ruler. A fundamental blindness on his part that I could exploit, though I hadn't yet determined exactly how. Ursula had been my captain long before she became my High Queen, and I'd experienced firsthand her canny knack for recognizing ability and placing people where they'd do the most good. She might have other flaws as a leader, but choosing the wrong person for the job, especially for an effort this key to the security of the realm, simply didn't play for me as an explanation. I could see that now, from the words she'd sent. *I picked you for good reasons this time, too. Not the ones you think. When boulders speak, they give good advice. I listened and acted accordingly.*

Kral also underestimated the depth of her relationship with Harlan, her personal boulder. Of course she would have discussed her plan with him. If she talked to no one else, she would ask the person she trusted as much as, if not more than, her sisters. And with him *being* Dasnarian? He absolutely would have explained the implications of sending women into the Emperor's court. Furthermore, she could have sent someone else. Many other ambassadors to Ordnung from various kingdoms, quite a few of them men, would have more diplomatic skills than Dafne did. Marskal, lieutenant of the Hawks, outranked me in experience and easily matched my scouting and fighting abilities. Zynda might be her trusted cousin with powerful abilities, but there were Tala men the High Queen could have called upon.

Considering all the puzzle pieces—and thinking like Ursula, as I'd tried to do—why send the offender with the very foreign dignitary she'd pissed off?

If she'd truly been angry, she could have simply sent me away from Ordnung on one of the many reconnaissance missions I myself had been fielding scouts on. We'd needed more trained observers out there. Why not send the disgraced head of her scouts to do that?

I picked you for good reasons this time, too. Not the ones you think.

It bore contemplating, which was what I did, making those words into a comforting mantra, moving through Danu's Dance, the twelve sword forms, and any other drills I could recall or devise for myself. Anything to keep moving in the dense, chilled air on deck and to test the limits of the flowing silk scarf that counted as a dress. In becoming adept at the wrapping, I'd improvised a few improvements that gave me greater range of motion. Kral shook his head at that, but I challenged him to point out how it differed in appearance from his way of doing it, and he conceded. I may also have distracted him by allowing him to unwrap the thing and examine my inventions. That paid off nicely for us both.

I finished a spin, coming up short and pulling the sweep of my blade when I caught sight of Kral. "I hear we'll be there soon."

"Yes, soon you'll be able to sight the harbor with those keen eyes of yours." He looked me up and down. "You've been at your exercises since dawn—haven't you had enough?"

I rubbed my hands up and down my bare arms, wishing I could do the same for my rapidly chilling feet. "Yeah, but if I stop moving, I get cold—and I'm a mountain girl. I thought I was tough. Why don't Dasnarian women freeze to death?"

His face blanked with some surprise. "I never thought about it. They don't go outside in the winter months, I suppose."

My turn to gape at him. "Say you're not serious."

"If you stayed in our cabin, you'd be warm enough," he pointed out. "There's coals for the brazier and blankets to wrap up in."

"So I could lose my mind with boredom? No, thank you."

He grinned. "No, that wouldn't be you."

"What *is* me is that I'm going to wear Zynda's cloak. I'll keep the *klút* on, but I'm wearing the cloak over it. It's pretty and flowing, so you'll approve."

"I'm sure I will," he replied, with unusual agreeableness, making me narrow my eyes at him. He snagged me around the waist. "Only a couple of hours until we have to pretend not to be lovers," he murmured, brushing my ear with his lips. "Want to put the time to good use?"

Oh, yes. Yes, I did.

12

Perhaps the harbor at Nahanau had spoiled me with its grotesque grandeur, or the one at Ehas so tropically lovely, but Jofarrstyr left me vaguely disappointed. No towering dragons carved from rock nor smoldering volcano angrily rumbling in the distance. No sunny blue waters cupped by palm trees and whitewashed houses tiered upon each other. Instead, a sprawling stone city, larger than I'd ever seen, lined the coast in both directions. Beyond the crowded shore, the land stretched flat and interminable, covered with more buildings as far as I could see, all under a gray sky that drizzled a mix of snow and sleet.

"Jofarrstyr," Kral declared beside me, unnecessarily, but with a tone of pride and triumph. "Jewel of the Dasnarian Empire," he added, and I turned my face away so he wouldn't see the dubious smirk I couldn't quite suppress. Maybe it looked better in the sunshine.

"Is that the palace?" I pointed to an elaborate structure, taller than the rest, with gold-tiled domes that glittered even in the dim light.

"No, the palace cannot be seen from the harbor. We'll take carriages there. That's the temple."

"Of Deyrr?" I eyed it with increased interest, studying it. I'd have to see it closer up, but it looked reasonably penetrable. Certainly it was no fortress, with all those balconies and widows' walks around the domes. An agile climber like myself could scale that pretty easily. Not in this outfit, but I had my other things packed and ready for just such occasions.

"No." Kral coughed out a laugh. "And don't throw that name around. That sect keeps a low profile, with no great edifices. If they meet, they meet in secret. That is the Temple of Sól, the one god."

Great. It would have been way too convenient to be able to find the practitioners of Deyrr in a big, obvious building. The disappointment irritated me enough that I didn't even bother to argue with the one-god assertion. Of course the Dasnarians would think something like that.

The *Hákyrling* sailed ever closer to Jofarrstyr, cleaving through the center of the crowded harbor, other ships making way with expedited movements.

Clearly everyone recognized the ship belonging to the Imperial Prince. The cheerful mood of all the men aboard palpably vibrated in the air. I supposed if I'd been trapped on the other side of a magical barrier and despaired of ever getting home again, I'd be . . . Oh, wait. That *was* me now. Better and better.

Recognizing that my own sourness tainted more of my mood than the sight of foreign Jofarrstyr, I huddled deeper into the cloak, taking comfort in its softness. What in Danu had my big mouth gotten me into this time?

"Warm enough?" Kral asked. He stood a decorous distance from me, wearing what must be his dress uniform. Not his signature color, but a deep blue, also embroidered over the breast with the Konyngrr fist, this time in silver and topped by an elaborate crown. Emperor Hestar's insignia, no doubt.

"With the cloak, yes." The fur lining gave the cloak exceptional warmth, and I'd found a *klút* to match the deep emerald velvet of the exterior. I sent thanks to Moranu that Zynda had brought the thing along and then had to abandon it. I'd been shortsighted in thinking my leathers would be enough, simply because they always had been.

Dasnaria, a land of many firsts for me.

Kral must have heard something in my voice, because he searched my face and actually gave me his human smile, the one he normally showed only after sex, or when I shaved or otherwise tended him. "The white fur suits you—sets off your dark skin and eyes, makes your lashes look even longer. You look both lovely and exotic. An excellent note to set with His Imperial Majesty and the court."

I was spared thinking up a diplomatic answer to what Kral undoubtedly intended as a compliment by the arrival of his officers, also all in the deep blue dress uniforms with the silver-threaded crest. "No armor?" I asked under my breath.

"Into the Emperor's presence, never," Kral replied in an equally low tone that nevertheless conveyed his astonished disapproval. "Only he and his guard are armored."

"Will it be a problem that I'm wearing my knives?"

He'd never said so, but I didn't want to make an obvious mistake on the first day.

"No." Kral shook his head infinitesimally, gaze back on the shoreline activity. "They'll be assumed to be decorative only. It won't occur to anyone that you know how to use them at all, much less so effectively."

Excellent.

"Don't look so pleased with yourself. I strongly advise you not to disabuse anyone of their assumption."

Probably wise advice.

Unlike in the harbor at Nahanau, where the *Hákyrling* had pulled alongside a long, empty dock, at Jofarrstyr we dropped anchor in the harbor and Kral's men rowed the select group of us to a landing area. I tried not to let that bother me, that I'd have one more obstacle to getting back to the *Hákyrling*. After all, it wouldn't make any difference if the ship was sitting at a dock with a convenient gangplank. I couldn't sail her by myself, and even if I could,

I couldn't recross the barrier without Queen Andromeda's assistance.

With every passing moment, I became more dependent on others, and I didn't like it. Of course, I could always take off, find a new place, a new job. I'd done it before; I could do it again. But that wouldn't get my mission completed and the information home.

Trying to shake off the gloomy mood, I studied the landing platform, distracting myself with memorizing details. If for some reason I did have to come back through here in a hurry, any mental maps I retained would up my odds of escape, if only fractionally. Festooned with sapphire silks hanging from a gold canopy, the platform appeared to be reserved for royalty and their entourage only. Guards—all men—in more of the deep-blue dress uniforms waited at attention.

Other landing areas ranged around the harbor area, some crowded with men, others deserted, all decorated in varying degrees of grandeur—both the people and the platforms. How did one know which platform to row to? I strongly suspected going to the wrong one would result in all kinds of trouble, particularly given the preponderance of soldiers everywhere, all in deep blue, though in different styles that might denote rank or responsibilities.

In such a concentration, they looked uncomfortably like an army. Perhaps Kral's boasting of the empire's might contained more truth than we'd wanted to believe.

Like all things Dasnarian, the platform was efficiently designed, so that a ramp lowered into our boat and allowed us to glide up it more or less regally. Less, in my case, as the drizzling snow made the surface icy slick. My silk slippers hit it and slid. I recovered quickly, with the balance of long practice, but Kral's hand cupped my elbow anyway.

"Don't make a spectacle of yourself," he ordered. "I told you the slippers were a bad idea."

I hoped Danu noted my heroic restraint to balance out my

many faults. Kral and I had argued about my footwear several times, and I'd conceded that my boots looked terrible with the *klút*. At the last minute, I showed Kral my little craft project: I'd made a pair of slippers with soles cut from my destroyed fighting leathers and silk uppers taken from the end of the *klút* I planned to wear. They matched, which is high fashion, right? Danu knew I wouldn't miss the forearm's worth of silk from the *klút*, as it had enough length to swathe a woman two heads taller than I. Which probably described most Dasnarian women.

Releasing me again and moving ahead, Kral swept through the landing area, ignoring the guards, who all bowed deeply, leading our little parade through an arcade of more silk, punctuated with various sculptures, all of the same man. Here brandishing a broadsword at the sky. Next on a horse, brandishing a broadsword. Oh, look, and here with a booted foot on a creature I didn't know, except that it appeared to be very large and very dead, no doubt due to the, yes, brandished broadsword.

I might have identified a man with a larger ego than Kral's. Of course, semi-divinity would do that to even the most humble of men, I supposed. Still, I seriously doubted Emperor Hestar had ever started out as modest kind of guy.

As instructed, I stayed by Kral's left side, lagging by a pace. I didn't mind the inferior status the position implied, as it allowed me to absorb all I could through peripheral vision and take my cues from Kral. At the end of the arcade, a grand carriage awaited. Seriously, outrageously ornate. Uorsin would have eaten his left arm in acquisitive envy. The thing appeared to be fashioned entirely of gold and silver, embedded with jewels. Six horses in equally lavish harness blew steaming breath. All six were perfectly matched, in an unusual silver-white, barely dappled with gray that matched their darker manes and tails. Stranger to me, however, the horses stood hugely tall—my head would barely reach their shoulders— and carried massive muscle bulk, as such an undoubtedly heavy contraption no doubt required. Probably necessary for carrying around the big Dasnarian men in their full armor, too.

I still awaited with keen anticipation my first glimpse of a Dasnarian female. Kral's improbable remark about them not going outside seemed to be validated so far—I'd not seen one woman. Now, I'd be the first to say I'm a fan of men. I like them, both specifically and in general. But to be exclusively surrounded by them? Danu, it gave me chills, and not the good kind.

The fact that every man in sight fell into immediate and deep obeisance to Kral didn't make me feel any better.

"Ambassador?" Kral held out a hand at the carriage, ostensibly to help me up the three incredibly shallow steps. Frozen slush coated the metal, however, so I swallowed my pride and took his hand. Better to look like I needed help than slip and bang out a tooth or something. Despite the leather soles, the chilly wet had soaked right through my slippers, freezing my feet further.

Kral handed me into a seat and settled opposite. When it became apparent that none of the other men would join us, I kicked off the slippers and tucked my feet up under me, worming them inside the silk so I could warm them against my skin. Predictably, Kral frowned at me.

"That's not a position for a lady to sit in," he informed me.

I looked around the ostentatious carriage, even peeked under a cushion and behind one of the velvet curtains covering the window, then gave Kral a quizzical look. He heaved out an exasperated sigh.

"Yes, we're alone, but you agreed to follow the rules of female behavior at all times. If you slip up and forget—"

"I'm not stupid, Kral." But I *had* reached my limit for the moment. "I'm capable of discerning when I need to assume the persona you taught me and when I can take a moment to prevent frostbite."

He gave the slippers a disgusted glance. "Like you listened when I told you those were a bad idea?"

"Barefoot would have been better?" I snapped back.

"What would be better is if you completely absorbed the man-

ners required of you here. You'd be in less danger of getting yourself in trouble if you behaved as a Dasnarian woman at all times."

"Not going to happen, Kral. I'll play the part, but I'm not going
to lose sight of who I am." The very idea settled dread in my gut.
I'd prefer to become one of Illyria's reanimated dead, shuffling
mindlessly to do her bidding. Actually, behaving like a proper Dasnarian female came pretty close to the same thing. Fortunately, I
understood Kral better now. Though he might berate me on
proper manners, it came from a place of concern. He liked the
woman I was, in all my brash and unmeek ways, whether he'd
admit it to himself or not. "I know you're concerned for my well-
being, but you're going to have to let me find my own way here.
You gave me the knowledge I need. Trust in that."

"Speaking of which," he said, twitching the curtain to glance
out the window, "you should start addressing me by my title.
Prince Kral, General Kral, or simply Your Imperial Highness.
And try not to sound sarcastic when you say it," he added with a
wry twist of his mouth as he glanced back at me.

"You're calling 'Your Imperial Highness' simple?"

"I'd particularly like it if you'd shout it while coming." He
grinned, eyes glinting.

That sense of humor saved him from being completely insufferable. If only he let it out more. Already my ardent, teasing lover
from the *Hákyrling*'s voyage seemed to be disappearing, walled
away under an increasingly hard and shiny shell that Kral fastened around him and held in place with the glittering Konyngrr
fist. Tension rode him, and he clearly chewed over how this return home would go.

Kral claimed he wanted nothing more than to get home, but
the brittleness in his eyes reminded me of the sound in Harlan's
words when he referenced his family and homeland. Something I
understood all too well. When I went home, I'd take Harlan a
bottle of *mjed* and we could drink it between us and commiserate
on the misery that was the Dasnarian Empire.

If I got home.

Kral had fallen back into the brooding silence that had increasingly overtaken him as we drew closer to Dasnaria. I twitched aside a bit of the curtain, angling to see what I could of Jofarrstyr. We traveled down a broad main thoroughfare with traffic going in both directions, fancy carriages—though none as ornate as Kral's—all drawn by those enormous horses. None, of course, as perfectly matched. Men walked along raised paved pathways separated from the stone-inlaid streets by deep gutters that appeared to carry sewage.

"Why is it all gray stone?" I asked.

"The province of Bjarg provides stone for the empire. Their granite is the strongest to be found anywhere in the world. Rough or polished, it lasts through the freeze and thaw cycles. And you shouldn't be looking out the window—you might be seen."

"I know how to look without being spotted," I replied in a mild tone. A five-year-old among my people knew how to do that much. "So, are these your horses, your carriage? Or do they belong to the Emperor's household or some such?"

"Assessing my wealth?"

Assessing escape routes, actually. Not that it would do me much good to talk Kral into giving me his carriage—or for me to steal one of his horses—if I couldn't leave Dasnaria itself. Perhaps there were other countries connected by land that weren't part of the empire. Seemed unlikely, given what I knew, but that might be the only solution if I couldn't go home. I couldn't spend the rest of my life in this place.

On the flip side, all of this made the possibility of getting myself killed on this mission look like an absolutely cheery prospect.

"I apologize," Kral said, apparently taking my reflective silence for offended sulking. Then he blew out a long breath. "I am on edge contemplating breaking the news to Emperor Hestar of the barrier and all that's transpired with the Nahanauns, including my failure to find their treasure. Yes, this carriage and the horses are mine. As the second son, I received considerable wealth and several estates from our father."

"Lots of houses to live in."

His lips twitched. "Which I don't, as I'm sure you're poking at me for with that remark. I'm always at the Imperial Palace or traveling, it's true."

"Why is that?"

He shifted, looking away from me. "My life is not my own. I must do as the Emperor commands me."

"The *Hákyrling* is as much home to you as anything, it seems."

He considered me with some surprise. "I'd never thought of it that way."

I shrugged. In truth, I missed the *Hákyrling* more than I would have predicted. The carriage jolted, the sudden jarring movement so unlike the rocking rhythm of the sea I'd grown used to. Part of me kept listening for the creak of the wood, the wind snapping in the sails, the water singing its song of good weather and bad. I'd never thought I'd care much for the ocean or sailing, but somewhere along the journey it had gotten into my bones. Could be just apprehension of what lay ahead for me feeding that emotion.

"I like the *Hákyrling*," I told him. "It's a lovely ship."

"Thank you," he replied gravely. "I designed and built it. It was the . . . the one thing I could call wholly my own, that I made instead of inheriting."

"Cleverly designed, Your Imperial Highness," I told him, struck by the sorrow in his gaze and kind of sorry I'd ascribed his earlier remarks about it to boasting, instead of to simple truth.

"That might be the first compliment you've ever paid me."

And I hadn't thought of it as a compliment to him. Hmm. Mostly I figured his ego didn't need any more stroking. "Well, you have a very nice cock, too, Prince Kral." I blew him a little kiss and he laughed, relaxing more.

I probably should have realized he'd be concerned about the news he brought to the Emperor, brother or no. I'd never forget that headlong journey from Windroven, when the Hawks accompanied Ursula to deliver news we all knew the High King would greet badly. Some of the Hawks even started a betting pool that she'd find a way to divert us, to avoid going before her father on what could have been a suicidal audience.

A bet I happened to win because I knew she wouldn't shirk her duties. Just as it wouldn't occur to Kral to gloss the news. Or to take the *Hákyrling* and sail off somewhere entirely new. For an unhinged moment, I nearly suggested it to him. Pictured myself climbing onto his lap, kissing him the way he liked, and whispering it in his ear. *Let's go. Turn the carriage around and take us away from this horrible place. We'll sail around the world and find out if granite really is the hardest stone. We'll battle fish-birds, have wild sex, and be only ourselves. Let's go.*

"What did you say?" Kral frowned. "Let's go where?"

I hadn't meant to voice that last and cleared the whisper from my throat. "Have you considered what you'll say to the Emperor?"

A line formed between his brows. "I'm hoping inspiration will strike."

"We're stuck in a carriage together for a long ride," I pointed out, "and I'm pretty sure you won't agree to whiling away the time the way we usually prefer to. I might be a commoner and a simple mountain girl, but I lived at Ordnung with a . . ." *Remember who you're talking to.* "A sometimes difficult High King. I've observed some here and there of how to present uncomfortable information if you want to talk out a strategy."

Kral shook his head, mouth in set lines. "It's not possible to predict how the Emperor will react to most anything. I have a certain amount of power, support within the court, so he'll be careful of that. Otherwise, I can only tell him the truth."

We rode in silence after that.

13

W e finally left the seemingly endless city behind and entered a
forest. It looked old, the trees towering to great heights,
gnarled with thick bark and sporting dense moss on the north
sides—I verified the direction with Kral, who seemed bemused that
I asked. It reassured me to see that some things held true no matter where in the world I might be. In a land where I'd not yet
glimpsed the sun, it helped to know I could guide myself with familiar tricks.

I couldn't decide if it was a mark of unreasonable paranoia,
smart planning, or force of habit that I watched our route so
closely, marking in my mind the direction we took and the roads
that branched away. All paved with stone, as Kral had promised,
even in this deep forest, which felt . . . odd, I supposed. Certainly
the smoothed stone made for a faster journey, but something
about it seemed soulless to me. And I was not a woman to fret
about soulfulness.

Maybe I simply hadn't been so before this because I'd never
encountered the feeling.

Shifting restlessly, I reached to check my drying slippers, using
the opportunity to stretch my limbs. I hadn't sat still this long

since the fish-bird injuries. If I'd been on foot or horseback, I'd have peeled off from the group to climb a tree and take a look around, then enjoyed a bracing run to catch up.

"Did you climb trees as a boy?" I asked Kral.

"Hmm?" He blinked at me, clearly distracted from deep thought.

I gestured at the forest. "Trees, you know. Did you climb them?"

"No." He seemed entirely baffled. "Why do you ask?"

I didn't know, so I shrugged it off. The sleety weather had at last converted to full-on snow, which fell in thin, sparse flakes, but at least looked prettier. "Passing the time, I guess."

"We're nearly there. I don't much like riding in the carriage either, but it adds a certain important pomp to our arrival. You'll have your first glimpse of the Imperial Palace in a moment." He drew back the curtains on one side.

"No worries about being spotted?"

"It's traditional to stop and enjoy this view," he said. "It's quite famous in all of Dasnaria—and a badge of honor to be able to say you've seen it for yourself."

Oh, well then! If it was a badge of honor to brag about, how could I resist? I drew back the curtains on my side also, while Kral knocked on the carriage ceiling and called out to the driver that we'd stop to show the ambassador the view.

We rounded a curve up a slight incline, and the trees thinned, then parted entirely, giving way to an immense circle of immaculate snow. A glassy lake sat in the middle, and inside it, a palace. The reflection in the water made it look bigger, I realized quickly, a clever trick to fool the eye into believing the edifice to be enormous. Really, it was only huge. I mentally snorted at myself for that one, because the Imperial Palace exceeded Ordnung by four times, at the very least.

Ordnung, with its many tall towers, was a vertical fortress. Some of that came from Uorsin's strategic intelligence—a smaller area for attackers to besiege made for better defense. Above a certain height, any fortress simply couldn't be effectively assailed. Even flight-capable shape-shifting enemies couldn't wreak as much damage as a ground-level siege engine. So, with its moat and external and internal walls, plus the inner castle, which could also be sealed up, along with being crowded onto a plateau hemmed by mountains rising around it, Ordnung boasted a fairly small footprint.

Of course, more than one joke had circulated about the thrusting towers compensating for Uorsin's manhood. Spoken very quietly, among discreet groups.

On the other side, King Nakoa KauPo's palace by the sea had been mainly flat, rambling over the terraces with as many of the rooms open-air as not. The sheer lack of secured doors and accessible balconies should have made it completely insecure, and yet the very openness of it meant I'd never devised a way to get Dafne out with no one spotting us. That would have been the case even if the *Hákyrling* hadn't been closely guarded and our only viable way off the island.

The same bottleneck to escape I still faced.

And now this.

"Is . . . is the palace *in* the lake?" My voice came out awed, though I truly felt terrified for my own future. The tone pleased Kral enough to run a hand over my hair, cupping my skull with affection.

"Yes. The most impressive feat of Dasnarian engineering ever accomplished. It sits on granite pilings sunk into the lake bottom and is inaccessible unless the single drawbridge is lowered. A marvel of impregnability."

I could see that as I surveyed the sheer walls that rose out of the water, polished to a high gleam. Not unlike Ordnung, no windows, doors, ledges, or other features interrupted the flawless rise of the walls for an extraordinary height. Anyone jumping into the water would be killed or at least maimed to the point of wishing for death.

Rising from above and behind those walls, the palace itself sprawled both outward and upward. Towers worthy of Uorsin speared the sky, and lower, longer portions looked like barracks that could house thousands of fighters. And likely did.

"Beautiful, isn't it?" Kral prompted.

"I've never seen anything like it before in my life," I said, glancing at him and adding a smile to cover the fact that I hadn't exactly agreed. It wasn't beautiful, no. It was cold, forbidding, and . . . well, soulless. I hated it on sight. "Is the lake natural?" The clearing around it, for easily a league in any direction, surely wasn't.

"Spring fed," Kral replied. "Then dammed and maintained at a consistent level by judicious release of water during high season."

Interesting. Could be the dam would be an exploitable weak point. Destroy it, drain all the water, and—what? Storm the even taller walls by slogging through lake mud? A strategy that wouldn't do me any good if I was inside those walls, regardless.

"Ready to storm the castle?" Kral's voice had a teasing note, but the way his eyes held mine made me feel like a fellow warrior about to do that very thing.

Although I feared I'd never see the outside of those walls again, I simply sent a fervent prayer to Danu for strength and agreed that I was ready.

It took longer than I expected to make our way around to the drawbridge, which had been positioned at the farthest distance from the first glimpse point. The road followed the boundary between the forest and the cleared area around the lake. Though Kral gave me a quizzical look, he didn't stop me from drawing the curtains on the other side of the carriage.

"It's only forest on that side," he noted. "Not much interesting to see."

Forest, indeed. Ancient, overgrown, thick with dense underbrush. Even if someone were to somehow escape the walls of the palace, swim the lake, then manage to cross the snowy expanse without being felled by a dozen arrows, the forest would be nearly impassable.

For most anyone but me. Get me to the forest and I could hide forever. Not that it would get me home, but I felt better to know that much. The Dasnarians might regard that overgrowth as daunting. For me it promised refuge.

Really too bad I'd never learned to swim. If I survived this, acquiring that skill went to the top of my list.

All along the road, guard posts faced both inward and outward, with men stationed to both scrutinize our approach—followed by deep obeisance to His Imperial Highness—and face steadfastly away to constantly scan the pristine clearing. Other outposts ringed the lakeshore, no doubt similarly manned to observe both water and snowfield. The walls would have guards also, either stationary or patrolling.

An interesting flaw in the security, though—not one guard challenged Kral as to my identity. Either His Imperial Highness could do as he pleased without question or they cataloged me instantly as female and therefore beneath notice. I sorely wanted to ask Kral which it was, but that would be tipping the direction of my thoughts too much. He worried about my revealing myself as a less-than-demure woman; I worried about his realizing I'd been sent as a spy who planned her clandestine escape.

One thing had become hugely apparent, however: Unless the practitioners of Deyrr visited the Imperial Palace, I would have to find a way to get out and go to them or I'd never find any answers to the High Queen's riddles. It made me tired to contemplate it.

"Almost there and you can rest," Kral told me. "I know it's been a long journey."

I opened my mouth to retort, then closed my lips over the words. No sense mentioning this hardly counted as an afternoon excursion to me. The closer we drew to the center of the fist of Konyngrr, the more Kral seemed to fall into his mental rut of seeing me like all females instead of the person he'd come to know so thoroughly. It would have annoyed me if it didn't work so well for my plans. I needed his help, yes, but not for him to suspect my true agenda. So I smiled. "It will be lovely to rest, yes."

"You need not attend court immediately. There's not much left of the afternoon's session. I'll present myself to His Imperial Majesty, then likely meet with him privately, at his discretion. You can be introduced at dinner. Or tomorrow, if you prefer to be fresh."

Oh, no, no, no. I definitely wanted to be there when Kral gave the first indications of his visit to the Thirteen Kingdoms. That would tell me a great deal, those initial moments and honest reactions before political masks could be re-created and donned.

"I'd feel much better sticking with you, Your Imperial Highness, and having you introduce me. That way I can be sure everything is handled according to proper protocol." I indicated the guards who waved us onto the freshly lowered drawbridge. "I can't help but notice that your rank and obvious importance pave the way for so much."

Too thickly applied? Perhaps, because Kral studied me, a slight line between his golden brows. "I'm relieved to see you shed some of your overconfidence. You'll proceed more wisely, being more cautious now. My rank and importance only go so far. I cannot defy the Emperor, much as I'd wish to. It would mean my death, too, or banishment. Please remember the stakes and keep your mouth, fond as I am of it, closed more than not."

With a shiver, I tucked my feet into the still-damp slippers and nodded.

We progressed across the drawbridge in fits and starts, as the guards lowered sections immediately before us, then raised them again behind us. At each stopping point, the guards hailed His Imperial Highness, bowed, and let me pass without a single question. I began to suspect Kral bringing an unknown woman into the palace wasn't unprecedented. The thought didn't make me jealous exactly—though before that moment I would have said I didn't have a jealous bone in my body—but it added to my unease.

"I think you were wise, Prince Kral, to clarify and disguise our relationship," I said quietly as we traveled a section between posts and couldn't be overheard.

He caught my eye and nodded slightly, fervent agreement and more of the man I had come to know in the look. Reassuring to know he still lurked somewhere inside the forbidding Imperial Prince.

We finally reached the walls, guarded by smooth metal doors that swung slowly outward over a ledge far too narrow for a siege engine. Presuming one could even get that far. They closed with a resounding boom behind us.

"What do you do with groups of more than one carriage?"

A flicker of grim humor at that. "One by one, Ambassador. One by one. Fortunately, the occasion rarely arises. Very few people come and go from the Imperial Palace. They either come to stay or never make the journey in the first place."

That explained some of why Karyn had never been to the palace. I didn't blame her a bit. She'd certainly hate me for having her dragged from her orchards to this grim prison. "Perhaps you should write your wife a letter," I said, abruptly enough that Kral raised an eyebrow.

"The question of our marriage can only be entertained before the Emperor. He created it; only he can end it."

I gaped at him. "Why did you agree to such a bet, with those kinds of stakes?"

He watched me intently. "You don't respect me and repeatedly question my honor. How could I refuse to meet the challenge you laid for me? I would only fall lower in your estimation."

"I didn't mean it to be like that, Kral."

He lifted a shoulder, let it fall. "You had a point. I wouldn't like Karyn's life. Knowing you . . . it's made me think. A marriage in name only punishes us both. I won't divorce her if she doesn't wish it, but if she does, then that is the honorable thing to do. Perhaps it will go some way to making amends for my role in Lady Mailloux's troubles."

Full of surprises, this man. It would be beyond merely interesting when Karyn—who hopefully wouldn't be some idiot who preferred being a celibate princess kept on her own lands like some flower preserved under glass—made the right choice, letting me cash in my favor.

And call upon Kral's exacting honor to help me escape this place.

The six horses pulled us into a crescent before more guarded and barred doors, these in the towering blank wall of the main edifice. Above, on a walk at the top of the wall, soldiers stood at severe attention. Even at his worst, Uorsin hadn't manned the walls with this density.

"Is Dasnaria at war?" it occurred to me to ask.

Kral flicked me a glance, face impassive. "Dasnaria is always at war. That is the way of things."

I'd be pleased to never hear that phrase again—only three words in Dasnarian, using the command tense—and employed with relentless finality. It seemed to echo everything hopeless about the place. The carriage doors opened, sending snowflakes fluttering in, as if seeking to escape the chill. Guards in a double line between us and the doors, forming an aisle, all bowed deeply, while a group of other men, servants it seemed, in simple gray robes with cowls, knelt in full obeisance, foreheads pressed to the slush-covered stone. Kral stepped out and turned back to offer me a hand. I took it, surreptitiously brushing his palm with my fingers, to make myself feel better, gratified when he closed his fingers warmly around mine, if only for the briefest moment.

Inside, more servants—all male, making me doubt that women even existed in this dour place—took my cloak, and also the slippers from my feet, giving them puzzled looks. The floors were entirely covered with plush rugs, woven in brilliant patterns in jewel tones, and blessedly soft and warm on my feet. Flowers, animals, abstract designs, repeated themselves and were regularly punctuated by the Konyngrr fist. Pretending to shift aside to allow room for the servants to help Kral with his outer garments, I deliberately stepped on one of those crests. A childish gesture, perhaps, but it made me feel better to grind my heel in it.

We stood in a long hall bordered with doors that were interspersed with enormous mirrors behind more statuary. Some looked to be replicas, or virtually so, of the ones I'd studied at the landing platform. From the high ceiling hung elaborate creations of faceted crystal studded with white candles. The heat of the flames made the crystals whisper against each other in faint chimes as they bounced the light among themselves, against the mirrors, and back. Stunning that the silence, born of servants who made no noise and the muffling power of the rugs, could be so complete that the cyrstals' quiet song was clearly audible.

An older man in an elaborate uniform—same crest and colors, different style and insignia—came down the long hall, his footsteps audible, but barely. I began to feel like a deer in rainy weather, jumpy at not being able to hear the predator's step on soft, wet leaves. Unlike the guards, this man studied me intently as he approached, before turning his entire attention to Kral, giving him that deep bow.

"Your Imperial Highness, Prince Kral, welcome home. A grateful empire shall sleep easy this night knowing you keep watch over her."

He said more, but I couldn't catch it all. He spoke Dasnarian, yes, but not the sort I'd become accustomed to with first the Vervaldr, then Kral and the other men aboard the *Hákyrling*. Some words I recognized, but they had elaborate suffixes added, or extra prefixes. Thank Danu that Dafne had spent the effort to teach me to listen for such things. At the time I'd considered it just revenge for all the knife-work drills I'd put her through. Instead it seemed we'd both prepared the other for impossible situ-

ations. The extra embellishments had an overall effect of sounding far more formal, probably adding political subtleties that
would escape me entirely. If all the court spoke this way, I'd be in
serious trouble.

"Baerr Lars," Kral said, and held out a hand to me in a gracious gesture. "May I present my guest, the ambassador from the
Thirteen Kingdoms, sent by Her Majesty High Queen Ursula to
convey greetings to His Imperial Majesty Emperor Hestar."

There was a lot more to it. They spoke to each other about me,
and I gathered that *baerr* meant the equivalent of our "chate-
laine" and that Lars, like Lise at Ordnung, ran the physical aspects of the Imperial Palace. In a place this size, that would be like
being ruler of a small kingdom, but with none of the glory. Lars finally agreed to pass the word of our arrival, bowed—deeply to Kral
and more shallowly to me—and left, leaving us to proceed more
slowly.

When Kral held out a hand to me, he again curled the tips of
his fingers around mine, then guided my hand to his rigidly held
forearm. "Baerr Lars recommended this presentation," he told
me quietly, in the way of speaking I'd become accustomed to. "I
did not give him your name, as it should be given to the Emperor
first, and it also occurred to me that I don't know your family
names."

Oh, great. I supposed Ambassador Jepp would sound awfully
brief in this place. Funny how Queen Andromeda had so recently
spoken my full name for the first time I'd heard it aloud since . . .
well, since I left home. "Jesperanda," I told him, my tongue numbly
twisting around the syllables, it had been so long. "Jesperanda im
Kaja."

He dipped his chin, acknowledging, with no inkling I'd handed
him a small piece of flesh from the interior walls of my heart.

14

I expected something like the throne room at Ordnung. Uorsin hadn't lacked for ego or grandiose aspirations himself, so the hall that housed his high throne was the grandest I'd encountered in any of my travels. When I'd first seen it, as the Hawks rotated duty being available to then Princess Ursula when she attended court, I'd been hard-pressed not to stare about like a Brynling taken to market for the first time.

That feeling rushed straight back into me, the old echoes of being that kid overwhelmed by the sight of houses, livestock, people, and goods, all piled on top of each other—overlaid with newer memories of High King Uorsin, center figure in a line of thrones, the golden marble, the fantastically patterned rose window of Glorianna.

Like that market had been in comparison, the hall at Ordnung seemed dim, dusty, even provincial, compared to the Emperor's throne at the Imperial Palace in Dasnaria. We moved through several antechambers filled with petitioners, their apparent rank, grandness of costume—and décor of the room—increasing with proximity to the throne room. We waited only a few moments in the final one, empty but for us, as a man in a uniform similar to Baerr Lars's took my name in advance.

"He'll have it whispered to His Imperial Majesty first," Kral told me in a low undertone, though we were perfectly alone. "The worst that can happen is he won't see you right away. In that case, I'll use my influence to get you an audience. So don't be disappointed if—"

"Quit worrying. I'm fine."

He stiffened. "I don't worry. Just remember to behave properly and keep your mouth shut. Keep in mind that I can't help you in there."

"Got it. You don't have to keep telling me." A solo scouting mission. Something I'd done hundreds of times before.

The man returned before Kral could admonish me further. He opened the double doors—each inlaid with the Konyngrr fist— and stepped aside to reveal the near-blinding grandeur of the throne room. I was glad I hadn't yet blown it with Kral, because I might have stood in stunned shock if he hadn't stepped forward, bringing me with him. We paused there, on a high platform with no railing, while the entire assembly arrayed below turned to scrutinize us at the announcement of first Kral's many names and titles, then my brief ones. The herald fell silent, as did the entire room. Unsettling that so many people could be so utterly quiet. If the platform was intended to instill a sense of peril, of the possibility of falling at the slightest misstep, it worked admirably.

Despite knowing I'd always land on my feet. *Bryn never look back.*

Directly across the sea of faces, Emperor Hestar sat on an ornate throne elevated so high that he looked down on our raised platform. Made of white and silver metals, embedded with crystals like more of those light fixtures that crowded the high ceiling above, the throne's back cupped Hestar in a replica of the Konyngrr fist, as if holding him in the palm, while giant fingers stretched out to curl around him. Sparkling wires, perhaps also encrusted with the crystals, radiated out, a massive spiderweb.

Each thread ran to some sculpture set in a niche on the towering walls. More of the ones I'd seen already—and now that I'd seen Hestar in the flesh—definitely of him executing heroic deeds, only in polished platinum. Everywhere my eye went, it collided with images of Hestar, the fist, and dazzlingly painful brightness.

Resplendent in the center, framed by a velvet cloak in a blue so deep as to be almost black, Hestar wore a silver version of the Dasnarian armor, polished to a mirror gleam. A modified helm served as his crown, inset with clear jewels. All the glare made it difficult to look closely at his face—which made me realize I'd forgotten to be meek.

I stared straight into Hestar's gaze, and he looked right back.

It grounded me, though, the hard, dark eyes of Kral's brother, taking my measure as I took his, one fighter to another. Though he couldn't be much older than Kral, Hestar's face carried deep lines from exposure to harsh weather, along with the pale skin of a man who no longer went outdoors. A short beard so white it looked almost as clear as the crystals seemed to be a product of age, compared to the more golden shades of blond of most Dasnarians.

As it was too late to appear deferential, I held Hestar's hard stare, thinking of Danu and her unflinching clear eyes.

"Brother," he intoned in a voice like a brass gong shattering the silence, without taking his eyes off of me, "you may approach. Bring the ambassador with you."

Kral turned to the side, where a flight of steep stairs connected—still no railing—and twisted to the floor below. Barely wide enough for the two of us side by side, the spiral stairs were another clever strategy. Uncarpeted and covered with slickly glazed tiles, they required concentration to descend, even in my bare feet. Kral's boots clattered loudly. It would be impossible for a force of any size to either steal into or storm the throne room. The sole entrance would be too high to jump from without injury, and anyone who managed to get this far without approval could be easily picked off the stairs by the innumerable guards ringing the hall. I began to see why Kral didn't worry about my wearing my knives—even if I managed to throw a few, the sheer number of armed guards would swamp me.

I could have planted one in Hestar's eye, however, from the vantage of the platform, if I didn't mind suiciding. An excellent backup plan for future audiences.

Instead, traveling down a center aisle as at Ordnung, we wended around the side by a path separated from the assembly area by a waist-high wall. The route forced anyone approaching the throne to pass a gauntlet of armored guards. As we made our way to the front of the room, I finally spotted some of the elusive Dasnarian females, distinctive in their bright *klúts* in a sea of mostly deep blue. I counted five, two so draped in jewelry that they had to be the Imperial Princesses. They all watched me with fascination—and with practiced peripheral vision. I gazed back at them directly, head held high, figuring I'd already blown it with the downcast eyes and unwilling to make it seem like a mistake by changing my demeanor after the fact.

All were tall, strongly built women with gorgeously creamy skin, of the kind that had never seen the sun, and hair they all wore long, in glistening blond cascades. Under other circumstances, and without that promise I'd made to Kral, I'd have contemplated wrapping myself in that silky hair while I explored all that lovely, soft skin. Okay, I still could fantasize. I'd never vowed to squelch attraction to anyone else. I wasn't *dead*.

Yet. And I very well could be soon, so I might as well be shot for attacking as for cowering. So I smiled at the women, dipping my chin in a kind of female solidarity moment. None of them betrayed their surreptitious observation by reacting, but one of the princesses leaned her head ever so slightly to the other, and I felt sure she said something.

I really wanted to know what. Which grounded me more than anything else. I was still me inside the *klút*—wanting to know the gossip, feeling randy, and fantasizing about someone other than Kral. All in all, I felt more like myself than I had since setting foot in Dasnaria. I'd told Kral I'd take his advice, and I *had* paid attention. But in my own thoughts I kept going back to why Her Majesty had sent *me*—and it surely wasn't because she figured me for doing well at acting subservient.

You are, and always have been, my best scout. I picked you for a reason five years ago. I picked you for good reasons this time, too. Not the ones you think.

The problem with the "not the ones you think" part was that every time I hit on what reason it could be, it occurred to me that it wasn't that, because I'd thought of it. Brain puzzles made my head hurt. I thought with my knives, and Her Majesty knew that about me. She wouldn't expect me to suddenly become a different person.

It all came down to that I was utterly alone, with only my own wisdom to guide me, meager though that might be.

Though I also had Kral's own example. I'd watched him in this same situation in reverse, approaching the High Queen on her throne, bluffing his way through the audience as if he weren't isolated from all support, trapped in a foreign land with no allies and only a hundred men. He might be an idiot on some things, but he knew how to lead, how to win. He might not recognize it, but he and I were much the same person under the skin. I could do far worse than emulate his behavior, though it would no doubt send him into a frenzy if I told him my reasoning.

Good idea or not, I would follow that. And my gut. Better than trying to be someone I wasn't.

We arrived at the foot of the throne, our heads not even reaching the level of Hestar's feet. Kral bowed low and I did not do the same, despite his painstaking tutoring. Instead I inclined my head in acknowledgment, more than Kral had done with High Queen Ursula at the outset.

Even from the remove and with the ambient glare, I clearly

saw Hestar raise his brows. *First blood.* "Why do you not bow, Ambassador Jesperanda im Kaja?"

Such a booming low voice. I'd thought Harlan's voice deep—Ursula's boulder—but Hestar's rumbled like otherworldly thunder. Were I given to much fancy, I'd almost believe in the semi-divinity. Certainly everything about his appearance conveyed that impression. But deck me out in enough shiny stuff and I'd look impressive, too.

Okay, maybe not *that* impressive.

"I bring you greetings, Your Imperial Highness, from Her Majesty High Queen Ursula of the Thirteen Kingdoms, as her ambassador and as a gesture of goodwill from a monarch of rank. However, I am her subject, not yours. My fealty belongs to her alone, a loyalty I would never betray."

A murmur ran through the otherwise astonishingly silent room, almost subvocal. Kral remained in his bent position, his forearm tense beneath my hand. I sent him a mental apology. Though, all things considered, his having to watch me be executed might be upsetting to him, but it wouldn't be nearly as terrible as my actually going through it.

If I could take it, he thrice-damned could, too.

I might have only a few people I respected, but my High Queen topped the list and I would not let her down by demonstrating obedience to some guy who thought he was a god because everyone treated him that way. Keeping my back straight and chin up, I held Hestar's gaze, even though the glare about burned my eyes.

"I have not heard of these Thirteen Kingdoms," Hestar finally said. "Only of the Twelve Kingdoms, which are rumored to be small and worth no notice."

"Indeed, Your Imperial Majesty, we were once the Twelve Kingdoms, united and ruled in the past by High King Uorsin. Following his death, his eldest and heir, High Queen Ursula, ascended to the throne, adding a thirteenth kingdom to her realm."

I sounded pretty good, keeping it simple, direct. No verbal embellishments, but Hestar wasn't using them either. Kral remained in his bowed position, which seemed ominous, however.

"Acquired through conquest?" Hestar sounded intrigued.

"Through marriage. The High Queen's sister married the king of the newest kingdom, allying the lands."

"I'm relieved to hear of a king. I'd begun to think this a realm made up entirely of women."

And here I was thinking the same in reverse of yours. I managed not to say that out loud, and simply inclined my head in slight acknowledgment.

"Rise, Brother," the Emperor finally said, sounding a bit irritated. "You have been long away. I expected you to bring me treasure, not . . . this person. Explain yourself."

"Many unusual events befell us, Your Imperial Majesty," Kral replied, not shaking off my hand as I'd more than half expected. "Much that you will wish to hear about."

"Is that so? I hoped you'd bring me the treasure I seek, not stories." Hestar's gaze flicked back to me, considering. "The ambassador's skin is quite dark—are her people of the Nahanauns? Don't tell me you never made it to the islands; I will be most displeased with you."

There they went, talking around me. I jumped in before Kral could speak, so I wouldn't have to compound my brashness by interrupting him.

"Your Imperial Majesty, the people of the Thirteen Kingdoms are many and varied." That ripple of reaction again, just audible, murmuring of shocked surprise—until Hestar glanced up and the room went utterly silent again and I soldiered bravely onward. "Depending on the region they hail from, their skin may be much darker than mine or as fair as the ladies of this court. But the Nahanauns have only recently become known to us. If they are related to our people, we have not yet uncovered the connection. Her Majesty High Queen Ursula will be most interested in any information the Dasnarian Empire might provide on the topic."

Especially since part, maybe most, of the archipelago belonged to her now. Probably not something to mention in our first meeting.

Anger stirred in Hestar's expression, muted behind neutrality, but recognizable as like Kral's. "You dress as a woman, Ambassador, but you do not behave or speak as one. Are you truly a man who comes to me in the guise of a woman, a wolf taking the fleece of the sheep he hopes to stalk?"

Very much too close to the truth there. Only I was a spy in diplomatic clothing.

"Your Imper—" Kral started.

"Silence. I'm asking her. This . . . *person* you brought into my court from a place no one cares about." Something canny in his eyes, however, made me think he knew more than he let on.

"I am a woman, Your Imperial Majesty, a woman of my people, which means how I behave and speak comes from who I am, not the shape of my body. His Imperial Highness Prince Kral has been gracious in guiding and advising me. I come before you in the garb of Dasnarian people as a gesture of goodwill, to demonstrate, ah, that we are all . . . brothers and sisters."

Okay, most of that had been pretty good. I kind of lost the thread there at the end. From the corner of my eye, I caught the crooked line around his mouth that Kral got when he wanted to throttle me.

Hestar leaned his chin on a fist. "Your people are peculiar indeed to send one such as you as ambassador to the great Dasnarian Empire. Should I perceive this as an insult?"

The room couldn't have gone more silent, but it seemed to. Not even a rustle of clothing. Did these people even breathe quietly?

"A strange question to ask, Your Imperial Majesty, unless your intent is to pay insult to me." Not diplomatic, perhaps, but I'd been insulted plenty of times. Calling a person on it usually elicited an apology from the right-minded who'd done it accidentally, and letting it go only encouraged the bullies to keep going. Which would Hestar be?

"In Dasnaria," the Emperor replied slowly—thoughtfully?—while stroking his beard, "a woman cannot be given insult because she cannot challenge to defend her honor." His gaze flicked past me, to his sisters—I would put money on it. "What say you, Inga?"

A rustle of silk, the chime of bells, and one of the blond women stepped up beside me, eyes cast down. Her scent swirled with the settling of the many folds and drapes of her *klút*, sweet as full-summer flowers in bloom. That was the thing about women. I generally preferred the hardness of a man, but a woman brought all that soft, redolent delicacy to sex. I hadn't been with a woman in a while and, given my luck with men lately, perhaps I should see if I couldn't be satisfied by sticking with women.

A bunch of women stuck in a seraglio together might be a great place to start. Fuck Kral and his rules.

Head in the fight, Bryn.

"Your Imperial Majesty," Inga spoke in a voice like a gentle rain, "it seems a woman may feel insult, but in the softness of her heart and spirit, she forgives. Thus, she cannot be injured by such."

Really? She had her hands folded over her belly, her eyes glimmering aqua blue behind thick gold lashes, as she peeked at me sideways. Her lush mouth curved slightly at the corners. Amused, then. Wielding her own blades, only invisible ones of wit disguised as agreeableness.

"As I thought." Hestar sounded satisfied. "A true woman cannot take insult; therefore, if you *have* taken insult, Ambassador, logically you are no woman. Yet you dress as such. For a man to dress as a woman or a woman to dress as a man goes against the will of Sól. As I channel his eyes, I cannot see such anathema. Go, Ambassador, and do not seek my audience again, until you decide which you are. And take heed: Should you be the incorrect person, I shall have to remove the offense you present from the world of the living."

Okay, so . . . which did he want me to be? "Your—"

"I cannot hear the voice of a non-person." Hestar looked through me, then turned to Kral. "Stay and observe court, Brother. You have missed a great deal. Later, you and I shall discuss your adventures in private."

I wasn't sure what to do. Retrace my steps to the platform and go wander about? Ooh, or I could simply leave. Find my way out of this prison of a palace filled with crazy people, send a message to Ursula to . . . what? Hope these people elected to stay on their side of the world. Depend on the barrier to keep them out as Annfwn had so neatly done to us for so long.

But no, I had explicit instructions. *Keep it simple. Do the job. Come home. Don't be a hero.*

Inga's hand brushed mine, her gaze snagging mine sideways. So, when she backed up into her previous row, I went with her, instead of following Kral. Two gray-robed servants—females by the slender shapes, though I couldn't see past their cowls—scuttled through the people ranked behind the princesses, bowed to me, and moved a few steps, then stopped, as if they expected me to follow.

"Go," Inga murmured to the floor. "We shall talk."

I almost would have thought she spoke to someone else, but she flicked a glinting sideways glance at me. Her sister edged her profile just past, adding her gaze, surprisingly penetrating for being from the corner of her deep brown eye.

Danu, I hope you're keeping watch on this enterprise.

15

I followed the two servants out another route, this one descending through a trapdoor in the floor I hadn't been able to see before, due to the people crowding it. Again, nothing to stop the unwary from falling over the sides, should court become unruly and press someone too near the edge. Indeed, the courtiers ringing the hole portrayed the nerves of people on the political downside of the reigning power circles.

Not good to be the one standing next to the servants' stair. Check.

We descended yet another very steep flight of stairs, though made of the same stone as the walls and not so likely to slip up the careless foot. Well-armed guards waited at the bottom. They tipped back the cowls on the servant girls, whose hair turned out to be shorn to the scalp, looked them and me over carefully, then unlocked the door via several strong bolts and let us through into a narrow, poorly lit passageway.

Hestar likely intended this as a fresh insult, sending me out the servants' way. I'd note it, keeping a mental accounting simply because he didn't expect me to, but this hardly bothered me. The status of hire-swords varied from kingdom to kingdom and among households. In most, the guard staff counted as servant class. During peacetime, the fighters typically doubled as workers, supplementing in various capacities according to skill—whether it be chopping wood for fires, digging latrines, hunting, helping in kitchens, what have you. Ursula always insisted her Hawks learn something of all those skills, and anyone with too much pride to do them didn't last long. We served as her elite guard, yes, but also in whatever other tasks needed doing. Growing up with a small nomadic tribe had been much the same, so I'd adapted to that ethic just fine.

Because I'd been injured, I'd been too weak to help with burning the undead, though many of the Hawks took on that horrible task when so many of the Ordnung servants simply couldn't cope. We'd had the advantage of being out of the castle, so none of the living dead were our own, unlike for most denizens of Ordnung. Even so, the Hawks who did speak of it called the experience the worst of their lives.

Suffice to say, moving in the world of servants comforted more than insulted. *Totally missed with that strike, Hestar.*

The passageway twisted, branched, and took sharp angles, all of which I noted as I would any rambling trail, mentally matching my position with the formal halls above. Buildings follow patterns, just as mountain ridges and washes do. The landscape below reflects the one above because they're part of the same whole. Understanding those relationships was the key to always finding your way.

Baerr Lars met us finally at a point below the first of the audience waiting chambers. No bow this time, but neither did he treat me as a servant.

"Ambassador," he greeted me with a neutral form of the word. "This way, if you please."

I followed him, the servant women falling in behind me. A little parade of subservience—how ridiculous. Still, I took advantage of the opportunity to study my surroundings, adding to my mental map of the endless palace. We took an offshoot hall that led to an entirely different wing. Added on later than the central section, judging by the abrupt demarcation from darker, worn stone to lighter and rougher. How did they haul it from Bjarg and how were workers vetted? Could be a portal of lesser security to explore. Especially given the more lax standards for the servants and the associated entrances and exits.

Not that my job was to plan an assault on the Imperial Palace. *Keep it simple. Do the job. Come home. Don't be a hero.* Still, it never hurt to file the information away, should I survive and should tensions between the realms come to that.

Rising in elevation, if not in the Emperor's good graces, I climbed several sets of increasingly grander stairways, following Baerr Lars through seven guarded and locked doors. Finally, he stopped before an unattended door and one of the servant women slipped around him to open it, the other following her through. One busied herself with lighting sconces, while the other set flame to a prelaid fire in a hearth inlaid with lovely jade-green tiles. Warmth would be good.

"As your status remains . . . undetermined, Ambassador," Lars said, actually clearing his throat over the words, as if they left a bad taste in his mouth, "I have placed you in the women's wing of the palace, but not in the main seraglio or any of the private ones. Hopefully you will not be frightened."

I paused on my way to the fireplace, glancing over my shoulder, then around the generously proportioned set of rooms. Plenty of space to work out—excellent, as I might be spending a fair amount of time locked in here, if I didn't miss my guess. At least during daylight hours. At night I'd find a way to do a bit of skulking about. "Frightened?"

He inclined his head and smiled, not unkindly. "Being isolated from other women can be unsettling, I understand. I'd prefer to house you as befits a woman, but the . . . uncertainty regarding you bars that happy solution. I do hope you'll understand and not fault the hospitality of the Imperial Palace."

Very interesting. So, not willing to completely antagonize me, should I turn out to be important, but also not willing to risk me with the fragile hothouse flowers of the Dasnarian Empire. As it seemed I'd lucked into at least one less set of walls, that worked for me.

"I do understand, Baerr Lars. These chambers suit my current position quite nicely. Thank you for your consideration."

Some tension left him then, his smile one of relieved warmth. "I'll leave you, then. Should you need anything at all, simply request it of Sunniva or Runa here. Her Imperial Highness Inga has assigned these *rekjabrel* to you for the duration of your stay. If they cannot immediately satisfy your request, they will come to me and I will do my best, so please don't hesitate to ask, no matter what you may wish for."

Even more interesting.

He left with an even more courteous bow, one I recognized as that of a servant—no matter how highly ranked—who lives and dies by the whim of those he serves.

Sunniva and Runa continued freshening the room, behaving as if they'd heard none of the conversation, though I knew better than that. Servants always heard the best gossip, because good ones faded into the furnishings and people forgot about them. In this place, female servants would be that much more so. Sunniva and Runa were about to become my new best friends, only they didn't know it yet.

I wandered the room, staying considerately out of the way of their freshening tasks, getting the feel of the place and considering the best approach with them. I had us figured for similar stations in life—close to the royals, though not of them—but they'd see me as much higher in life. A suspicious character, with this whole bizarre gender-confusion thing, real or constructed to make my life difficult. And a foreigner, with strange ways. Hmm.

To my surprise, the room boasted two windows. I rambled past those first. Narrow and glazed, then covered with thick tapestry curtains, they were still big enough for a person my size to pass through if I shattered the glass. The drop, naturally, yawned below with alarming distance. No ledges on this face, either. I was a good enough climber to find hand- and footholds in the joins. If not, a stone courtyard far below would be happy to dash my skull to smithereens. At least I'd die fast. A fall from this height wouldn't leave me simply disabled.

Still, someone who could fly could get in and out, which it seemed the Dasnarians had not considered. And, hey, I just happened to know some people. Not anyone usefully in the area, but all options are good options. Beat zero options by leagues.

Twitching the tapestry back into place, I resumed my explorations. One wall had no openings, being solid stone between me and the neighboring room—or so it appeared. I'd check for secret openings or passageways once alone, particularly as the big, heavy headboard of the bed abutted it. I'd learned that much about Dasnarian design from Kral's cabinets on the *Hákyrling*. The second wall seemed to contain only the door we'd entered through, while the third, the one with the fireplace, had two doors, one leading to a closet and the other to a bathing chamber with actual drains for waste.

Runa hastily followed me in and poured water into a basin for me, cringing away as she did. "Apologies, Ambassador, that it is not yet warm."

My first opportunity. I smiled at her, keeping my expression kind—easy to do, as I felt for any person clearly so cowed. "That's all right. I know my arrival was unexpected. You and Sunniva may be unafraid, as you'll find that my needs are few and simply fulfilled." The Dasnarian language made my little speech stiff. It was much easier to phrase commands than reassurances, but I seemed to get my point across, as she nodded and smiled tentatively, still not meeting my eyes, however.

"Would you like hot water for a bath, Ambassador?" She indicated a dry, deep stone basin. Sized for someone even like Kral.

"Yes, please, if it's no trouble."

She glanced sideways at me, a flash of curiosity before she damped it. "Ambassador, you can be no trouble. We have no other duties but to see to your happiness—in every way."

Something about that last remark worked under my skin. Along with one of Kral's references when we argued about Nakoa abducting Dafne, when he said that it wasn't any different than what any dignitary might claim. I had my fun playing handmaiden, and I wouldn't turn down anyone who wanted to play sex-slave to me— but for a night maybe and only for games. The possible reality lay slick and heavy in my gut. Baerr Lars had called them *rekjabrel*. I rated my own bed slaves, apparently.

"Hot water, food, and some wine—or *mjed*?—would be most welcome. Thank you."

She slipped out again, a ghost of a woman, and I shut the door behind her. Privacy to answer the call of nature, positively luxurious to do indoors, though most prison cells boasted that capability, and also to examine the drains. The bathing chamber shared a wall with the fireplace. Presumably the flue for the smoke went up and the drains likely paralleled that going down. Smoke one direction, shit the other—and a tight fit either way—but still a possible escape option.

Probably I'd end up with shit, as that would lead to the lake, and being on the roof with the smoke wouldn't do me any good.

When I emerged, Sunniva and Runa had already manifested buckets of water from nowhere, heating them on a brace over the fire. My things from the *Hákyrling* had also arrived, such as they were, and I entertained the whimsical notion that their journey had been as laborious as mine, with all the stop and go of entering the palace. The whimsy transformed quickly into annoyance as I noted everything had been searched, and not neatly either. And Danu take it! My big knife had gone missing. Bastards. I'd have worn it if there'd been a place for it in the *klút*. Or made one, if it had occurred to me that they'd take it. Kral could have thrice-damned warned me. I'd have given it to him to keep for me.

"Is all well, Ambassador?" Sunniva asked, drawing edgily near and wringing her hands, face hidden in the cowl.

"Fine." I kept most of the snarl out of my voice. It wasn't their fault. I'd take it up with Kral.

"Shall I put your things away?" she asked with such hesitation that I ground my annoyance down, finding a smile for her. I wanted their trust, not their obedient fear.

"Yes, thank you." Deliberately walking away from my bags, I demonstrated to myself how I'd let go of the issue. *Only things.* The knife wasn't my mother, and regaining it wouldn't bring her back. A carafe of *mjed* sat on a table by the fire, promising comfort, so I poured a healthy portion into the single cup provided. I savored it, standing and staring into the fire, letting all my roiling thoughts and emotions pass through me and settle out. Danu taught that a muddied mind could not see clearly.

Had my mother felt this way? Cut off from the tribe, from me, from even her true self, masquerading undercover as a spy. Though her shieldmate had told me the story, several times, until I could say it back and reassure him that I'd always remember my mother's legacy, I'd never quite considered what it must have been like for her. At least I didn't have a daughter back home waiting for me to return. I'd feel a particular kind of despair over facing my death inside enemy territory, knowing I'd be letting her down by never going back to see her safely to maturity.

And Kral asked why I didn't have a husband or children. Fool. One pain less was . . . well, one pain less, I supposed.

I turned away from the fire to find Sunniva glancing down quickly and Runa studying me with open curiosity, only averting her gaze when Sunniva nudged her. Both looked much alike, beyond their similarities in coloring. The high, intelligent foreheads and broad cheekbones that marked them likely kin to Harlan and Kral—and Hestar. Special servants to the Imperial Princesses, too. I'd put money down that these were some of those royal byblows, bred for a life of servitude.

"Problem?" I asked, addressing them more as I would one of my scouts, mostly out of habit, but that seemed to startle at least Runa out of her habitual meekness.

"Are you truly a man wearing a *klút*, then, Ambassador?" she asked.

Sunniva elbowed her harder. "She means no offense, Ambassador. We are simply uncertain how to . . . care for you. Shall we address you as a man or a woman?"

Curse this place that it had messed with my head enough that I didn't have a ready answer to the question. Once the bath was ready and they saw me naked, the obvious gender aspects would be cleared up, but that addressed only part of the conundrum. According to this culture, I kind of *was* a man in thought and behavior, wearing a woman's body.

Ha! Wait until I told Kral that particular theory. If he didn't leave me here to rot, which would be an admittedly simple solution for him.

"What makes you ask at this moment?" I tried, mostly as a stalling tactic.

Runa dipped her forehead at the carafe of *mjed*. "Only men drink this liquor, so therefore you must be a man." Her forehead crinkled as she studied me more boldly. "But you *look* like one of us, even with your dark skin. Except your hair is short, as if it was shorn for service. Perhaps you were a servant and elevated?"

Sunniva made a sound halfway between a snort of derision and a whimper of despair. "These things are not our business, Runa! Mother always said your curiosity would be the death of you."

Aha. My pathway in. "Let me show you something, Runa." I poured more of the *mjed* into the empty cup and held it out to her. "Take a sip."

Her mouth dropped open in horror—and avid curiosity.

"Don't!" Sunniva hissed at her. "Women cannot drink of it. It is of Sól and therefore of men. Too much *svida* will cook a woman's nature."

"But the ambassador told me to," Runa hedged, then sidled to me. "Surely a tiny sip won't be enough to cook me."

Sunniva slid a look at me that immediately darted away. I nearly laughed. Clearly she wanted to comment on the quantity of my feminine nature. "But it's poison to a woman," she whispered, wringing her hands.

"It won't kill me, will it, Ambassador?" Runa asked, taking the cup gingerly in her hands, holding it like she might an injured bird.

"It won't." I said it to reassure Sunniva as much as Runa.

"Runa . . ." Sunniva wrung her hands.

"Maybe a bit of cooking will be good for me," Runa said to her sister, a bit sharply. Her gaze lingered on me, and the daggers in my armbands. She brought the cup slowly to her lips. Sunniva watched in fascinated terror, the way people look witnessing executions, making a squeak of anxiety as Runa swallowed. They looked at each other, waiting with obvious apprehension in the one, delighted anticipation in the other—which turned to consternation as color flooded her pale face. Runa coughed, then coughed again, harder. Running to her, Sunniva put her arms around her sister's waist and buried her face against her neck. "Don't die, Runa! You can't leave me here alone."

Absurdly, Runa giggled. "It burns! Oh, it burns, but in such a delicious way. Try it, Sunniva."

Sunniva's blue eyes went wide and she took Runa's face in her hands. "You're not cooking."

"Of course she isn't," I said, adding more *mjed* to the cup Runa still held. Getting them a bit tipsy could only help with our little bonding ceremony. "Sure you don't want to try, Sunniva?"

She did want to, left out of the fun now, but shook her head. "The water is hot for your bath now, Ambassador. Let's assist you with that."

"I can take my own bath."

"Oh, no, we must help you," Sunniva insisted, with a determined set to her chin that reminded me vividly of Kral. Stupidly sending a pang through me of missing his company. Days of near-constant companionship would do that, I supposed. He might be annoying, but he never bored me. Not something I could say for my other lovers. Probably I'd get tired of Kral, too, over time, given enough opportunity. That pang demanded the opportunity to try. Alas for the impossible.

"Sunniva." I studied her, then Runa, who still held the *mjed* cup, eyes wide with trepidation. "Are you under orders to see what I look like naked?"

Both women cast their eyes down, golden lashes fluttering, in subservient apology. They didn't speak, but that was answer enough.

"Fine." I shrugged and began stripping off my knives. They'd see me for myself and carry back the tale. Let the repercussions be what they were. They followed me into the bathing chamber, helping me unwrap the *klút*. It was kind of nice to have their expert assistance. Kral might have known the basics, but these women possessed serious expertise. I set a few more daggers on the edge of the bathing cistern as I took them off, then posed naked for them, even turning in a circle. "Well?"

They looked me over, exchanged glances. A great deal of unspoken communication between them.

"Do you want me to bend over so you can look between my legs?" I meant it jokingly, but Sunniva cocked her head.

"Ambassador, if you would . . ."

"Allow us to bathe you," Runa inserted with a nod at her sister. "That will suffice."

Bemused, I stepped into the water, which felt deliciously warming indeed. They set to scrubbing me with scented soap of the same varietals of the lotion Kral liked. I'd never been washed by another person before—at least, not literally as opposed to as an excuse for foreplay—and the women did a thorough job of it. I tried to take it philosophically, that following their efforts, they could be in no doubt of what I did and did not possess, anatomically.

It wasn't unpleasant, but definitely not remotely sexy. Hopefully it was the situation that dampened my ardor, and my tepid feelings had nothing to do with Kral ruining me for anyone else. Was he meeting with Hestar even now? Frustrating that I couldn't get ears into that conversation. Hmm. Unless Sunniva and Runa found out from their *rekjabrel* cousins in Hestar's service.

Runa scrubbed my hair, massaging my scalp as she did—an exquisite experience—while Sunniva scrubbed my feet and trimmed my toenails, not quite as soothing. This being tended to, however, could get addicting. "Ambassador?" Runa asked tentatively.

"Just ask," I told her with my eyes closed. "I'm nearly impossible to offend." Ha! Just as Hestar said of women, but for entirely different reasons. "I know you have no intention of insulting me," I added, in case that tidbit made it back to someone else.

"I can arrange for a wig for you, if you like. Some women do, once elevated from service or punishment, while their hair grows out."

I squinched open one eye and she hastily brushed the suds away before they could sting. "My hair is exactly the way I like it. I keep it cut short on purpose for three reasons—because I like how I look this way and it's easy to take care of, because it's wildly curly and if it gets too long, I look like a *hystrix* on a bad day—"

Both women burst into a fit of giggles at that image. Not so funny if you actually saw it, though. Actually . . . maybe it was. I waffled a bit on the third reason, as the information would likely be carried out of the room, but my gut said go, so I did.

"Third, I'm a fighter and long hair makes a too-convenient handle for an opponent."

They fell silent at that, Runa rinsing, then combing my hair with a comb made of spicily scented wood, Sunniva polishing my toenails with some kind of rough pad. She'd remarked on the ugly state of my feet and set to work on prettying them with grim determination.

"How . . . how can you fight?" Runa finally asked. "Surely not against men."

Sunniva said nothing, but she filed quietly, hanging on every word.

"Against men, yes, or other female fighters." I decided not to mention fish-birds or shape-shifters, as that might overload their already stretching sensibilities. "Having good weapons and knowing how to use them makes all the difference. Everyone has a weakness. The trick is to get past where they're strong and strike where they're weak."

Good words to remember. Sometimes I was smarter than I knew. "And . . . these are good weapons?" Sunniva asked, with a nod at my nearby daggers, which both women had been careful not to touch. "They are so much smaller than swords. It seems odd to think they could do anything much."

"Excellent weapons. A broadsword suits a fighter like Kr— like His Imperial Highness Prince Kral—but, while I can lift one, it's not the best choice for me. See? I'm shorter, lighter of body; my strength, like for most women, is in my hips and legs. It changes how I fight. I'm fast, so a light, sharp weapon suits my style."

"Women are strong in their lower bodies," Sunniva affirmed with a brisk nod, surprising me. "The men, they don't know that. But they don't see what it takes for a woman to carry and birth a child. They moan over their aches or their winter coughs, but they don't lie there for days, laboring, wracked with pain, bleeding their lives away while their children are born."

Not something I knew much about, but I believed her. Not many of my good friends had given birth to babies—most of the female fighters shared the herbs that let us avoid getting pregnant in the first place, as it could mean the loss of a job at best and dying in a fight at worst—and I tended to wander away from those conversations where women started trading labor horror stories instead of battle tales. Still, I'd been at Windroven when Queen Amelia nearly died giving birth to her twins. The Hawks had even secretly consulted over a strategy to handle Ursula if her sister died and she lost her mind with grief. The High Queen could handle most anything, but the chink in her armor undoubtedly was her sisters. Fortunately, it hadn't come to that.

"I can teach you," I told them. "A few little knife tricks. I have some extra daggers you could have."

They actually jerked their hands off me, as if I'd burned them. "We could not," Sunniva said with great firmness, glaring at her sister. "Never."

Runa nodded unhappily. "Never."

16

They wouldn't talk more after that, except to comment on the state of my nails—both hands and feet—my skin, my unpierced ears. At least they gave up on the hair.

"Your hands are so rough!" Sunniva cried in a tone of real despair. It seemed now that they'd determined me to be a genuine female, the state of my beauty posed a real problem.

"Calluses," I told them, rubbing my fingers together, thinking of how they represented a real fetish for the Dasnarian men. Ursula had confided it to me, that day Kral arrived at Ordnung, taking me aside after they'd signed the treaty and were ready to celebrate, explaining that Harlan liked hers—one of those few times I saw her flustered—and that Kral seemed to be equally intrigued. She'd asked me to pass the word to any of the female Hawks who might be interested in playing, but I'd kept that nugget to myself. And made sure Kral felt mine. I'd wanted him from the moment I laid eyes on him. All that Dasnarian muscle, with the mind of a shark. The opportunity to present myself for gobbling had been too good to miss.

It had worked like a dagger to the heart. He'd fastened all of that exuberant sexual vitality on me, and the evening progressed exactly as I'd hoped. As can happen with the morning after, it only got rocky after that.

"Calluses from using weapons," I clarified. "Don't try to polish them off. I need them, to keep my hands strong for using knives and swords, even a bow." And also for tantalizing my lover. Where in Danu was Kral? Entirely possible he'd vanish into the bowels of his family and never reemerge. That withdrawing and personality change as we drew nearer to this spider's nest could have been him deliberately putting distance between us. Probably politically savvy on his part. Understandable, if so. Shouldn't bother me.

I'd get myself out of this mess without his help, if I needed to. It wasn't as if we enjoyed a deeper bond than sex. Maybe a rough kind of friendship. Being in the Imperial Palace, however, brought home that any friendship we might enjoy fell second place to the fact that we served rulers who would be enemies without a fresh treaty. One Hestar might not even ratify. He hadn't sounded at all happy with Kral.

Sunniva and Runa finally declared my hands and feet as pretty as they could make them without hours' more work—and that was better than they'd looked my entire life—and wrapped me up in a *klút* I hadn't seen before, this one in patterned silk of dappled greens, like a forest. The colors suited me, they said, and I liked them just fine. They debated the problem of the extra length briefly, then solved it by Runa cutting off quite a bit and Sunniva hemming the cut end with silk thread and stitches that whipped so fast her fingers blurred. I refrained from pointing out that Runa's sewing shears were basically a pair of sharp, one-sided blades. But I made mental note of her dexterity. I could teach her to use those as a weapon quite readily.

Whether due to their expertise or the lack of surplus material, the new *klút* flattered me far more than any of Kral's. The deeper colors did suit my darker complexion, and the greens somehow made my brown eyes interesting. And the expertly draped silk emphasized my figure in all the right places. If only Kral could see, alas. Though he couldn't act on it, I'd still enjoy watching him simmer in his frustration. Small joys.

The women had discovered I possessed no jewelry—not even for my feet, to their great dismay—and were deep in discussion of what to do when it belatedly occurred to me they were fixing me up for more than an evening alone in my room. Would I be going to the dinner Kral mentioned? After Hestar's banishing me from his sight, that seemed highly unlikely.

"Ah, Sunniva, Runa—what am I getting decked out for?"

They gave me astonished looks. "The Imperial Princesses' visit, naturally!" Sunniva replied.

Ah, of course. How interesting. Runa cocked her head, listening. "Here they come now."

They both withdrew at the polite tap on the door, vanishing with the practiced ease of good servants. "Come in," I called, remembering to use an invitational phrasing, rather than the male command variety.

Another servant girl in gray robes opened the door, sidestepping behind it as Inga and her sister swept in. Eyes no longer lowered, they examined me with bold curiosity. I'd put money down that they'd come to my rooms directly from court.

"Ambassador." Inga inclined her head, her brown-eyed sister hovering slightly behind her. "We have not been introduced. I hope it fits within your cultural values for us to introduce ourselves. Among women here, we tend to be less formal."

Though she didn't phrase her words as a question, the tone of her voice made them into one. I figured Sunniva and Runa had managed to pass the news of my verified femaleness during one of their errands for supplies, but Inga seemed to be allowing me the benefit of the doubt behavior-wise. Interesting. I could see why Dafne found paying attention to language and words enlightening. But how would she handle this—was less formal good or bad?

Eh, back to being myself.

"Less formal is fine with me, Your Imperial Highnesses," I

replied, "though what I consider to be informal could well be perceived as impertinence."

Inga's lips twitched into a wry smile. "Ah, but women cannot be insulted, can they?"

Sarcasm was the last thing I'd expected from the Imperial Princess. "So I've recently been informed," I replied, sharing the head-shaking moment. I could like this woman.

"Leave us," she called out, and all the serving ladies slipped out of the room like water disappearing down the drain.

Once the door shut, both Inga and her sister visibly relaxed, giving me genuine smiles. "I am Inga, and this is my sister Helva. We generally dispense with titles when in private."

Again the implied question in her tone. "Please call me Jepp, then."

Helva's smile broadened and she stepped forward to take my hands, squeezing them almost painfully tight. "Jepp, I greet you as one woman to another. Tell me, if you will—have you news of our baby brother, Harlan?"

I must have looked shocked, because Inga laid a hand on my shoulder. "Please don't think ill of our impatience. It has been many years since we've heard news of him and longer since we've spoken with him. Rumors had traveled to us that he had taken his mercenaries to a place called the Twelve Kingdoms, along with other, more dire possibilities. Forgive our driving straight to the core of our concern, but—"

"But have mercy on our hearts and don't keep us in suspense," Helva cut in. "It's so rare for us to access information from a reliable source. Do you know of him and if Jenna is with him?"

Talking to the Imperial Princesses had a rhythm similar as with Sunniva and Runa, so much so that it was tempting to tease them about it. But I wouldn't indulge that amusement; they both seemed so urgently distressed. Besides, they might not take it well.

"Harlan is fine. He's . . . a friend." That was fair enough. I doubted Harlan would argue the point, though we were more loose acquaintances than anything. "Who is Jenna, though? I don't know anyone of that name."

The relieved smiles that had brightened at my news crashed at that last, and they exchanged long, worried looks, the familial similarity to Sunniva and Runa even more pronounced.

"Would you care to sit? I'm happy to tell you what I do know." I gestured to the chairs by the fire, trying to channel what little lady-like social behavior I'd observed from Queen Amelia. Ursula would usually just point to a chair. Belatedly I recalled the forbidden *mjed* on the table, but it was too late to hide it.

Helva picked it up with a sly grin. "We heard tell of your request. I approved it when Baerr Lars inquired. You have them all terribly confused."

The information network moved blazingly fast. Something to keep in mind. Hopefully if I told them what they'd come to find out, they'd share some information with me. "Would you like some?"

They exchanged conspiratorial smiles and Helva poured for three. "The men think we don't drink it," she confided. "The heat is considered to be unhealthy for a woman's watery, yielding nature."

"Ah." I decided against giving away that Sunniva and Runa had explained the very same. "But you are not concerned?"

They both snorted, a sound very like their brothers'. At least Harlan and Kral. Hestar might shatter into a pile of crystalline spiders if he laughed. "We all snuck *mjed* together in our youth. Why the men think we change when we are confined to the world of women, I have no idea."

"Men can be obtuse about women," I suggested, thinking of how Dafne, Zynda, and I had gotten to be friends commiserating over men. And Kral had his blockheaded ways. Certainly his ideas of proper female behavior didn't reflect the reality of his sisters' lives. *When we are confined to the world of women.* How much did he even know of their lives?

"True are your words," Inga said, raising her cup. "You are most welcome to Dasnaria, Jepp. We have long awaited your arrival without knowing we did."

"True are your words," Helva echoed, clinking her mug to Inga's and mine. "Now, tell us—did Harlan truly seduce a king's daughter and stage a coup?"

I managed not to choke on my drink—the stuff did burn going the wrong way—and began to set the story straight by telling it as I knew it, beginning with the return from Windroven with Ursula, to find Uorsin had hired the Vervaldr as mercenary guards. Relating such a tale wasn't easy. I couldn't forget my listeners were more than concerned sisters. For all I knew, Hestar had prompted this visit to dig information out of me. How much of Uorsin's insane paranoia should I relate as the reason for bringing in the Vervaldr? Should I mention Illyria's presence? No, I thought not, but then I reached the point of explaining how Ursula fled Ordnung to save her life, at Harlan's urging—and found myself tripping over my own story feet.

They caught my slips, too, both Helva and Inga listening intently, interrupting occasionally for more specifics on Harlan's words and actions. Despite the intervening years, they knew him well and their questions tended to pinpoint the areas I attempted to blur. Fortunately, I could plead ignorance on plenty, as I wasn't intimate to much. Sure, I overheard a great deal and observed more, but I could dodge mentioning my own speculations. I told them of Ursula's return, fudged a bit on Uorsin's demise at her hands—though emphasizing that Harlan did *not* do it—and described the glorious coronation in great and, I hoped, impressive detail, winding up with Kral's arrival at Ordnung.

They sat silent for a bit when I finished, turning the story over in their heads.

"So," Inga said thoughtfully, "our brother did meet with Harlan. I wonder what he'll tell us about it?"

"Do you suppose he swallowed his pride enough to ask Harlan about Jenna?" Helva retorted.

I doubted it, as Kral hadn't mentioned this mysterious Jenna to me, the cagey bastard.

Inga snorted. "You know Harlan would no more betray his vow now by discussing her than he did back then."

I listened to this with great interest, though I attempted to appear casual, in case I alerted them that their conversation revealed secrets of their own.

They turned on me, however, with all the intensity of mountain cats spotting a crippled deer. Those females hunted in groups, too. "So," Helva said, pouring me more *mjed*, "tell us of this High Queen of yours. How did she seduce our baby brother?"

"She didn't, thank you," I replied, a bit too annoyed to be diplomatic. "Her Majesty is not the seducing sort."

Inga waved that off. "*Every* woman is the seducing sort when she spots a man she wants. And why wouldn't she want Harlan? He's the best of men. Always has been."

"*Luta.*" Helva wiped away a tear. "I miss him so."

"What kind of woman is she?" Inga demanded. "Do you find her admirable—as a person and as a ruler? She truly does rule?"

"Pretend you're describing her to us for a marriage match," Helva urged. "Tell us why she suits our brother."

"Yes—what do you like about her as a person? We'll never meet this wife of his, so what you tell us is all we'll ever know."

"Kral met her," I said without thinking. Too much *mjed* perhaps. Or too much of these wily lionesses stalking information. How much would Her Majesty want me to reveal? "You may yet get him talking."

"You call him by his name," Helva mused.

"And you traveled here with him on the *Hákyrling*," Inga fit her words to Helva's.

Dangerous territory. I needed to get them off my relationship with Kral, lest I find myself in even deeper imprisonment as his *rekjabrel*.

"Yes, High Queen Ursula truly rules. You would like her." Funny to see it, how these women from such different cultures would understand each other. "She grew up as her father's heir, eldest of three daughters. He had no sons."

They exchanged a look at that. Oh, yeah, they got it.

"She's a warrior. Blazingly fast. No one can beat her—not even Harlan. They spar a great deal, always seeking to one-up the other."

Inga's pretty aqua blue eyes sparkled with excited wonder. "Truly? A woman who can hold her own with a man the size of Harlan, with all his skill? Yes. Yes, I can see he would be fatally attracted to that."

"You are a warrior, too." Helva gave a knowing nod to the armband sheaths I'd strapped back on. "Everyone is saying those daggers are only exotic jewelry, but they're not. You can use them."

I shrugged that off, but Inga fixed me with a glittering gaze gone imperious. One I well recognized. "Show us."

"What do you want to see?" I hedged. More important, what skills did I want to keep secret?

"Something. Anything you like."

"A parlor trick, perhaps," Helva chimed in. "Something impress—"

She broke with a gasp when the dagger I'd drawn thunked into the wall behind her, pinning a painting of a dancing girl in the eye.

Inga regarded me thoughtfully while her sister gaped, looking between me and the dagger sunk into the wall.

"I barely saw you move," Helva finally said.

"Her Majesty is faster," I replied, in all honesty—and maybe just a bit of pumping up my own ruler's semi-divinity. Ursula's shape-shifter blood made her faster than any mossback like me could hope to achieve. But I held my own.

"No wonder he picked her for a wife," Inga murmured.

This I felt I could clarify. They'd made it clear in formal court. "They are not husband and wife," I told them.

"They . . . have no permanent attachment?" Helva asked in a

faint tone, a bit of rising outrage behind it. "He is her male concubine? Surely not a *rekjabrel*!"

Inga pinned me with an accusing stare. Oh, wonderful, my first diplomatic incident. At least, the first official one.

"Her Majesty is the High Queen of the Thirteen Kingdoms," I explained, feeling my way. "She cannot marry the prince of another empire. And no, Harlan is not her concubine or *rekjabrel*. We don't have slaves. He's a free man who's pledged himself to her of his own will. She never asked it of him."

"Pledged himself?" Helva fastened on that. Inga had gone still, as if moving might interfere with her understanding of important information.

"Is there any sort of . . . salute or gesture he makes to her?" she asked, attempting to sound casual, but I knew that sort of body tension. While my Dasnarian might be barely serviceable, I was fluent in the language of the body.

Kral knew it, so why not tell Harlan's sisters? "The *Elskastholrr*, yes."

"*Luta*," Inga breathed. "This is extraordinary, indeed. Little rabbit, what in Sól are you thinking?"

"He always did go for the dramatic gesture," Helva remarked, lips curving in a nostalgic grimace. "That's why Jenna—"

Inga cut her off with a lifted hand. "Do your people understand the significance of the *Elskastholrr*?"

"It's not common knowledge," I hedged.

"But Kral knows."

"He explained it to me, in fact."

"Not entirely, I imagine," Helva inserted.

"No wonder our brother Kral seeks to protect you," Inga said, watching me for a reaction.

"Does he?" I kept my tone light. "His Imperial Highness agreed to escort me here as ambassador, as part of the treaty he signed with Her Majesty the High Queen, and made a personal promise to Harlan to assist me, as a way of making amends for past wrongs."

They both stared at me, far more arrested than if I'd confirmed that I'd spent a great deal of the *Hákyrling*'s voyage doing their brother every way anatomically possible. I reviewed what I'd said, feeling my calm fray at the edges. I should have stuck to throwing knives.

"A treaty?" Helva squeaked, brown eyes going to Inga, who shook her head minutely.

"No doubt he discusses such with His Imperial Majesty even now," Inga said in a quelling tone. "This explains why dinner was canceled."

Aha. Which explained why the Imperial Princesses had the leisure to visit me. No, let's be honest, to interrogate me with all of Kral's determined obstinacy and none of his finesse.

"Amends for what, exactly?" Inga inquired conversationally, pouring us all more *mjed*.

I could drink most people under the table, but I suspected these women had been weaned on the heady stuff straight from mother's milk. I wouldn't go into a knife fight drunk, so I didn't pick up my cup. "I wouldn't know. I'm not Harlan's intimate, by any stretch. Our association is primarily through his relationship to Her Majesty." And the comingling of the Vervaldr and the Hawks, but that seemed a reasonable line to draw.

One that didn't fool Inga for a moment. "Jepp." She leaned forward and laid a hand on my knee. "You have no reason to trust us. I understand that. But let me lay out a few ideas for you. Kral may have agreed to help you, for whatever reasons"—and here her tone made it clear she thought I hadn't told her all of them—"however, I can vouch that the Emperor will be greatly displeased that Kral signed any kind of treaty. The more you can tell us, the more we can assist you and him both. Regardless, you have already annoyed His Imperial Majesty, whether by design or not, and Kral will be in at least some level of disgrace for that. Not to mention for returning without the Nahanaun treasure. That means *we* are your help here."

Helva nodded, a bit ruefully, but in total agreement.

"We *want* to help you," Inga continued, "for several reasons that I can explain. I am asking you to take a leap of faith and exchange stories with us. Conversely, we can also use our influence with our eldest brother, along with the confirmation that you are as female as any of us, to have you confined to the seraglio."

"Threats?" My fingers twitched to draw a blade, though my head knew it wasn't that kind of fight.

Inga tilted her head in acknowledgment. "You have your weapons. I have mine. I'd far rather agree to be allies."

"And in return?" I asked, feeling as if I'd been treed by the felines who circled beneath.

She lifted a shoulder and let it fall, in that fatalistic Dasnarian way. "I believe *hlyti* guided you here and now for a reason. We need you. In return, we can tell you things you and your High Queen need to know. We can use our influence to ensure you the freedom to do whatever your real purpose is here."

My real purpose? I couldn't think of a response that didn't sound either disingenuous or a confirmation.

"Come now, Jepp," Inga said briskly. "We are all women here. If Harlan has given the *Elskastholrr* to your queen, he places his loyalty to her above all things, which means he told her to send *you*. Our brothers may be thickheaded, but they are not stupid."

"Ban is not so smart," Helva murmured, and Inga flashed her an amused look.

"Harlan and Kral are not stupid," she clarified. "Harlan could have sent you himself, knowing us well and that we would have this conversation. He asked Kral to aid you in return for amends, both of them knowing the import of that request. So." She rubbed her hands briskly together. "It follows that you're a spy. What are you here to discover?"

17

I really should stick to knives. This entire conversation had me drowning. What would Dafne have said at this point? Danu, I should be guarding the door while she talked to these she-lions. Everything had gone upside down.

"Let me tell you a story," Inga said more gently. "Have some *mjed* and listen. Then decide if we are friends or enemies."

Because I really wanted a drink to take the edge off, I did.

"There are ten of us, children of the former Emperor, seven boys and three girls, born to His Imperial Majesty's three wives. Helva and I are half sisters."

"But Harlan, Hestar, and I are all full siblings," Helva put in.

"And Kral is our half brother, his mother's only son. She also bore a daughter. Jenna."

I began to have a bad feeling about this.

"The birth order is important because right to rule depends on it," Inga continued.

"For the males," I clarified.

"Aha. Not exclusively. See, Hestar was born first. Then Jenna, only a month later, with Kral born a year after that. Then my mother bore me. Harlan is the youngest of us all. It gets trickier, however, because Jenna and Kral's mother was first wife, Hestar's was second wife. That affects their rank as well."

"Okay. That's a lot of kids born in quick succession."

"Our father, the former Emperor, of course waited until he was crowned, then married his three wives and began getting heirs as quickly as possible," Helva explained.

"Of course. And on his concubines, too?"

Both women nodded. "It's good for a new Emperor to demonstrate virility," Inga said. "His Imperial Majesty has five children by his three wives now. They don't leave the seraglio, however, so you would have to meet them there."

I was having a difficult time keeping it straight. Dafne would be making a chart.

Inga waved a hand in the air. "We have scholars who devote their entire lives to tracking these bloodlines. The salient information to this story is that, by being firstborn and also born to the first wife, Jenna posed a threat to Hestar becoming Emperor. Jenna and Kral's mother was a high-born princess, from a family dynasty that predates the Konyngrrs. Had Kral been born first instead of Jenna, there could well have been a division of the house, possibly civil war. A month's time in birth rank compounded by a family as powerful as theirs makes the heirs very nearly equivalent."

"Except for gender."

"Yes, except for gender. But, as it was, Jenna and Kral's mother, with the help of her family, conspired to have Jenna betrothed to the king of one of the more powerful kingdoms in the empire—and one of the most recently acquired."

Restive, then. Not unlike in our realm.

"With that alliance, the subsidiary kingdoms could have applied enough pressure to raise Kral from second in line to heir to the Emperor, something his mother and his mother's family wanted badly. Positioning a son of their family to be the next Emperor was the entire reason for her marriage. And she'd raised Kral to want it, too. She's a . . . strong personality. Kral could never please her by giving less than all of himself to that purpose."

Helva smiled. "We are a family bloodthirsty for power. It comes down in our father's seed and our mothers' milk. We crave power like the air we breathe."

"Except for Harlan," I said, puzzle pieces shifting in my head. "He left Dasnaria and said he'd never go back."

"Indeed." Inga nodded. "But did he ever say why? I'm thinking not, if you've never heard Jenna's name."

"Jenna was eighteen." Helva leaned forward, the expression on her face urgent. "She'd never even been outside the Imperial Palace. The king she was to marry was in his seventies—and his previous four wives had all perished. He only married girls who weren't yet twenty, and still none of them lived past thirty. Do you understand what I'm saying?"

The bad feeling only grew worse.

Inga put a restraining hand on her sister's shoulder. "Harlan was a boy of fourteen, but already so steadfast in his character. An empathetic person, from the beginning."

"That hasn't changed."

Inga nodded, unsurprised. "Jenna did not want to marry that man, but she had no ability to stop the wedding. No recourse to refuse the match."

"What did she do?" But I could guess. Knowing Harlan, knowing what I would have done.

"*She* didn't," Helva said. "She couldn't do anything."

"Harlan did," Inga confirmed. "He arranged to accompany her on the journey to her new home, and helped her to escape along the way."

"Where did she go?" I asked, amazed that Harlan had never mentioned this. It would have made for a terrific campfire tale. Although the campfire smoke often shrouded more unspoken stories than the ones told aloud.

"Nobody knows."

"Nobody? Surely Harlan does."

Helva pursed her lips, frowning. "Somehow I don't think he does."

"He refused to tell any of us any details," Inga said. "No matter how we swore to keep the secret or begged. He told us once that he'd given her the best chance he could to be free, then refused to say another word on the topic. No one could get it out of him—and believe me, they tried. Until he ensured they couldn't."

"By leaving?"

Inga looked surprised. "No, by undergoing the *skablykrr*. I suppose he wouldn't have spoken of that if he kept the *Elskastholrr* secret, too. It's a . . . hmm."

I nearly taunted her about keeping secrets, but she'd knit her brows, perhaps uncertain how to explain.

"Part philosophical training, part martial system," Helva put in. "Anyone who completes it has demonstrated they can make and keep a vow so that it will never be broken. Harlan completed the training in secret and vowed never to tell anyone anything more about Jenna than that he'd given her the best chance he could to be free."

"I thought when he left that he'd go to her, though. Take her with him on those travels of his," Inga retorted.

"Not if he doesn't know where to find her either," Helva pointed out. "All he did was see her free. Not safe. Not cared for."

"But that would be unconscionable! How could she live without care and protection? He wouldn't have done that to her. He might as well have put his own sword to her throat and left her corpse by the side of the road."

I cleared my throat. "Can I clear up a misconception here?"

"You do know where Jenna is!" Helva brightened. "Oh, thank Sól."

"No, not that. I think Harlan kept his word on that. He never spoke of her, or any sisters at all. I, ah, heard he had brothers before Kr—His Imperial Highness arrived." Of course, the females of my acquaintance had been primarily interested in Harlan's brothers and if any were available. A hotly debated campfire topic, in fact. Sisters hadn't been a topic of conversation. Not something I thought politic to mention to Helva and Inga, however.

"I know Harlan would have sent you to us for a reason, though," Inga obstinately maintained. "He knew how much we'd worry, about both of them."

The reason slowly dawned. Maybe not so much what I could tell them—or Dafne or Zynda could have, for that matter—but what we could show them.

"Maybe," I said slowly, feeling my way through, "Harlan wanted you to know that in the world outside Dasnaria, women live well without care and protection. They have their own incomes, decide their own marriages. I've never had a man to take care of me. My mother died when I was young. I lived on my own, earned my own way. Jenna, wherever she is, could be doing the same."

And I'd suggested that very thing for Karyn. Why hadn't Kral said anything about his missing sister then? The Imperial Princesses pondered my words, uncertain, puzzled even, but with the expressions of someone tasting a new food that they found quite palatable.

"So, how does His Imperial Highness Prince Kral play into this?" I asked. "You said at the beginning that his thirst for power played into the story, and his making amends."

Inga lifted a shoulder, let it fall, and took up her *mjed*. "Our father and his mother made Kral's life miserable in the aftermath of Jenna's departure. He went after them both, dragged Harlan back, and did everything possible to get her location out of him. Our father promised Kral would be his heir if he could restore Jenna to her husband."

"Husband—they had already married?"

"Oh, yes—and thoroughly consummated," Inga said.

"He was cruel to her," Helva whispered. "She came back to us weeping and we could do nothing but clean her up and send her back for more."

It made me sick. I would embrace magic if it would be a kind that would let me go back in time and help Jenna escape, too. For a secret like that, even I could learn to keep my mouth shut. "And Kral would have forced her back to that."

"He didn't have a choice. His mother and her family . . . Well, he had the promise of infinite power on one hand and, on the other, the half existence he now lives, with the Emperor's boot heel on his neck and his mother's family refusing to help, out of their anger." Inga pushed back her hair without disturbing her jeweled headdress, stretching her neck. "They failed in the bid for the throne, and the Emperor has never forgotten it. He's done everything possible to crush Kral's fighting spirit, so that he cannot pose a threat. Thus he became general of Dasnaria's armies— a figurehead position that mocks his powerlessness because he can only relay Hestar's orders—and ruler of nothing."

"You know he already has a wife, and he's only allowed one," Helva said, not a question. "He is not allowed to have heirs. I don't know what promises he might have made to you, but . . ."

"No promises." I might have said it too hastily, because they both sported dubious expressions. "Beyond the ones to aid me here in the Dasnarian court."

The sisters exchanged a long look; then Inga turned back to me, all business. "Jepp. I like you. I will consider your thought, that Harlan predicted I would, that Helva would, too. But in bringing you to court today, Kral showed . . . unusual behavior. You say he signed a treaty in Hestar's name, which you must understand, knowing this story, the Emperor will view as seditious. A challenge to the throne. He could be using you as a distraction, bait to keep Hestar from killing him outright."

"We thought perhaps he promised you a place in his household," Helva added. "As second wife, concubine, or *rekjabrel*."

"Why else allow him to use you so?" Inga asked, studying me. "Unless it furthers your true purpose here."

Did it? My head swam, overloaded with intrigue. Any knife fight, even an assassination, was more straightforward than this. I wasn't at all sure what Kral believed my goals to be, or his plans for me beyond vigorous, casual fucking. *Keep in mind that I can't help you in there.*

Danu—he'd meant that in all seriousness. I'd believed him but hadn't quite gotten that he not only couldn't; he *wouldn't*—because he'd be watching out for his own neck. He'd known he'd be in grave trouble for signing that treaty with Ursula. I wasn't an ambassador; I was one of his *byndes*, easily sacrificed to gain ground for pieces with more power. And I'd played right into it.

Well, I had used him, too, in all fairness. And I still held my trump card for forcing his honor, if Karyn complied. Maybe I could rally Inga and Helva to help there, too? Though it would require their believing that Karyn would be all right on her own in the world.

But how much to confide to these women of my mission? I wasn't devious enough for this. I had to toss these lionesses some meat. They both watched me, blond manes gleaming gold in the firelight, gazes keen with hunger for information. Their one commodity, I understood: the network of female communication.

"Let me tell you about the treaty and why Kral signed it. I don't know how much of this he'll confide to His Imperial Majesty, but as far as my High Queen is concerned, this is a matter of public record." I had a copy in the documents Dafne had brought along, believing it to be perfectly legal. Or rather, I hoped I did. Would Kral be devious enough to have searched for and removed it? Possibly. I hadn't hidden it, which now seemed to be a glaring oversight. Kral had played a deep game with all of us. Maybe I'd kill him and save Hestar the trouble. Only, thrice-curse it, I'd promised not to.

"Excellent." Inga beamed at me as if at a favored student. At her nod, Helva, who'd taken possession of the carafe, poured more *mjed*. "That will do nicely for an initial exchange of information."

"There is a barrier surrounding the Thirteen Kingdoms, a magical curtain that prevents anyone from passing through it. His Imperial Highness, along with everyone aboard the *Hákyrling*, found themselves trapped inside the barrier and unable to return to Dasnaria. They appealed to the High Queen for assistance. She agreed, in exchange for an agreement of peace between our realms." There. Nice and succinct.

"What are the details of this treaty?"

I should have read the cursed thing. "They're all written down."

"Hmm." Inga tapped her nails on the chair arm, her many rings and bracelets flashing. "How did the *Hákyrling* get inside this barrier in the first place if none can cross it? How did Harlan and the Vervaldr do so, for that matter?"

Not unlike dueling with someone with a much bigger sword. I needed to be quick on my feet. "The barrier, ah, moved recently. It used to cover a much smaller territory."

"Moved?" Helva asked, loading the one word with deep doubt.

"It's a magic thing. It . . . extended to a new perimeter, and everyone inside that perimeter when it happened got stuck inside. Most everyone was fine with that." Except for Nani and her people. And others we didn't yet know about. "Except for the crew of the *Hákyrling*."

"And our brother was sailing through the Nahanaun archipelago when this occurred?"

"That's what he's said."

"Did he fail to find the *gyll* or simply claim he didn't?"

"I don't believe he did."

"And yet he returned home, at great cost, signing an illegal treaty that could mean his death or disinheritance, banishment, as happened to Harlan, without what Hestar sent him to get. He could have remained in the islands and continued to search." Inga pointed all of this out with calm logic, finding every flaw.

"There were complications," I explained. Weak. She had me on the run, backing up on uncertain footing. She knew it, too, so pretty with her jewels, white skin, and golden hair. So lethal.

"Such as?"

Danu take it. I couldn't change reality, only deal with it. Did Ursula ever feel this way? Probably. Another reason not to want a crown. "The barrier goes through the archipelago now, which means the islands belong to the Thirteen Kingdoms by default. At least, all the ones on that side of the barrier. High Queen Ursula plans to negotiate with King Nakoa KauPo to explain all of this. I think that's in the treaty, too."

Helva sat back in her chair and rubbed her forehead. Inga closed her eyes briefly, as if in prayer. May her goddesses help her more than Danu had me.

"Perhaps Kral did find the treasure but gave it to your High Queen in return for passage home." She fixed me with that gimlet stare again.

"I doubt that. Like I said, I think he didn't find it. I don't even know what it was."

"What do you think it is?"

"I'm not privy to His Imperial Highness's thoughts," I snapped. "He didn't say, so I don't know."

"And you don't know the details of the treaty. You're an extraordinarily strange choice for an ambassador, Jepp."

Didn't I know it.

"But you are an excellent choice for an assassin. Or a spy. Which is it? Both perhaps?"

A triple hit. She might as well have planted three daggers in my breast, purring as my lifeblood spilled over the floor.

You are, and always have been, my best scout.

When pinned by the enemy, nothing to do but bluff your way through and hope to survive. "I'm a scout," I told her, meeting her gaze as a duelist, letting her know I had killed before and would again. "I'm good at surviving. Her Majesty sent me to find out what I could about our new allies. If you turn out to be enemies, I'll give her that information instead. You, both of you, Imperial Highnesses, have to appreciate the value of information."

Inga blinked long and slow, the lioness lazing in the sun, heating to move, hot and quick to take down her prey. "A spy, then. And a reasonably clever one. If you decide to trust in us, I might be able to assist you in acquiring the 'information' you seek, so long as it doesn't undermine anyone I care about. As a gesture of good faith, I'm going to help you with the part of your role that you, so far, have not been good at."

I didn't even want to know.

18

So it came to pass that I found myself dressed in the most exotic approximation of my normal clothing no one from home could have dreamed up.

Calling in a virtual army of *rekjabrel*, the Imperial Princesses had examined my usual fighting leathers, along with the ruined bits of my best ones, then culled through a virtual mountain of silks, velvets, satins, and even dyed leather. Telling the story of the fish-bird attacks that caused the ruination of my best leathers at least kept them entertained—and allowed me to speak freely. The story also helped to accomplish two more things I hadn't managed thus far: convincing them of both my fighting skills and the existence of magic.

All because the rents in my formerly best leathers could not be mistaken for anything but something resulting in wounds, so saturated with my blood and so neatly shredded. The women held the leathers against me for comparison, smoothing soft fingertips over my skin beneath, noting no matching scars. I caught Inga watching me consideringly after that, perhaps with a revised opinion of my relative foolishness. Little did she know.

It took hours, but the ladies worked wonders, creating a form-fitting version of standard fighting leathers—but made in crimson leather, scarlet silk, and satin decorated with bloodred daggers. Several of the *rekjabrel*, including Sunniva, embroidered the fabric, examining my smaller knives and replicating their delicate, lethal curves with great artistry. Helva thought they should be in silver thread, but Inga insisted on subtlety. In my opinion, they'd left subtlety behind several hours before when they settled on shades of red for me. I'd liked the forest greens—far better camouflage—but the Imperial Princesses overrode me with breezy ease, Inga finally pointing out that it was far too late for me to expect to hide from notice.

Bryn never look back. But I regretted some of my past choices. Not that regret did me a thriced bit of good at that point.

They sent for food, and we ate, drank, and exchanged stories, while the *rekjabrel* sewed, trying pieces out on me and whisking them away again to tailor the outfit even more perfectly. By the end of the evening—well past midnight—they'd performed a miracle, even transforming my boots to fit their vision. The soft leather and embroidered satin pants fitted me like a second skin. A crimson silk shirt with flowing split sleeves mimicked the drape of the women's *klút* but gave glimpses of my arm and wrist sheaths, also recreated in embossed crimson leather. An embroidered satin vest hugged my waist and ribs, lifting and emphasizing my breasts. My boots had been decorated and bejeweled much like the Imperial Princesses' bare feet, an echo of their artful designs.

The various sheaths dripped silken scarves and ribbons, ones I meticulously adjusted to keep my draws clean and unfettered, the roomful of women watching in glowing-eyed fascination as I checked each one. My mother's jeweled belt would have matched perfectly, a thought I put aside with equal precision.

"Good," Inga finally pronounced, exchanging a satisfied nod with Helva. "You are dressed as a man, and yet completely feminine. No one can mistake that you are, indeed, a woman, but with the personage of a man."

I cast a rueful eye at my cleavage—much more of it than I'd

ever thought to have—and had to agree. "But . . . aren't these awfully close to Kr—His Imperial Highness's personal colors? I don't want to seem too closely aligned with him."

"Jepp . . ." Inga hesitated, choosing her words, but Helva stepped in with an impatient shake of her head.

"You may not wish to admit to the nature of your relationship with our brother." She held up a painted and bejeweled hand to stop me from saying anything. "That's your prerogative. However, it's obvious to anyone with wit that there is a relationship, and, besides, you walked into His Imperial Majesty's court on his arm. He may not have officially declared you to be under his protection, but he did enough to give everyone pause. I don't know what game he's playing, and I think you don't either. Suffice to say that—"

"That you're already aligned with him in the minds of everyone here, including his, is my guess, and you might as well use it to good effect," Inga finished. "Now we'll let you rest and we shall see what the morning brings. Send Runa to me should you need anything, not Baerr Lars, understand?" She waited for us both to acknowledge, then bade us to rest well and be ready for whatever was to come.

They determined I should attend breakfast—a formal meal in the Imperial Palace, apparently—as only family would be present, and not the Emperor, so it wouldn't violate his edict that I stay out of his sight. And so, barely hours after I'd finally been released to sleep, Sunniva and Runa awakened me to bathe yet again and dress, yet again.

Seriously, the campaign trail made for an easier life than this silken world of women.

Kral had not visited—though how could he with my rooms packed with people?—nor had he sent any message. I assumed if Hestar had executed him, the network of gossip that had me in its bosom would know all about it. Inga and Helva, who appeared at my door with bright smiles and wearing colorful *klúts*, brought no news to that effect.

We three walked together, the Imperial Princesses bracketing me as they chatted about absolutely nothing at all, retracing our way through the series of locked doors. It would make me crazy to live behind so many walls, so thoroughly contained. Maybe it made them crazy, too.

The Dasnarians might all be a bit mad. It would explain a great deal.

Speaking of madness, some surged through me as we entered the large dining hall. Glazed but uncovered windows looked out over the lake in three directions, with glimpses of the road. Mountain peaks rose in the far distance, ones that had been screened from view when I'd traveled under the canopy of the evergreen forest but now clearly visible from this particular vantage. The sight of them gave me a pang of homesickness and made me want to smash the glass, leap from the window, swim for shore, and run for the dense woods as fast as my fancified boots could take me. Insane thoughts, indeed, that tempted me to disregard all the obstacles that made the fantasy impossible.

"Good morning, Ambassador," a rough-warm voice breathed over the nape of my neck, raising the short hairs and tightening my nipples. Speaking of fantasies.

I turned, putting my back to the window ledge and the far-too-tempting view, to take in the sight of Kral, alive, well, and more handsome than I cared to admit. Someone had shaved him and trimmed his hair. Probably some of his *rekjabrel*. An irritating thought. He looked good, though, wearing the deep blue of the highest-ranked nobles, glittering with silver stitching and icy blue jewels that matched his hard eyes—just as the dark uniform echoed the shadows under them.

Looked like he hadn't gotten any more sleep than I had.

Ridiculous that I wanted to stroke that newly shaven cheek, to lean against him both to give comfort and be comforted. For all I knew, he planned to throw me to his wolf of a brother in order to save himself. He could have already done so. Somehow, though, it didn't bother me all that much that he might be my enemy. After all, I'd known that about him the first time my scouts brought me word that he approached Ordnung, with his battalion of one hundred men under his toothy-fished banner. Amid this barrage of the exotic, knowing him for that familiar man became a steady rock in a stormy sea.

He would likely laugh at the comparison. Even as I smiled at the thought, it occurred to me to wonder why Kral had approached— and sailed the *Hákyrling*—under his own banner and colors instead of under the blue and silver of the Konyngrr fist.

Kral looked me over in turn, actually taking a step back to do so. His gaze flicked to Inga and Helva, chatting nearby with several other noblewomen, judging by their finery, staying close to me without hovering. His haunted expression cracked to show a glint of that feral smile that meant he was thinking of sex, the hard, vicious kind in particular. Danu help me that my body responded instantly. I'd missed the cursed man. We'd gone barely a full day and night without fucking and I was starving for him.

"You look good," he murmured under his breath. "Both deliciously edible and also dangerous. I see my sisters have been at you."

"Inga and Helva have been most kind." There. I sounded all polite.

Didn't fool him. "I thought Baerr Lars wouldn't put you in the seraglio, that you might be given rooms in . . . neutral territory."

"That is indeed the case, as I understand it. Not in the seraglio, but not far from it. Your sisters came to me. They had many interesting tales to convey—ones I'd never heard before."

He narrowed his eyes. "Such as?"

"Oh, you know." I accepted a steaming beverage a servant handed me. Sweet, creamy, with a cinnamon bite. "Brothers, sisters. Family squabbles are fascinating, don't you think? So many parallels across cultures."

"Why are you talking like that?"

I'd been trying to use more formal Dasnarian, badly, but still. "I'm being ambassadorial, Danu take you."

"Ah. You are still you inside that exotic getup." He cut a men-

acing look to Inga and Helva, who smiled, giving him coy sideways glances, and growled in the back of his throat. "You play a
dangerous game, taunting me with family secrets."

"Yes." I met his eyes defiantly. "A game you started. Don't
blame me if I choose not to be the *bynde* for you any longer."

"What does that mean?"

"How did your private audience with His Imperial Majesty
go? I'm available to discuss the treaty you signed with the High
Queen any time he wishes."

Kral took my elbow, moving me a short distance away from his
sisters, just far enough to be out of earshot. "Don't listen to everything the gossiping biddies tell you. You and I need to talk. Not
here."

"This is your territory. Plus I'm going to guess that *you* are not
being kept behind locked doors. Tell me when, where, and, most
important, *how* to get there, and I'm happy to meet with you. To
talk, of course." Okay, I shouldn't be flirting. The man brought
out the worst in me. I couldn't seem to help myself.

"Stop smiling at me like that. People will get ideas."

Smiling like what? "Your sisters already suspect we have a . . .
connection. They seem to think your behavior toward me is unusual."

"They are women," he dismissed, but he also dropped his hold
on my arm, putting ceremonious distance between us, and folded
his hands behind his back. "Women are forever preoccupied with
imagining love affairs, arranging marriages, and such."

"I'm a woman," I pointed out. "A fact I believe has been validated
and transmitted to the Emperor." Inadvertently, I glanced at my own
cleavage again and looked up in time to catch Kral's avid gaze there
also. I took a deep breath, just to torture him. Gratifyingly, he followed the movement, then wrenched his eyes to my face.

"I sent a messenger to my wife this morning," he said in a
more conversational tone, though his jaw had tightened, the blue
of his eyes fulminous. "I'll expect her tomorrow."

Why had he agreed to that bet? Knowing what I did now

about his history with Harlan and Jenna, it seemed increasingly unlikely that it had been entirely because I'd challenged his honor. "I look forward to meeting her."

"You shall. In the meanwhile . . ." He cleared his throat and straightened. "Good morning, Sister. I understand you've been making the acquaintance of the ambassador. Yours was ever the generous heart." He managed to make the supposed compliment sound like an accusation.

Inga threaded her arm through mine, affectionately squeezing me to her side as she did, glancing up at Kral sideways. "Indeed I have, Brother. Such an interesting woman. It's not fair for you to monopolize her company." Her voice oozed with insinuations. "Did I hear you say that Karyn will be paying us a visit?"

"You've always had excellent hearing, as well," Kral replied without other inflection. "I was just about to offer the ambassador a tour of the Imperial Palace after breakfast. She's traveled a great distance to learn more about us, and His Imperial Majesty wishes the ambassador be completely educated in the might of the Dasnarian Empire."

"A reflection of his favor, then, that you are tasked to do so."

The air between them hung so heavy with barbed words, I wanted to draw a dagger to deflect them. Instead a male servant broke the tension, calling the group to sit and eat. Kral inclined his head, not quite a bow.

"Until after breakfast, Ambassador." He turned on heel with military precision and headed to a long table where the men gathered. Inga led me to another table, round and low, with silken pillows to sit on.

"Women don't get chairs?" I eyed the men's table, their voices boisterous as they passed platters of food.

"There will come a time for you to make that play, but not yet," Inga soothed. "Besides, it's good for our shark to taste a bit of blood in the water and be unable to eat."

"Word is," said one of the ladies I didn't know, giving me a thorough side-eye as I settled myself, "that His Imperial Highness refused his *rekjabrel* last night. There was much disappointed weeping."

I sipped the warm, spicy-sweet drink, selfishly pleased at the disappointed weeping. At least Kral hadn't gotten laid either.

"And he's sent for Karyn," Inga announced to the table, sending a flurry of astonished expressions my way. The ladies gave up all pretense of casting their eyes down once the men moved away, eyeing me with bold assessment.

"She won't get Karyn to approve," one said to her neighbor.

"Maybe she will. Karyn won't care."

"His Imperial Majesty, however, certainly won't approve," the first replied with a decided sniff in my direction.

"Approve of what?" I asked, tired of the giggling insinuations.

Helva, seated on my other side, patted my hand. "Our brothers' wives assume that you seek to become Kral's second wife, a role that requires the approval of the first wife. Why else would our brother send for she who's never been sent for?"

I groaned mentally. Either Kral was oblivious to female politics—entirely possible—or had factored this in when he agreed to my foolishly proposed bet.

"I do not seek to become anyone's wife." I stated it clearly, as a man would, without any apologetic embellishments. "I'm here to do a job and go home again. Alone. And unmarried," I added, just in case any doubt remained.

"Tell that to my brother." Inga tilted her head toward the men's table. Following the direction she indicated, I caught the hot blue flash of Kral's eyes on me before he looked quickly away. "Be very careful, Jepp," Inga continued under her breath. "You may be fierce, but you are only a woman, which means you have no power here, despite your foreign queen. Learn from the stories we've told you. What a man, particularly an Imperial Prince, no matter how out of favor, chooses to take, he may also choose to discard. Your best lawful security would be in gaining status as his wife. I would not be so quick to dismiss the honor."

As promised, Kral claimed me after the meal—one that had been so enormous, I nearly cried with relief at the opportunity to walk some of it off. Not anything like a real workout, but after nearly a full day and night of doing nothing but sitting, I craved movement of any kind. Treating the excursion as a formal tour, Kral took me through all the public areas of the Imperial Palace, explaining their functions within the Dasnarian court and the peripheral government. He'd shrugged on the persona of His Imperial Highness, with that remoteness of the man I'd met in the carriage, so unlike the lover I'd come to know on the *Hákyrling*.

He took me through a vast series of meeting halls, bordered by smaller rooms for more intimate conferences. "These are where new laws are debated and signed into effect," he explained. "The studies are for those wishing to influence those laws one way or the other to meet and attempt to persuade those with voting power."

"Doesn't His Imperial Majesty have absolute power, then?"

Kral lifted a shoulder and let it fall. "It is a balance. The Domstyrr contains representatives of all the subject kingdoms who are in good standing. As a condition of that standing, they tithe to the empire and enjoy the opportunity to influence the laws that govern us all."

"Why couldn't the Domstyrr decide to elevate one of their own as Emperor instead?" I thought of Kral's mother and her machinations to make her son Emperor over Hestar.

"The Emperor is no fool." Kral laughed, an indulgent smile for me with it. "Anyone so presumptuous as to put forward a law without His Imperial Majesty's sanction would find himself out of favor at best and summarily executed at worst."

So not *that* much opportunity to influence the laws. More of the figurehead sinecures, such as Kral being general of nothing in reality. The tour continued along those lines, with ample demonstration of how the Domstyrr operated under Hestar's aegis.

I put up with it all for some time, at first curious to determine what agenda Kral followed, then increasingly bored. Understanding the Dasnarian judicial system had not been on the list of what Her Majesty wanted me to find out, and I seemed to be no closer to the things that were. No sign of the Temple of Deyrr or High Priest Kir, nor any way of researching the Star of Annfwn. If only someone would draw me a map.

"Are there any temples on the Imperial Palace grounds?" I asked, hoping to sound casually curious.

Kral flicked me a glance, my question an interruption of his theme of law and the passing of judgments in an amphitheater currently empty but capable of holding tens of hundreds. Tiered benches looked down on a central platform with a pole, large enough to hold one person. The accused, presumably, who would be tethered.

"All temples are in Jofarrstyr proper. In the Imperial Palace, only His Imperial Majesty holds divine right on these grounds. Though other gods may be elevated above him, it would be an insult to do so in his presence. Why? If you seek a temple of your goddess, Danu, you won't find one in Jofarrstyr. I've told you, she is considered but a minor deity."

And Danu's followers didn't build temples to her anyway, other than those of our bodies. "Ah, I see. I shall have to observe her upcoming high holy day on my own, then." A total lie, as the Feast of Danu occurred at midsummer and involved mostly feasting, drinking, and—for the celibate—an unusual amount of licentiousness. For those of us who regularly indulged in the more carnal side of life, the day became simply an excuse to have fun. Kral didn't know that and, shrugging in agreement, continued the stultifying tour.

At least it gave me the opportunity to better learn the grounds of the Imperial Palace. What parts connected, what did not. Dead ends, blinds, and improbable bridges. By matching up my mental maps, I determined which tower held my rooms. A tall, isolated one. Not helpful knowledge yet, but perhaps someday.

"Kral," I finally said as we walked over an exterior bridge that arced dizzyingly high above a stone courtyard where soldiers drilled with rigid precision, the solitude my first opportunity to speak frankly with him, "why this tour?"

He glanced down at me, an eyebrow raised. "So that you can be educated in the—"

"Yes, yes, the might of the Dasnarian Empire." I stopped at the high point of the bridge. A chill wind tore at my silk scarves and flowing sleeves, ripping the words from my mouth, but we could not be overheard. "You said we needed to talk, Kral, so say something worthwhile already. What's going on? What did Hestar say about the treaty?"

Kral set his jaw, temper in his eyes. "You have such a lovely mouth. How do I forget so quickly the sort of words that come out of it?"

"You seem to be excellent at self-delusion," I retorted. "You promised to help me. You can start by telling me what's going on."

"There is no treaty," he ground out. "I was not empowered to sign any such document, not to save myself or my men. The Emperor does not believe in the barrier and suspects me of making up the story to prevent him from acquiring the Nahanaun archipelago and your Thirteen Kingdoms."

Aha. Verification that Hestar knew perfectly well where I came from.

"What treasure did you seek there, Kral?" I asked it softly, but the question surprised him still. "Were you looking for Jenna?"

He snapped back as if I'd slapped him, recovering quickly, fingers flexing as if he longed to lay hands on me. "If you value your neck, don't throw that name around. I don't care what my meddling sisters told you."

"I'm not flinging it around. Only you and I can hear." I gestured at our isolated eyrie. Though the wind bit sharper than a fish-bird beak, it felt better to be outside, out of the cloistered warmth of the stone palace. "What was your plan—to find her and drag her back to her husband?"

He laughed, bitter, a shadow of something in his eyes. "Is that what they told you? What you must think of us and our family scheming. With Harlan cast in the role of loving brother and great-hearted hero, while I am . . . what? Ever the shark. Circling the water. Tasting for blood. Going for the kill. Yet another reason for you to withhold your respect."

He leaned in as he spoke, not touching me, as the eyes of the wary guard were ever upon us, but face lined with tension and silent violence.

"I only have one side of the story," I said evenly. "Tell me the rest of it."

"Forgive me if I decline to confide my greatest pain."

Fine, then. "All right. Confide something useful. If there's no treaty, what's the upshot here? Does Hestar intend to wage war on the Thirteen?" If so, that would take precedence in the mission. I'd also owe it to King Nakoa KauPo to warn him that Hestar's eye wandered in the direction of complete conquest. He'd treated us as guests, aside from the whole business with Dafne.

Kral was staring over my shoulder, jaw muscles working, gaze hard as glaciers. "When I know, I'll attempt to tell you. Though you won't be able to do anything in that case."

"I can travel home, pass along the message of Dasnaria's might that your Emperor so clearly wants me to perceive."

"You can send a letter."

"And that will get through the barrier how?"

"Hestar doesn't believe in the barrier, I told you."

I threw up my hands. "Does his belief change your knowledge of reality, Kral? You know the barrier exists whether your idiot of a brother listens to you or not."

His jaw clenched, eyes icy as the wintery sky beyond, midnight cloak snapping in the whipping wind. "Shut up, Jepp. Don't be so cavalier about His Imperial Majesty."

"Or *what*? Will he strike me down in his divine and righteous wrath? I owe your Emperor no loyalty, no vow. I have made vows to Danu's service, several of which I've managed to violate in rather spectacular fashion, and she has yet to visit punishment on me." Though it occurred to me that this entire fiasco of a mission could be Danu's final attempt to teach me a lesson.

"You are a fool," Kral gritted out. "After all I've shown you these last hours, how can you not be cowed? Observe the might of Emperor Hestar as a man, even if you don't have the wit to recognize anything else. Your goddess might not strike you down, but His Imperial Majesty surely will if you continue to provoke him. What will it take to get through to you?"

Ah, at last! An explanation for the tour in all things penitential. And a glimpse of the Kral I knew best. Perversely, his furious lecturing turned me on. "I'm not sure I can be cowed. But if you can find us one of those private spots you mentioned, you are welcome to try."

19

Danu bless the man, thickheaded though he might be in other ways, he picked up the challenge quickly enough, lust melting the icy blue as his gaze dropped to my prodigious bosom, his voice going from grit to velvet. "Let me show you the stables, Ambassador. I'm sure you're keen to see how Dasnaria houses her steeds."

"Oh, yes, I understand her stallions are exceptional specimens," I agreed, adding a few formal flourishes to the words. "Virile, handsome, and ever ready in the service of the empire."

Kral nearly laughed, choking on it, his tense anger diffusing. "You will be the death of me," he hissed through his teeth as we passed a row of young soldiers at attention, waiting their turn to enter the training grounds.

"The little death, at the very least."

He didn't respond to that taunt, showing me through a pair of doors large enough to admit a carriage twice the size of his. The smell of a stable in winter swarmed over me, steaming with horse warmth and sweet with hay and grains. The scent and feel of the place grounded me, too, something the same everywhere. Never mind that the Dasnarian horses lived better housed than most people I knew.

Kral took us through the wide aisles between stalls, ostentatiously lauding the might of the Dasnarian horses, emphasizing the fecund, willing mares in such florid formal terms that the muscles in my cheeks began to ache from suppressing the grins that wanted to crack free, and my lungs full to bursting with trapped laughter.

By the time he'd taken me through the extensive tack storage, waxing on eloquently about the value of the elegant multistrapped bridles for bringing out the best performance in a mare and the best saddle to maximize a comfortable seat, particularly when riding a frisky, even fractious filly, tears of repressed mirth leaked from the corners of my eyes.

He'd imperiously dismissed all the stable lads as unworthy of the Ambassador's elite presence, a gambit I didn't love, but appreciated when no one witnessed Kral pulling me into an unlikely cramped closet behind rows of oiled saddles. The pitch darkness of the space had me stretching out my hands to prevent a collision with something unpleasant, but no sooner had the latch snicked into place than Kral pulled me back against him, snugging my ass against his raging erection, his hands everywhere at once.

"Ah, *cvan*, I missed this," he growled, sinking his teeth into the side of my neck, sending all blood flow from supplying my brain to flood my groin instead.

"No marks," I gasped, remembering that it was important, but not exactly why because yes, yes, yes—he felt so good and I ached to have him inside me. Or, okay, yes, his brutal grip on my body. That worked, too. He spun me about, pressing my spine against some wooden shelves, brushing aside the rest of the silk shirt and filling his hands with my breasts above the tight vest.

"This outfit," he muttered, dropping his mouth to follow the path of his hands, "you planned it to drive me insane, yes? I hate it here. I'd forgotten how much. And not having you only makes it that much worse. Tormenting me with what I cannot have."

"You seem to be having it just fine." I worked to free his cock, not easy with him bent over to feast on my bosom with teeth, tongue, and hands, driving both of us wild. We might as well have starved for each other for months. "Here. Wait—let me."

He let me go long enough for me to undo the series of buckles on my leather pants but lost patience as I shimmied the tight fit of them down my thighs. "Enough," he grunted, spinning me again and taking my wrists to guide my palms flat to the wall. I'd barely oriented to the new position when his fingers delved into my cleft from behind. I choked on the cry of agonized pleasure, biting back calling his name in a prayer that would bring far worse down on us than a punishing deity.

"Like fire, like water," Kral murmured in my ear, biting the rim and soothing with his tongue as he stroked me below, his other arm wrapped around my waist to hold me still. I wanted to spread my legs, but couldn't, trapped by the tight leather. "So hot, so wet. Mine."

"Please, Kral, let me—" I lost it on a groan as he pushed a finger inside me, then another.

"Plenty of room. You let *me*, little mare. I'll cover you so well that you'll never again snicker at the might of Dasnarian stallions."

At another time, such talk would have had me rolling with laughter, but something about the continuation of the previous jokes, all under cover of discretion I barely knew how to practice, only intensified it all. Not a game. Life and death. Don't laugh. Don't cry out.

Oh, Danu. And *don't* scream his name when he thrusts his thick cock into you. Though I was wet as I'd ever been, the constriction of my closed thighs made him huge in me, dragging against my burning tissues with such friction that a sob forced out of me and I dropped my head to both quiet myself and suck in air as he drew back, giving me enough space in my body for a desperate attempt to draw breath.

Aborted when he thrust in hard, forcing out all the air I held on a high keen of unbearable pleasure. He clamped a hand over my mouth, and I smelled my own arousal on his slick fingers, licking, then biting their fleshy pads so he snarled in my ear.

"No sound, *hystrix*. Shh. Listen," he hissed in my ear, slowing to pump in and out of me, the tension building so that I shook with it, the grit of stone digging into my hands, the world narrowing to his rough-dark voice and the hugeness of him filling me. "So fucking beautiful. So dangerous. And mine. My lovely Jesperanda. No matter what."

The force of his thrusts lifted me to my toes and higher, his flexing thighs catching the backs of my own and raising me, the thick-thewed arm around my waist keeping me steady. I lost my mind entirely, mewling against his hand, biting down hard with each sharp-edged stab of pointed ecstasy.

Until I unraveled, thrashing mindlessly in his grip, feeling him so deep inside me it seemed he'd invaded every part of my being. Until I throbbed with him in every blood vessel, this man I shouldn't want so very badly. *Kral*, my blood whispered with each pulse. *Kral*, my heart thumped. *Kral*, my soul wept.

"Jesperanda," he grated in my ear. "*Cvan*."

And convulsed, mouth hot on my neck, wet, fierce. A kiss without teeth.

Surprisingly tender.

He lit a candle stub so we could reassemble ourselves into a semblance of propriety, my task more considerable than his, and I briefly envied how easily he tucked himself away again. Fortunately my shirt laced again with only a little trouble, the vest having held the rest of it in place, the loose sleeves and ribbons accommodating to a man's impatient hands.

"There." I finished and posed. "Does this look right again?"

He cupped my breasts, the lines of his face sharp in the slim flickering light. His thumbs brushed my taut nipples through layers of silk, not teasing, but more tasting. My need, however, was apparently no less for the recent fucking, because I had to close my eyes against the surge of it. I'd become unexpectedly vulnerable to him. Thin-skinned. As if I bore a bruise only he could touch and the slightest brush of his hand or flick of his icy gaze made the place throb with feeling. And, just like a bruise, though it pained me, on some level I also couldn't seem to resist testing it. Did it still hurt? Yes. Still? Yes.

" 'Right' is not the correct word," Kral said quietly, dropping a kiss on my temple, and I had to dredge up the memory of what question he answered. "You look like a cross between a sword fighter and an emperor's concubine. Lethal, lewd. Compelling. Beyond enticing." He dropped his hands to my waist under the snugged-in vest, caressing the flare of my hips. "I think it was a mistake to bring you here."

"It wasn't exactly your choice," I pointed out.

"Perhaps not at the time," he conceded, "but now I have something of one. In this place, I may not wield the power of the Emperor, but I have enough to send you away. Perhaps to one of my estates. I could keep you there. Safe. Protected. It's killing me that I can't protect you here."

My blood simmered delightfully under his stroking hands. But not enough to addle my brain. "My mission in life is not to become your *rekjabrel*."

"What is your mission in life—to run around from job to job, man to man?"

Not a good time to mention my recent brainstorm of switching to women exclusively, to simplify my life. But good to revisit at least my current mission.

Determine if Ami's annoying friend who visited her before we did can be found. Do not engage. Recon only.

What do they know of a special jewel, how badly they want it, plans to acquire, plans to use. The why is critical.

"I like my freedom. You try to lock me up, I'll escape."

"I'll make you my wife." His lips brushed my temple. So sweet. "Between us we'll find a way. You'll have power, wealth you never dreamed of. With an alliance with your queen, we could—"

I put a hand on his chest, enough power behind it to back him up a step. "Is that what all this lovey-dovey seduction is about— your scheme to become Emperor in Hestar's place?"

He scowled, putting a hand over my mouth. So not sexy under these circumstances. "You put us both in grave peril saying such aloud. Even hidden here, we could be overheard."

I bit down hard, and he yanked his hand away with a quickly muffled curse. "And yet you're willing to risk peril by fucking me here."

"It was your idea," he whispered, harsh in the shadows, holding up his hand. "You drew blood."

"Good. I hope it stings," I replied evenly. "Maybe that will serve as a reminder that I'm not a *bynde* in whatever plan you're working. Tell you what, leave me out of it. With a friend like you, I'm only adding one more enemy."

I pushed past him, reaching for the door, and he caught me around the waist. Not punishing, but embracing. He buried his face in my hair. "I apologize, *hystrix*. Truly. Don't abandon me."

Holding myself rigid, I contemplated that. The great and powerful Kral apologizing? Probably another power gambit.

"No words?" He sounded truly concerned, big hands on my back, pressing me to him. I did not unbend. Or speak. When the silence dragged on, he released a long breath. "I'm not in the habit of sharing my thoughts and secret plans with anyone."

"Not even your mother? I understand she schemed plenty."

He lifted his head and cupped my jaw in his hand, holding me still with the other, turning my face to study it in the sputtering candlelight. "Sól save me from the plotting of women."

I held his stare. "I think you'll want a goddess's help for that. Try Moranu; all things of shadow and tricks fall to her."

"But can I trust in her—or you, for that matter?"

"You don't have much of a choice." I unbent enough to lean into him, then followed instinct—and desire—turned my chin in his hand to press a kiss to his palm, holding his icy eyes all the while. "I already hold your secrets, and you vowed not to kill me."

He brushed a thumb over my bottom lip. "I'm a doomed man," he murmured, more to himself than to me. "I don't know what it is about you . . . But we can't talk now. We've been out of sight too long and will be sought soon. Meet me here tonight. Two hours after the midnight toll. Can you get here without being seen?"

Using a move from Snake Slithers, I extracted myself from his hold, neatly proving to both of us that I could have done so anytime I wished. "Of course." For good measure, I tossed in a jaunty Dasnarian salute. It made me feel better, to mimic my usual cockiness. How I'd get through all those locked doors, I did not at all know, but it was high time I did some exploring on my own.

It wasn't like Kir would come knocking on my door, ready to tell the tale of Deyrr and the Star of Annfwn.

Kral only shook his head at me. "Perhaps I will make a blood sacrifice and burn a prayer—but to your Danu, in the hopes I won't yet see you face execution."

I patted him on the cheek. "Don't worry, honey. I wouldn't expect you to watch."

After another hour of the formal tour, during which Kral returned to his most stultifying self, blandly ignoring any opportunities I presented him to engage in a few double entendres, I finally returned to my rooms. Taking advantage of the meek female postures, I observed each locking mechanism without seeming to. They played upon various iterations of the same three basic locks. One kind required a key to be inserted, another a pattern of finger presses on an inset panel, not unlike the cabinets in Kral's cabin, and the final kind a heavy bar that demanded considerable strength to move. Not impossible to get back through, but not a walk in Glorianna's rose garden either.

Perhaps Danu smiled upon me at last, because, as luck would have it, Inga arrived to invite me to observe an entertainment presented during the evening meal, for the Emperor's extended family. There had been no midday meal—not that I needed to eat, after that groaning breakfast—so this served as the second social repast of the day. Hestar would be present, but the ladies would observe from behind a screen, so I would not violate the edict by crossing his sight.

All I needed to do was contrive not to be locked behind the doors again once it was over. Sunniva, Runa, and their cohort had been busy—when did they sleep?—and presented me with yet another version of my enhanced leathers, these clearly designed for more formal wear. Still in shades of crimson, these included more jewels, intricate embroidery, and a stiff skirt that belted to my waist and flared behind me. It seemed silly and extravagant, but left my legs free to move as I needed, plus gave additional coverage for a few more daggers, which Sunniva and Runa efficiently helped me secure. Ribbons make decent temporary sheaths—tie them the right way and they hold well enough without too much jostling. Turn the blade and a clean slice means an even faster draw.

All the red wouldn't be ideal for sneaking about should I get caught in the light, but I could work with it.

Turned out the stiff skirt was lousy for lolling on the silken pillows, too, though the gallery of women gave a nice vantage point for scanning the assembled men below. The screen allowed me to observe as much as I liked, which worked out well, as talking while the musicians played was rude. We all had to listen in utter silence and attentiveness, which only made me want to yell and dance about.

I kept an eye on Kral. Hey—that was just being smart, paying attention to my own interests. Even though he looked especially striking in his formal garb, glittering with charm as he moved about

before the concert started. Once, in conversation with some decorated man, Kral glanced up at the screen, his eyes narrowing before
he returned his attention to the other man. He stopped his glad-
handing the moment Hestar entered, retreating to an unobtrusive
location near the back of the assembly.

Not a flash of pink cloak anywhere. Surely, even if none of the
temples kept a presence at the Imperial Palace, Kir would want to
be here. What was political collusion if it involved none of the
governmental power? The Temple of Deyrr played games between kingdoms or Ursula wouldn't be so concerned. Their people had to be here somewhere. Possibly I wouldn't recognize Kir
if he dressed as a Dasnarian and not as his High Priest self. That
happened in hunting at times. A woman could be so focused on a
particular search image that she failed to see easy prey of another
kind.

Biding my time, I watched the people, studying faces to match
my memory, much as I'd observe deer from a blind. So oblivious
these men, in their preening and fat complacency, placing the
women they so easily dismissed above and behind their backs.
Could I throw a knife through one of the openings in the carved
screen? Maybe. I aimed for the final target, not the trajectory, but
it could be done. The shirikins would work best, with their sleek,
polished lengths. They doubled nicely as hairpins, which would
be handy if I had hair to put up. Perhaps Sunniva and Runa could
devise something.

It would be ideal to practice the tricky maneuver. Maybe I
could sneak back to do that. This entertainment hall boasted considerably less security. From an angle to the side, I could likely
place a shirikin right in Hestar's throat. He'd die before the musicians stopped playing.

A happy thought, though not what I'd been sent to do.

Still—would Her Majesty censure me? Killing the rabid bear
before he left hibernation was nothing more than smart planning.
It had nothing to do with wanting to help Kral. Not much, anyway.

I caught Inga's eyes on me, glittering like the jewels she wore. She appeared as languid as all the other ladies, but I knew better. I gave her a half smile and she dipped her chin in acknowledgment.

I had no idea what she thought we colluded on.

When the concert finally—thank Danu!—concluded, Inga led the parade of ladies back toward the tower of feminine imprisonment. As we made our way, I dropped to the rear of the group. Easy enough to do, with the ladies keeping their eyes down and their attention on their murmured conversations, which did not include me. Helva glanced back at me once, met Inga's sideways glance, and deliberately turned away again.

As we rounded a bend passing through yet another fussy sitting room, I dawdled as if to examine yet another portrait of Hestar in some remarkable feat that appeared to involve riding some sea creature, while brandishing a broadsword, naturally. When no one noted my tardiness, I slipped behind a tapestry, staying put without stirring long enough for all the ladies to be secured behind locked doors and my absence noted, if it would be.

If anyone came searching, I'd simply step out and plead confusion. Such a lovely room; such a stirring portrait! I'd become absorbed, looked about, and, gracious me, had lost the group, then got completely turned around.

I didn't think they would come looking, however. As with most security, the guards focused on keeping people from going in. So far as I could see, none kept a tally of who'd emerged and not returned.

Sloppy, if you ask me, but I wouldn't be consulting for the Dasnarians on the subject.

Gradually the sounds of the palace quieted. A servant entered the sitting room and doused the lamps. At Ordnung, a few torches in main hallways would be kept alight for the night guard and anyone wakeful in the small hours. As Ursula had often been one of those people, I'd been about during those times, taking my turn among the Hawks at keeping a surreptitious eye on her. Marskal's idea, but one I supported. Knowing Ursula, she'd likely been aware of our presence, but between us we kept up the subterfuge that she enjoyed the privacy of her night rambles, and we rested better knowing we kept watch.

Of course, that had changed once she took Harlan to her bed. No more restless nights. No need for anyone but him at her back. What might that be like, to trust someone so utterly? *But can I trust in her—or you, for that matter?* Kral's question made me smile. Unlikely Moranu would trouble herself for a Dasnarian. For that matter, I didn't place my trust in Danu. Justice might seem straight as a blade, but wisdom worked in sneaky ways. Danu could be a fickle bitch, as anyone on the losing side could attest.

As my mother had learned.

When I judged things to be quiet, I crept out, sticking to the shadows. I'd made mental note of the areas of the palace Kral had *not* shown me, so those would be the first I'd visit. I debated leaving the skirt behind in the sitting room, to reclaim it later. It would be too suspicious if I did get caught and anyone recalled that I had been wearing it before. My planned little-foreign-girl-lost ruse might not work, but the chances went way down if I looked too much like a thief in the night.

But then, my chances of not getting caught went way up without that wide profile. Committing fully to the gambit, I shed the stiff skirt, along with the most conspicuous jewels and most dramatic scarves, hiding them all behind my favored tapestry, then giving Hestar's overblown face a pat on the cheek. If only I could get the ladies to make me something in basic black.

On the walls, the watch called the midnight hour, which gave me a quarter hour shy of two to spy about the palace. That might be pushing it to make it to my tryst in the stables, but Kral would wait at least a little while.

Making my way through the dimmed halls and empty sitting rooms reminded me of moving through a forest—an alien one of overstuffed velvet draped to disguise unforgiving stone. Another ramification of the Imperial Palace's impressive security: The guard in all their multitudes had grown lazy. No one could penetrate the palace defenses, and all knew it. If one didn't perceive a threat, the guy next to him would, or the ten guys after that.

Give me a hyperaware and paranoid scout to patrol a wide perimeter, knowing if anything got past her it would be entirely her fault.

As it was, I evaded both the stationary guard and those walking their rounds with relative ease. I wouldn't relax my vigilance, however. Getting comfortable killed many a scout and spy. Still, my heart remained level and my nerves steady, even as I penetrated the men's section of the palace. In that tower, the bulk of men kept their rooms; Kral had told me that much. Higher rank drew higher rooms. Servant men lived in the lowest tiers, in the portions below lake level. Sounded damp to me.

Then the entertaining salons. Kral had revealed that much before clamping his mouth on the answer to my question of what sort of entertainment. My guesses proved spot-on as I circled the rooms, peeking in from a dark corridor. Not everyone had gone abed, it seemed, though no one seemed worried about observers.

Oh, actually, it seemed they expected voyeurs. All along the corridor, curtained alcoves allowed people to peep through eyeholes at the proceedings from shadowed surroundings. It only clicked for me when I chanced upon a male servant pleasuring himself in one, his face nearly glued to the wall. With his back to me and his attention fully riveted on whatever he witnessed, he never noticed my presence.

Despite my native curiosity, usually piqued by anything that promised to be sexy, I had to force myself into the next alcove to take a look. I didn't like this. But being a good spy meant observing all I could in pursuit of my elusive prey—even that which turned my stomach.

It wasn't all bad. Some of the women, and numerous young

men with shorn servant hair, appeared to be enjoying themselves. Others faked it, to my practiced eye, with fixed smiles and dramatic groaning. None of the dominant lovers, if you could call them that, seemed to care. They availed themselves of the bodies with careless arrogance.

Sick at stomach and heart, I scanned that room and every other for Kral's presence. Some salons accommodated larger groups, some only intimate couples. Perhaps some rooms existed without access for voyeurs, among whom I now uncomfortably had to count myself, but I obviously couldn't look into those.

The deeper in I made it, the more royal the participants and, very often, the more disturbing the sights. I'd never counted myself as sexually squeamish about much of anything at all. In fact, I once would have boasted that I'd seen and done everything anatomically possible.

Some of the things I witnessed that night left me feeling like a shaken virgin.

Resolving to find a way later to purify my mind and heart— perhaps I *would* become one of Danu's celibate priestesses—I persevered. *Bryn never look back.* Moving like a ghost, making myself look, then sending regular prayers for this girl or that boy to survive what they suffered, I found my way to the innermost salon.

The corridor ended in a loop there, forming a nearly complete circle around a good-sized chamber. Various *rekjabrel* collapsed in naked, and sometimes bleeding, heaps about the room. Some lay alone; others clung to each other. All had been heavily used, probably for hours. I'd put a lover or two through his or her paces all night more than once, but this . . .

I shook my head to clear it.

Two men and a woman sat in a loose grouping of chairs in the center of the room, in various states of undress. Hestar, surprisingly pudgy without his shining armor. The woman I didn't know, though she was recognizably Dasnarian with her robust height and golden coloring. Her eyes, however—those I knew well. Coal dark and deathly, like Illyria's had been. Even to my magic-numb senses, she glowed with cold power. It dripped off her, and, in the shifting torchlight, her straight waterfall of hair seemed to writhe of its own accord, as if composed of snakes like the monsters of the old stories my gran liked to tell over the campfire.

The other man, older than I recalled, his hair white, face lined, and chest thin in the swathe revealed by the black robe he wore— gotcha, High Priest Kir. A naked young man knelt trembling at his feet. Kir toyed with the long blond curls, every once in a while tugging so the young man winced. Never a word of protest, how- ever.

They talked quietly among themselves, too low for me to over- hear much beyond the tone, which was distressingly like that of lovers in afterglow.

I should go. Leave them to it. Not my job to do more.

Do not engage. Recon only.

Besides, my internal sense of time ticked toward my meeting with Kral. To find out his plans. No way I'd do him that night. I'd never felt less like having sex in my entire life. In all truth, I only wanted a jug of Branlian whiskey and an unoccupied cave to hide in. I might never stomach the taste of *mjed* again, the sweet smell of it hung so heavy in the air.

Or that could be the smell of death. Not fresh, bloody, well- earned death, but old and corrupt. I studied the used-up *rekjabrel* with newly opened eyes. One young woman who lay nearest me on her back, legs still splayed, her face turned toward me, stared with blue eyes that blinked only occasionally. The stupor she lay in, what I'd taken for the languor of hard use, all could be signs of that undead life. This magic looked to be more refined than Il- lyria's, whose techniques led to living dead with no remnant of personality, no native intelligence, and bodies that crumbled about them. This woman knew enough of her state for despair to fill her otherwise blank stare. But her chest did not rise and fall with breath.

None of them breathed. Not even the blond man at Kir's feet.

A clammy chill washed over me. Time to get far, far away from this corruption. I moved silently as always, but a slither of warning slimed over the edge of my awareness.

Almost unwilling, I looked.

To find that priestess of Deyrr staring directly at me.

20

I'd been pinned by a predator's gaze before. Danu knew—I'd stared into the eyes of an enraged bear. None had terrified me like this.

But they'd all taught me to do better than stay rooted to the spot.

I lost no time disappearing myself from that poisonous awareness. Moving with extra care, because I recognized my own panicked state, I retraced my path only far enough to take the first branching corridor that would lead me away from the salons. A scout who fears being spotted will be. Something about that frantic state sends up alarms to every animal sense. *Prey,* it screams. *I'm afraid. Come and take me.*

So I calmed my heart, steadied my breathing, and thrust aside all I'd seen, along with the slick, viscous sensation of the priestess's gaze. When servants and guards passed, I hid easily in time, my hearing and the fine hairs of my skin attuned for the least sound, the slightest hint of alarm.

It never came.

I went to the stables, partly because that had been the plan and my scattered wits couldn't quite assemble enough to settle on another. Also because, if the priestess did alert the guards to a trespasser, I'd do better to not be anywhere they expected.

Also, the sweet warmth of hay and horses helped immeasurably. The sound of their hooves scraping through straw as they shifted, the whuffing of their great lungs at rest, all of it so grounded in the natural world that it steadied me as little else could.

Except the fierce strength of Kral's arms enfolding me.

I might have trembled a bit, allowing that purging of the fear and tension. Hopefully he'd mistake it for my usual lust. Okay, maybe not, as I clung to him, breathing in the clean scent of man, even his daily Dasnarian spiciness a comfort in the face of the rest.

"Did you have a close call?" he whispered against my hair. "You're so late I feared you'd been caught. Having you meet me was foolish. We won't do it again."

"No. Well, yes. But not what you think."

"What, then?" Kral took my face in his hands, tipping it up though he couldn't possibly see me in the pitch darkness. His thumbs brushed over my cheeks. "Are you weeping?"

"No. I never cry." I dragged myself away from him. No leaning on him. Especially him. For all I knew, he'd been in that chamber of horrors, doing those . . . I couldn't think about it. Scrubbing my cheeks dry, I did the same for my scalp, hoping to stimulate the wits within. "I need you to tell me something."

"Isn't that what we're here for?" He sounded wry. "As the throwing-yourself-into-my-arms portion of our entertainment appears to be over."

I shuddered at the word "entertainment," the rich desserts I'd consumed because I'd been bored listening to music—bored!—rising sour in the back of my throat. "Yes. Yes, it is. But first I'm going to ask you a question and you'd better answer it honestly."

"I've never lied to you." He sounded somber, darkly grave.

"You've also judiciously refrained from giving me the whole truth. That's understandable. So have I."

"Is that so?" His voice had gone icy, and I imagined the chill blue of his eyes. For a moment I regretted letting go of him. His body, at least, would provide a compass for the man inside. I hoped.

"When you came to Ordnung, you told Her Majesty that a man in pink robes had been glimpsed in Dasnaria."

He was silent a long moment. "And she told you this."

Well, not me directly, but close enough. "Yes. She asked me to ascertain his presence here."

"Then you're a spy. This explains much. I perceive the plan now—Lady Mailloux was to play distraction as ambassador while you skulked in the shadows, spying out information I freely offered as a matter of goodwill. And the shape-shifter . . . A pity, there. I suppose that you've also lost her sorcery. Was she meant to fly you both away again once you stole what you needed?"

More's the pity, all right. I'd give a great deal for Zynda to spirit me away from this piss hole, though Kral wouldn't know she didn't have an avian form large enough to carry even Dafne's petite frame. I scrubbed my scalp again, wishing the slick sickness away. "You recognized the priests of Glorianna at Ordnung and found one's presence at the Imperial Palace, consorting with the Temple of Deyrr, as odd as we did. Don't try to dazzle me with your protestations of goodwill, Kral. It served your purposes to dangle that tidbit."

"Why are you coming clean now?" he asked out of the darkness, one of his swift interrogation strikes.

I almost didn't answer. No way could I trust him. But somewhere around that bruised place in me, something whispered that I couldn't afford to not trust him. That I'd already made that potentially fatal choice. If he were part of all this—if he'd done those things I'd seen, knew what Hestar dabbled in—then I might as well be dead. I couldn't fight that priestess, not without allies. She'd looked right through the wall and known me for who I was. My gut screamed the truth of it. I'd rather find out now than wonder if this man who'd smiled at me and kissed my hair, touched my body, had also taken undead *rekjabrel*. If he had, I'd break my own vow and try to kill him; then he'd be free to kill me without voiding our pact.

I might suffer in some hell of Danu's contrivance, but the bower of Glorianna's arms had always sounded oversweet and deadly dull to me anyway.

"Jepp." Kral took me by the arms, which absurdly made me feel better, though it should have bothered me that I hadn't realized how close he'd remained. "What happened tonight? I know you were at the concert."

"Did Inga tell you I would be?"

"No." He went quiet. "I swear I can scent you. I get a whiff of forest-fresh air, a taste of the heat of your skin." He stroked my arms, shoulder to elbow, skimming over the knife sheaths. "It makes no sense, and I am a man who relies on that which makes sense."

"Then you won't like what I have to tell you."

"Tell me anyway." He drew me against him, cupping my head so I once again leaned into his strength. Call me a fragile female, but I took the comfort offered. In a few minutes, I would learn to stand on my own again.

"I saw him. The priest, a man we suspected when you mentioned his presence. His name is Kir."

"I have never heard this name. You saw him inside the palace, or have you grown wings of your own so that you flew off to Jofarrstyr to espy him?" His tone made it partially a joke, with a thread beneath that suggested he considered it a real possibility. Funny that it reassured me that he was no more certain of me and what might lurk in my head.

"In the palace, yes. In one of the private entertainment salons with your eldest brother and a priestess of Deyrr." It seemed wiser not to say Hestar's name, though I couldn't say why.

Kral's grip vised on me, nearly crushing me, so tight I couldn't draw breath for a long minute. Perhaps he'd kill me right then. The enemy spy caught in her own web. At this point it would be a mercy killing. *I'd sooner put a blade to my sisters' throats than allow them to be so abused and unprotected.* In light of what I'd witnessed, I could see Kral's point in preferring to kill a woman he loved than see her subjected to . . . that.

"You are a fucking fool," he finally whispered, his hands easing, stroking over me as if checking for injury. "You could have died right there and I would never have known what happened to you. Or worse, I'd—" His words choked off.

"Worse, you'd encounter me as an undead *rekjabrel* in your own entertainment salons."

"Don't even say that." His voice had gone ragged. "You have no idea what they could have done to you, if they had any idea that you'd seen them. You're beyond lucky that—"

"*She* saw me. She looked right at my hiding spot and recognized me."

"How could she have?" He sounded reasonable, rational and logical, but fear surged beneath.

"I don't know. How can you smell me across a room? I'm telling you she knew."

"But I've heard no alarm. If she'd mentioned your presence there, my brother would have this place swarming with guards."

"Okay." I took a breath, let it out slowly. "Okay, that's what I figured. So she's playing her own game. That means I have time."

"Time for me to smuggle you away. Surely now you see the need; you'll let me protect you."

"No." I shook my head against him, then pulled back. Not all the way, just enough. "I have a job to finish. Karyn arrives tomorrow, yes? Give me until then. Once you've released her from the marriage, I'll smuggle myself out with her and make my own way from there."

"You're so confident she'll want away from me." He sounded grim, and somewhat bereft.

"I understand now why you didn't want her here, but yes. I do think she'll make that choice. I think you believe that, too, which is why you agreed to the plan. Do you think she'll lead you to Jenna?"

"How could she? Jenna is gone forever. I don't know what my sisters told you, but there is no reason to think she lives. So many searched for her, including me. I resigned myself to her death years ago." His voice sounded hollow. "I'll carry the guilt of that forever."

"Which guilt—that you failed to protect her or that Harlan was the one to save her, when you would have condemned her to an abbreviated life of misery?"

"All of it. I acted in my own selfish interests, yes, but she would have been better off married and safe than at the mercy of the cold world. That is the way of things."

"Kral." I dug my nails into his skin, just enough to command his attention. "Stop saying that stupid phrase. It's just an excuse not to see things differently. You've been in the larger world. If anyone would, *you* would know that the worst awaited her in this place. Or at the hands of the man who'd murdered four wives."

"We don't know that." Kral at his most stubborn. "Gossip and tale-telling. Besides, he died only a year later. She would have outlasted him and stood to gain a huge fortune, several estates."

"Enduring what evils until then, and after all that, controlled by who?"

"Me, I suppose," he admitted grudgingly. "But I loved her. My only full sister. I would have seen her safe and protected . . ."

"Yeah," I said, when he trailed off. Perhaps his skull had thinned; that sense might be leaking through it and penetrating his brain. "She would have gone from one keeper to another. Some things are worth more than all the wealth in the world. Freedom is one of them. Harlan knew that."

"Harlan." Kral spoke his baby brother's name as if tasting it anew. "Ironic that the one of us who least craved power fell into the lap of it."

I let that go. Harlan had gained what he did because he didn't want power, but Kral likely would never see that, thinning skull or not. "Is that what you crave, what you want more than any-thing—the power?"

"Of course," he answered. Too quickly to my mind. "Power allows all else. The promise of becoming Emperor has been the only bright spot in my life since Jenna disappeared. The only thing that has kept me going day after desolate day. Who knows, perhaps even my blessed mother will receive and forgive me then, if I finally achieve what she's given her whole life to gain."

"Is it even possible to unseat him?"

I felt him lift his shoulder and let it fall in that fatalistic Dasnarian shrug. "Who can say? I have the loyalty of a good portion of Dasnarian armies behind me, despite how I've been hamstrung, a grave mistake on my brother's part. He thought to make me figurehead of nothing, but he handed me a gift there. I thought to fund my efforts with a portion of the Nahanaun treasure I'd hide from him, but there is none to be had. Still, I have plenty of wealth, as you noted, and not all of it in obvious places. I also thought to capitalize on you and your queen, to destabilize my brother. Now it seems he does likewise, reaching across the sea to link the power of your priesthood to the darkest of ours." He sighed heavily and laid his cheek against the top of my head. "I cannot understand it. My brother was ever ambitious, forever self-absorbed and convinced of his divine right to triumph and rule, but he never sank to these perversions before."

"We need to know more."

"I'm telling you that—"

"Listen. At Ordnung a priestess of Deyrr worked magic on our former High King to twist him more than he was already." Never mind that he'd been fertile ground for it. Apparently so was Hestar. "It could be they've done the same here. The temple has been working a long game. Here and in our realm. Whatever their plan, it involves us all, the twisted and the innocent—and those of us who lurk somewhere in between."

He chuckled and it helped my heart, to hear him less in despair. "I need time," I told him. "And access to the temple, to find out about one more thing. Where do you think she'd be living in the palace?"

"Almost certainly in the seraglio. That would explain why I wasn't aware of her presence. Though it seems the women would have carried tales, so perhaps not. Still, better to stay well away from her."

"This priestess might be my only way of discovering what I need to."

"And what is that?"

"I think it's better if I don't tell you."

He tensed under my hands and I burrowed them under his shirt, stroking him as he had me, soothing him with my rough fingertips. We'd connected first and best this way. "If you don't know, you can't be made to tell. The priestess has mind powers."

"*You* know," he pointed out.

"Right—but I can't unknow it at this point. Take this small protection."

"While you won't let me protect you at all. It is impossible for me to live like this—everything in me, all I was taught and have learned is screaming inside my head to take action, to do . . . I don't know. *Something*." Anger infused the words, but he remained pliant under my hands.

"I'm not helpless. I'm not a girl raised in the ignorance of the seraglio to go meekly to my fate, with no way to defend myself. You can't get me out of here without triggering suspicion. The court already gossips that we have a liaison. You can't jeopardize all you and others have worked for to protect a *rekjabrel*."

"You have never been only that to me," he said, rough and quiet. "I—"

"I know. We click. Amazing sex, and we make a reasonably good team, too. Who would have guessed we'd make excellent political bedfellows, too? But you have important things to do. You could become the Emperor of all Dasnaria." I made sure to pitch my voice low there. "From what I've seen, they thriced need you to be. As much as I like you, Kral, I'm a scout, a hunter, a daughter of the hill tribes of Bryn. I am not the woman for you except in the right now. We both know this. Lock me up in one of your beautiful prisons and I'll die."

"You'll die an uglier death if you're caught. I won't be able to stop it. Not without the power I need, and I can't get that power if I act to save you." He groaned for the lethally circuitous problem.

"Fast or slow, death is death. I'd rather take mine on my feet, blade in hand."

"Like your mother."

He said it softly enough, almost reflectively and after a long pause, that I almost didn't hear, but that wasn't what caught me up short. "What?" I didn't remember telling him that.

"You said that about your mother, when I asked how she died. You dodged the question and only answered, 'Blade in hand.'"

"I didn't dodge."

His hand caressed my cheek. "A blatant dodge."

"I don't think so."

"How did your mother die, *hystrix*?"

"How did yours?"

"She didn't. Hasn't. She yet lives in the seraglio, where I may not see her. Not that she'd agree to meet with me, the son who sent her only daughter to perish at the whim of the cruel world."

He and I both, eternally chasing after the living and dead ghosts of our parents, trying to become the person they wanted us to be, someone they'd be proud of. "I have a bit of irony for you. My mother was a spy. No, don't say anything yet. I've only told one other person this story, so it's shy of being heard.

"Before Uorsin became High King, the twelve kingdoms fought among themselves, often bitterly. When the Great War concluded, that put an end to the overt strife. However, pockets of violence and resistance remained—I'm sure you can imagine."

He made a noncommittal sound. Odd how this cozy darkness made it easier to tell the story, like the smoke-shrouded low light of a campfire.

"I was born less than a year after the Great War ended. My mother used to call me her victory prize." I coughed a little for

Kral's sensibilities. "Apparently there was a great deal of . . . cele-brating."

"I thought you told me the women of your people knew how to prevent pregnancy." His hand dropped to my belly. "You're not—"

I slapped his hand away. "No, I'm not and I'm not going to be, so shut up. She chose to have me. She said she wanted to bring some life back into the world after dealing so much death. Any-way . . . maybe this story doesn't matter." I'd lost track of why I'd wanted to tell it, to him, hiding in a tack-room pantry when the next hour could bring my death.

"I want to hear it. You owe me a secret. Who is the one other person you've told?"

"Ursula," I admitted. "When she was only captain of the Hawks at the time and the day seemed impossibly far away that she might become High Queen."

"Tell me. The war ended, but not all was peaceful. Your mother returned to her people, birthed and raised you. Then departed again, leaving her young daughter behind."

"Don't make it sound like she abandoned me. I had a grand-mother, plenty of aunts, cousins, and so forth to put meat in my mouth. Plus she had no choice in going. I mentioned that our peo-ple roamed the low mountains in the western part of Noredna, northern part of Duranor."

"Depending on who sat on the throne."

"You pay a lot more attention than you seem to."

"It's not good for a woman to believe a man listens to her—she begins to think to influence his opinions."

"You're insufferable. I don't know why I haven't killed you yet, simply to shut you up."

He readjusted me to slide within the brace of his muscular thighs, moving his hips suggestively. "I know why. Besides, you promised not to. Stop stalling with the story."

"Stop interrupting me," I countered. He had the right of it, though. I was dragging my feet, and that wouldn't make the cam-paign trail any shorter, only slower. "My mother owed allegiance to Duranor, the kingdom that arguably started the Great War. Uorsin rose to power as a general in the Duranor armies, then somehow managed a switch that made him High King of all the defeated kingdoms."

"Interesting." Kral sounded contemplative. "Quite the feat."

"Magic," I said, as if the one word explained everything, which I supposed it did. "It was rumored that Salena, Uorsin's queen, had enabled this unlikely change in the power structure, and Duranor didn't rest easily with it. Their king, Teodor, sent my mother as part of their tithe of fighters to serve at Ordnung. And to be a spy. She was to report back anything and everything she could discover about Salena and the two young princesses."

"You know all of this because her friend brought you the tale, along with your mother's knife."

"Yes. Her friend, lover, and also a spy." I replaced the stale air and plunged onward. "My mother managed to insinuate herself into High Queen Salena's personal guard."

"Like mother, like daughter."

I shrugged. "She was highly skilled, and Uorsin preferred Salena had no male guards about her."

"At last," Kral said in a dry tone. "Something I can understand."

"Ha-ha." But the levity helped the tightness in my chest. "My mother became friends with Salena, though the queen had nearly lost her mind by then. She'd always been strange with her witchy ways, a Tala sorceress and shape-shifter, but marriage to Uorsin destroyed her, bit by bit."

"Not all marriages have to be that way," he countered quietly.

"Tell that to Karyn," I retorted, and he sighed. "No one knows what she found out, but my mother had told her friend that Salena had confided in her, that she had information to take back to King Teodor. My mother waffled, however, feeling guilt over betraying the woman who believed her to be a friend, and delayed, apparently with some wild thought to persuade Salena to leave with her."

"Truly?"

"My mother thought that Salena, as a Tala, would thrive in the mountains and forests of our people, that she might regain her sanity. A second-place solution, as she couldn't go home."

"Would she have—left the security of her home, her husband?"

"No, but not for the reasons you're thinking. I don't think my mother could have known it, as I only discovered much later that Salena could have gone home to Annfwn at any time and chose not to for her own reasons."

He didn't say anything, but his silence was speaking.

"This story is taking far longer to tell than it should. My mother was discovered, exposed as a spy, and Uorsin set to make an example of her. She outwitted them, wrested free, stole back her knife from a guard, and cut her own throat."

Kral's breath went out in a low whistle.

"In that moment before she—" Danu take it, my throat actually clogged with the old grief. The sights of the evening had really gotten to me. "She called out to her friend to bring me the knife with her blood on it, to tell me this story, so I'd know she'd died as she wanted to, blade in hand, to preserve what she believed in." I wiped the heel of my hand hard against my nose. "That's why I told Ursula. I wanted her to know . . . who I was. So I wouldn't be serving her under false pretenses."

"How did she react?"

I laughed, the sound a little watery though my eyes were dry. "She called it an interesting tale and left it at that. With her you don't always know what she's thinking."

"So I recall." Kral sounded somewhat amused. "A born queen, then, knowing how to play the strategy, to never reveal the wins or the losses within."

"Like you. You're not an easy read either."

"Perhaps." He sounded like he was thinking of something else. "And I know why you told me this story tonight."

Oh? I didn't. Not really. Except . . .

"This is why you won't leave. You think to stick until the end, to find the information you're meant to, perhaps to save Karyn, perhaps more of them, as your mother wished to save Salena."

"Perhaps," I echoed him. "I know I can't save them all, but I can't do less than my mother did. She died, blade in hand, for what she believed in."

"She died an empty death spying for a king she didn't love, leaving a young daughter behind to fend for herself." Kral's voice had gone harsh. "And you'll do the same—cut your own throat rather than choose wisely and take your chance to escape."

"Which reminds me—someone searched my bags and took my mother's knife—can you get it back for me?"

He laughed, without humor, and laid his forehead against mine. "You are the impossible one. You want me to hand you the blade of your own self-destruction?"

"A dramatic gesture is worthless without good emotional resonance," I agreed. "If that priestess tracks me down, I want every weapon possible at my disposal." I kissed him, partly to stop further argument, but mostly savoring the taste and feel of him. At least we'd had this, this thing that burned so hot between us, against all reason. This was clean and real enough to sear away all that ugliness.

21

Kral accompanied me back, stubbornly arguing that, if we were caught, he could spin a better story about late-night— or early morning, I pointed out—meetings than I could to explain my wandering about. Fortunately, we made it to my sitting room cache undetected, Kral frowning at me as I dug out the discarded pieces of my costume.

"You left a fortune in jewels behind a tapestry in the common area of the palace?"

Oh, had I? It really hadn't occurred to me one way or the other. "I didn't know they were real."

"Of course they are. Would I have you outfitted with anything less?"

I would have hit him, but I was occupied with buckling on the dratted skirt. "You're not supposed to be outfitting me in anything, Your Imperial Highness. We have no relationship, remember? You're really quite bad at this secrecy thing."

He sighed out the breath of a man clinging to patience. "I brought you here. You're my responsibility. That would be true regardless of any other . . . activities."

Said activities still had me throbbing and mentally breathless.

My certainty that I wouldn't want to have sex again any time soon had been shattered by Kral's searching kisses and devastating touches. I hesitated to apply the phrase, but we'd made love in that little closet with an intimate urgency and emotional intensity I didn't care to examine too closely. Except that what I'd seen had rattled me so thoroughly that I wasn't my usual self.

Nor was he, in some way I couldn't quite put my finger on.

Neither of us had spoken much since, particularly about that. Still, I had the impression that he had been as taken by surprise as I. We'd lingered far longer together than we should have, unusually reckless for us both, and yet I couldn't regret it. Dread hovered at the edges of my vision, a sense of impending doom that whispered I'd better enjoy what I could while my head remained acquainted with my neck.

Also, I felt human again. Maybe that was the thing about human contact—it reminded you what you fought *for*. That was a common pitfall among warriors of all stripes, to focus always on the battle while failing to remember the very thing we thought worth fighting for in the first place.

"Hurry." Kral cocked an ear at the sounds from the walls. "The dawn guard is changing over. The day patrols won't be so lackadaisical."

He'd noticed, too, then. "That's everything. Now what?"

"Too late. Sit." He pushed me toward a chair, quickly splashed wine into two cups, poured the rest of the bottle into an urn, set the empty on a table between us, and sat in the chair opposite me. "Drink."

The wine tasted oddly sour to my morning mouth, but I did as he said, observing over the rim how he loosed his clothing again, giving himself the look of a man who'd sat up in conversation all night.

"That said, Ambassador," he began in a loud voice, loading it with exasperation, "His Imperial Majesty has made himself perfectly clear on the subject and I cannot—what?" He snapped the last at a startled guard who opened the door.

"I beg your pardon, Your Imperial Highness." The guard bowed deeply. "I did not mean to interrupt your meeting."

Kral waved a disgusted hand. "Just as well. The ambassador and I will not reach an understanding anytime soon. Arrange to escort Ambassador Jesperanda back to her rooms. I must dress for court."

"Yes, Your Imperial Highness." The guard came to stand by me, clearly torn between observing decorum and dragging me bodily out of the room. I saved him the trouble of making that decision—and the dagger wound I'd inevitably deal him if he tried—by rising and stepping out of his reach. Discretion be thrice-damned, I had run out of patience for diplomacy. I wanted to kill things and this guy would do nicely for a start.

"Thank you, Prince Kral, for your time tonight." Because I couldn't resist, and by Danu if I couldn't kill something, I could at least dance along another edge, I added, "We may not have reached an understanding, but I myself am quite satisfied with this night's work."

I turned and walked out before he could articulate the sharp-edged thought that glinted in his eyes, leaving the poor guard to catch up in order to "escort" me. At least he saved me having to test my skills at avoiding the door guards and working the locks myself. When I reached my rooms, Sunniva met me with perky greetings, as if I hadn't been away all night, and began filling the bathing cistern with water she'd had heating by the fire. She'd likely been tending it all night, which gave me a pang of conscience. Still, I hadn't asked her to do it. I *had* asked my pair of *rekjabrel* to leave me be, but that clearly wasn't going to happen. They weren't exactly my jailors. I felt sure they reported on my movements, however.

Hopefully only to Inga.

While Sunniva worked, I lingered at the window, studying the changing of the guard and the landscape beyond. Letting the crisp predawn air clear the last dregs of horror from my mind. Once, in a former life, if I found myself awake at this hour, I would have gone out to hunt, the animals and I moving through the crepuscular light in our ancient waltz of tracking and evasion. They'd be out there in that dark forest.

But I would not.

My quarry lay inside stone walls and corrupt minds.

Shaking off the melancholy, I forced my thoughts into next steps. Karyn should arrive later that day. I needed to speak with her. *If* I could convince her to take the chance at freedom, I'd offer to help, and escape with her in her entourage the next morning. I deliberately set aside worries of where I'd go. If I could escape the Imperial Palace, I would. Then I'd think about how to get my information back. It all relied on a very big "if" at this point. I'd been so certain that any woman in her right mind would jump at an opportunity to be free, to live her own life, but some of these women seemed far from rational in their calm acceptance of their lives. How much did Inga and Helva, for example, know of what went on in the entertainment salons?

Quite a bit, I hazarded, from hints they'd dropped. People would turn a blind eye to a great deal of suffering, so long as they never felt the pain themselves. Not a charitable thought about the sisters who'd been only kind to me. Still, plenty of very nice people allowed atrocities to occur by pretending they didn't know, or that they couldn't do anything. It's not *me* doing these things, they tell themselves. *I* am kind and generous.

Sometimes it took the people like me, the ones who aren't so nice, to take a harsh stance and destroy the pretty salons where the powerless suffered.

Which I couldn't do if I left. Thinking of it that way, whichever Karyn chose, my own options would narrow to a single course. For the moment, I needed to focus on the day ahead, the next hours. No matter how events shaped up, this could be my last opportunity to dig up information on the Star of Annfwn.

A sound at the door pulled me away from the view and my thoughts. A sleepy Runa, waking up to take over so her sister could sleep, answered and took something from a male servant. She brought it to me, a box wrapped in silk and tied with bright ribbon.

"You have an admirer, Ambassador." She smiled shyly. "Perhaps you will find true love and a husband here yet, then stay with us forever."

I managed a reasonable smile in return, by dint of clamping my molars together to suppress a shudder of horror. But I had to ask. "And what of you—do you have an eye on someone to marry?"

She blanked with shock, then slowly shook her head at my ignorance. "Daughters of concubines do not marry, Ambassador. We live to serve only."

"In the entertainment salons," I finished, though she hadn't left me an opening.

She blanched, casting her eyes down and twining her fingers. "You have been there? I know some women go, to savor rather than to serve."

Like that fucking priestess. What others? "Not to participate," I assured her, unwilling to have her afraid of me in that way. "But I observed . . . some extreme sex play."

She canted her head, part releasing tension in her neck, part shrugging off some thought. "It's not so bad. If one is obedient, docile . . ."

"Enthusiastic," Sunniva offered in a sharper tone, emerging from the bathing chamber.

"That," Runa agreed. "Then we are spared the inner salons. And we need serve only a few times a year and are otherwise left alone."

Sex only a few times a year, and the rest a respite. It curdled my gut. *Like mother, like daughter.* Maybe so, but whether my idea or some legacy of my mother's—I wanted to rescue them all. Instead I opened the box. The big knife lay nestled inside. Kral had moved quickly, a gesture that touched me more than any admirer's gift might. I'd take its return as a good omen. That's why my heart felt lighter. With a feeling of setting my feet on the right path, I fitted the blade into its sheath and added that to the belt I'd wear later. Let them try to take it from me again.

"Will there be a formal breakfast this morning?" I asked.

"Not today. The ladies are taking their meals in the seraglio, anticipating the arrival of Her Imperial Highness Karyn Konyngrr," Runa answered. "There will be a reception and an audience with Hestar tonight, so they rest in preparation for that."

"Would it be possible for me to join them, when Karyn arrives?"

"I'll send a message. I'm sure the Imperial Princesses will all be pleased to entertain you."

Suppressing a shudder at that word—"entertain" would never mean the same to me again—I gratefully sank into the hot water.

I ended up falling asleep soaking in the tub. What came of gallivanting all night, along with being up most of the night before. Oh, well—I could sleep when I was dead. Which might be sooner rather than later. Something to look forward to!

It worked out all right, as Runa woke me after a nap of a couple of hours with the news that Karyn had already arrived, and I should finish my bath, then join the ladies at my leisure. The water was surprisingly still warm. Runa'd been adding to it, she confessed, so it wouldn't cool. Distressing that I'd been so out of it I hadn't awakened at that.

I finished bathing in short order, dressed, and we left Sunniva to sleep off her own night's vigil. We turned in the other direction from my rooms, proceeding through a final door.

I don't know what I expected. More of the same, I supposed. Instead we entered a place that, had I awoken within it, I'd never have imagined to be inside that ornate stone edifice I'd been memorizing.

The seraglio did not lie in the tower as I'd mapped in my head. In retrospect, seeing the real thing, I understood that I'd entirely mistaken how very large the seraglio was. It would never house so many women in such luxury, placed on the upper floors of my towers as I'd imagined it.

No, instead of ascending, we went down a set of stairs that wound squarely around the center of the tower. So far that I lost track of levels. The flights of stairs didn't match the height of the floors on the other side of the internal walls, so parsing the difference wasn't easy. Surely we descended below lake level by the end, the mass of stone and water looming over my head with oppressive weight.

"Is there another way out of here?" I asked Runa, who looked surprised.

"That wouldn't be safe," she said, by way of not exactly answering the question.

"I don't like this," I muttered to myself, but she replied.

"Nobody does at first, who wasn't born here. But once they see how beautiful, they learn to love it."

And then we stepped into paradise.

Of a sort.

Perhaps it was the unrelenting oppressiveness of the endless gloomy stairway, but the seraglio served itself up before me like an unexpected oasis in the heart of the Aerron desert. Stone columns held up a high ceiling, tiled in shining blues and golds, so mirror bright they reflected light like the sun. More of the crystalline lamps hung from the tiles, but fashioned to be smooth, so they glowed rather than refracting the light in jagged pieces as they did above. An enormous lake filled the center of the room, also tiled in shimmering colors, so the shallow end showed aqua as Inga's eyes and the deep a blue like darkest midnight.

Warm as summer in Elcinea, the room allowed women to loll about in all states of undress. Some swam naked, while others relaxed on the bordering tiles. Flowering plants and trees with feathery palm fronds as in Nahanau scattered throughout, creating intimate conversation areas or larger communal spaces. Everywhere women wandered barefoot, in *klúts* or less, smiling and talking in soft tones. Fruit actually hung from some trees.

"See why some choose to never leave?" Runa murmured. "This is far better than the world of men."

"No wonder you all have such white skin," I replied. "Even I would turn fair left in here long enough." I hadn't meant it as a joke—far from it—but Runa giggled.

"This direction to meet the Imperial Princesses," she said, taking my hand, lacing her slim fingers with mine in a familiar way. A strange place with different manners entirely, the seraglio.

She led me through another section, screened off from the rest, boisterous with the shouts of young voices. Children. Hundreds and hundreds of them, boys and girls, playing games, swimming, and dashing about with the reckless, careless glee the young of other people often showed. Among my people, children were expected to spend free time refining their skills. Any games involved thinly disguised lessons in tracking, making weapons, building strength. These children simply played, making me realize I'd missed their presence in the palace above, that silent and sterile place.

The princesses, other wives, and several older women I hadn't yet seen sat in an alcove at a polished table inlaid with colorful mosaics. One side of the alcove opened to the lagoon, and the other three walls were graced with paintings so vivid and lifelike that, if I didn't know perfectly well we were under tons of rock and beneath a lake, I'd have believed we overlooked bountiful orchards and a calm, tropical sea.

Illusion, all of it. The insidious kind that again layered loveliness over brutal reality.

Inga rose to meet me, taking my hands in hers, Runa slipping away in her invisible fashion.

"Beautiful, is it not? You are, of course, welcome to take rooms here, Ambassador." She indicated with a wave of her hand the balconies and walkways that bordered the high walls, warmly lit hallways leading off to various apartments. "Though I know your important work requires you to be more convenient to court and your various meetings. It's good of you to take time to visit us here."

Her words, as always, carried layers of meanings. Probably if I had nothing else to do but lie by an artificial lagoon all day, I'd think of clever ways to drop hints also. Or, who was I kidding? I'd be more likely to spend my time chipping with my dagger at the weakest spot I could locate, whether it drowned us all in freezing lake water or not.

"Your Imperial Highness is most gracious." I tried a smile to match hers. "I understand you have a visitor for me to meet."

"Indeed." She led me to the table, and a young woman rose. Exceedingly nervous, tremendously lovely, she kept her eyes firmly fixed on her knotted fingers. Instead of the pallor of the other ladies, her skin glowed with the kiss of the sun, her blond hair a marvel of colors from deep gold to bleached white. "This is the Imperial Princess Karyn Konyngrr af Hardie," she said, confirming my guess.

Karyn's eyes flicked up to mine, a gorgeous deep blue, full of sick fear. "Ambassador Jesperanda," she said, her voice barely above a whisper, then fell silent. Apparently my reputation—and plenty of gossip—had preceded my arrival.

"Shall we eat?" Helva interjected in a cheerful tone, tugging at Karyn's hand, urging her to sit. "This is Karyn's first visit to the seraglio of the Imperial Palace also, Ambassador. I believe you two have much in common."

"More in common than Kral's wife knows," one of the other ladies snickered, and I, still edgy with wanting to kill something, had to restrain myself from throwing a knife at her. Just to slice off one of her pretty curls, perhaps nick her fair cheek to draw a bit of blood, as she tried to do with her cruel words to Karyn. Indulging my restlessness and not above intimidating the nasty one, I pulled one of the shirikins I'd added to my costume, to acquaint myself with their heft and weight again.

Made of sleek, squared-off metal for most of its haft, the shirikin narrowed to a wicked point, finer than one of Runa's sewing needles. Slimmer than my smallest finger, it moved with speed when thrown and danced gracefully as I idly spun it. All the ladies' gazes fastened on the flicking glint of it, though Inga raised hers to mine, a wry acknowledgment in her lovely eyes.

"How did the journey treat you, Your Imperial Highness?" I inquired. "It seems you arrived quickly."

"As always, Dasnaria's roads were impeccable. And I, of course, hastened to answer my husband's summons with all alacrity. It would not do to disappoint His Imperial Highness Prince Kral." She met my eyes then, something of defiance in them, not quite in accordance with her subservient word choice. "Whatever he requires of me, I will be happy to offer him. His happiness is mine."

Yeah, mine, too, but not in the same way. Ha! "Perhaps after we eat, you and I can walk about the seraglio together, to explore its many charms." Danu, I began to sound like these women. I couldn't get out of here fast enough. How difficult could swimming through icy lake water be?

Inga and Helva took over the conversation, asking Karyn for gossip from the outside world, which she knew distressingly little of, beyond her own lands, and offering their own, which mainly involved other wives and children. I listened for any clues relevant to my own interests and watched for a woman who looked like the priestess. If I didn't spot her, I'd have to take Inga or Helva aside to ask them directly.

It could be that all spies reached a stage where pointed questions yielded greater return than subtle scouting. Perhaps that's what my mother had finally done. Not a promising path, in that case.

Though Karyn dawdled over her meal, finally she could delay no longer. At Inga's encouraging nod, she rose and walked with me to a path strewn with flower petals that seemed to circumnavigate the vast hall.

"I know you are my husband's concubine," she said, admirably—and surprisingly—leading with the attack as soon as we walked out of earshot. "He may not have signed the contracts, but the ladies assure me it's true."

I'd already weighed out how honest to be with her. Obviously Kral's ideas of secrecy didn't factor in the way speculation traveled like static bursts from woman to woman in the seraglio. For a sequestered group, they sure knew a whole lot about relationships in the palace. Came of having invisible female servants everywhere, not much else to think about—and a huge stake in the outcomes.

"He's been my lover, yes," I told her, and went straight for my core message, which I'd emphasize as often as necessary to get her to believe. "Where I come from, women are not concubines. We take lovers as we wish, to keep or release. I want you to know I never intended any insult to you or your marriage bonds. When I first took Kral to my bed"—that phrasing made me absurdly happy—"I had no idea he was married."

"If you had known, would you have refused him?" She posed it as a question, but the challenge in her voice made it clear she thought otherwise.

"I don't know." I really didn't. "I like sex and Kral's a handsome man. I thought it would be a onetime deal. It didn't occur to me to think about his life beyond that one night. I didn't expect to become embroiled in it. But causing you pain was never something I wanted, then or now. If you ask me to never touch him again, I won't."

She cast me a surprised sideways glance. "Then you do not seek to become his wife?"

Always with this. "No. I don't want to be anyone's wife, least of all His Imperial Highness's."

Stopping midstep, she surveyed me with astonishment. "Why bed him if not for that?"

I wanted to roll my eyes at her. *Virgin,* I reminded myself firmly. Lately I seemed to be surrounded with these women who'd never shared a campfire with anyone. "For sex, Karyn. It's fun, great exercise, infinitely interesting. A great way to feel good and make someone else feel good at the same time." And that sense of connection, that feeling that hummed still deep inside, as if Kral had left something of himself behind.

"I wouldn't know," she replied, understandably bitter, and resumed walking. "But the stories I have heard don't mesh with that."

"People like to tell bad stories. When we have time, I'll tell you a few juicy ones."

"We have time now, don't we?"

I followed her gaze to the group of children playing some game as an older woman perched on a bench kept watch with an affectionate smile. Looking on this scene, it seemed as if time didn't move. As if the sands weren't slipping away until evening, when Kral would pose his question to Karyn.

"We don't. I don't, that is, and I'm afraid I've drawn you into this." The immense selfishness of my actions hit me then. I had no idea if Karyn liked her life. The women here sure seemed to. Who was I to impose my values on her? Maybe the freedom I cherished would feel as terrifying to her as being imprisoned in this place would be to me.

"Let's sit." She picked out a small, pillowed sofa under a tree whose branches wept with pink blossoms. How did they encourage the plants to bloom like this? "Tell me," she commanded, all regal princess, despite that she must be at least five years younger than I. "I detest dithering."

I bit back the retort that I never dithered. At least, not with knives. Difficult conversations apparently posed an entirely different challenge. "Tonight Kral will offer you a divorce if you wish it. He'll release you to do whatever you want to with your life. You can go anywhere you like, marry again or not, have sex, have children. It will be your choice. The freedom to decide."

She sat, stupefied, then burst into tears. And not ones of joy.

22

It sucked up a lot of precious time, calming her down again. Especially as no one came to my aid, though plenty watched us sidelong and fell into murmuring conversations. I could only guess at what they speculated: what the evil witch of a man-stealing foreign concubine had done to the innocent and lovely Imperial Princess. Helva lurked nearby, eavesdropping, no doubt thinking I hadn't seen her.

Danu save me from female Dasnarians, too.

Another area of skill I sadly lacked, comforting a weeping woman. I'd never been the hold-her-hand-while-she-cried kind of friend—I was more there for the phase of "let me help dispose of the body."

Unfortunately, in this case, the culprit to be killed was me.

"And you say you don't want him for your own," she finally accused through watery sobs. "You aspire to displace me entirely! You don't want to be concubine or second wife; you want to be an Imperial Princess." Her tears made the last almost unintelligible, but I got the gist.

"Oh, stop it," I snapped, taking her by the shoulders and shaking her a little. If only I could shake actual sense into her. "I swear by Danu's clear eyes and bright blade, I do not now, nor will I ever, want to be an Imperial Princess of Dasnaria. Quite frankly, I'm utterly bewildered why *you* want the job."

She blinked at me. "But . . . but, I am the fourth-highest-ranked woman in the Dasnarian Empire."

"You can slap a crown on my head and call me High Queen, but if I can't even decide for myself who I want to fuck, where I want to live, and what I want to do with my life, what in three hells does a title matter?" I'd raised my voice and was waving my hands, but I didn't care. "Line a cage with embroidered satin and shiny jewels, but it's still a cage. Even animals know that. Why can't you all see it?"

"When you're born in a cage and live in it all your life, you don't see it for that," Helva said, finally moving around to sit with us. "You call this a cage and we see safety. You speak of freedom and we hear only warnings. Terrible things befall the fairer sex in the larger world."

"Terrible things befall them here, too." I may have said that too sharply, because Helva flushed and couldn't meet my eyes. Oh, well, I had no stake in convincing her. "Tell me, Karyn—do you enjoy your life?"

"I have everything I need. A beautiful home, a royal husband, wealth, servants, rank."

"That doesn't answer the question. Are you happy with your life?"

"How do I answer such a question?" she retorted, eyes snapping with impatience. "I don't even know how to assess that."

I pointed a finger at her. "Exactly!"

She and Helva regarded me with identical expressions of bemusement.

"What do you mean?" Helva finally asked. "How is a person even to know what might make them happy if they've never done it?"

"That's why I say 'exactly.' No one can discover what feeds their soul, what truly makes their life complete, until they've tried things. That's what freedom is about—being able to make mistakes, to screw things up and get hurt. Because only then do you figure out what works right for you, what feels wonderful and joyful. How can you know what makes you happy if you've never done *anything* at all?" Belatedly I realized I'd ended up with pretty much Helva's same question. A great orator I'd never be. Kral had made that crack about the relatively long speech I'd given about what I respected. Apparently when I got wound up by my topic, I could go on at length, even if I didn't say it particularly well.

Though, in my defense, it was notably difficult to address the subjects of personal happiness and freedom of choice in the Dasnarian language, particularly in the feminine forms. I'd defaulted quite a bit to male terms, *Hákyrling* style, not horrible formal-court version. Which no doubt accounted for the knitted brows and worried finger knotting of the other two women.

"Anyway," I finally wound up, far from a brilliant finish, "it's your choice, Karyn. If you decide on divorce and freedom, I'll help you in any way I can. I'll go with you, give you advice, protect you, hunt for food—whatever we need to do."

"Why would you do that?" She found her tongue at least, though still completely perplexed.

"I'm not staying here. I have to go home sometime. You might as well travel with me."

"I understand why you work to remove me as Kral's wife, but not why you'd then abandon your prize."

"Believe me, honey, he's no prize." I said it reflexively, a joke. General Lunkhead, a prize indeed, but she stood, fists clenched at her sides in impotent fury.

"His Imperial Highness Prince Kral is a great man!" she declared. "Handsome, noble, brave, intelligent, kind, honorable. How dare you besmirch his reputation!"

I rose to face her, holding peaceable palms out to quiet her, making sure not to crack a grin. If I hadn't already known she'd barely spent any time with the man, that summation of Kral's character would have given it away. "No one is besmirching anyone. I simply meant he's a man. One I happen to be fond of, but he's not a trophy in some tournament we're all fighting in. Whatever you decide—and allow me to reiterate that this is your choice—I'm not staying here. His Imperial Highness is up for grabs to any taker, so far as I'm concerned."

"I'm to decide this, in only a few hours? How do I know what to choose?" Karyn looked on the verge of tears again, fragile, and Helva put a supportive arm around her.

So spoke a woman who'd never made her own decisions. My temples throbbed. I should never have dragged her into this. She had no foundation for this, no ability to critically examine her options. I'd been learning to decide between stay or go since my mother first put a dagger in my hand and taught me how to be predator instead of prey.

"You don't have to decide," Helva told her, giving me a dark look. "Simply go on as you always have been."

I heroically refrained from pointing out that deciding not to decide counted as a decision, too.

"I'm the fourth-highest-ranked woman in Dasnaria," Karyn told her, as if we all didn't know that.

"Yes, you are." Helva squeezed her shoulders. "You never know. Sól preserve His Imperial Majesty and all his line, but should the unthinkable occur, you could be Empress someday."

Meanwhile the current Empress never left the seraglio, and even her own son hadn't seen his mother, the previous Empress, in years. But at least Karyn had stopped crying. "That's right." She turned on me with a defiant tilt to her chin. "And you are nothing and no one. Not even a concubine, or a proper female at all. I will tell my husband tonight that I will fight to keep him. I will not approve you as a second wife or in any capacity. You might think me young, stupid, and innocent, but I come from a line of Emperors. I was born for this and I won't let you take it from me."

Inexpressibly weary, I nodded. So be it. That decided my path. At least it gave me more time to hunt for information on the Star, dig up what I could of Kir's plans. Maybe I'd come across a reasonable escape plan.

For the first time it penetrated my own thick skull that I would lose my bet with Kral and he could claim any favor of me. He'd promised not to request anything that would make me unhappy, but his stubborn belief that I could be happy locked up on one of his estates might make him pick that. Horrifically shortsighted of me.

Heh, maybe if I could get a message home, I could request they carve that on a memorial plaque for me.

I left Helva and Karyn to console each other and discuss what they planned to wear to the reception that evening. From what I'd heard, it would be held in the hall where the concert had been, which at least meant I could observe from behind the carved screen. Maybe I could assassinate Hestar for Kral as my favor. I couldn't see my way to killing his sons. They were innocent of action, if not thought, so far as I knew. Kral would be on his own there.

Somehow I didn't think Kral would be a child killer either.

Were those boys here somewhere? It sounded like male children left the seraglio after a certain point, and none of the boys I'd seen looked older than ten or so. Not that I was much of a judge of children's ages—and I had no idea how old Hestar's heirs were, for that matter. Immaterial. I'd be willing to kill the Emperor and I could do it. Maybe in return for the assist, and the sacrifice of my life, Kral would be willing to get a message back to Her Majesty for me.

Would they have a wake for me and toast my noble death in the service of the Crown? That would be gratifying. Maybe I could send instructions that the toasts be made with Branlian whiskey.

It made me feel better to contemplate that party. Maybe I could pen a little farewell speech. Or write a glowing tale of my heroic deeds for someone to read. Surely my old friends would see to that much.

I rounded the bend of a little lagoon, following my mental map to where the stairs to above should be. Up ahead, a woman sat trailing languid fingers in the water, an icy fall of bone-straight hair hiding her face. My short hairs stood on end, my scalp prickling with warning, even before she looked up and looked at me with coal-dark eyes.

"What have we here? A little mouse," she crooned, her voice so quiet I should not have been able to hear her as clearly as I did. "Did you crawl through these walls also?"

I stopped, not going any closer to her, my instincts clamoring at me to run. Old chills coursed in my blood. The smell of the dry cave, the rumble of the waking bear. Run. *Run!* But running only led the bear back to the people you loved. I'd learned that lesson the hard way. At least one mistake I'd never make again.

"Priestess," I greeted her, proud of my even tone. Might as well inform the bear that I knew she was awake.

A smile tilted the woman's mouth. "Are you a follower of Deyrr, little mouse?"

"No. The goddess Danu holds my spirit in Her hands."

"An interesting choice of words. Do you imagine your spirit safe there? I think you recognize something of who I am. If so, you know that I can pluck your will—and your slender reed of a soul—from the uncaring hands of your feeble mockery of a goddess."

"Danu is the goddess of wisdom and the bright blade. These are shining strengths. Perhaps you are the fool to think Her feeble."

The priestess laughed, the delighted sound of a sensual woman. It should not have turned my stomach as it did. "You call me a fool. How amusing. I am not the one who believes in something that does not exist. Danu is a fabrication. A figurehead assigned certain moral qualities to guide people too stupid to think for themselves. You seem like a practical woman, if not a very intelligent one. Why do you put faith in a story made up to soothe children?"

"I'm not the one who believes in her religion so strongly that she became a priestess. Through that glass, that makes you the greater fool."

She cocked her head, tucking the stream of hair behind her ear. A beautiful face, nearly poreless, but repellent as a venomous snake with those dead black eyes. Otherwise she looked like any Dasnarian woman. What foul magic turned her eyes so dark?

"Deyrr is not a god or goddess. It's as real as the magic that clings to you. Where do you come from that you have this shine of magic? It's not ours, but it tastes somewhat like." She flicked out the tip of her tongue, licking at the air between us. "What is that flavor? I know it from somewhere."

I shouldn't have any magic. Firmly a mossback in all my blood. Unless living within the umbrella of magic had left something of it on me. Not unlike rolling in an old carcass could leave a distracting stink on the wily hunter. Or the Tala healing had stuck to me. That must be it.

"I can easily find out, you know." She trailed her fingers through the water, smiling at me with closed, curving lips. Something nudged at the back of my skull. "So you might as well tell me. Everyone tells me what I like to know, and then they forget I'm here."

"Why waste my breath on you, then? Ask someone else."

A bright, avaricious light filled her eyes as she narrowed them. "The Star of Annfwn. You've seen it. Touched it."

Had I? I supposed I'd handled Ursula's sword from time to time, holding it for her when she borrowed my knives or some such.

"Yes. Right there," she breathed. "I see it through your eyes. In the hilt of a sword all this time?" She shook her head, laughing again, and flicked the water from her fingers. "How rich. And I'm the one to discover it. I knew I bided my time here for a reason. That fool priest gave us nothing useful, but you, my little mouse, you walked right up and nibbled at the cheese."

"What do you want with the Star?" My thoughts clunked with muddy feet, but I retained enough sense to recall that part of my mission, even though I lacked the wit to be subtle in asking.

"Everything." She smiled, sunny, full of lethal charm. "If you don't understand its power—as surely neither does your mistress or she wouldn't *wear* it in a mundane weapon—I'm not going to enlighten you. I'm so glad I didn't kill you last night. I knew there was a reason not to. Now, run along, little mouse, and forget about me while I follow you back to your hole. Don't worry about a thing. I'll see you again soon."

I walked along the lagoon, smiling at a group of towheaded young boys who dashed past, laughing and tossing a ball. Could Hestar's heirs be among them? I didn't even know how old those princes were, but I wouldn't kill them for Kral, even if I'd happily assassinate Hestar for him, to repay the favor I'd owe now that I'd lost our bet. Had he asked me to, though? I didn't recall him actually saying so, but the thought felt so familiar. I reached for it, my fingers brushing the tip of the memory before it vanished like a cat's tail around a corner.

No, a mouse going into its hole.

Never mind. Chasing memories never worked well. I'd lie in wait for it to stick its nose out again. *Little mouse.* The image made me shiver when it shouldn't have. Mice could be a nuisance, but I'd never harbored a fear of them, as some did. And why in Danu was I strolling along the lake in the seraglio thinking about mice? I needed to—

"Ambassador Jesperanda." Inga stepped into my path, speaking in the tone of a woman who'd repeated herself several times already. Not good, for me to be so unaware. I put away the twin daggers I'd drawn without thinking and rose from the fighting crouch, Inga observing with wary amusement.

"Apologies, Your Imperial Highness. You startled me."

"Now I understand why my brother refers to you as a porcupine."

I blinked at her, reassessing. "You've discussed me with him?"

She fluttered fingertips, dismissing the relevance of the question. "The Dowager Imperial Majesty requests that you attend her in her rooms."

It took me a moment to sort through the chain of Dasnarian honorifics. The former Empress? As in Kral's *mother*? Daughter of a powerful family and schemer for the throne of the empire. Oh, no, no, no. "Actually, I have a number of meetings to . . ." What? My mind was so strangely blank.

"Jepp," Inga interrupted, not unkindly, and quite easily because I lost the thread of my thought. I'd been on some errand but couldn't quite recall what. "This is not an invitation even you can refuse."

This was a fine reason I'd avoided romantic entanglements. I'd never yet had to face a lover's mother. Not that Kral and I were entangled in exactly that way, but somehow I'd ended up dealing with both an angry wife and now his mother. Danu kill me now. Not really, I hastily added in a sincere prayer to the goddess. She might not be any more real than Hestar was a god, but it never paid to . . . Wait, since when didn't I believe in Danu? After the session with the Dowager Empress, I'd do a bit of a workout in my rooms, get myself centered again.

Inga had already slipped her arm through mine and guided me companionably back the way I'd come. A pretty blonde with very straight hair and dark eyes lolled by the water's edge. She smiled and fluttered her fingers at me, and I nodded vaguely back, though I didn't recognize her. Had she been at lunch?

"You handled Karyn most kindly," Inga was saying. "Not many in your position would have."

No secrets in the seraglio. Something to remember. "I'm not sure sending her into hysterical tears counts as kindness," I muttered.

Inga waved that off. "She is young and lacks experience. Her family has kept her quite sheltered. Their estate is rich in its bounties, and she's like a pampered, spoiled child still. It's to their advantage, you know, for her not to grow up and see the world critically. She's their link to the royal household. A bargaining chip. It's led her to believe she has more influence on the world than she does."

I glanced at Inga, but she kept her gaze ahead, face serene. Inga was no fool, and she played a deeper game than perhaps even Kral did. "Whose side are you on?" I asked her bluntly, a surprise strike under her guard.

"The one that wins." She flicked me a sideways glance, aqua eyes guileless. "It's always best to be on the side that wins, I've found. Your Imperial Majesty," she called through an ornate doorway, with pale yellow curtains drawn back on either side, held in place with silver chains. "I've brought Ambassador Jesperanda to see you, as requested. I'll just leave you ladies alone to chat."

She backed out with a sly smile, undoing the chains so the curtains closed.

"Ambassador Jesperanda." The gravelly voice came through a doorway. "In here, if you will."

Nothing to do but follow through. *Bryn never look back. They follow you back to your hole.* A wave of illness passed over me, for no reason whatsoever. Maybe I'd eaten something bad for lunch. Cheese. No, there'd been no cheese. Why in Danu was I thinking about cheese? Surely I wouldn't pass out.

"Are you all right, child? For all that your skin is darker than *svasshnut*, you look quite pale. Here, sit. Have some tea."

Svasshnut again. I still hadn't seen, much less tasted, the stuff. Must be a family thing. At least it wasn't cheese.

I lowered myself to the knee-high table and took the cup she pushed toward me. Not glass, not metal, it seemed made of something in between. Like the fired clay mugs from the fens, only infinitely thinner and more delicate. Fortunately, the heat of the liquid through the fine shell slowed me from gulping, as the "tea" contained more *mjed* than anything else. Still, the potent burn caught me unawares, and I nearly choked on it. At least my stomach settled somewhat, and the wave of dizziness passed. Also, cupping the fragile vessel in my hands gave me the opportunity to collect my wits and study Kral's mother over the rim—a basic habit of observation I normally would have done the moment I entered the room.

Her hair, intricately braided and coiled, gleamed the platinum of age, though her pale skin remained perfectly unlined. She had to be twice my age, likely more, but it didn't show in her face. I could see Kral in the sensual line of her lips, in the long, clever fingers, and in the remorseless ice blue of her eyes.

She studied me in turn, seeming most interested. "I see why my son is drawn to you, Ambassador Jesperanda."

Because he went for witless women who became faint and ill at the least provocation? "Please, Your Imperial Majesty," I said, unable to think of a better response to fill her expectant silence. "Call me Jepp."

She smiled, ever so faintly, an echo of Kral's happy, sated smile. "Then you must call me Hulda."

"Is that proper?"

She lifted one shoulder and let it fall, an almost girlish gesture on her. "Oh, dear Jepp. Don't try to convince me that you're much concerned with protocols. The gossip has yet to settle on why your queen picked you as ambassador, but it's quite clear to everyone that she did not choose you for your politeness or deft social skills."

"I don't know—maybe everyone in the Thirteen Kingdoms is terribly rude and I'm the best of the lot."

Her smile widened, though not enough to reveal her teeth. There her age showed, if only slightly, lines bracketing her mouth. "Fighters are never the best diplomats. They'd rather resolve problems with their swords and fists than through conversation and compromise. Though I'm given to understand you prefer knives for your weapon. Would you indulge an old woman and provide a demonstration? That tapestry on the wall over there, can you—"

Without looking at the hanging, I pulled a dagger and put it through the eye of a strangely cavorting white deer. That was better.

More my usual self. The Dowager Empress didn't look impressed, exactly, but she did eye me with intensified interest. "Can you kill a man that way?"

"Man or woman, in that way or in any number of other ways," I returned evenly. "But only if they deserve it."

"And you are the one who decides that?"

"While I'm out here in the wilds of the Dasnarian Empire, who else can decide for me?"

"At least you're wise enough to recognize the Imperial Palace as more dangerous than any wilderness, and wildest of all is its heart, in the seraglio. The men don't know this, but I think that perhaps you do."

Little mouse. I shook the whisper out of my head. "Are you asking me to kill someone?"

She laughed, a husky sound. "Yes, I do see the attraction. I haven't spoken with my son in some years, but even so I could have predicted he'd be fatally attracted to a woman like you. If I did ask you to kill someone, would you? What if Kral asked you to?"

"Kral does his own killing just fine, and, no offense to you or your rank, no, I wouldn't kill someone because you asked me to."

"What if I persuaded you they deserved it?"

"I'd still have to decide for myself."

"Would you do it out of love for my son, perhaps?"

"That goes for Prince Kral, also." The subject of our private bet shouldn't enter into this conversation.

"Hmm. What did you think of Karyn?"

"Excuse me?" Hopefully these two topics weren't connected. No way would I hurt that girl. Slap her upside the head, maybe, but I'd set out to help her, not end her life.

"I understand that my son will offer her a divorce. A fascinating development—one that you obviously must have orchestrated, as it would never have occurred to him to do so on his own. That boy thinks with his sword, not his wits."

Absurdly, I wanted to defend Kral. As many times as I'd insulted his intelligence, I'd only done it out of . . . a kind of affectionate frustration, I supposed.

"Don't like me disparaging your lover?" Hulda sipped her tea, wickedly amused. "Another fascinating development. Are you truly in love with him, then?"

23

Now I truly did choke on the tea. From Hulda's wide smile—finally revealing yellowed teeth—she'd timed her question precisely for that. This was the woman who named her son for a shark, then dunned ambition into his head so thoroughly, he valued nothing else. And who sold her daughter into marriage to a murderous, cruel husband.

"Well, it's been wonderful meeting you, but I have a number of meetings to attend before tonight's ceremony. Thank you for the tea." I set my cup down.

"If you assassinate Hestar, I'll see to it that Karyn experiences a sudden illness that will lead to her unfortunate demise. My son will be the next Emperor and you the Empress."

I shook my head, blowing out tension on a laugh. "How would you manage that?"

"Her death or your marriage? I'll address both. Poisons are my weapon, and I believe I am as proficient in them as you are with your little daggers. With Karyn sadly gone to Sól's lap, Kral will need a new first wife. He will do as I tell him and marry you."

So many responses sprang to mind that they tangled on my

tongue. This worked in my favor, as none of them managed to tumble out. Finally I settled on one that didn't seem too obnoxious. "If you're so good with poison, why not kill the Emperor yourself?"

"Oh, come now. You might be soul mate to my son in thinking with your knives instead of what's between your ears, but you're not that obtuse. Nor is Hestar. He knows very well what I'm capable of and has everything tasted. If you move quickly—and it will have to be at the reception this evening, as you've been flaunting your skills more than you should—you can take out Hestar before they realize how dangerous you really are and disarm you."

It took some doing not to finger one of the shirikins I'd secreted on myself with exactly that possibility in mind. I'd still really like to squeeze in a trial run, but that might not be possible. Restless, I rose and went to the tapestry, plucked the dagger out of the deer's eye. I spun it between my fingers, contemplating.

"If I do this thing," I said, trying to sound as if I hadn't already planned it all out, "everyone will know it was me. I'll be executed, conveniently freeing you of the obligation to make me Empress. Which"—I continued as she opened her mouth—"I don't for a moment believe you can arrange. There's no one to sign me over, and Kral doesn't listen to you. You two don't even communicate; he told me so."

"Did he, now? Afterglow is excellent for extracting confessions."

I didn't reply, disconcerted that she'd voiced something I'd said many times. She and I were nothing alike, and yet people loved to say that men went for women who reminded them of their mothers. Even though Kral's attraction to me was purely sexual, this whole line of thinking bothered me.

I needed to get out of this crazy-making place.

Hulda gave my silence a slight, wry smile. "Talk to my son and tell him what we discussed. I can tell you exactly what he'll say. The moment Hestar dies, Kral will become Emperor by default, which means he can protect you and the legalities will be irrelevant. The best and fastest way to secure your safety—something that will be of paramount importance to him—will be for him to immediately marry you. You can tell him you have my approval." She said that last as if she'd bestowed a great boon on me.

"I won't have Karyn's approval."

"You don't need it, if you have mine. The chit possesses far less power than she thinks. Then she'll be dead and you can be first wife and Empress."

"And I'll owe it all to you."

She waved a negligent hand. "Consider it a wedding gift."

Oh, right. I sheathed my dagger. "I'll talk to Kral."

"So will I. You may relate to him that I'll attend the reception this evening. After all, Karyn is like a daughter to me."

She really did think I was stupid. But I managed a confident smile. "I'll have Kral tell you what we decided then."

"Not necessary. If you refuse to do as I ask, I'll tell the Emperor that you came to me to bargain for my approval, as Karyn refused to give it. A foreign assassin, placed like a viper at the heart of the Dasnarian Empire. My poor son, duped by an evil temptress, more man than woman. You'll die, Jepp. Quite painfully, in the entertainment salons. There will be many who will enjoy exploring your tolerance for torture. I understand they're quite skilled at keeping their victims alive for days, even weeks, testing their limits until the poor things finally give up their lives. The spirit breaks long before the body."

I pretended the threat didn't make my skin crawl, that the image of myself suffering what I'd witnessed didn't terrify me. Being at the mercy of . . . The memory dashed away, as if equally frightened. "Ah." I cocked a jaunty hip. "So it's either death by sexual torture for me or becoming Empress of the Dasnarian Empire."

She smiled thinly, lips sucked in over her aging teeth. "I like my bargains to be exceedingly clear, so there are no confusing gray areas."

The stale, damp murk of the stairway leading out of the seraglio hit my senses like mountain air on a spring morning. If I never went into that thrice-cursed satin-lined nest again, it would be too soon. I made it back to my rooms, pushed past a startled Sunniva, and closed myself in the bathing chamber. Putting a finger down my throat, I made myself puke up everything in my stomach.

Maybe it wasn't poison that had made me feel ill, but I wasn't taking any chances. Weak and a bit shivery, I sat on the stone floor, back against the door for good measure, and breathed in Danu's Cycle to energize my body to kick out any dregs of poison, if there had been some. I only knew something was wrong with me, and with my fucking life hanging on the line, I needed to get myself right again thriced-fast.

"Ambassador?" Sunniva tapped on the door. "Are you ill?"

I really looked forward to being alone again someday. To being Jepp who communicated best with her knives again. "I'm fine." *Go away*, I thought fiercely at her, unwilling to be that brusque with her, but on the verge of it.

"I can arrange for—"

She broke off when I flung the door open. "I'm fine," I repeated. I needed to think and I did that best moving anyway. *Thinking with your knives instead of what's between your ears.* What Hulda didn't understand, with her spiked tea, indolent existence, and luxurious prison of pillows, was that the mind is part of the body. Movement of my muscles moves my brain. "Help me push these chairs out of the way."

"But why?" Sunniva set to work moving another of the chairs to the wall.

"I need space. Stay back." Because I had it again, I drew my mother's knife, the bigger haft and satisfying weight more centering than my smaller knives. Settling into Midnight Form, I let the movements take over. When my mind cleared of the noise, I'd review my options.

Such as they were.

I'd verified Kir's presence, so I'd fulfilled my mission. I could escape, find my way home somehow, and take back that news. Her Majesty wouldn't blame me for that. Really, I could have left as soon as I'd found that out. Why hadn't I? It seemed like there had been something more I was to do—but what? She'd sent that note, and I'd committed it to memory. I'd never forgotten orders in my life.

Determine if Ami's annoying friend who visited her before we did can be found. Do not engage. Recon only.

There had been more. I could see it in my mind like something in a dream. Leaving Kral snoring, going to my own cabin, the small room a tumbled mess of my things and Zynda's, a few of Dafne's that she hadn't needed on Nakoa's tropical island. I'd sat at the desk she'd used and laid the scroll out flat. My muscles sang with renewed vigor as I moved, my mind clearing. A still pond for the memory to rise through and settle upon the surface. Letting me see it in my mind's eye.

> *Got word from our shifty friend. None of it your fault. You did good. Don't beat yourself up for the dragon king's actions. That's an order. Things will work out. I'm handling it. Maybe even better this way. Know our librarian relayed some of what she and I spoke of, but she may have been uncertain what to keep secret.*
>
> *In case there's doubt:*
>
> *Determine if Ami's annoying friend who visited her before we did can be found. Do not engage. Recon only.*

~~~~~~~~~~~~~~~~~~~~~~~~~~~~~~~~
~~~~~~~~~~~~~~~~~~~~~~~~~~~~~~~~
~~~~~~~~~~~~~~~~~~~~~~~~~~~~~~~

> *Keep it simple. Do the job. Come home. Don't be a hero.*
>
> *You are, and always have been, my best scout. I picked you for a reason five years ago. I picked you for good reasons this time, too. Not the ones you think. When boulders speak, they give good advice. I listened and acted accordingly.*
>
> *If this finds its way into a fire, all the better.*

No matter how I focused my mind's eye, those few lines remained blurred. The rest of Ursula's crabbed hand stood out bright and black. Those lines, though; it was as if some finger had rubbed them through. Had the scroll been tampered with? That would have stood out in my memory. I would have been concerned, not frisky and cheerful enough to make the sign of Glorianna and hum her morning song while I burned the letter.

My memory of my orders had changed. It had to be Hulda who'd done it—tampering not with the scroll, but with my mind. I didn't understand it, and there shouldn't be magic here, outside the barrier, but . . . there it was again—that funny feeling that I should know something.

I stopped without finishing all twelve forms, wiped the sweat from my brow, and sheathed the blade. Sunniva sat in a chair by the window, the tapestry pulled aside for better light, and watched me as she embroidered.

"That is truly miraculous to see, Ambassador," she said with quiet reverence.

"It's a skill like any other. Like your embroidery. I can't do that, so it looks miraculous to me."

She giggled, surveying her work. "But I could teach you to do this—not that such a humble task would be worthy of you," she added hastily.

"Tasks themselves can't be more or less humble. They simply are. It's the person who decides they're too special for some job or another. Where I come from, everyone learns to do everything."

"Not embroidery," she pointed out, then flushed at her boldness. "I apologize. I—"

"No apologies necessary. You're absolutely right." I prowled over to the window. Behind the overcast sky, the sun would be declining, bringing an end to the short winter day. Perhaps my last. *Danu grant me a clean death.* I maybe didn't deserve it, but I hoped for it. "We didn't have that skill, or I would have learned it. I can sew enough to keep myself clothed. No better than that."

"Then you already have the beginning," she said, snipping off a thread with her shears. "The rest is simply refinement and elaboration."

"I could say the same to you." I nodded at her shears. "You already have the beginning, with your own knives."

She held up the sewing shears as if she'd never seen them before. "You think so?"

"I know it. Bring them here and I'll show you."

Following that impulse, I showed her a few basics. There wasn't time for much, so I built on what she already knew, her customary grip on the shears, using them in a new way. The memory of that morning at Ordnung came back with painfully nostalgic clarity. Ursula teaching Dafne basic self-defense, using Harlan as the practice dummy and me as a second. That had been a good day, fun, full of laughter and being with good people I cared about.

Upon further thought, I hoped they wouldn't mourn my passing overmuch. I'd had a good life. A longer one than my mother's, though not by much. I'd done some useful things and had a great time in general. This would be a little gift to the women of Dasnaria. Hard to say what Harlan had hoped for. In the end it didn't matter.

I'd given what I had to give, and that would have to suffice.

Sunniva and Runa helped me dress early for the reception. They'd sent a message to Kral for me, requesting a meeting beforehand. Hopefully he'd agree and that would get me back out into the palace proper with enough time to check my aim through the screen. I hadn't yet decided on my course of action regarding Hestar. It really depended on what Kral wanted for his favor.

If he asked me to kill the Emperor, I would. Of course, I was honor bound to do whatever he requested for his prize, but I wasn't above trying to talk him out of something I didn't like. I wouldn't marry him, however. Neither of us wanted that, and I wouldn't consign either of us to that particular damnation. We danced an uneasy line of love and hate as it was. All we needed was to be metaphorically imprisoned with each other to push that firmly into lifelong hate.

And I really didn't want Karyn dead. When she declared her decision to remain married to him, he needed to send her home immediately. If Kral could save my ass—provided he'd do so by at least letting me escape, if not actively assisting me—then I'd ask for that. If he couldn't, I'd ask for a clean death. Maybe I'd have time to do it myself. With my mother's blade, as she did.

A fitting end.

Arrayed in my crimson clothes, complete with the stiff skirt, festooned with even more jewels and the addition of a dramatic silk cloak, I paced, waiting for the summons from His Imperial Highness. At least the delay let me practice moving with the headdress Runa had designed, a decorative band that let me slip extra shirikins in as part of the overall effect. She and Sunniva had very much wanted to use a fake hairpiece, but—big surprise—nothing in the Imperial Palace matched *my* hair.

Finally, a page arrived to conduct me to the meeting with His Imperial Highness Prince Kral. I surprised Sunniva and Runa by kissing them and giving each one of my small daggers. I couldn't wear all of them on my body, much as I'd tried. If I didn't return, my belongings would be tomorrow's trash anyway.

Carrying the scroll I'd written, I went with the page, counting the doors and locks, noting that the patterns remained unchanged. If I needed to get back through them, I probably could. Nothing like a plan to be executed under immense pressure with zero practice.

Kral had arrived in the ladies' observation salon ahead of me, pacing around the place like a caged lion, exuding resigned impatience. He, too, had already dressed for the reception, his deep blue cloak flaring around him as he strode, his lean, muscled body garbed in enough silver to shine like the Emperor's.

He dismissed the page and greeted me briskly, "Ambassador Jesperanda. An odd choice of locations. Men do not typically enter this chamber."

"I'm pretty sure you won't contract a disease as long as you don't touch anything."

He barked out a laugh and stopped just out of arm's reach, looking at me like he'd love nothing better than to put his hands and mouth on me. Danu knew I wanted it, too. A shame that it seemed unlikely we'd ever have each other again, regardless of how the evening went.

"You look good, *hystrix*. If only I could peel off some of your blades and uncover that soft belly beneath." The low pitch of his voice, for my ears alone, shimmered over my senses deliciously. "Maybe later tonight, we can meet in our—"

I cut him off with a lifted hand. It hurt too much to think about that, to flirt with him when I couldn't have him. We were never really supposed to have as much as we did to begin with. I'd have to be satisfied with the memories if I lived. Hopefully those wouldn't get erased, too.

"I had an interesting day," I told him. "I spoke with Karyn. And with your mother."

"Oh?" He went from lover to warrior in an instant. Hulda was the fool, if she couldn't recognize that her son's mind was sharper than any blade he might wield.

I summarized it for him, as I'd report on any information-gathering mission. He listened intently, without interrupting, showing no sign of reaction to his mother's plan. When I finished, he raked hands through his hair, disordering the perfect styling, then gave me a rueful smile.

"I told you Karyn wouldn't take freedom over rank."

"You didn't tell me she was an idiot," I retorted, then felt a little bad. Karyn wasn't stupid, just a product of her upbringing.

Kral sighed and picked up my hand, turning it over to stroke the calluses. He shouldn't be touching me, but so far no one else had entered the room, and I didn't have the heart to stop him. I really needed to be touched, if only that much.

"She is not like you," he said quietly. "You have so much boldness, so fierce in everything you do. I don't think you understand what it's like for someone to be afraid of losing everything. People will suffer a great deal simply to hold on to what they have, even if they are miserable, for fear of having nothing at all."

He was wrong. I did understand. The spectre of losing everything prowled at the back of my mind like a starving bear in a cave, seizing on any scrap of hope and devouring it.

"What do you want for your favor, for winning the bet?" I asked him, with equal softness, bracing myself for the answer.

"Can you do it? Kill him from here?"

I glanced at the carved screen. No room for doubt. "Yes."

His gaze glittered with ambition. "You would do this for me, no questions asked."

Shaking my head a little, I studied him. He'd make a reasonably good Emperor, better than Hestar. No worse than others. "You won the bet," I pointed out.

"And my mother's plan to make you Empress?"

"Count me out. Karyn is your wife; she deserves to be one in truth. With this change, you can bed her. Give her a full existence, children for you both. You won't be so lonely then."

His hand tightened on mine. "I don't want her. I'm . . . Jepp, I don't see ever wanting another woman again. You are the one I crave, that I see in dreams and wake longing to touch."

The words coiled through me with answering need and keening regret. "Well, of course. Once you've had the best, all other women pale."

He didn't laugh or smile, however. "It's more than that. These last days—I hear something interesting and I look to see what you think of it, and it drives me crazy that you're not there. I want you with me. At my side, like we were on the *Hákyrling*."

That gave me an actual, physical pain. I missed that time, too. Maybe it was the awfulness of being in the Imperial Palace, but those days aboard the *Hákyrling*, the nights with Kral, had taken on a certain glow. They might have been the happiest days of my life. But . . .

"Things can't be like that again, Kral," I said, as gently as I knew how. "Your place is here."

"They *can* be like that, here," he insisted. "If you don't want Karyn dead, if you don't want to be Empress, I can make you second wife. You could live here with me, in my rooms even, if you don't like the seraglio. Be my bodyguard. Be my lover. We're good together. You can't deny that."

I pulled away my hand, unable to bear that meager contact any longer. His heat, his spicy scent, beckoned to me too strongly. We were good together. The best I'd ever had. *We seldom marry our great passions.* I shook my head again. "You know that would never work. We had a good run, you and I. Let's call it good. If you want to do something for me, be . . . be kind to Karyn. Be a generous lover. Take your time and teach her what she doesn't know. She's intelligent and pays attention. She can be a good wife and lover. Just don't let your mother poison her."

"I can handle my mother," he said grimly, though most of his unhappiness was for my refusing him, the pain clear in his eyes. "What will you do, then?"

Drawing the scroll from my belt, I gave it to him. "If you can't save my life tonight, I'm asking you to send this to the High Queen."

Of course he unrolled it, scowled at it. "I can't read it."

"No," I replied with what I figured was admirable patience. "It's in Common Tongue." And the Hawks' shorthand style.

"I'm not sending back unknown information to a foreign monarch, not even for you."

So much for protestations of eternal devotion. "Fine." I snatched it back. "If I get out of here alive, I'll find a way to get it back."

"And I'll find a way to keep you alive and safe. Trust me that my mother's threats are empty ones." He lifted a hand to touch my cheek but dropped it before making contact. "Then we'll talk more."

"I can't stay here, Kral." I felt a little desperate at that moment, because part of me—a surprisingly large part—wanted to be with him badly enough to forget all other considerations. But that was my libido thinking. All along I'd been weak where he was concerned, letting lust lead. Making the same mistakes, over and over. I'd die in this place, even if my body lived, my heart and spirit withering day by day. "I don't belong here, living in that seraglio or not, worrying about every bite of food or drop of liquor that passes my lips, served by people who are slaves. I hate everything about this place. I hate that there are locks on everything, that I can't hunt in the forest without passing through umpty-million guard stations. That there are people in those entertainment salons being tortured and humiliated because it gets someone else off." I had to drag in a long breath because I'd run out of air, and Kral took advantage of the pause.

"I could change things. Once I'm in power, I could—"

"Change an entire society? You can't even change your own thriced mind about how women should be treated. I love you, but I can't live here, even for you."

He looked like I'd thunked him between the brows with the hilt of my big knife. "You . . . what?"

I threw up my hands in silent exasperation. Time was slipping by, and any moment now someone would enter the room. "We don't have the luxury of a big heart-to-heart right now."

"I don't care," he growled, grabbing my arm and yanking me closer. "You said you loved me."

"Don't you see? It doesn't matter. Sure—against all reason and rationality, I love you. Or something like it. Like I would know. You rock my personal boat like no one else I've ever met. But it doesn't change anything. You might be the great passion of my life, but there's a saying my mother taught me that we seldom marry our great passions. I cannot give up who I am for you." I wrested out of his grip to wipe my eyes.

"You never cry," he said, looking wrecked.

"I know. See how bad you are for me?"

He set his jaw. "I'd like the opportunity to try to be good for you. I would like to do something to make that list of people you respect."

I laughed breathily, my chest tight. "You want to do something—send Ursula this message. I promise there's nothing in it to compromise the empire. It's . . . it's what she asked me to find out, and I don't want to die having failed in that."

"You're not going to die." But he took the scroll and tucked it in a pocket of his cloak. Something settled in me for at least one task accomplished.

"I don't want to die, so I'm counting on you for that. If it looks bad, just get me out of the Imperial Palace. Across the lake would be nice, but I'm not choosy. I can handle myself from there."

He blew out a breath. "I know you can. I wouldn't believe it of anyone else, but I have no doubt you'd find a way home."

"Sweet talker." We stared at each other a long moment, and I very nearly threw myself into his arms for one last embrace. Fortunately, Danu still smiled on me enough that I didn't.

24

Inga, Helva, and Karyn, trailed by a wake of other ladies, entered the room, stopping short in surprise at the sight of us.

"Your Imperial Highness," Inga said, recovering her poise and shooting me a sharp sideways glance. "We apologize for interrupting your meeting with the ambassador."

"No need," Kral replied, drawing on imperious arrogance like another cloak. "We needed to speak prior to the evening's activities, and this location served the purpose."

"What purpose is that, my lord husband?" Karyn practically snarled, thrusting herself between us and even risking a glance at him. "To flaunt your foreign *rekjabrel* under my nose to humiliate me and my family that much more?"

"Careful, little wife," Kral murmured. "The law does not stand with you in this matter."

"Because the law cares nothing for women or their fragile hearts!" she cried, then burst into copious tears. "I have been ever faithful to you—still a virgin, praying six times a day that someday you will come to me and give me children. And this is how you reward my loyalty?"

Kral met my gaze, and I gave him a rueful smile. "You're right," he said to her. It shocked her enough that she stopped crying, like a kid caught out midtantrum. "You're right," he repeated, "and I was wrong to treat you so. This day marks a change between us."

"How?" She breathed the question, startled hope in her face almost painful to witness. "The Emperor's edict binds us."

"I will petition His Imperial Majesty to change his edict. I have reason to believe he will." Kral glanced at me again, then set his jaw and concentrated on Karyn. "I will be a better husband to you, as faithful to you as you've been to me. Ambassador, ladies, I must go. Karyn, would you allow me to escort you, along with the Imperial Princesses?"

She nodded, hesitantly taking the arm he offered. He left without looking at me again. Inga and Helva fell in behind, both giving me raised eyebrows of inquiry. The other ladies ignored me as always—well, ignored me to my face, but no doubt made me the topic of their whispered conversations. They picked out their favored seats and I wandered about the room, picking my vantage point and calming my mind for the task ahead.

Below, people assembled. Hulda arrived, causing quite a stir of interest, and went up to speak to Kral. Interestingly, Hulda did not bother with casting her eyes down. Instead, she spoke for some time, while Kral maintained an expression of polite interest that told me nothing. Karyn still clung to his arm, doing an admirable job of appearing serene. She looked right beside him. Beautiful, even regal, in her elaborately embroidered and draped *klút*. I hadn't noticed before, but she wore the deep blue that matched Kral's uniform, bewitchingly stitched with silver-thread spiderwebs and studded with crystals so she sparkled like the crystalline lamps hanging from the ceiling.

Hestar arrived with his entourage and took note of the Dowager Empress's presence, tellingly scanning the room for threats. Not a foolish man. He moved to greet both her and Karyn, even taking Karyn's hand, saying something that made her smile. The four spoke congenially for some moments; then all laughed at some joke. Just another happy family.

Then Hestar raised a hand and everyone fell silent, even the ladies around me, though they slid expectant looks from me to Kral and Karyn and back again. Suppressed excitement vibrated in the air. Hestar took his throne.

"Brother, I understand you have a petition to make, but first let me welcome Her Imperial Highness Princess Karyn Konyngrr af Hardie to the Imperial Palace. You are most welcome in this visit."

He emphasized that last ever so slightly, a repressive eye on Kral.

Karyn curtsied, chimes on her outfit ringing delicately in the expectant hush. Taking her hand, Kral bent over and kissed it, simply oozing with polished charm. "Your Imperial Majesty, when we wed at your direction, we pledged to you, our family, and all the people of Dasnaria that our marriage bed would remain pure and untainted until you established your heirs."

"And we are grateful for the peace you've guaranteed with your sacrifice," Hestar replied. "However, if you are considering requesting that I allow you to consummate your marriage, let me prevent you from making such a grave misstep that would anger me greatly. The inheritance of the throne of Dasnaria must remain undisputed if we are to have peace."

"Her Imperial Highness and I understand and appreciate that position. We would not ask for such a thing."

Karyn shifted, her hand tightening on Kral's, but otherwise did not react. I had a clear path to Hestar, from my position near a largish opening in the screen. Left eye or right?

"In my travels, I've had much time to contemplate," Kral was saying. "My first wife is a beautiful young woman from a powerful family. I am lucky to have called her mine. I have come to see, however, that it has been unfair of me to ask her to continue in this celibate marriage. Karyn has her entire life ahead of her, children she could bear to another husband. Therefore, I'm offering her freedom before Your Imperial Majesty and all our family, including my cherished mother, the Dowager Empress Hulda. Karyn, should you wish it, I will agree to annul our marriage."

I scratched my head, slipping a shirikin into my palm, readying myself. Karyn, though, hesitated. The ladies around me held as still as rabbits under brush as the coyote goes by. Then she raised her chin and met Kral's gaze. Letting my breath out to steady my hand, I focused on Hestar's right eye. Once Karyn declared herself content to stay, I'd throw.

"Thank you, my lord husband," Karyn said. "I accept your offer. I will take my freedom and resign all claim to the Konyngrr name."

Utter chaos exploded.

Hestar sprang to his feet, shouting in outrage, spoiling my carefully planned shot. Kral stared at Karyn, utterly flabbergasted. The ladies around me sent up a caterwauling of consternation, dire predictions, and wails of terror. Even Hulda looked astonished.

Of them all, only Karyn seemed unmoved, though she swallowed hard.

"Silence!" Hestar roared, everyone instantly obeying. "Karyn Konyngrr af Hardie—are you in your right mind in this decision, free of coercion?"

"I am, Your Imperial Majesty. I'm willing to accept the consequences of my decision. I realize that I'll be banished from the Dasnarian Empire, but it's a price I'm willing to pay."

My mind raced to reframe my options. I no longer owed Kral a favor. I'd won our foolish bet, so cavalierly made back on the *Hákyrling*, with so little thought to the ramifications. I could escape with Karyn's entourage and call on Kral to help me, to send the *Hákyrling* to convey me to this side of the Nahanaun Islands. I could then make my way to the barrier and find a way to send a message, so someone would come to help me cross.

Hope flooded me, a bright counterbalance to all the dread that had haunted my day, all the grief of parting from Kral.

"I grant the annulment," Hestar was saying, an unpleasant

smile creeping through his beard. "And, Karyn af Hardie, lest our other women seek to emulate this disloyal, unfeminine course, I sentence you to death. Guards, take her to the tower. She will burn at dawn."

Hope shattered again.

I still had the shirikin in my hand, but no clean shot. I'd hesitated too long. The guards dragged off a hysterically weeping Karyn. Hestar departed in a cluster of his own guard. Kral remained where he was, as if frozen to the spot. Hulda spoke sharply to him, but he seemed not to hear, then glanced up at our eyrie. Gathering herself, Hulda strode in our direction, and I became aware that all the ladies stared at me, whispering viciously among themselves.

One thing was certain: I did not want to be there when Hulda arrived.

I sheathed the shirikin in my headdress and slipped out the far door, finding myself on an open balcony that led onto yet another observation salon. Figuring I should be directly above one of the waiting areas that led to the throne room, I stripped off the hindering skirt, stuffed it behind a curtain, then climbed over the ornate railing. The curlicues made for excellent handholds as I shimmied along, working my way to the massive crystalline lamp that hung from the ceiling I clung to. Hot wax dripped on my hands as the thing swung with my weight, careful as I was, but I ignored the sting, concentrating on not setting myself on fire. Quite the drop to the floor below, still.

Hulda's demanding voice rang from above, intensifying my incentive. I let go.

The plush carpet cushioned my drop and roll, allowing me to gain my feet and dash into the next salon. A startled guard shouted at me to stop, and I put a dagger in his throat. As much as I'd wanted to kill something all day, I didn't enjoy having to do it.

I should have killed Hestar when I had the chance. Now I had no choice but to rescue Karyn.

With no planning, no knowledge of where they were holding her, and no allies.

I didn't know what I'd done to piss off Danu so badly, but the bitch goddess clearly had it in for me.

A point further proven when I rounded a corner to nearly collide with Inga. She narrowed her pretty aqua eyes at me, then glanced curiously at the ceiling. "Ambassador. How did you manage to be here already?"

"Fleet feet," I answered. "And I'm afraid I can't linger."

She sidestepped to block me. I'd have to be rude to get past her, and I really didn't want to gather more enemies on my trail. "What did you think of what just occurred?"

"Some surprise from Karyn there."

She sighed and stepped to the side of the hall, drawing me with her with a slim hand on my elbow. "I believe she feared she'd be poisoned if she stayed," she told me in a low voice.

Ah. "There are no secrets in the seraglio."

Inga tipped her head in acknowledgment. "Unfortunate that none of us predicted the reaction of His Imperial Majesty."

And that I hadn't taken him out when I had the chance. With Kral stepping into Hestar's shoes, Karyn would've been safe instead of facing a death I brought to her as surely as if I'd killed her myself. I had to take the chance. "Do you know where they're holding her?"

Inga studied me. "Yes. Do you mean to liberate her?"

"If I can, and if you'll tell me where to look."

"Tell me what you came here to discover."

Canny wench. But I had no time to put her off. My neck itched with the surety that Hulda would be upon me in a moment. Not to mention the penalty looming for that dead guard in the other room. I spoke fast and low. "There's a man here, Kir, who sometimes wears pink robes. He's a companion to the Emperor."

She nodded. "I know this man. A priest of Sól."

I snorted at that. "Where is Karyn being held?"

"Why do you care about this priest?"

"Can we walk and talk?"

"No." She added a serene smile.

Danu take her. "We believe he means to cause trouble for the Thirteen. That he's here to collude with . . ." Damn it, I slammed face-first into that weird memory hole.

"The Temple of Deyrr," she supplied. "I agree. He's friendly with the High Priestess."

"I don't know her."

Inga looked faintly surprised. "Surely you do. She greeted you by name in the seraglio earlier today."

The pretty blonde who'd waved right before I felt ill. This was bad. She'd done something to me, I felt sure of it. Not Hulda. Deyrr. I needed to escape this place.

But not without Karyn.

Shouts echoed down the hall. My time was up. Inga's eyes flicked to it and back to me. "The third tower, top cell. It won't be easy. I'll wish you luck anyway."

"Thank you." I almost didn't ask, but . . . "You could come with us."

She shook her head, as if she'd anticipated me. "I'm needed here. However, if you do get out and care to . . . establish an exchange of information? You know where to find me."

Impulsively I kissed her, then gave a cheeky grin at her startled expression. "If you feel moved to distract my pursuers . . ."

"Go."

Her laugh followed me down the hall as I took off at the fastest pace that wouldn't make it look like I was running away from something. Third tower. I might as well head there directly. It could make sense to hide out until the wee hours, but instinct shouted that every passing minute brought me closer to discovery and Hulda's revenge.

No, the smartest bet was to get to Karyn before it occurred to anyone that's what I'd do.

I ducked out of the main hall at the next intersection, then found a narrow stairwell to the servants' corridors. Once there, I moved faster, following my mental map through the branching passages, making my way to the warren of supply rooms that lay far under the third tower. I passed any number of servants, who looked surprised by my presence but only bowed and did not question me. At least I had that much advantage.

I hadn't been in the third tower yet, though we'd passed it on Kral's tour of all things jurisprudence. Should've guessed that's where they'd hold prisoners, convenient to all those judgment and sentencing halls. If they planned to burn Karyn, that would almost certainly be outside. Wouldn't want to stink up the Imperial Palace with the stench of burning human flesh. I'd had plenty of experience with that miasma, even if I hadn't actually helped burn Illyria's living dead.

Illyria. Deyrr. Something there, but what? Maybe I should find that fucking High Priestess and kill *her*. I could make a rampage of it, run around the palace killing as many of the people who'd pissed me off as I could before they took me out. A reasonably fine way to go.

If I didn't owe it to Karyn to get her out.

Danu, if you get me out of this alive, I'll never try to fix anyone's life again. Or make bets. Or fuck married men. Or any men.

About twenty other character flaws occurred to me to promise to fix, but I didn't want to overcommit. Besides, I'd reached the narrowing part of the tower and had to exit the servants' corridors again, so I needed to focus on stealth.

Would it have killed Sunniva and Runa to make me a black costume?

Keeping to the shadows and quieter halls, I made my way floor by floor, altering the stairwells I used, though always choosing the dustiest. Once I was forced to hide behind a larger-than-life bust of Hestar holding scales, apparently dispensing justice, markedly without his broadsword. That artist had a vivid imagination. The noblemen passed by without noticing me, laughing as they discussed their plans for some hunting excursion. Lucky bastards. I had no idea how I'd get Karyn out, over that drawbridge. Maybe she could swim. I could chuck her into the lake, wave good-bye and good luck, and then . . . what?

Maybe she could swim and drag me with her. Ha!

Finally I reached the top floor, which seemed to contain more than one cell, thank you, Inga. However, guards in full armor stood before only one of the solid doors, at the end of a long corridor. With no convenient alcoves to hide me. Wonderful. Nothing to do but brazen it out. I hadn't followed through with my plan to rescue Dafne from Nakoa's palace; by Danu, I'd get Karyn out or die trying.

Bryn never look back.

They follow you back to your hole, another voice whispered in my head.

On the plus side, if I died, I wouldn't have to worry that I was losing my mind.

Palming several daggers, I pumped breath in Danu's Cycle, then burst into the hallway, running at top speed and yelling a Bryn war chant.

One guard goggled in shock, but the other drew his sword and ran straight for me. Fortunately for me, he didn't take the time to drop his visor, so I felled him with a dagger in the eye. Should've been Hestar. The other guard recovered and pulled a broadsword from his back sheath, taking a fighting stance. Just like the good old days, sparring with the Vervaldr and their bloody big weapons. Without pause, I engaged. The surprise helped. These Dasnarians always expected fighters to square off. *Come hunt Tala criminals in the hills with me sometime and I'll teach you not to square off.*

The Vervaldr never wore this hard armor, though, so it took me a few tries before I found a chink in the join between plates. With me inside his reach, the guard couldn't quite get his sword into me, but he was smart enough to punch me with a mailed fist. Rang my bell pretty good. Didn't hit me hard enough to knock me out, though, and that was his last mistake. I got my big blade under the chin guard and through his throat before he could clonk me again.

Thank you, Mother.

I waited a moment, to see if my noise would bring anyone running, but my luck—such as it was—held. The key to the locked door hung conveniently nearby. I wouldn't be able to count on this level of complacency for much longer. The mechanism worked much as on the other doors I'd observed, so I got it open quickly to find a wide-eyed Karyn backed against the wall of the windowless chamber, looking like a cornered doe expecting the arrow to hit home.

"I'm here to rescue you. Let's go."

She gaped at me. "Why would you—"

"I hate the stink of burning person," I snapped. "We can have a long conversation later. Move."

She moved. Surprisingly fast, too. Still wearing all of her jewelry, she chimed as she ran beside me, otherwise reasonably quiet on her bare feet. We made it to the disused stairwell, and I made her stop. "We need to lose the bells. As much of the glitter as possible, too."

For once she didn't argue, efficiently stripping off bracelet, armbands, and the jingling chains that decorated her ankles and feet. I prowled down to scout out the level below. Quiet and empty. Good news, and yet . . . I didn't like this.

Karyn had tucked up her *klút*, tying the tails between her legs.

"Good idea," I said, somewhat surprised.

She grimaced. "Country girl. Better for running, riding, and climbing trees."

"Smart. I don't suppose you can swim?"

"Of course."

Of course. Okay, all I needed to do in a pinch was get her to a point where she could jump in the lake. Hopefully the dark night would cover her from all the guard. I'd take her through personally if I could, but that would be the last-ditch effort. I explained the plan to her as we made our way from floor to floor.

"I can't jump in that lake," she hissed at me. "It's ice water. I'll die before I reach the shore."

"Possibly freeze or definitely burn—take your pick. I called it a last-resort solution for a reason."

"What's the first resort?"

"I don't know yet," I muttered.

"I couldn't hear you."

"I'm working on it. Now, be quiet." Mostly I was praying to Danu for some kind of divine intervention, and look how well *that* had worked out so far.

The servants' corridors had to be the best bet. If we could work our way around to the side of the palace where the stables stood, we'd at least be out of the main defensive areas. Once they discovered Karyn's escape, they'd focus on that damn bridge, knowing we'd have to cross it. Even if we made it to the bridge before they were onto us, we'd never get through all those guard posts. We'd be swimming for it regardless. It was the only way out, which meant I'd have to do it. All kinds of animals swam—how hard could it be? And the exertion would keep us warm. Water shouldn't be any different.

We ran through the maze of the corridors, astonished servants flinging themselves to the ground to bow before Her Imperial Highness. At least they didn't dare try to stop her, if they even knew what had happened. We were one level below the open deck that led to the stables, so I turned us into an empty stairwell that went up.

And ran straight into a pack of guards.

These were on alert, visors down and swords already drawn. I thrust Karyn behind me and went on the attack. There were too many. I went into a Whirling Wind pattern, big knife in one hand, smaller blade in the other, but their armor made it nearly impossible to get any kind of damage in. They moved together, boxing me in and trapping me against a wall.

"Run!" I yelled at Karyn. "Run for the lake!"

But they already had her, several guards holding her while she fought tooth and nail, a spitting, hissing wildcat of a woman. Too bad we'd both die now—I could have taught her how to use that fighting spirit.

The guards had me at sword point. Behind them, Hulda came down the hall, more guards with her. I knew then with crystal clarity why my mother wanted me to have her knife, wanted me to know her story. *See you soon, then, Mother.* I lifted the knife to my throat with a sense that all my life had headed straight to this moment.

25

"No!" The thundering voice rang out. And—fuck me—I faltered at the anguish in Kral's shout. Just enough hesitation for a guard to knock the blade from my hand. They seized me, one ruthlessly yanking my hands behind my back, binding them there. I struggled, but too late.

Kral stopped before me, stricken. "What have you done?" he whispered hoarsely. *Don't make me watch you die.*

"Crimes for which she will face His Imperial Majesty's justice," Hulda announced, threading her arm through Kral's. "It seems you will suffer the loss of both wife and *rekjabrel* by morning. Take her to face judgment."

Shaking her off, Kral put a hand on my arm, leaned in. "I asked you for one thing."

"So did I. Why did you stop me?"

"I . . ." He gathered himself. "It wasn't a conscious decision."

"Your Imperial Highness," a guard began, but Kral cut him off with an impatient jerk of his hand.

"For my favor," I whispered with urgency, "if they don't execute me cleanly, have someone kill me. Don't let them send me to those entertainment salons."

His expression broke into something I'd never seen on his face. A kind of agony that hurt me to see. "I can't—"

"You owe me," I spat in his face. "If you care anything for me, for your honor, you'll see to it."

He drew in a ragged breath, dragged a hand over his face. "I'll find a way to stop this."

"That would be nice." Absurdly, I laughed. Better than raging or weeping, but Kral looked at me strangely. Oh, yeah, I'd definitely lost my mind. "If you can't," I told him, "I mean it. A clean execution. You don't have to watch. That is, Kral . . . Just don't watch, okay?"

"Enough of this," Hulda declared. "The Emperor will be waiting. He won't be happy to have been dragged from his entertainments."

They took me to the great hall of judgment, tying me to the post on that little platform. Very quickly the tiers of observation seats filled, entirely with men. Then Hestar arrived. Kral did not.

Which was fine by me. I'd told him not to watch, and I'd meant it. I could probably get through this with my head held high, but watching him suffer might break me. In a surreal way, the moments ticking by felt like afterlife already. I should have died the moment I put my mother's blade to my own throat. All of this time after felt borrowed. Not an extra life anymore, not for this kitty cat. Somewhere along the way I'd lost count and used them all up.

Hestar interrogated. I stayed silent. He threatened, and I prayed to Danu.

Not for rescue, because I knew that to be impossible, but to die a good death. Not broken and begging. And I prayed that the goddess would guide my queen, that the Thirteen wouldn't fall to these people.

Hestar slapped me across the cheek. A weak blow for a guy

that big—I'd bet Karyn could hit harder—but he got me exactly where the one guard had punched me. Nothing like a big abrasion and forming bruise to scream, "Hit me here." I'd forgotten about it, but it stung like Danu's tits.

"Do I have your attention now, Ambassador?" He sneered.

I spat in his face.

The crowd of men went into a frenzy. Apparently one does not spit in a semi-divine being's face. Slowly and with a horrifically icy gaze, Hestar wiped my spit from his cheek, then smeared it over mine, grinding the heel of his hand into my bruised cheekbone, my skull into the hard post.

"I'm glad it's come to this, man-woman," he crooned, quietly enough that no one could overhear, though they'd fallen into silence once more. "I'm going to kill you myself, after I've had my fill of you. I'll find out exactly what you have of a woman, and then I'll cut them off piece by piece. All this lovely dark skin—but I'll bet you have pink bits, too. You'll have more in another hour. You like knives. You'll enjoy mine as I peel this skin off."

I glared into his face, wishing beyond reason that I could free just one hand long enough to pull the shirikin from my headdress and plunge it into one of those hate-filled eyes.

"Harlan gave me a message for you," I said.

That gave him pause, just a moment's worth, but enough that I registered it as a direct hit. "I have no interest in a traitor's words. His or yours." He started to turn away.

"He told me a story, about a woman named Jenna." I don't know what possessed me to say it, but that stopped him. "He set her up as a queen in a foreign land, where she commands armies of shape-shifters. Dragons fly at her bidding and sorcerers work powerful magics. Rooms filled with treasure. She's coming for you, Hestar. Harlan told me to tell you that. Her forces are beyond mighty. She'll kill you, and all of your children, then take her rightful place as Empress."

He didn't look at me, the line of tension across his shoulders speaking volumes.

"I find her guilty," he announced to the room, who politely applauded. "Take her to the entertainment salons."

I fought them, of course, but they were wise to me, piling on enough guys that I couldn't get away from one without running into another. Finally they had enough rope on me that I couldn't move, and one simply flung me over his shoulder and carried me there.

If I got a hand free, I'd use a shirikin to kill myself. Not as easy, but the desperation should help. Unfortunately, they took me to a central interior chamber and chained me to a raised platform, spread-eagled on my back—including a band around my throat—before cutting away the last of the ropes. Though they left me there, no matter how I strained against the cuffs, I couldn't get a hand near my head.

To fend off utter despair, I studied the room, planning how I'd escape if I could. I recognized the place, of course, and remembered seeing Kir there with Hestar. And someone else, whose face remained a blur. It had to have been her, she who messed with my mind. *She greeted you by name.*

A door opened behind me, where I couldn't see. Terror, brittle as ice, shredded my gut.

"You'd better kill me fast, Hestar, because I will fucking destroy you at the first opportunity!" I shouted.

"Always with that smart mouth."

Kral.

He strode past me, taking the key from the wall, and came to the platform, rapidly unlocking the cuffs. I couldn't quite process what was happening. Unable to keep up with events, my emotions stayed with terror. So I handled it as I always did. "You know, you Dasnarians shouldn't leave keys so near prisoners. It makes things too easy."

He flicked an icy, unamused glance at me. "Once we're safely away from here, you can bitch about 'too easy.' " He helped me sit up. Yeah, I was a little woozy. He ran his hands over me, expression full of that concern that undid me every time. "How bad are you hurt—can you run?"

"A mere scratch." I gave him a cheeky grin and hopped off the table.

"So tough." He handed me a bag holding my knives, including my mother's. Danu love the man. "Hurry."

"What's going on here, Kral?" I asked as I quickly strapped them all on, something I could do with lightning speed, even with a woozy head.

"I know you're usually the one playing hero, but even you should recognize a rescue when you see it. Put this on." He handed me a servant's cloak.

Good idea, one I should have thought of. I pulled the cowl deep over my face. "Kral—"

"We can converse later. Move."

An uncanny echo of my earlier, and disastrous, rescue of Karyn.

"What about Karyn? We have to—"

"Hush. Move."

I moved, following him out the door he'd come through, saving any more questions. Hopefully he had a plan, because I was fresh out. I followed him through the halls, keeping back a servant's respectful distance, face down, eyes up only enough to see his boots, flashing with their ebony shine.

Since terror seemed to be working for me, I didn't fight it. Just let the high song of fear run through me, my blood hot with it.

No matter what, I resolved, they would not take me alive again.

Kral greeted some guards, gave orders, and we were outside, the winter night bracingly frosty. Snowflakes whirled around Kral's boots, stirred by his forceful movement. We passed the stables, went to the wall.

"Can you climb down?" he asked.

Looked like I'd end up in the lake after all. "Yes." I ditched the cloak and swung a leg over the balustrade.

"Not right there." Kral pointed. "The boat is over here."

A boat. I could have wept with relief. "I take back everything I ever said about you being an idiot. Thank you for this. And goodbye. I, ah—"

"Save it," he cut me off. "I'm going with you." He chucked my servant's cloak into the water and swung his own leg over the balustrade.

I climbed down as fast as I could and still find decent toeholds in the darkness. Kral went faster, and I marked the distance to the water by the sound of his boots hitting wood, the rustle of water as the boat shimmied, the murmur of a woman's voice.

"You're there. Let go, I've got you." His hand closed around my ankle in a reassuring grip. Beyond grateful, I dropped into his arms, never more appreciative of his steady strength than in that moment. He lowered me to a bench, handed me a cowled black cloak—dry, thank Danu—and put one on himself.

Karyn peered at me from the depths of hers, her face pale with fear in the glow of torches from the walls, but a wry smile on her lips. "Kral's plan is much better than yours."

"I'm not going to argue that."

"Jepp got you out of the cell; I only kept you out of it," Kral grunted, rowing.

"Is there another set of oars?" I asked, feeling around.

"You can't swim, but you can row?"

"How hard can it be?"

Kral laughed, a soundless huff. "You'd be surprised. Let me do it. You rest. And be quiet. Sound travels over water."

I resigned myself to it, feeling useless, but too glad to be away from that place to find fault. If we were spotted, I could drown myself. The icy water should make it relatively painless. A cold hand touched mine, and Karyn squeezed. "Thank you," she murmured, leaning her head to me.

I had too many things to say back to her, too many questions, so I simply squeezed back and held on.

It took only a few minutes to cross the lake, but it felt like hours. I kept my gaze on the palace, watching for any sign they'd spotted us. No way I could get a knife in one from this distance, but they could easily skewer us with their arrows. The little row-boat glided from the deep shadows into paler ones between two of the lakeshore outposts, glowing rings of light around them. I reversed myself on the bench, keeping hold of Karyn's hand, to observe those guards. They faced away, watching the snowfield. Ever wary of attackers from outside, not fleeing prisoners from within. Lucky for us.

"Are you going for brazening it out or sneaking through?" I asked Kral as quietly as I could.

"Sneaking, then brazening if caught." He gave me a fierce grin, all shark.

"Kral. You can drop us on shore and go back. If you're—"

"Shut up, Jepp. How's my alignment?"

I held up a hand to show him to guide the boat more to my right, and he followed, keeping his eyes on me, slowing the oars to make their motion nearly silent, using them mostly to change our direction, letting us glide to shore. Odd how much we'd come to trust each other. Something I could never have predicted—that I'd need rescuing and that he'd be the one to do it. I only hoped he had a plan for getting back into the Imperial Palace and cover-ing his actions. Perhaps Hestar would not suspect his brother of rescuing me and Karyn, but Hulda would, I felt sure.

We neared the shore and I flattened my palm to indicate slow-ing, Kral understanding as if we'd worked on this signal system for years. The boat scraped ice bordering the lake edge, a sound that ricocheted in my sensitive ears. My eyes flew from one guard outpost to the other, a knife in my hand, though I doubted I could throw that distance. Karyn let go of my hand and lifted a bow, nocking an arrow, to my vast surprise.

"Country girl," she murmured. We all waited a moment longer, but the night remained quiet.

"No splashing," Kral warned us, quietly and unnecessarily. I wouldn't hold it against him, though. My nerves were screaming with the tension, too.

Moving with surprising stealth for such a big man, still wearing his fancy dress uniform under the shrouding cloak, he eased himself into the water, going in thigh deep, clenching his jaw at the iciness. He held out arms to Karyn and she crept to him, rocking the boat ever so slightly, holding her bow against her. He lifted her into his arms and waded onto shore slowly, ice cracking beneath his boots nevertheless.

Every second, every sound, ticked us closer to discovery, so I braced myself and imitated Kral's technique, shimmying myself into the water. Not unlike crawling over the balcony railing as I'd done hours and forever ago. The Imperial Palace shone brightly, like a jewel reflected in the waters, impressively beautiful lit up at night, showing no sign of the ugliness within.

The freezing water took my breath, the shock of it more than I'd expected, especially as it soaked through at my waist and belly. But I made myself move slowly, joining Kral and Karyn where they crouched on the shore.

"I was coming back to get you," Kral muttered.

"Now you don't have to." I'd do everything I could to make sure he didn't have to rescue me anymore.

The snowy expanse stretched before us, more lit than not by the bordering guard posts on each side. "Skulk, then run if they send up an alarm?" I asked.

"They'll shoot first. You'll have an arrow in your back before you can dodge."

"Then we run, zigzags, all at once but not together. Like birds scattering in a flock. Confuses the predators."

"This time *we* are the fish-birds," Kral said, and we shared a moment over that reminiscence.

"Meet you in the forest."

Kral grinned at me. "Bet you I make it first."

"You're already down one bet with me," I retorted. "Sure you want to lose again?"

"You two were made for each other," Karyn muttered. "Can we run already?"

"Yes." Kral put a hand behind her head and kissed her on the forehead. Then did the same with me, only lavishing the kiss on my mouth. "Good luck, ladies. Go."

I ran. Faster than I'd ever run in my life.

It's counterintuitive, zigzagging rather than running flat out. Every instinct screams that you're exposing yourself, your back itching like the target it is. You have to force yourself sideways, from this pool of shadow to the next, pace slowed by the crunching snow collapsing with the unwary step. As Kral predicted, before I heard any shouts, an arrow thunked into the snow next me, just as I'd darted to the side. Then the alarms rang out, passed from tower to tower. Arrows came at me from the ring I approached now, but I kept my eyes focused on the dim corridor between them.

I drew my mother's blade, though, just in case an arrow brought me down but didn't kill me.

Ahead, two men each ran from the guard towers flanking my escape route, leaving an archer on both to shoot at me. I poured on the speed. *Please don't let me break an ankle.* Karyn was doing the same in bare feet, and I was sure, country girl or no, she wasn't in nearly the athletic condition I was. Kral was slower and made a bigger target. I refused to be the one not to make it through.

One of the guards running toward me followed my dart, lining himself up nicely in my range, getting a knife in the throat. More had to be running up behind me, but I couldn't afford to look. Eyes on the prize, head in the fight. Get to the forest.

An arrow tore through my cloak, much too close. At least the fluttering silhouette had confused the archer's aim. I took down another guard, then a third. The last one, smarter than the others, stopped trying to intercept me and instead took a stance between me and the forest, dead center between the guard posts. If I went around him, I'd veer closer to the archers. With his armor, visor down, broadsword ready, he'd get me before I could get a knife into him.

We were all dead. How could any of us pass this gauntlet?

At least I'd die on my feet, blade in hand.

I ran straight for the guard, counting on his proximity to at least dissuade the archers. Thank Danu the rain of arrows did indeed stop. The man swung his sword in an arc, readying himself for me.

Then lowered it. Saluted, and stepped aside.

What in Danu?

But I took the break, dodging around him out of caution, skidding across the ice-covered stone road, plunging into the dark embrace of the forest.

26

I kept going, as fast as I could while making no noise. The night had gone as eerily silent as Hestar's court. No more shouts, no crashing of guards through the trees. Nothing.

Too easy.

We should have set a meeting place more specific than "the forest," but I supposed there hadn't been time. One day, as my chances of surviving this seemed to be growing, I would once again operate on a solid plan of action. That would be sweet, indeed.

Without that luxury, I angled toward Kral's and Karyn's trajectories, as I'd last seen them. If I didn't intersect with them, I'd wait for first light—which should actually be not much longer according to my time sense—and then I'd track them. Never mind that potentially thousands of imperial guards would be tracking all of us. At least we were out, against all odds.

And I was in my element.

It centered me again, to be in the forest. Even an unfamiliar one. Many of the trees were the same, and the underbrush. How did that happen, that the same kinds of plants grew on different sides of an ocean? I'd bet Dafne would know.

Once I reached where Kral should have come through, if he'd traveled in a straight line, though of course he wouldn't have, I began circling back. He'd been to my right and Karyn beyond him. If either had been wounded but had made it to the cover of the woods, they'd likely have hunkered down somewhere. For myself, I was happy enough to keep moving, as my soaked silk and leather pants would no doubt freeze the moment I stopped.

I crept through the forest, so silently I very nearly stepped on a doe curled in the bracken for the night. She bolted, sending my heart crashing through my ribs. I listened to her passage, ears attuned for any shouts or sounds of men going in that direction.

Nothing.

I began to worry as I slipped through the trees again. Which isn't in my nature, so I wasn't very good at it. If Karyn had been recaptured, did I owe it to her to go back and try for another rescue? Probably, but I might not possess enough courage. Now, if something had happened to Kral . . .

I'd skin that deer once I brought it down.

Why in Danu's clear eyes hadn't he gone back when he could? He'd be missed by now, guards certainly would have recognized him, and he'd be branded a traitor. Even if he managed to bring down Hestar, the Domstyrr would never ratify him as Emperor. Or deify him or whatever. *It's all I've ever wanted. The only thing in my life that means anything to me.*

Maybe he had a plan. He'd better have one.

A grunting sound came from ahead, just to the right, strumming my nerves to high alert. Human. But who?

Taking my time, I circled wide to the left, making sure plenty of forest remained open for escape. If I had to run, it would not be in any direction that would lead me back to the palace. Keeping a low profile, I crept closer to where the sound had been. There, a bit of movement in the brush, shadows upon shadows. Too dark to see much.

A whisper of steel.

My heart hammered energy through my system. Blade in hand,

I readied myself. If it wasn't Kral or Karyn, this person would die quickly. I edged in. Peeked through.

Thank Danu.

"Kral," I called softly, my voice rough with the crashing relief. His head jerked around, and he whirled, short sword in hand.

"Thank Danu," he breathed, echoing me, then sheathed his sword and, in two strides, seized me. His mouth came down hard on mine and I drank him in, crawling up to wrap my legs around his waist.

We were alive. We were together.

Nothing else mattered in that moment.

Except maybe Karyn's polite cough.

Chagrined, I unwound myself from him, noting the pained expression that crossed his face, if fleetingly. The sky had begun to lighten. In the distance, a bird called, a lonely, haunting sound.

"Are you hurt?" I asked him.

"A mere scratch," he answered, with a warm smile, his special one. "I'll be fine."

"He has an arrow in his back," Karyn said. "I managed to break it off, but he won't let me pull it out."

"No, that's right. Better not to. Let me see."

"Even your cat's eyes can't see in the dark," Kral grumbled, but he turned his back to me, bracing his forearms against a tree and leaning his head on them.

"Want to bet?" I retorted. "Besides, it's not even night anymore."

The arrow shaft stood out from his shoulder, solidly set into the meaty part of it, broken off about my forearm's length out. "I can cut it off closer to the skin, so it won't catch on anything. It'll mean that we'll have to cut it out when we get to safety. Can you get away with not using that arm if we leave the arrowhead in there?"

"Do it," Kral grunted. "Once we get to the *Hákyrling*, Trond can deal with it."

"We're going to the *Hákyrling*? Brace yourself—this will hurt."

I put the edge of my sharpest blade against the wood of the shaft, holding it still with the other as I circled it, cutting a continuing groove. It would take time, but we'd get there. "Isn't that the first place they'd look for you?"

"Do you have a better suggestion for getting out of the empire? If we're caught, we're dead."

"Worse than dead," I agreed glumly, and Kral reached a hand back to pat me on the hip.

"It didn't happen," he said. "That's the important part. You're away from it. We got you out."

"Why did you?" I asked quietly. Karyn moved away, giving us privacy, crunching too loudly in a pair of guard boots whose previous owner must be dead. Better than losing toes to frostbite.

"I promised." He sounded bleak.

"I only asked you to get me out, not to throw everything away by coming with me. I just hope you have a plan for how you'll go back."

"No." He laughed, not exactly bitter, but hollow. "There's no going back. But I made other promises, to you, to Harlan, to Jenna, both implicit and explicit. I decided to start keeping some of them."

"I don't get it. Being Emperor was all you ever wanted."

"I thought so. But being away so long, seeing Harlan again, seeing him happy, seeing my home, my mother, through your eyes . . . None of it looked the same anymore. You once told me that some things are worth more than all the wealth in the world, worth more than power." He took a long breath, let it out again. "I realized you were right. I want more."

The one time the man listens to me. "You could have gone for a less drastic choice," I told him. "You didn't have to throw away your entire life."

"You said you loved me. You called me the great passion of your life. Were you lying?"

Just great. One day I would learn to mind my tongue. "No. I also said that we had no future together, if you'll recall."

"No future together in Dasnaria," he corrected.

The blade cut through the arrow, the shaft coming off in my hand. I stared at it stupidly. "What are you saying, Kral?"

He turned, backed me against a tree. "When you asked your questions, I told you that the promise of becoming Emperor had been the only thing that has kept me going day after desolate day. I realized this wasn't true anymore. Even when I was angriest, the most frustrated with you, I looked forward to seeing you, arguing with you, touching you. You're mine. You're also the only person in the world, in my entire life, who's said they loved me. I'm not letting go of that. You're mine, and I plan to be yours."

"Where? How? We're impossible together and you have some fantasy that we'll settle down in some little cottage and raise babies? We'd both go insane from boredom inside a year."

"We'll figure something out." He kissed me. "Stop arguing. You know I'm more stubborn than you are."

"What about Karyn?"

"Annulled by the Emperor," she reminded me from the log she'd chosen. Not all that much privacy. "You can have him. You two are like something out of a Dasnarian ballad, star-crossed lovers, epic drama. At the end you'll either die in each other's arms or kill each other. I suppose both could happen," she added.

"With that decided," Kral said, releasing me, "we should go. There should be horses waiting for us not far from here."

"There should?" I tried to wrap my brain around that, as Karyn stood to join us.

"I sent word to men loyal to me. They'll get us to the *Hákyrling*, which will be ready. I *plan* my rescues," he emphasized with a sly grin.

"Shut up," I muttered. "It could have worked."

"Why didn't you come to me?"

"I didn't think you'd help. You warned me umpty-million times that you couldn't and wouldn't."

"I wasn't going to let Karyn burn."

"Thank you," Karyn said in a fervent tone.

"Let's fight about it later." I scanned the quiet woods, no sound but the faint calls of that one bird. "Were you two pursued into the forest?"

"No. Once we made the perimeter, the guard fell back. We haven't seen any since."

"That makes no sense. This was way too easy. I don't like it."

"I have an arrow in my back and you call this easy?"

"Yes. And you told me I could bitch about this once we were safely away. Crossing that outer ring of guard posts—I wasn't going to make it. An armored guard had me dead to rights, but he saluted and stepped aside. And now no one is chasing any of us. I don't like this."

"Maybe they don't know who we were and decided to let us go," Karyn put in. "Aren't they mainly concerned with keeping people out of the Imperial Palace?"

"If they didn't know who we were last night, they know it now," I said darkly. "Why aren't Hestar's people combing the countryside for us?"

"Probably he's just as happy to have me gone," Kral replied. "I was but one more threat to his power. Now he can declare me as banished as Harlan. Can't you just be glad of it?"

"No, because I have a suspicious nature," I retorted. "See what you'd have to live with?"

"I look forward to it," he replied, sounding like he meant it. "That alone will keep me from going out of my mind with boredom."

Karyn snickered.

We made it to the road a few hours later, then only had to walk the edge of it from the cover of the woods for another hour before coming across Kral's men, hiding in wait for us.

They gave us hot food, warm *mjed*, and dry cloaks. We traveled in the colors and under the banner of a noble house local to the area.

And made it to Jofarrstyr by nightfall without incident.

Too easy, my mind whispered, along with other snaking thoughts that I couldn't quite pin down. But I didn't say it aloud.

We hid until full darkness, then snuck out to one of the lower-rank pavilions and walked onto a boat piloted by sailors from the *Hákyrling*. As Kral had promised, the ship was ready. The moment we boarded, men below put out long oars as they had when they rowed us through the Sentinels on the way to Nahanau, forever ago. With no lamps lit, the only sound the dipping of the oars and the men's soft grunting as they worked, we glided out of the harbor.

I stood at the rail, snowflakes falling thick around me, watching the few lit lanterns in the harbor grow smaller. Jens stood ready to pilot the ship, Kral beside him, Trond having dispatched the arrowhead with relative ease. Sailors crawled in the rigging, prepared to set sail once we left the calm waters and hit open sea. Everything was falling into place.

Too easy.

Karyn stepped up beside me, golden hair in a long braid over her shoulder, warm cloak wrapping her. "Good-bye, Dasnaria," she whispered.

"I'm sorry," I said to her.

"Are you—why?"

"You have to leave your home, without even saying good-bye to any of your friends and family. I know nothing can make up for that, but if I can do anything for you, you have only to ask."

She cast me a puzzled look. "You risked your life to save mine. I think that makes us even."

"Your life wouldn't have been in danger if not for me," I countered. "I wish I hadn't goaded Kral to offer you an out from your marriage." It gnawed at me that maybe my motives hadn't been as pure as I'd convinced myself. I'd never been a jealous or possessive lover, but I hadn't liked Kral belonging to someone else. Now he'd given up everything to be with me, the crazy idiot, and I had no idea what to do with him.

"I'm glad you did. You were right. I would have lived there in my childhood home for the rest of my life, never knowing the joys of the marriage bed, children, anything beyond those lands. Maybe *blyti* guided you in this. It was meant to be."

"You Dasnarians are a fatalistic lot."

"Are we? You're the first person I've ever met who wasn't Dasnarian. Are all your people like you?"

I didn't have to give that much thought. "No. That is, it depends. There are lots of women fighters like me, scouts. But otherwise— not really."

She giggled. "That doesn't surprise me. You strike me as an . . . unusual woman."

"Do you mind, about Kral?" I took the plunge in asking her, feeling that I really should attempt to be generous. "I think he'd honor the marriage, no matter what Dasnarian law says, if you asked him to."

She gave me an incredulous look. "When all the while I'd know he pined for you? No, thank you. I have a chance for a real marriage now. I don't want one with a man desperately in love with another woman." She shuddered delicately.

"I don't think he's in love with me." He certainly hadn't said so outright. The concept of Kral in love seemed . . . bizarre and impossible. I imagined him mouthing impassioned words, like the minstrels did, and snorted.

"Jepp." Karyn faced me, very serious. "I might not have lived with Kral, but I know him quite well. The first time I met him, he told me of his sole ambition, to become Emperor. He wanted me to know before I agreed to the wedding. A great risk on his part, as I could have revealed what he said, but it meant that much to him, to take that chance. For years, he schemed to that end.

"Then he gave it up without hesitation for you. After the guards took you away, he was like a crazed man. He pretended to accompany me back to my cell, saying he'd see me safely imprisoned, then the moment we were alone, he killed all of my guards. You should have seen his face—terrifying to behold. The rest of it . . . he clicked through one step after the other. I knew nothing would stop him. Even when he had me wait in the boat and told me if he didn't return in an hour to row myself to shore, I knew he wouldn't fail. With the fire burning in him, it simply wasn't possible. If that's not love, I don't know what is."

The ship lurched as the hard crosswise current of open sea caught us. Men above passed shouts, the lines creaking and the sails flapping, then snapping full bellied.

I glanced back to find Kral watching me with his usual intensity. They'd lit a lantern, now that we were away, and the flickering light cast sharp shadows across his face. No, he would never be the romantic, but then neither would I. If he expected me to have babies, well . . . we'd have to fight about that one. The prospect made me oddly cheerful. A rousing argument with my Dasnarian lover made for far better fun than easy times with anyone else I'd known.

I smiled at him and cocked my head in question toward his cabin. He nodded once, long and slow.

Karyn followed the exchange and laughed. "If that's not love, I don't know what is," she repeated, sounding wistful. "Maybe *hlyti* is guiding me to mine. Perhaps he's in your Thirteen Kingdoms, wondering where I am."

"If we can get back, I'll help you look. We'll introduce you to every eligible man—or woman, maybe you'll discover—we can find, I promise. Like I said, anything you need, just ask."

"Will you teach me to use knives like you do?"

"Absolutely."

She gazed back at the sprawl of Jofarrstyr along the coastline, the thousands of flickering lamps. "I feel bad about them, all the ones still stuck there."

"I do, too." I thought of Inga, saying she was needed, offering to set up an exchange of information. It might be possible. Suddenly more things seemed possible than before. "Maybe we'll think of something."

27

The sky gleamed misty blue through the windows over Kral's bed. A good omen, I hoped. The smell of sea air and the sounds of the ship surrounded me with comforting peacefulness. All quiet. Racing before a good wind, by the feel. No sounds of alarm.

It couldn't be that we'd gotten away clean, but it seemed we had. Too easy.

Little mouse. The whisper echoed, then scampered away like the creature itself. I twitched, wanting to reach out and physically grab at the tease of memory.

Kral turned restlessly and pulled me against him. "Why are you awake? We've hardly slept."

It was true. We'd made love with ferocious hunger for hours, giddy with being alive, with being free, falling asleep as the watch called out the early hours. "Sorry. I popped awake. You go back to sleep."

He levered up to peer at me, rubbing a finger over my lower lip. "Something's wrong. You've been awake for several nights running; you're injured, exhausted, and you need rest. You should be sleeping like the dead."

Like the living dead. I shivered, looking into his blue eyes, shades lighter than the sky beyond, still unable to put a mental finger on it. "Can I tell you something?"

"Is this the thing you wouldn't tell me before?"

I frowned at him, trying to bring up the exact memory. We'd had that conversation, and I clearly remembered deciding not to tell him something—arguing with him about it—but by my mother's blade, I could not recall what secret I'd withheld.

"You still don't trust me," he said, taking in my silence, face settling into stark lines. "How can you love me but not trust me?"

"The one has nothing to do with the other," I snapped, and tried to wriggle away, but he held me against him.

"No more of that," he said. "No more walling me out. You and I are in this together. Talk to me."

"You're not exactly easy to talk to, and I'm not much for confiding my feelings." I pushed against his chest.

"So we'll both work on that." He set his jaw in that obstinate way of his.

"Kral." I gave up and leaned into the embrace. "You made this huge sacrifice for me. I'm grateful for my life—and more—but I'm not worth it."

"You're saying you think *we* are not worth it. This thing you believe about not marrying your great passion."

"You have to recognize the logic of that." Despite myself, I traced the lines of his muscled chest, my stupid heart fluttering when he kissed my hair in response. "What we have is fire and sex and . . . not the things that make daily life. Now neither of us has roots, no place to live. Even if we did, I'm not that kind of woman."

"So we live on the *Hákyrling* until we find a place we want to be. No, don't interrupt. You accused me of having a fantasy about a cottage and babies, but I never said that. Maybe I wanted to be Emperor for too long, but for now I want to simply *be*, without ambition. And I want to do that with you. Whatever we're doing. If we do have babies, we don't need some cottage to safely raise them in. Not with such a fierce mother and fearsome father." He pulled back and grinned at me. "Who could get through us to harm our children? There is no law that says marriage and children come with settling down in one place. That is *not* the way of things."

I blinked at him, astonished. "We'd . . . just sail around?"

"Well, we have things to do. Many games are afoot. I thought we'd start with finding a way back through the barrier and rescuing Lady Mailloux."

"Look at you," I said drily, "making amends all over the place."

"And I shall keep doing so," he said resolutely, "until I make that list of yours."

"You're already on it," I confessed, my heart gone to mush.

"Good." He grunted it, but the softness in his eyes showed how much it meant to him. "Because I cannot love a woman who doesn't respect me."

"Right back at you." I narrowed my eyes at him for good effect. Couldn't have him thinking I'd gone soft on him.

"I'm learning, *hystrix*. I'm learning. Now tell me your secret, so we can add it to the list."

"That's the problem—I can't remember it. Don't scowl at me." I sat up and scrubbed my hands over my scalp. "There's something I'm forgetting, and it's important." Urgent, even, and my trick of giving the memory time to emerge would take too long. "But it's connected to something else I'd forgotten and then remembered, which might help. I met a High Priestess of Deyrr. Inga thought I knew her because she called me by name, but I don't remember meeting her before that moment."

"You told me you saw her with Hestar and Kir in the entertainment salons."

"I did?" That explained that curious fuzzy spot. "What did I say about her?"

"Nothing more than that. You refused on the grounds of protecting me." He slid me a half-annoyed, half-affectionate glance.

"Okay." I pressed my fingers to my temples, willing the memory to form. "Okay, I remember saying that, but not what I was thinking about. I'm pretty sure she messed with my head. There was something Ursula tasked me to find out that had to do with Deyrr and I failed to. Or I found out and forgot."

"Perhaps it will come back to you, now that you're away from her influence."

"Maybe. But I can't shake the feeling that it has to do with how easily we escaped."

A call from the lookout of a ship sighted, followed by footsteps and a knock on the cabin door, requesting the captain's presence. With a sigh, Kral was up and yanking on clothes. I followed suit, grumbling about having nothing but the exotic crimson version of my leathers to put on.

"I like them," Kral remarked, patting me on the ass. "Very you."

We made it above to find the *Hákyrling* going fast at full sail. As one, we climbed the rigging and I got a flash of our future together. Maybe it could work. I loved the shipboard life more than I ever would have guessed, and sailing from place to place would satisfy my footloose ways.

At the crow's nest, Ove nodded and grinned at me, handing Kral the long-distance glass. Three crows also croaked greetings at me. He'd replaced the ones lost to the fish-birds, which made me smile. That, the bright sun, and the sheer freedom of the seas—and maybe that strange warmth of knowing Kral loved me and would always have my back.

"What is it?" Kral was asking, a fine form as he braced himself against the sway of the mast.

"Ship approaching on an intercept course," Ove replied. "From the direction of the islands."

I held out my hand for the long-distance glass and looked also. My throat grabbed with unexpected emotion. Look at me, a mess of feelings these days. The ship flew Ursula's hawk, along with the new one for the Thirteen Kingdoms, with thirteen interlinked rings forming a chain within the three overlapping circles of the goddesses. She'd come after me. "Ursula," I managed to say. "Um, that is, Her Majesty the High Queen."

Kral grabbed the glass back and looked again. "How did she get through the barrier?"

"Maybe Queen Andromeda helped her?"

The crows sent up a cawing warning at a great seabird swooping overhead. It landed with a whoosh of wide wings and shimmered into Zynda. With a salute, Ove climbed down the rigging to make room for all of us in the small space.

"Jepp!" Zynda seized me in a fierce embrace. "Thank Moranu you're all right. We got your message, but we've been sailing around forever looking for you. Where have you been?"

"Message?" Kral asked in a dry tone, giving me a narrow look.

"I may have asked Nani to relay an update for me," I told him with an innocent smile, then turned on Zynda. "Did you meet with her? I promised to help her back across the barrier."

Kral smacked a hand to his forehead. "Of course you did."

"Imperial Prince Kral." Zynda nodded to him.

"No longer. Plain Kral will do," he said.

She gave me a bemused look. "Indeed?"

"A *lot* has happened," I said. "We'll have to catch up. Is that really Her Majesty on the ship? Did Queen Andromeda bring you across the barrier?"

A mischievous look crossed her face. "Ursula, yes. Andi, no. We've discovered something new about a certain jewel." She slid a cagey glance at Kral.

"You can say it in front of him." I put an arm around Kral's waist. "I trust him. He's on our side now."

"You and I are on our own side," he corrected. "But we can evaluate alliances along the lines of the loyalties you still hold, on a case-by-case basis."

Hmm. We clearly would not lack for things to argue about. But then, he wouldn't be my Kral if we did.

Zynda flashed me a wicked smile. "I should have guessed all the good advice in the world wouldn't stop you from this particular destiny. At any rate, yes, the Star of Annfwn allowed us to cross the barrier."

The phrase echoed in my head in that same weird way. *The Star of Annfwn. You've seen it. Touched it.* I remembered . . . something. Not enough. *In the hilt of a sword all this time.* But it wasn't in Ursula's sword—not since Uorsin died.

"Does Her Majesty have it?" I asked. "I thought it was lost from the sword."

"It was, yes, because she swallowed it and it's resided in her belly ever since."

"Can that be healthy?" The thought kind of appalled me, though I knew of spies who'd resorted to those techniques to smuggle things out. But with the intent that they'd pass through, not stay in them forever. Magic was so strange.

Zynda wound her long hair back from her face, coiling it so the wind wouldn't whip it in her eyes, and fixed it with a jeweled pin. "She seems to be fine. Even better, we'd been sailing around the archipelago, tracing the edge of the barrier, when she discovered by chance that they could sail right through it, with no difficulty whatsoever. Many of the crew are Tala, but plenty are not. Including Harlan." She slid Kral an assessing glance. "We think it's because of the Star."

"She left Dafne with—"

"Queen Dafne Nakoa KauPo," Zynda corrected with a grin, "very happily married to her husband. They negotiated a treaty, another alliance by marriage, with Dafne declared an adopted sister to Her Majesty."

It took me a moment to wrap my head around that. "Then she bedded him with . . ." I slid a glance at Kral, who looked far too smug, as if he'd been proved right. "No force? Are you sure?"

"Ursula is sure, and you know she wouldn't stand for any coercion. She's satisfied that Dafne loves and is loved in return."

I whistled. "Good for our little orphan girl."

Zynda returned the smile. "There's more to tell you. But for now, Her Majesty is anxious to speak with you." She slid another speculative glance at Kral. "And to hear all your news in return. Can we pull the ships up beside each other?"

I threw the question to Kral, who lifted his shoulder in that fatalistic shrug. "Why not?"

Much as I looked forward to reporting in and delivering myself of my mission, apprehension crawled up my spine. What couldn't I remember?

Little mouse.

We pulled the two sailing ships up beside each other, the Tala ship light and feral compared to the heavier *Hákyrling*, reflecting much of the differences between the two races. The Dasnarians used clever devices to hook the hulls together and another to make a sort of bridge that we could cross.

"Excellent for boarding a captured vessel," Kral told me with an avaricious smile. "Not that I've ever done so."

"You? Never, I'm sure."

He caught me to him for an intense kiss, and when I surfaced from it, I faced the High Queen and Harlan across the short distance of our ships, both of them watching us without any surprise at all—and possibly satisfaction.

We crossed and I gave Ursula the Hawks' salute out of habit, then remembered myself and bowed. She shocked me by pulling me into a hard embrace.

"Thank Danu you're all right," she whispered fiercely.

Beside us, Harlan and Kral exchanged a back-thumping hug, full of manly shouting. I rolled my eyes, then laughed to find my queen doing the same. So good to be among friends again. Almost enough to defray that intensifying sense of foreboding.

She held me at arm's length. "Look at you. You look like one of those minstrel tales of pirates sailing the high seas. And you seem to have captured a ship as well. I have someone for you to meet."

She beckoned to a Nahaunan man who hung back, wide dark eyes cast down shyly. His long hair tied back with a colorful ribbon whipped in the ocean breeze and he clutched a silk packet I immediately recognized as the one Ursula had given Dafne, to hold her small daggers.

"This is Akamai," Ursula said. "Dafne hoped he might help you in Dasnaria."

"But the timing did not work out," he offered in a solem voice, flicking his gaze up to mine and away again, lush lashes fluttering like butterfly wings.

"You can read Dasnarian?" I guessed.

"Yes. Among a few other languages."

That *would* have been useful. Still, if we were to maintain contact with Inga, maybe it still would. He studied the silk packet, holding it tentatively toward me. "Queen Dafne Nakoa KauPo said that you might teach me to use these." Dafne sending me a new pupil. It made me smile. And it would be no trouble to train him along with Karyn. "I think maybe that—"

A shout of alarm from Ove, back in his crow's nest, almost immediately echoed by one from the Tala lookout, who burst into bird form and took off flying in the direction we'd come.

"What's going on?" Ursula demanded.

"The lookout flies to determine what closes on us." Zynda shaded her eyes. "Another ship?"

I followed the direction of her gaze, toward Dasnaria. Or a pursuer from there? But there was nothing but empty sea and sky. Just like looking at the barrier. This was all wrong.

And then it was upon us, as if out of nowhere. A Dasnarian sailing ship. Far too close and already sliding up to the other side of the Tala ship, Tala and Hawks alike racing to engage, popping into animal forms and drawing blades.

Terror seized me as the memories came back in vivid clarity.

Forget about me while I follow you back to your hole.

Once again I'd led the rampaging bear right to the people I loved.

Ursula had already drawn her sword, and I realized I had my daggers in my hands. Our many defenders surged, diving into the sea or flying off. "Don't let them!" I shouted to Zynda. "It's too dangerous. Tell them not to go. To come back!"

I didn't think she'd understand my order, but she cracked into bird form and zoomed to give warning. Akamai fled below.

"Who is it?" Ursula asked, crisply in command, Harlan stepping up behind her.

"A High Priestess of Deyrr. She followed me here." She'd messed with my head, made me forget, and now I'd endangered my captain and queen. *Head in the fight. Keep to the facts.* "She's very powerful and wants the Star of Annfwn."

"Well, she can't have it," Ursula snapped, sending signals to the alert Hawks and Tala guard, who'd come swarming to protect her.

"We have to get the ships apart," Kral urged. "We can't maneuver with—"

"Too late," I whispered as the scent of death washed through the air, sinking into my muscles and freezing them with nauseating chill. Helpless to stop them, everyone seemed similarly incapacitated, watching as the Dasnarian vessel set the grappling hooks and a black-cloaked woman crossed the bridge between ships.

She strolled up to us with a gentle smile on her lovely face, brushing away the straight blond hair that whipped into eyes like dark holes in her head. "Ambassador Jesperanda," she cooed. "How lovely to see you again. And this must be Salena's daughter. I believe you have something that belongs to me."

Ursula had taken a fighting stance but, like me, like all of us, remained frozen in it. Her throat strained against the strange paralysis, creaking out, "I've killed one of your ilk before. I'll do it again."

The priestess laughed. "Illyria? That pup. A handmaiden. A mere *bynde* to test a rumor. We had to know if all your High Priest Kir had told us was true." She shook her head, walking around Ursula, her gaze flicking to Harlan, who was straining to move behind her, and away again. I used her inattention to reach for the meditative state that allowed Danu's power to flow. I couldn't quite pump my rib cage to activate Danu's Cycle, but I worked what breath I could. Presumably she gave us that much space, so as not to suffocate. She couldn't simply kill us all until she had what she wanted. The Star. If she slipped at all, she'd be dead. Just give me a hair's breadth of opportunity.

In bits and nibbles, the energy flowed, thawing me ever so slightly from inside. Something else connecting to it. That bright green healing energy, still pooled in my tissues, that magic she'd sniffed but hadn't identified.

"Such a pitiful excuse for a priest," the High Priestess was saying as she studied Ursula, circling her. "No power at all. But Hestar had grown fond of him, the pair so alike in their perversions." She laid a finger alongside her nose. "Though I doubt Kir will realize the power Hestar promised him, when the empire takes over all your realm."

"Over my dead body," Ursula snarled.

The High Priestess laughed again, rich, sensual, and horrifying. "Well, yes. And sooner, rather than later. Deyrr will have what is rightfully ours. The Nahanauns can no longer keep the treasure from us. The old scribes awake, and this time they cannot hide from us."

"You won't reach them," Ursula said, a bead of sweat running from her temple as she strained to move. "You can't penetrate the barrier."

Sweat poured off me, too. My muscles still would not respond, but—it could have been my imagination—it felt as if my chest moved more easily.

The High Priestess shrugged that off with impatience. "All of you so ignorant. This is why the Star belongs in better hands. So kind of you to bring it to me. Where is it? Close. I can smell it. Not in the sword anymore, obviously. Aha!" She stepped up close to Ursula, just ducking the sharp edge of her upraised sword.

I fought to move and couldn't quite. Harlan's face contorted with stiff and slow rage, a growl of menace rolling from him, twin to Kral's, but neither of them moved. Gnawing away at the sorceress's hold like the mouse she'd named me, I could almost shift my grip on the knives I held.

The High Priestess's hand melted like wax and reformed into a claw. With that, she laid it almost gently over Ursula's belly. With a sick hiss, the queen's flesh parted, abdomen falling open so blood poured in a waterfall, the contents of her stomach acrid to the air. Dizzy with the gruesome memory of how that felt, I howled, joining my cry of agony to Ursula's, Harlan's a deeper echo. While I thrashed, a mouse flailing against the grip of the trap, the High Priestess reached into the cavity of Ursula's ribs with her other hand and plucked out the topaz, round and glowing with incandescent light through the smear of bright blood.

Ursula croaked as her eyes rolled up in her head, white with death, but could no more fall than any of us could move.

With a triumphant smile, the High Priestess held the bloodied jewel up to the sun. "At last," she purred. "Kiraka, we will meet again."

A blur of white swooped through my peripheral vision, the great seabird. Zynda! As large in that form as the High Priestess, Zynda slammed into her, knocking her off-balance. As graceful as any swordswoman, her wickedly pointed beak stabbed out one dead-dark eye. The High Priestess, staggering, screamed in rage. Zynda seized the Star in her beak, wide wings beating furiously toward the open sky.

Hand clapped over her eye, which streamed blood black as tar, the High Priestess flung a bolt of some violet magic after Zynda. It struck, glowed, and dissipated, Zynda flying still higher, unaffected.

In that short space of time, the magic hold finally slipped. Without thought, I threw the two daggers in rapid succession, one into her remaining eye, the other to the base of her throat.

The second knife cut off her scream and the rest of her magic—unleashing a torrent of sound and motion from the rest of us. Like a sail with ropes severed, Ursula dropped, Harlan diving to catch her.

Kral swung into decisive action, moving in front of me, his broadsword singing as it sliced through the empty air where the High Priestess had been. At his back, I scanned the open sea for where she'd gone. But she, and her ship, had disappeared as if they'd never been, the boarding bridge and hooks still rocking with their abrupt dislocation.

A howling Harlan cradled Ursula in his arms, a widening pool of blood around them.

28

With a snap of great wings, Zynda landed beside me, taking human form and pressing the bloody Star into my hands in one startling movement. "Guard it with your life." In the next blur of movement, she was at Ursula's side, trying to wrest her from the crazed creature that was Harlan. "Kral! Jepp. Help me with him!"

Kral obeyed her first. I clutched the Star, sticky slippery with Ursula's lifeblood, stupidly searching for the High Priestess to descend upon us again. At least I had the sense to tuck the jewel into a pocket, to have both dagger hands free. I wasn't swallowing the cursed thing, nor would I be gutted again.

The Tala healer who'd been with Andi had Ursula on her back now, heedlessly kneeling in the pool of blood. Kral sat nearby, his arms around Harlan, holding him against his chest, muttering something in hushed Dasnarian. Harlan had quieted, his gaze fixed on Ursula and the green glow emanating from the healer's hands, electric blue surrounding them both from something Zynda did.

Even as he calmed Harlan and helped him hold vigil, Kral stared at me with haunted eyes. *Don't make me watch you die.*

For the first time I understood how it would be harder on the person who had to watch.

Marskal found me keeping my useless watch. Too slow, too late. I blinked at my lieutenant, too numb to be surprised at his presence. "Jepp, to me," he snapped, grabbing my attention and habitual obedience through the shock.

"Sir." I gave him the Hawks' salute, though I didn't sheathe my knives.

"We have to uncouple the ships and sail through the barrier," he said, spacing his words. I'd talked thus, to skull-rattled warriors. "We'll be safe there and the Tala healer needs the magic. Take charge of the Dasnarian vessel, Scout."

I sought Kral's steadfast gaze, his somber nod cutting through some of the dumb haze. He had to stay with Harlan. I got that. And at least I had something to do. Jens, a step ahead of me, already had sailors in the rigging and men ready to pull up the bridge. He set course, the *Hákyrling* surging ahead, the Tala ship wheeling to follow.

With nothing better to do, I climbed to the crow's nest, searching the glittering horizon in all directions, straining every sense I possessed, searching for the High Priestess to reappear. I held the Star in one hand, in case its magic helped, and a set of throwing knives in the other—in case I had the pleasure of blinding her again. Ove set his crows to searching and watched from the long glass also.

From time to time, I checked on Kral. Harlan had moved, sitting with Ursula's head in his lap as the healer stayed nearby. Kral kept close to his brother, but always he held his face turned to me as the ships raced for the barrier side by side, until I lost the sight of him when night fell.

I started when Zynda appeared beside me, my focus had been so far away.

"Easy," she said, her face calm despite my blade at her pulse point.

"Apologies," I muttered, dropping the knives from her throat. "Ursula?"

"Alive, but barely. We need you to bring the Star, so we can cross the barrier. Hurry."

"Just take it." I thrust the jewel at her and she held up her palms, fingers spread wide.

"It's not for me. Come on."

"Like it's for me?" I called after her, but she didn't reply or pause in her descent.

I followed her down the rigging, a memory of doing the same while the fish-birds attacked assailing me. She stopped at the rail and flashed me a slight smile. "At least that piece was easier. Grab on."

I frowned at the surging sea between the ships. "Grab on to what? We need to pull up, hook the boarding ladders."

She shook her head, climbing over the rail and clinging to the side of the plunging vessel. "We can't afford the time. Hold on to my waist. I'll try to make it a clean dive."

Danu save me. Kral was teaching me to swim at the very next opportunity. With a heartfelt sigh, I pocketed the Star again and sheathed my knives. Climbing onto the rail behind Zynda, I wrapped arms and legs around her slender body, her long hair cold and damp between us. Impulsively I kissed her cheek. "If you drown me, I'll come back to haunt you."

She laughed, the sound turning into an uncanny song as her skin shifted into sleek scales under my hands. I squeezed my eyes tight as we plummeted into the water. Her muscular mermaid body undulating beneath me felt every bit as strange as it had looked, but she kept my head above water long enough to get me to the Tala ship and to Kral's strong grip, handing me up the ladder.

He stood with me in the prow of the Tala ship as we sailed into Glorianna's dawn, one arm around me and sword in the other, stabilizing me against the pitch of the waves. The *Hákyrling* held judiciously back, but we raced at full sail for the barrier. No tentative approach this time. Zynda assured me it would be fine, but

I felt like an idiot holding the glowing topaz in my hands, bracing to crash into a wall I couldn't see.

"I asked about Jenna," Kral said in my ear, cheek close to mine.

Surprised, I looked up and back to search his face.

"It was a long vigil." He lifted a shoulder and let it fall. "It seemed better to distract with old arguments than let him stew with worry. You were right about one thing, though—he loves her."

"Jenna?" I asked. One day I'd have enough sleep and my brain would work again.

"No." Kral squeezed me with affection and kissed my hair. "Your queen. Ursula. If I never again see a man so wrecked by the prospect of a woman's death, I'll die a happy man. Don't you ever do that to me."

"I'm trying my best. What did he say about Jenna?"

"He couldn't say directly because of his vows, but he hinted that the knowledge might be found on Nahanau—and that Dafne might be of assistance."

"Interesting."

"I thought so, too."

"So we're still headed for Nahanau, Nakoa, and Dafne—if we make it through the . . ." I gasped. "I see it."

There—a curtain of shimmering magic, between me and the rosy sunrise, taking on all the glorious colors and shining with promise.

Kral studied the horizon over my shoulder. "You and your sharp eyes."

"Best in the Hawks," I boasted, flashing him a grin over my shoulder. "We made it. She didn't get us."

He took the opportunity to kiss me, long, hot, and deep. Oh, yes. And like that, we slipped through the barrier, only a sparkle of magic on my skin to reveal that we'd crossed.

I had to take one more mermaid ride back across the barrier to bring the *Hákyrling* through. Kral went with us, cleaving the waves with strong strokes as he swam beside us with enviable ease. We both scanned the horizon with tense awareness, until the last inch of the stern glided through the barrier, only then able to breathe a final sigh of relief.

"Perhaps she's truly dead," Kral said, as unwilling as I to speak of the High Priestess of Deyrr aloud.

"Danu make it so," I agreed with a fervent prayer. Hopefully Danu would understand about me not following through on all those desperate promises to give up men, or sex entirely. Really, She should know me better. I wasn't giving up Kral, not even for Her.

A day later, surrounded by the calm seas of the Nahanaun archipelago, we all stood on the deck of the *Hákyrling*, saying our good-byes. Ursula looked her usual self, tanned and full of vigor. For his part, Harlan carried a wan and haunted expression that I suspected might take some time to shed. However, Kral thumped him on the shoulder, cracking some Dasnarian joke that had Harlan's face lightening. Ursula gave Kral a slight nod and he grinned back at her. Would wonders never cease.

"Your Majesty." I held out the Star. "I'd like to return this to you."

To my astonishment, she held up a hand, refusing it. "Keep it. That's a command from your High Queen."

I gaped at her, the jewel burning in my hand. "But it's not mine. I have no magic, and Salena gave it to you."

"And I nearly lost it at the cost of my life." She shrugged. "Think of this as bodyguard duty."

"What in Danu am I supposed to do with the cursed thing?" I asked, wracking my brain for an argument sufficient to make her take it back. I'd gotten sleep, but not nearly enough.

"I'm asking you, Kral, and the crew of the *Hákyrling* to do what you can to help people back and forth across the barrier. I'd like to send Akamai with you and Dafne will coordinate your efforts from Nahanau. I understand you have some questions for her anyway." Her thin lips quirked in wry amusement. "I believe she has access to a wealth of information. Any that you need."

We exchanged long looks, Kral and I. Maybe we could do something about establishing a communication channel with Inga after all. I didn't like not knowing whether Deyrr might still come after us. "You up for it?" I asked him. Maybe I could embed the Star in the hilt of my mother's blade. The thing was not easy to carry about.

"With you by my side? Absolutely." A flash of the shark, while his hand cupped the back of my head in a brush of affection.

"All right then, Captain. I suppose I'm still a scout, and a spy," I added for Kral, batting my lashes at him. "Just with a wider range."

Ursula gave me the Hawks' salute. "You are, and always have been, my best scout."

They left, crossing back over the grappling bridges and sending Akamai to us, then waiting as our crew pulled the bridges up. We watched as the Tala ship turned back toward Annfwn, Kral and I leaning on the rail.

"I'm surprised Karyn elected to stay with us," Kral commented, profile sharp against the glittering blue sea. "And the Nahaunan boy."

"I'm going to teach them how to use the knives. And Karyn is interested to help find Jenna. Apparently Helva and Inga spoke to her about it at length in the seraglio."

He shook his head in consternation. "Always working the angles, those two."

I snugged myself between him and the rail, shimmying against him and watching his eyes warm with interest. "Runs in the family," I said. "Want to work my angles?"

His hands tightened on me. "When I'm done with you, *hystrix*, you'll be all soft belly and no angles at all."

Sweet talker.